1. This book may be kept three weeks. It is to be returned on / before the last date stamped below.
2. A fine of 25c will be charged for every week or part of week a book is overdue.

THE GRANVILLE SISTERS

Recent Titles from Una-Mary Parker

THE GRANVILLE SISTERS

Una-Mary Parker

This first world edition published in Great Britain 2005 by
SEVERN HOUSE PUBLISHERS LTD of
9–15 High Street, Sutton, Surrey SM1 1DF.
This first world edition published in the USA 2005 by
SEVERN HOUSE PUBLISHERS INC of
595 Madison Avenue, New York, N.Y. 10022.

British Library Cataloguing in Publication Data

Parker, Una-Mary
   The Granville sisters
   1.   Sisters - Fiction
   2.   London (England) - Fiction
   3.   Domestic fiction
   I.   Title
   823.9'14 [F]

   ISBN-10 : 0-7278-6258-8 (cased)
               0-7278-9145-6 (paper)

Typeset by Palimpsest Book Production Ltd.,
Polmont, Stirlingshire, Scotland.
Printed and bound in Great Britain by
MPG Books Ltd., Bodmin, Cornwall.

Prologue

The five legendary Granville sisters first became famous for their beauty in the mid-thirties. The daughters of banker Henry Granville and his wife, Liza, they cut a swathe through high society, with the debut of Rosie and Juliet in 1935.

Photographs of them appeared in magazines and newspapers. They were the talk of the town for their stylish fashions, fabulous jewels and extravagant parties.

But they also attracted gossip as they became embroiled in scandals that included deception, betrayal, illegitimacy, adultery, divorce and suicide, which even their rich and influential parents were unable to cover up.

Then World War II began and nothing would ever be the same again for a family who believed they were indestructible.

Extract from the *Bystander*, May 1956
By Richard Warwick

PART ONE

Aspects of Revelry

1935

One

T he rivalry between the two elder Granville sisters had started when they were small, but had escalated into open hostility by the time Rosie turned eighteen, when Juliet was nearly seventeen. Whilst Louise, Amanda and Charlotte, who were much younger, lived in harmony up on the third floor with Nanny, a battle of wills was being faught in the large first-floor drawing room, driving their mother to distraction and their father to say he'd call off their coming out altogether if 'things went on like this'.

'But it's *so* unfair,' Rosie raged, eyes blue like dew-drenched hyacinths, blonde curls quivering. 'I should be coming out by myself. Juliet's far too young.'

'You're afraid I'll outshine you,' Juliet protested, knowing that she would, without even *trying*. She was also tall, slender, with blonde hair and pale skin, but her eyes were the shade of aquamarines, and very slightly slanting, and someone had remarked to her father that she had a mouth that would launch a thousand cheque books.

'Seventeen really is rather young to be a débutante,' their mother, Liza Granville, demurred. She was slightly scared of them both, with their natural assurance and self-confidence.

'Think how much money it'll save,' Juliet said swiftly. 'We can share one coming-out ball, instead of giving two.'

But money, as they all knew, didn't really come into it. They lived in one of the grandest houses in Mayfair, had a large Georgian house in Surrey set in twenty acres, and Henry Granville was chairman of Hammerton's Bank.

What mattered to Rosie was that Juliet possessed what everyone was calling S.A. Even she could see that sex appeal emanated from her sister like exotic perfume from a lily. It was there in the way she smiled, the look in her eyes, and the

4

natural sway of her hips when she walked, especially in high heels. Men turned to look at her in the street, and her father's male friends raised their eyebrows and said she'd 'go far'. Nobody had ever said Rosie was going anywhere.

'Mummy, you can't bring Juliet out. Who ever heard of sisters, a year apart, coming out together? It'll look so *twee*!' Rosie said, a note of panic in her voice.

'It won't look twee at all,' Juliet said disdainfully. 'It's not as if we look alike, and I certainly don't intend to dress like you.'

'What's wrong with my clothes?'

'Boring! You dress like everyone else. I intend to be different.'

'Listen, girls,' Liza cut in anxiously. 'This quarreling has got to stop. Daddy's already threatened to cancel any of us doing the season this year if you go on like this.'

Juliet smiled, realizing at that moment that 'doing the season' and presenting her daughters at court meant much more to her mother than it did to either of them. In fact, this was a moment Liza Granville had been secretly looking forward to for years, and Juliet knew it.

'Mummy,' she said sweetly, 'I'll never say a cross word to Rosie again if you'll let me come out. I'll be as good as gold, and do whatever you say, but please, please let me go to all the parties too.'

Liza wavered, avoiding looking at Rosie.

'I know Rosie's your favourite daughter,' Juliet continued wistfully, 'and I promise you I won't get in her way, but I would so love us to do it together, like a proper family.'

Her mother flushed guiltily, because what Juliet said was partly true, but Rosie was only her favourite because she was docile and needed to be supported, whilst Juliet would always be able to look after herself.

'I don't have favourites, Juliet,' she said, in a clipped voice. 'All five of you are equal, to Daddy and me.'

Rosie preened slightly. She *was* closest to their mother.

'Then can we come out together?' Juliet begged.

Liza gave a heavy sigh. 'Very well then. But no more fighting.'

Juliet beamed and Rosie glowered, and neither of them looked at each other.

'We'd better go to Norman Hartnell about your wardrobes,' Liza remarked. 'The season only lasts for three months, you know, from May to July, but there are up to five parties a night. You're going to need ball gowns and cocktail dresses and outfits for Ascot, Henley and Wimbledon. Not to mention masses of shoes and hats and handbags.'

The sisters' smiles widened in proportion to the rise of enthusiasm in Liza's voice, for they were also aware she'd need a new wardrobe too, even bigger and grander than theirs, and that was what she was finding so thrilling.

'The only reason the London season is during May, June and July is because the men have nothing to kill during those months,' Nanny Granville explained to the three younger sisters as they sat at a table in the middle of the day nursery having breakfast.

There were bowls of porridge for the children, and they drank their milk from silver-crested mugs, while Nanny and Ruby, the nursery maid, tucked into cups of strong Indian tea, poured from a sturdy brown teapot, and gobbled up slices of toast and marmalade.

'What do you mean?' Charlotte asked, wide-eyed with horror at the mention of killing. She was five, and as pretty as a doll, with long blonde hair, and the same blue eyes as Rosie. 'Killing what? What does Daddy kill?'

'All the gentry go shooting and fishing and stalking,' Nanny said in a reproving voice. The ways of the upper classes were dear to her heart. 'From August until April they look after their country estates and shoot pheasants, partridges, quails, woodcock –' she ticked them off on her plump fingers – 'snipe, hares and rabbits.'

'Like Peter Rabbit?' Charlotte asked hollowly, turning pale.

'I don't think you should be telling her all this, Nanny. She'll have nightmares,' said Amanda disapprovingly. She was eight, rather prissy, and so short-sighted her eyes were permanently screwed up like a mole, because her mother refused to acknowledge she needed glasses. 'When I grow up, I'm *never* going to shoot. Or fish, or hunt, either. It's all terribly cruel.'

'Don't be ridiculous,' Nanny retorted robustly. 'How else do you think the gentlemen are going to amuse themselves? Why do you think your father keeps a gamekeeper?'

Louise, as sweet and calm as a summer's day and just turned ten, gazed at Charlotte with sympathetic eyes.

'It's all right, Charlotte. They're not pets like the dogs at Hartley. Daddy would never hurt an animal. When they're shot, it's so quick they don't feel anything.'

Charlotte's bottom lip quivered.

'Now, come along girls,' Nanny said briskly. 'Ruby has to walk Louise and Amanda to school in ten minutes, and you've got to practise your reading, Charlotte.'

On the floor below, Juliet let out a thin high-pitched scream, turned over violently in bed, and then awoke, trembling.

She sat up slowly and covered her face with her hands. Would these nightmares never stop? It had been ages since she'd had one, and she'd hoped . . . but no, her dream had been so vivid, so terrifying, that it was going to take her hours to shake off the hideous images.

Then she noticed her dress for her presentation tonight, hanging outside her wardrobe. It was oyster satin, cut on the cross, with shoulder straps encrusted with tiny pearls. There was also a velvet train that would trail behind her, and white kid gloves reaching to her upper arms.

Her passport, she reflected, to creating another persona. An entry into a grown-up world, where she would be able to leave behind the person she'd been and become the person she wanted to be. A step towards freedom, and an ability to take control of her life from now on.

She could hardly wait.

Down the corridor, Liza was sitting up in bed, enjoying her morning cup of China tea, which Parsons, the butler, had brought her earlier, on a small lacquered tray.

As she lay back against the downy pillows, in her glamorous pink bedroom with its antiques and rich pink brocade hangings, she wondered if she'd ever thought, as the only child of a badly paid teacher and his seamstress wife, now both dead, that she'd one day be married to a rich man who lived in a palatial house in the most fashionable part of London? That she'd have eight servants? A chauffeur and a Bentley at her disposal? And a safe stuffed with the Granville family jewels, and her own lady's maid to take care of her clothes?

Henry Granville had fallen deeply and passionately in love with her when she'd been a companion to an old lady back in 1913. She'd been eighteen and the old lady had turned out to be his great-aunt, whom he visited regularly. Liza simply couldn't believe her luck when he'd proposed, and eventually whisked her away to a world she'd only ever dreamed about. But at first she'd refused him.

'I'll never be able to keep up with you and your family, Henry,' she'd protested, sure she'd be out of her depth, especially after she'd met his mother, Lady Anne Granville, whose father had been the Earl of Hanley.

'You'll be fine, my darling,' Henry promised. He was dashing, tall, with broad shoulderes, fair hair and a moustache, and the brilliant blue eyes their daughters had inherited. 'I'll look after you. I promise.'

Although she was wildly in love, Liza had still been doubtful. 'Suppose I say the wrong thing in front of your friends?'

Henry told her to be herself. He'd also promised that their different backgrounds would never, ever, cause problems. 'I love you and I want you as my wife,' he'd said with sincerity.

They'd been married the following year, just before the Great War started. Henry, who had joined the Guards, was sent to the front after the first few idyllic months, and Liza went to stay with Lady Anne, at Hartley Hall. Her mother-in-law had welcomed her warmly, taking her subtly under her wing, and Liza learned fast, desperate to make Henry proud of her.

Never intellectual, nor over-bright, she nevertheless grew into a sweet and attractive woman of shallow depths and few persuasive abilities but great charm. As their five daughters were born, so also was her ambition that they should marry as well and as happily as she had.

Henry realized this was what was behind her wanting the girls to make 'good matches'. And if he secretly wished her ambition was less obvious, he said nothing, but took it as a compliment, for it meant she had found happiness with him.

'I'd have gone to the loo before we left if I'd known we'd have to sit here for hours,' Rosie grumbled.

It was the 8th of June. The four of them had been sitting

in the car for two hours, and they were still stuck in the Mall, several hundred yards from the gates of Buckingham Palace. 'We should have left home earlier,' Henry remarked heavily, looking distinguished in black knee breeches, stockings with buckled shoes, and his war medals. 'All that fussing with your headdress, Rosie, has made us dreadfully late.'

'It's much more difficult to fix the feathers with this new short hairstyle, than it was when one's hair was long,' Liza said placatingly. Wearing a silver lamé dress, with a silver lace train, and a dazzling diamond tiara and necklace, her face glowed with happiness. 'As long as we're in the palace by eight o'clock, it'll be all right,' she added, smoothing her gloves.

Juliet smiled smugly. Her long thick tresses, which she'd refused to have cut, had been arranged into a Grecian knot, so the hairdresser had had no problem in pinning the three white Prince of Wales feathers into *her* hair. She was just cross that she hadn't been allowed to borrow one of her mother's tiaras.

'Only married ladies are allowed to wear them,' Liza had explained.

The long line of large black cars, like hearses on their way to a morticians' convention, edged slowly forward. The route was lined by thousands of people, agog to see the ladies in their finery and blazing jewels.

Juliet loved this attention, but Rosie looked embarrassed.

'For goodness' sake, don't wave back, Juliet,' Henry said at one point, as she raised a white gloved hand to acknowledge the crowds. 'You're not royalty.'

Royalty. Juliet savoured the word and imagined she was some foreign princess, accepting the adulation of her subjects.

Newspaper photographers had started taking their pictures now, through the car windows.

'I didn't know it would be like this,' Rosie said, appalled, while Juliet smiled flirtatiously into the lenses.

'The women come to see what people are wearing,' Liza observed, blasé. 'It's like a fashion show to them. They haven't come to see *us*.'

Getting out of the car when they arrived was a hazard neither of the sisters had forseen. Trains had to be draped over their left arm, heads had to be ducked so they wouldn't break their feathers, bouquets of gardenias and roses must be carefully clutched.

When a liveried footman offered his white gloved hand to support Juliet, she grasped it with the fervour of someone thrown a lifeline as they are about to drown in a rip tide.

'Gosh!' she murmured, climbing up the steps that led into the palace.

Once inside, Rosie and Juliet had never seen such a blinding mix of scarlet and gold in their lives, with a carpet that stretched ahead of them like a red ocean.

'Golly!' Rosie echoed, with awe.

'What happens now?' Juliet asked her mother.

'Follow us,' Liza whispered, leading the way with Henry up the grand sweeping staircase, past ranks of Yeomen of the Guards, until they reached the top, where powdered footmen collected Liza's white fox cape and Juliet and Rosie's ermine wraps.

Whilst the men greeted their friends, gentle preening was going on amongst the mothers and daughters, like doves attending delicately to their toilette.

Then they moved forward into the White Drawing Room, which was already crowded. To one side there were rows of gilt chairs.

'Go and sit there,' Liza told them. 'You've got your cards of command, haven't you?'

They nodded, clutching the precious cards bearing their names, without which the court usher would not allow them to go forward to be presented.

'Where are you going, Mummy?' Rosie asked in alarm. 'For goodness' sake, don't leave us.'

'I have to go ahead of you, darling. You'll follow, with the rest of the girls, in due course.'

They took their seats and watched for what seemed ages as their mothers disappeared through the far doors into the adjoining Throne Room. Then it was the turn of the débutantes.

Rosie moved with determination to be in front of Juliet, her blue taffeta dress and train echoing the colour of her eyes, her cheeks flushed, and her hands trembling with nerves.

Moments after, it was Juliet's turn.

'Miss Juliet Granville,' boomed the usher.

This was it. Juliet's moment of glory. With her head held

high, she swept forward to present herself before the King and Queen of the British Empire, an Empire so vast it was said the sun never set on it.

Gripping her bouquet, she dropped into a deep curtsey before the King, and then moving on, curtsied to the Queen. And suddenly it was all over.

She found herself in the Blue Drawing Room, where Rosie and her parents, looking proud, were waiting for her.

'What now?' Juliet asked.

'When the King and Queen leave the Throne Room, there's a champagne supper, and then the car will come to collect us,' Henry told her.

Juliet's face fell. 'Is that all?'

'No, we've been invited to a party at the Savoy, where, if you're lucky, you can dance the night away,' he replied, smiling.

'Oh, Daddy, how wonderful!' she exclaimed loudly, flinging her arms around his neck to kiss him, much to the horror of the other girls and their parents.

'I think we'll reserve the hug for later, sweetheart,' Henry said, good-humouredly extricating himself.

'We mustn't forget where we are, dear,' Liza said in a stage whisper.

Juliet looked unabashed. 'Well, I don't know about you, but I feel absolutely at home here.'

On arrival at the Savoy, the cloakroom was crowded with mothers and daughters shedding their trains and feathered headdresses, bouquets and gloves. The formality was over. The mothers were dying for a strong cocktail; the debutants were dying for a strong man to sweep them on to the dance floor.

Seated at a long table for thirty, Liza took a quick look at the other guests, congratulating herself on having cultivated Lady Carmichael for the last twenty years, including making her Rosie's godmother. She'd known all along that Trudie Carmichael, having a daughter the same age, would be entertaining lavishly during the season of '35. Whilst the Carmichaels weren't as rich as the Granvilles, they seemed to know a large number of 'young things', and so it was with satisfaction that Liza noted that both Rosie and Juliet had eligible young men on either side as they took their seats for supper.

11

Carroll Gibbons and his band livened the atmosphere with romantic popular music, and couples crowded on to the dance floor to the strains of 'I Cover the Waterfront', and 'Dancing in the Dark'.

Juliet looked sparkling and confident, Rosie looked hopeful.

'Isn't this a dashed good party?' remarked the young man on Juliet's right, who had introduced himself as Archie Hipwood. 'Been to Buck House, have you?'

Juliet nodded. 'Do you think I can have a sip of your wine? My parents are here, and I'm not allowed alcohol yet. Such a dreadful bore,' she added, imitating his drawl.

'How dashed unsporting of them. Here, swapsies!' He pushed his glass surreptitiously towards her, and took her orange squash.

'How angelic of you!' Juliet said flirtatiously.

The man on her other side leaned towards her. 'Hello. I'm Colin Armstrong. You must be Juliet Granville.'

Her eyes widened. 'How did you know that?'

'News travels, when there's a new beauty on the scene. Like to dance?'

Juliet took a quick sip of wine. 'I'd adore to. I just *love* this tune.' And away she skimmed in her ivory satin dress, with his arm around her waist, as she looked up laughingly into his plain but charming face.

Further down the table, Rosie was talking to someone called Charles Padmore.

'So where do you live?' he asked.

'In Green Street.'

'Enjoying your first season?'

'Yes. It seems to be great fun.' She looked towards the dancing couples with envy, especially when she saw Juliet swinging past as the band played 'Let's Make Hay While the Sun is Shining'.

'Do you ride?'

'Not so much now, but we had ponies when I was young,' Rosie replied, looking towards her mother for help. Why wasn't she having as much fun as Juliet?

She turned to the man on her other side, hoping for better luck. 'Hello, I'm Rosie Granville,' she introduced herself shyly.

'Hello there. I'm Peregrine Carnegie.' He smiled affably.

'And ... erm ... do you go to lots of these parties?'

'Not really. Aunty Trudie roped me in for the evening. I'm at Oxford, reading economics, actually. I don't have time to go to parties. Isn't your sister Juliet Granville?'

'Yes,' Rosie replied icily.

'Thought I recognized the name. Word's already got around, according to my aunt, that she's a smashing beauty who might become the Deb of the Year!'

'I'm never *ever* going to go to the same party as Juliet again,' Rosie exploded, on the verge of tears, as she and her mother went to powder their noses later on.

A look of panic floated across Liza's face. This was only the first night of a season; another twelve weeks lay ahead of them.

'There's your joint coming-out ball next week, darling,' she stammered, flustered, knowing now she had a real family crisis on her hands.

The atmosphere in 48 Green Street was charged with a mass of conflicting emotions on the morning of the ball.

Liza was up early, nauseous with a mixture of nerves and excitement. She looked at herself wistfully in the mirror.

Why was it that the way she *thought* she looked and the way she actually looked widened with every passing year?

Downstairs was all hustle and bustle. Boxes of flowers were borne aloft into the house like floating herbaceous borders, and the caterers had already delivered a load of little gilt chairs with red velvet seats.

In the kitchen, Mrs Fowler, the cook, was casting a beady eye over the food being prepared for breakfast for the two hundred guests, while she remained jealously in charge of the menu for the dinner party for twenty-five before the ball. She was a whippet-thin little woman, with a tired face framed by whisps of ginger hair, and when she smiled, she bared her teeth in a canine grin.

'Put the hired crockery and glasses in the passage outside the skullery,' she commanded in a rasping bark. 'Don't go bringing no crockery in here.'

Meanwhile Parsons, the butler, cast a worried eye over the dozens of cases of champagne, and wondered how long they'd last.

To add to the chaos, removal men had arrived to clear the drawing room and morning room of furniture, so there were frequent collisions in the hall between what was going out and what was coming in.

Even the nursery was in turmoil, as Charlotte kept jumping up and down, exclaiming, 'I want to *dance* with Daddy tonight!'

'We *are* going to be allowed to watch people arriving, aren't we?' Louise asked anxiously.

'We'll see what your mother says,' Nanny retorted.

'But I want to dance with Daddy,' Charlotte wailed.

Louise said comfortingly, 'I'll dance with you on the landing, where no one can see us.'

Charlotte's bottom lip quivered. 'But Daddy won't be on the landing,' she gulped.

Nanny spoke crisply now. 'Charlotte, if you don't eat up your cereal, you won't be dancing with anyone.'

The triumphal cascade of pink champagne, flowing from the top of a pyramid of wine glasses into a base of white marble, drew gasps of delighted amazement from the guests who arrived to have dinner before the ball. It was the *pièce de résistance* of the evening, and the first time anyone had seen the like at a débutante ball.

'It's too, too divine!' exclaimed Lady Sibyll Lygon, who wrote articles about society parties for *Harper's Bazaar* magazine.

Lady St John of Bletso, gazing at the sparkling pink display, agreed. 'Too marvellous for words, my dear. Do you suppose it will keep flowing all evening?'

Behind her even the Aga Khan looked impressed, while the Duke and Duchess of Rutland 'smiled appreciatively', according to a report in the *Tatler* magazine.

At the top of the stairs, Louise, Amanda and Charlotte, in white organdie party frocks with blue sashes, peered down through the bannisters, fascinated by what was going on.

'They all take after you, Liza,' Lady Diana Cooper, a famous beauty herself, remarked. 'You really must get them painted by Philip de Laszlo. He's done an exquisite portrait of Princess Elizabeth, you know.'

It seemed to Rosie, beautiful in a white lace dress and long white gloves, that the whole of London was taking part in her coming-out ball tonight.

Unfortunately, she raged inwardly, so was Juliet.

It had all started to go wrong before the dinner-party guests had even arrived. She was waiting with her parents to receive the guests when Henry spoke.

'Where's Juliet?'

Rosie shrugged. 'I haven't the faintest.'

'She's ready, isn't she?' Liza asked, fanning herself nervously.

'I've no idea, Mummy. She's been cooped up in her room all afternoon.'

'Oh, for goodness sake . . . !' Henry sounded rattled.

'I wanted her to see the champagne cascade and the flowers before anyone arrived,' fretted Liza. 'She *must* be ready.'

She herself had been made-up, hair curled, and tiara in place for *hours*.

'*Juliet!*' she called, a touch frantically.

'She'll never hear you, darling,' Henry pointed out. He strode over to the bottom of the stairs, a distinguished figure in white tie and tails.

At that moment they heard footsteps and, looking up, saw Juliet descending at a leisurely pace.

For a moment Rosie looked bemused. Juliet looked taller than usual and glamorous like a Hollywood film star. A spray of white velvet roses, which certainly hadn't come from Norman Hartnell, but more likely the bargain basement of Selfridges, lay over her left shoulder, the central rose so large that when she lowered her chin, all you could see were her aquamarine eyes, which seemed to be heavily fringed in *black*.

'What have you done to your face, Juliet?' Liza remarked in horror. 'And where did you get those dreadful flowers?'

At that moment Juliet turned to face them, and to her mother's shock she saw Juliet had cut what had been the modest V-line of her dress into a plunging ravine, which exposed her deep and provocative cleavage.

Liza gave a thready scream. 'You *can't* appear like that!'

But Juliet smiled, her scarlet-painted mouth so voluptuous that Henry felt quite taken aback.

15

'Go and scrub that muck off your face at once,' he whispered angrily, 'and cover yourself up with a scarf or something.'

'You look like a *tart!*' Rosie stormed, tears rising, cheeks flushing.

'That's better than looking like a washed-out drab!' Juliet snapped back.

'Now, girls . . .' Henry began agitatedly.

As Juliet told Louise the next morning, 'I was literally saved by the proverbial bell. Lady Astor arrived at that moment in one of her *five* tiaras, so Mummy and Daddy had to shut up.'

That night, Juliet seemed to reach a new peak of beauty and allure. Watching, Liza realized with disappointed pang, that her precious Rosie really was going to be overshadowed by her sister. Rosie might be blonde and exquisite in a gentle way, but Juliet had something else. An indefinable charismatic quality, and sexuality that made her outstanding.

'Isn't Juliet a stunner,' people kept saying. The older men eyed her wistfully and wished they were thirty years younger, and the young men gazed into her eyes and wondered if they were in with the chance of a kiss.

But Liza frowned worriedly. Bringing the girls out together had been a dreadful mistake.

'It's so unfair, Mummy,' Rosie had whispered, when they went upstairs to powder their noses.

'Oh, sweetheart . . .' Liza sympathized.

'Can't you *stop* her?'

'What can I *do?*'

Mother and daughter looked at each other blankly, racking their brains to think of a way Juliet could be stopped . . . but stopped from doing what, exactly? Being her natural self?

Liza was about to tell Rosie to be more assertive, but what was the point? Rosie wasn't the assertive type. 'I should have forced her to wait until next year,' she said lamely.

Rosie's pretty pink mouth drooped at the corners. 'Well, it's too late now. She's going to spoil the *whole* summer for me. I just know she is.'

Liza had a sinking feeling Rosie was right.

As Henry watched the proceedings anxiously, he saw his mother, Lady Anne, taking a seat with a group of other dowagers.

'Hello, Mother. You're looking very splendid.'

'Thank you, dear.' She nodded as Juliet swung past in the arms of her partner. 'She's a little minx, isn't she? But so enchanting,' she observed, amused. 'I've always liked her spirit.'

He smiled, raising his eyebrows. 'She's unsquashable.'

'But there's a lot of good in her. She'll be much happier now that she's growing up.'

'I've never thought of her as being unhappy.'

'Haven't you, Henry? Oh, I have. The child hasn't been happy for a long time.'

'Mother, what do you mean?'

Lady Anne shook her head, her drop diamond earrings trembling.

'The child's been troubled by something since she was quite small.'

'I can't think what,' he replied doubtfully.

Lady Anne patted his shoulder with her gloved hand. 'Don't worry about it, my dear. She'll be all right.'

'Yes, Mother. But will Rosie?'

The next edition of the *Bystander* dubbed Rosie and Juliet Granville as *The most beautiful débutantes to grace the London scene since Margaret Whigham in 1930*; while the *Sketch* summed up the party as *The coming-out ball of the year*. The *Tatler* went even further: *Rosie and Juliet Granville, the sublimely exquisite débutantes of 1935, are destined to make brilliant marriages.*

'Look at all these thank-you letters!' Liza exclaimed. 'Aren't people sweet?'

'Look at all these bills!' Henry said drily. 'How can the hire of a hundred and fifty gilt chairs come to almost as much as if we'd *bought* the damned things?'

In the aftermath, bickering in the family kept flaring up at intervals because everyone was tired. A sense of anticlimax was permeating through the house like an epidemic of influenza.

Nanny complained the young ones had become 'spoilt little brats' overnight; Mrs Fowler had thrown a saucepan at a

17

scullery maid because it hadn't been cleaned properly, and even Parsons, normally calm and measured, had a sharp word for a parlour maid because she laid the table for luncheon incorrectly.

To top all this, the servants were clamouring for time off to go and watch the Silver Jubilee celebrations of King George V and Queen Mary.

The streets of London suddenly blossomed in a flurry of Union Jacks and bunting. Patriotism swept through the city like a contagious and feverish euphoria. Liza and Henry were invited to the Jubilee Ball at Buckingham Palace, but, to Juliet's fury, she and Rosie had not been asked.

'It's for the grown-ups, darling,' Liza explained. 'You'd be dreadfully bored.'

'So when can I go to the palace again?'

'I expect you'll be invited to one of the garden parties, in due course.'

Nanny was determined though, that Louise, Amanda and Charlotte should see the King and Queen travel in procession in their golden carriage from the palace to Westminster Abbey. Liza was doubtful because of the vast crowds. The children might so easily get lost.

'You must take Parsons and Ruby with you, Nanny,' she said firmly.

'Very well, ma'am,' Nanny replied obediently, though she knew there was no need. Once the children were dressed in their best pale-blue linen coats, red shoes and white socks, in the style of the King's granddaughters, Princess Elizabeth and Princess Margaret Rose, they'd be given special treatment by the crowds, who would doubtless think they were the offspring of some European monarch.

Her scheme worked. Flanked by the butler and the nursery maid, Nanny managed to manoeuvre the girls to the front of the crowds, so that when the procession passed them in the Mall, they were in a perfect position to appreciate the magnificent carriage, with the elderly King and Queen sitting inside.

'Look!' Charlotte screamed with excitement.

'Hush,' remonstrated Amanda.

Nanny said nothing at all, because by now the tears were streaming down her plump cheeks.

'Well . . . !' she said, when she could say anything at all. 'Did you ever . . . ?'

'Beats the cinema any day, if you ask me,' Ruby agreed.

'Quite,' said Parsons.

Nanny blew her nose. 'Children,' she said as they walked home through Green Park, 'this is something you can tell your grandchildren about. You'll never see a grander sight, not nowhere in the world,' she added with stout patriotism.

'Holland Villas Road is so *out* of town,' Liza observed. 'Who has invited you to dine with them there?'

Rosie glanced at the letter asking her to join a dinner party before Lord and Lady Heysham's ball. 'It's signed Cynthia Bartlett. The dance is at Holland House, so that's very convenient, actually. Who's Juliet dining with? Not with the same people, I hope?'

Liza hesitated. Juliet had actually been invited to dine with the Londonderrys. It was rather a feather in Juliet's cap because the Marchioness of Londonderry was one of the most spectacular hostesses of the era, only rivalled by Lady Astor.

Rosie looked at her mother anxiously. 'Who *is* Juliet dining with?'

'Lady Londonderry,' Liza replied casually.

'Why has she asked Juliet?' Rosie exclaimed petulantly.

Liza looked guiltily embarrassed. 'It's only for dinner, Rosie,' she said soothingly. 'Once you get to the Heyshams' ball, it won't matter who you've dined with.'

Rosie looked particularly ethereal that night, in a gauzy pink dress with gold beaded shoulder straps and pink and gold topaz earrings. Her skin was flushed like a sun-ripened peach, accentuating the blue of her eyes. She was determined to talk to more people, dance more dances, and generally to shine more than Juliet. She knew she looked good, too, because when she arrived at Mrs Bartlett's house, her hostess's eyes flashed and her thin lips vanished completely. It was obvious that Rosie was going to outshine Flora, her plump and rather plain daughter.

Once they arrived at Holland House, Rosie hung around in the cloakroom for several minutes, a trick she'd learned from Juliet, so that by the time she entered the ballroom, Mrs Bartlett

19

and her other boring dinner-party guests had scattered.

Having been received by Lord and Lady Heysham, and Prudence, their daughter, Rosie spotted one of her friends, Megan Hamilton, sitting on the far side of the ballroom on one of the little gilt chairs provided for débutantes to sit on until someone asked them to dance. But before she'd reached Megan, a tall, broad-shouldered young man with dark brown hair and the dark sentimental eyes of a spaniel, came up to her as if he already knew her. Lady Heysham stepped out of the receiving line and for a moment Rosie thought she was going to whisk him away, but instead she smiled charmingly.

'Rosie dear, may I introduce you to Alastair Slaidburn?' Then she turned to the young man as if she were about to describe a rare jewel. 'And this is Rosie Granville,' she told him.

'How do you do,' he said gravely, shaking her hand.

'How do you do.' Her heart felt as if it was being deliciously squeezed, like gentle fingers testing a plum for ripeness.

'Would you like to dance?' His smile lit up his face, crinkles of laughter lines forming around his eyes.

'I'd love to.' They took to the floor and, as they trotted around to a quickstep, Rosie realized in a moment of crystal clarity, almost like second sight, that this was the man she wanted to marry. Happiness flowed over her like a comforting warm wave as she managed to keep up with his intricate footwork.

When he suggested a glass of champagne and somewhere to sit out for a few minutes, she accepted with alacrity. He led her to an anteroom, and they settled with their drinks on a sofa.

'That's better, much cooler,' he remarked, smiling at her. 'So, do you enjoy being a deb?'

'I'm having a wonderful time,' she replied inanely, sipping her champagne. Mummy had told them both they must only have soft drinks, but this, Rosie felt, was a special occasion. 'Do you go to many of these parties?' Her tone was hopeful.

'Not if I can help it,' he replied, amused, 'but Alice Heysham is my cousin and I promised to give her a helping hand in bringing out Prudence.'

Lucky Prudence, Rosie thought, wishing she could think of something witty and amusing to say, so he'd stay by her side for the rest of the evening.

'Tell me about yourself,' Alastair asked, easily and confidently. 'Where do you live?'

The ice was broken. Rosie relaxed and she told him about her parents and the house in Green Street, how she loved to play tennis, and what sweet little sisters she had. Somehow she forgot to mention Juliet.

They danced together some more, and then, excusing himself reluctantly, he said he simply had to do a couple of duty dances, namely with his cousin and with Prudence, but would she save a dance for him after that?

'Of course,' she agreed blithely. She decided to spend the time powdering her nose, putting on some more lipsalve, and talking to the wallflowers who always congregated in the cloakroom rather than face the humiliation of sitting around the dance floor, hoping somone would ask them to dance.

Just as she was leaving the cloakroom, Juliet swept in, wearing a dress Rosie hadn't seen her wear before. It was peacock-blue satin, with yellow and red silk butterflies scattered around the shoulders, and she looked amazingly exotic, with her long hair swept up into coils at the nape of her neck, interwoven with ropes of small pearls.

'*There* you are!' Juliet exclaimed, her blue eyes rimmed with black, like a cat. 'Been in here all evening, have you?' she asked with false sympathy.

'No, I haven't!' Rosie snapped frostily, suddenly feeling overblown and dowdy.

Juliet gave an amused shrug, raised her plucked eyebrows and said, 'Oh, well . . .'

Rosie hurried back to the ballroom, but Alastair was still steering Prudence around the floor; her expression was bovine, his bored. *Damn*, she thought; who can I talk to until he's free?

'Hello, Rosie,' said a voice in her ear. It was Charles Padmore, lanky but exquisitely groomed. White tie and tails are definitely flattering, Rosie reflected. They make any man look handsome.

'Like to dance?' he asked.

'That's sweet of you, Charles, but my shoes are hurting me dreadfully; can we just talk for a few minutes?' She fluttered her lace fan whilst keeping a surreptitious watch on Alastair's movements.

'If that's what you want.' He sounded disappointed, and she

21

was aware of him looking at her breasts and then sweeping down to her hips before he looked into her face again. 'Can I get you a drink?'

'Yes, please.'

When he returned from the bar with two glasses of fruit punch, he droned on about the Derby the previous day and how the Aga Khan's horse had won, until, to her relief, she saw Alastair coming towards her again.

'Would you excuse me, Charles?' she asked sweetly. 'I promised this dance to Alastair ages ago.' She made it sound like some time last year.

Crestfallen, and about to say he thought her feet were hurting her – but then thought better of it – Charles turned away, muttering something about wanting another drink anyway.

As Alastair spun her around the floor, twisting and swooping her through a tango, his hips pressed hard against hers, his hand deep into the small of her back, his brown eyes held a triumphant expression.

'You're a good dancer,' he remarked.

Rosie, breathless, smiled back. She didn't dare say a word because all her concentration needed to be focused on her feet.

Eventually Mrs Bartlett came up to her, husband in tow, while Alastair went to fetch more drinks.

'I don't think it's very nice the way you've comandeered Lord Slaidburn all evening,' she said coldly. 'There are other girls at the party who want to dance too, you know. Anyway, we're leaving now, so come along; we'll take you home.'

Alastair had come back with their drinks and Rosie turned to look at him. She longed for him to take her home later – much, much later – but she knew that wasn't allowed, and she also knew he'd never even suggest it, for the sake of her reputation.

For a wild moment she thought of telling the Bartletts she was staying on longer and then going home with her sister, but, as she hesitated, Mrs Bartlett made it plain she was in no mood to argue.

'Now, come along at once, Rosie. Flora's got a bad headache, haven't you, dear?' she asked her daughter, who looked as if she'd had a miserable evening.

Rosie said goodbye to Alastair and then walked away, but she couldn't help turning and looking back at him. She knew nothing about him, not even where he lived, and yet she already felt a sense of loss at no longer being by his side.

He was still standing where she'd left him, and their eyes locked. For a split second she felt like turning and running back. Then he smiled and her heart shivered with longing.

'Are you coming, Rosie? The car's waiting.'

Rosie wondered with a chill of desperation when she'd see him again, as she obediently followed Mrs Bartlett into the waiting car.

Lying in bed, Rosie relived the evening from the moment she'd arrived at the ball until she'd been forced to leave.

Then she was struck by a dreadful thought. Juliet had still been at the party when she'd left. Supposing she'd met Alastair? Danced with him too? She'd heard Juliet returning a short while ago. With one bound she was out of bed, and tapping on her sister's door.

'What is it?' Juliet mumbled, opening the door. She was standing in white satin-and-lace camiknickers, and her silk stockings were held up by white satin suspenders. 'What do you want, Ros?' Her mouth was full of hairpins and her arms were raised as she pulled the ropes of pearls out of her hair.

'Did you . . . did you have a good time? You're home very late.' Rosie tried to keep the querulous note out of her voice.

'I thought it was a dreadfully dull evening. They really shouldn't invite all the old fathers, too. They're such a lecherous lot. In the end Archie took me to the Astor in Berkeley Square. We couldn't get in to the Embassy.'

Relief washed over Rosie like an Atlantic roller, leaving her feeling weak and bruised. 'Archie . . .?' she croaked, seemingly interested.

Juliet shrugged. 'Archie whatever. You know, the man with the slicked-down hair.'

'Oh, *Archie!*' Rosie repeated as if he were a life-long friend. Hysterical giggles were not far from the surface. 'Oh, well, I'm glad you had a good time.'

Juliet's eyes narrowed. 'You got out of bed at three o'clock in the morning to ask me if I had a good time?'

'I . . . erm . . . I couldn't sleep. I just wanted to make sure you were all right.'

23

'Since when? What are you up to, Ros?'

'Why should I be up to anything? I bet Mummy doesn't know you spent most of the evening in a nightclub, alone with a *man*!'

'And of course you're going to tell her?'

'No. I'm not.' Hoping she looked dignified, Rosie turned and went back to her room, where, having carefully closed her door, she did a wild little jig of happiness.

Two

'Oh, how divine! Are those for me?' Juliet reached out from the morning-room sofa, where she was lounging with a copy of *Vogue*, as Parsons bustled in carrying two bouquets of flowers, one of lilies and roses, and the other of carnations, peonies and orange blossom.

Rosie, writing thank-you letters at a table, looked up resentfully.

The butler seemed to be having difficulty with his mouth, which kept twitching to one side.

'They're both for Miss Rosie,' he replied primly.

Rosie flushed a deep pink. No one had ever sent her flowers before. 'Who are they from?' she asked eagerly.

He indicated tiny envelopes nestling among the sweet-smelling blooms.

'Thank you, Parsons.' She ripped open the first envelope. 'Oh! How sweet,' she remarked without enthusiasm.

'Who's it from?' Juliet asked.

'Charles Padmore.'

'*What* an excitement. Who are the others from?'

Rosie's hands were shaking so much she could hardly open the envelope. A moment later she gave a gasping laugh.

Her sister watched her closely. 'So? Who sent them?'

Rosie shrugged elaborately. 'Alastair whatever,' she said carelessly. 'Parsons, can you get these put into vases, please? I think I'll have them in my room.'

When Rosie was alone, she read the note again. *Hoping to see you again soon. With love, Alastair.*

'Oh, my God . . . Oh, my God . . . !' she kept repeating to herself. It was too good to be true. She must tell Mummy. This was a secret she couldn't keep to herself a moment longer, and she certainly wasn't going to tell Juliet.

Hurrying up the stairs, Rosie rushed into the room adjoining her parents' bedroom, which Henry referred to as 'Mummy's Holy-of-Holies'. This was Liza's sitting room, where she attended to her correspondance and made her telephone calls. It was a bright chintzy room, with a desk, a couple of armchairs, and a mantelshelf groaning with invitations. To see these stiff white cards, with their copperplate engraving, gave Liza a warm feeling of happiness. Especially the ones from Buckingham Palace, with the crown printed in gold at the top. She even allowed herself the indulgence of keeping out-of-date invitations propped up amongst the others, so it looked as if they were going to even more parties than they actually were.

Rosie's words came tumbling out as she told her mother about Alastair and the flowers.

'Slaidburn. Alastair Slaidburn,' Liza kept repeating, frowning in concentration. 'Wait a moment, darling.'

As she spoke she reached for her 'bible', *Debrett's Peerage*, flipping through the flimsy ricepaper pages, until she came to the entry she was looking for.

Rosie watched with bated breath.

'Rosie,' Liza said at last, as she examined the impressive coat of arms. 'Have you any idea who he is?'

'Mrs Bartlett referred to him as Lord Slaidburn.'

'Darling, he's the Marquess of Slaidburn, aged twenty-seven, his family seat is Ashbourne Park, and he ownes most of Worcestershire. His family are not RCs, so *that's* all right.' Liza leaned back in her chair as if she'd been felled. 'Rosie, you're made! He's one of the most eligible bachelors in the country.'

Rosie felt stunned, her eyes wide with amazement.

'Now,' said Liza, pulling herself together. 'This is what you must do. Be discreet. If it gets out he's interested in you, he'll run a mile. Don't flirt too obviously and don't even let him *kiss* you until he's made some sort of declaration, and I don't mean a note with a bunch of flowers. Let him hold your hand, but only in private, and the only presents you can accept from him are chocolates, and maybe a good book. D'you understand, Rosie? This is really important.'

The thought passed through Rosie's mind that all this sounded more like a military operation than the beginning of a love affair, but she nodded happily, promising to do exactly as her mother said.

When Henry returned from the bank that evening, weary after a long and tiring day, Liza couldn't help babbling on about Rosie's new swain, and what it could mean. He poured himself a large gin and vermouth, and then dropped heavily into a chair.

'Liza, have you any idea what is happening in the real world?' he asked heavily.

His wife bristled. She never knew what he meant by the 'real world'. Surely their world was real enough?

'What do you mean?'

'I had lunch with Ian today. Things are very serious.'

She looked at him nervously, reached for a cigarette, which she placed in her long jade holder before lighting it. Ian Cavendish was Henry's oldest friend. They'd been to Eton together, and then Trinity College, Cambridge. Ian was now high up in the Foreign Office, and, in Liza's opinion, a boring old gossip.

'So, what did he have to say today?' she asked, a touch resentfully.

'You know Winston Churchill has been warning the House about Germany? Ian told me that the FO have received information from MI6 that Hitler has called for conscription, and ordered air-raid shelters to be built in Berlin.'

Liza frowned, not wanting to hear all these things. It scared her to think there could be a repeat of the 1914–1918 war with Germany.

'I don't suppose it means anything?' she said weakly.

Henry looked strained. 'But can't you see? It means war is inevitable. The Nazis have been building up the Luftwaffe, we've already lost air parity with Germany, and they're calling Churchill a warmonger.'

Liza dragged on her cigarette, saying nothing.

26

'Ian met Churchill for luncheon last week. Do you know what he told Ian?'

She shook her head, knowing he'd tell her even if she'd said she already knew.

'Churchill said the present situation is the most serious this country has ever faced in its long history. We're simply not prepared for war. If Germany strikes out at us, we're finished, and so is the rest of Europe.'

'So, what can we do?' A sudden note of fear had entered her voice. Could the situation *really* be serious?

Henry shrugged, and reached for his briefcase. 'I read something today that just about sums up the situation.' He pulled out a copy of *Punch*.

'Listen to this.' Henry started to read aloud.

'Who is in charge of the clattering train?
The axles creak and the couplings strain,
And the pace is hot, and the points are near,
And sleep has deadened the driver's ear;
And the signals flash through the night in vain,
For Death is in charge of the clattering train.'

'Oh, Henry!' Shocked, Liza looked at him, her eyes filled with tears. 'That's the most horrible thing I've ever heard. I can't believe we'll really . . .' She clapped her hand over her mouth.

'We're all on that clattering train, my darling.'

'Then what's going to happen to us?' she sobbed.

Henry got up and went and put his arm around her shoulders. 'Try not to get too upset, darling. It'll be some time before anything happens, anyway.'

Her expression brightened. She wiped her cheeks with a tiny handkerchief. 'Really? Truly? And perhaps Hitler will change his mind, don't you think?'

Rosie was madly in love. It was a bright shining love, new and fresh and thrilling, and it absorbed her night and day. When she was at home she withdrew into a world of golden daydreams, inhabited only by Alastair Slaidburn and herself. She hated going to parties if he wasn't there, and feared going to parties if he *was*, in case he showed an interest in someone else.

27

'He's so attractive, Mummy,' she confided. 'I'd marry him tomorrow if he asked me.'

'Maybe he will,' Liza replied with ill-concealed excitement. She couldn't resist her own bit of daydreaming: 'My daughter, the Marchioness . . .' Chatelaine of Ashbourne Park . . . the first débutante of the season to marry . . .

'*Mummy!*' Rosie said impatiently.

'Umm?' Liza tore herself away from her delicious fantasy. 'What is it, darling?'

'I know he's going to the Wheatleys' ball tonight. Which dress should I wear? He's seen all my ball gowns,' she added ingeniously.

'Then we'd better get you a new one, but it'll have to be off the peg, I'm afraid.'

Rosie smiled happily. 'I saw a beautiful apricot chiffon dress in a shop in Bond Street. It was only eighteen guineas. And Mummy . . . ?'

'Yes?'

'I also saw a divine jacket made of squirrel, but dyed to resemble sable, for eight guineas; it would go terribly well with an apricot dress, wouldn't it?'

Liza was about to point out that Rosie already had a white ermine cape and a blue fox wrap, but thought better of it. After all, to make sure her daughter looked good was a long-term investment, and worth every penny.

It so happened that Liza and Henry had also been invited to the Wheatleys', and as soon as she saw Alastair Slaidburn, she was deeply impressed.

'Don't you think they're well suited, Henry?' she whispered, as Alastair took Rosie off to dance.

Henry started, appalled. 'Well suited? Good God, Liza, she's only known the man for five minutes. I don't want her rushing into marriage at her age. Anyway, isn't it presuming rather too much?'

Liza smiled at him with her secret cat-like smile, as if she knew something he didn't. 'I gather he's rather keen on her.'

'You shouldn't encourage her, Liza.'

'Get me another glass of champagne, will you, darling?'

Henry stomped off to the bar wishing he'd never agreed to

this débutante nonsense. His sister hadn't come out, because of the Great War, and so he hadn't fully realized what they were getting into with Rosie and Juliet.

Now he felt angry. He did not want his daughters going to the highest bidders, as if the season was some bloody cattle market. When it came to Louise's turn, he decided to put his foot down. The money would be better spent sending her to a finishing school in Switzerland.

'... *And you'll find us all, doin' the Lambeth walk, Oi!*' Juliet led the '*Oi!*' Everyone roared and they all made the thumbs-up signal over their right shoulders. Then she flung herself at Colin Armstrong, giggling helplessly.

While guests at the Wheatleys' ball were behaving like Edwardians, across town in Grosvenor Crescent the Martineaus were holding an altogether less formal dance, and Juliet was having the time of her life.

'Let's get a drink,' Colin shouted above the din.

It was a warm night, and they took their drinks out on to a balcony, where Juliet perched herself on the balustrade, looking coquettish in a pale blue evening dress with a little flirty feathered cape. Crossing her ankles, she swung her feet with their dainty silver high heels to and fro.

'Can I have one of your gaspers, Colin?' she asked.

'Right-o.' He opened his gold cigarette case and offered her a black Sobranie.

'Thanks.' She took one and held it to her scarlet lips for him to light. Then they sat side by side, his arm round her waist, in companionable silence for a few minutes.

'Why don't we go on to the Hennessys' dance?' he suggested suddenly. 'This one's beginning to drag a bit, isn't it?'

Juliet nodded. The party had already peaked, and she'd been seen by everyone she'd wanted to be seen by. 'There's just one snag, Colin. I don't know them, and it's the one party tonight I haven't been invited to.'

'Neither have I,' he chortled. 'So who cares?'

Juliet's eyes sparkled like blue crystal. 'You mean ... ?'

'Why not? It's at the Dorchester. If we're not allowed in the front entrance, we'll sneak in through the kitchens.'

Juliet shrieked in delight. 'What a lark! Let's do it.'

29

They slipped unnoticed out of the house without saying goodbye to Lord and Lady Martineau, or their dinner hostess.

Once out in the street, she gave a deep sigh of relief, smelling freedom. She was now, for the first time, without a chaperone, and completely alone in the company of a young man, in the middle of the night.

Colin grabbed her hand. 'Let's walk. It's not far.'

Juliet agreed, feeling daring and naughty. She squeezed his hand, and he stopped walking for a moment to turn and kiss her lightly on the mouth.

'You're so adorable,' he murmured, fixing her with his bright eyes.

Juliet giggled happily. Walking in the fresh air had made her realize she'd had quite a lot of champagne, and that felt marvellous too.

When they reached the ballroom entrance of the hotel, she held her head high, and sailing past the two uniformed commissionaires, entered the lobby.

'I'll leave my wrap,' she told Colin, but at that moment a red-coated master of ceremonies came up to them.

'May I see your invitations, madam, and sir?' he asked with exquisite courtesy.

Juliet smiled sweetly. 'You've already seen them. We went out to have a cigarette, and now we've come back again.' And with that she disappeared into the ladies' cloakroom. Here she bumped into several fellow débutantes.

'Hello,' she greeted them. 'Isn't this a marvellous party? *such* divine music.'

If the others wondered why they hadn't seen her all evening, no one challenged her. When they left to go back to the ball-room, Juliet went with them, careful to let them surround her. There was no sign of Colin, so she stayed with the girls as they chattered amongst themselves like a flock of brightly coloured birds, until she saw Edward Courtney, who she'd met at a party the previous night.

'Edward . . . !' she exclaimed joyfully, as if he were a long-lost friend. Then she linked her arm through his and looked up at him with a beguiling smile. 'Isn't this . . . Oh, gosh! That's my most favourite tune. Oh, do let's dance, Edward. I can never resist this music.'

Unable to resist her, Edward allowed himself to be dragged on to the dance floor, and a moment later they were doing a smart quickstep. Edward was transfixed by her animation and sense of fun. At one point his girlfriend re-emerged from the cloakroom, looking for him, but he found it no hardship to cut her dead.

As for Colin, the last time Juliet had caught sight of him he was drinking at the bar; he'd suddenly become the most easily forgettable young man she'd ever met.

'You're up early, Mummy,' Rosie remarked in surprise, when Liza stalked into the dining room as she and Juliet were having breakfast the next morning.

'I'm up early,' her mother snapped acidly, 'because I was awakened at *dawn* by Lady Fogarty, your dinner hostess and chaperone last night, Juliet, phoning to say she and her husband spent twenty-five minutes looking for you last night, to escort you home. Lord and Lady Martineau had no idea where you'd gone either.'

Juliet looked sorrowfully at Liza. 'Mummy, I had a raging headache. I think it was a migraine. I was almost blind with agony. All I wanted to do was creep home and go to bed, so I slipped away. Got a taxi right outside their front door too.'

Liza raised her finely plucked eyebrows and pursed her lips. 'Then where were you when I looked in on you, at twenty past two? Your bed was empty.'

'I might have been in the bathroom,' Juliet ventured. 'I had a terrible hunt for aspirins. With all these parties, Mummy, you really should make sure there are aspirins in every bathroom.'

Rosie looked across the dining table at her. 'People only need aspirins if they drink too much,' she said smugly. 'Anyway, I thought I heard you coming back at about three thirty.'

Ignoring this remark, because Liza had no idea how to handle the situation if it were true, she proceeded to lecture Juliet on her rudeness, and told her she must write letters of apology immediately after breakfast.

When the sisters were on their own again, Juliet turned on Rosie with venom. 'Why did you say I wasn't back until three thirty?'

Rosie sipped her coffee. 'Because you weren't. What were you up to?'

'Mind your own business, and why are you looking so pleased with yourself?'

With studied nonchalance, Rosie dropped her crumpled table napkin on to the table, and rose. 'No particular reason.' Then she walked slowly out of the room and into the hall. Once out of sight, she rushed up the stairs, taking them two at a time, until she reached her mother's bedroom.

'Mummy?' She tapped urgently on the door.

'Come in.' Liza was sitting at her dressing table, which was cluttered with silver-topped jars, brushing her hair.

'You'll never guess . . . !' Rosie began. 'I didn't have a chance to tell you last night because Daddy was in a bad mood, and I knew he'd object, but Alastair has invited me to a luncheon party in the ladies' annexe of his club. There's going to be twelve of us, so I can go, can't I?'

'Of course you can. When is it?'

'Today.' Rosie was breathless with excitement. 'Now, what shall I wear?'

Had she known it, in the days to come her wardrobe would be the least of her worries.

It wasn't long before Rosie was certain Alastair was about to propose. Loving him more every time she saw him, she responded to the warmth of his manner, his intimate glances and the occasional squeezing of her hand. He held her close when they danced, and told her she was 'beautiful' and 'wonderful'.

She was slightly worried, though, that it was now July, and the season would end in three weeks.

'There's always the little season, in October,' Liza said soothingly. 'Everyone comes back to London, refreshed from their stay in the country, and we might give a party ourselves. Just a little one, so Daddy doesn't get cross, but don't worry, darling. It's obvious Alastair's crazy about you; he hasn't looked at another girl all summer, has he?'

'No. He never leaves my side at parties.'

'Well, there you are, darling! He's obviously besotted with you.'

*   *   *

Meanwhile, to liven things up, gatecrashing had become Juliet's latest craze. She and her friends made bets to see how many parties they could crash in a week, without getting caught. Cecil Beaton, she'd been told, had crashed a ball in the twenties with his sister, Baba, and had been forcibly ejected.

Juliet thought this was terribly smart and it hadn't done *his* reputation any harm, had it? Everyone was clamouring to be photographed by him these days, and he was invited to all the best houses . . . at least once.

The thrill of dashing through tradesman's entrances, or side doors, or climbing over railings and walls with Edward, James, Colin, Andrew, or whoever was her accomplice on that particular night, added a frisson to what might otherwise have been a round of fairly dull parties.

By the third week of July, the débutantes who had been popular when they came out had blossomed, made lots of friends and were looking forward to the little season in October. Those who had not, had promptly gone back in again, saying they were missing their horses in the country.

There was only one more dance before the mass exodus from London, and both Rosie and Juliet had been invited.

Juliet, getting ready in her room, felt an unexpected twinge of regret. Going out every night had become a part of her life. She was no longer a girl in her teens who had nightmares, no longer 'Rosie's younger sister', but a young woman in her own right, certain her head would always rule her heart, and that she'd have complete control of her destiny from now on. For the rest of her life, she intended to remain in charge of her feelings and actions. It was, to her, a way of making sure she never got hurt.

In the next room, Rosie was putting the finishing touches to her face and hair. She'd decided to wear the white gown she'd worn for Queen Charlotte's ball, because Alastair had said how much he liked it. Tonight she had the strangest presentiment something stupendous was going to happen.

Juliet arrived at the ball before Rosie. Within moments she was surrounded by a galaxy of handsome young men, offering her a drink, a cigarette, or a dance.

'Later, perhaps,' she replied, smiling with the lazy assurance of someone who knows they'll be asked again.

Then she became aware that a man she'd never seen before

was staring at her. He was tall and broad-shouldered and looked much more self-assured than the other men. She also liked the fact that there was a certain charismatic slow-burning rage in his eyes, which was both sexy yet scary. Intrigued, she watched as he stood talking to Edward Courtney and suddenly realized they were discussing her. Amused and flattered, she averted her face so they could see her profile, which she knew was her best angle.

'I'll introduce you,' she heard Edward say. 'She's top hole in the looks department, isn't she?'

Juliet feigned surprise when Edward appeared in front of her.

'Hello, Juliet. May I introduce . . .' Edward affected an introduction, most of which was lost, as the band struck up at that moment.

'Would you like to dance?' The young man's voice was almost a croak.

'I'd love to,' she said lightly, languidly stubbing out her cigarette in a glass ashtray.

Edward watched them as they drifted into the art deco ballroom. They made a striking couple, Juliet so femininely alluring, with her delicate hand resting on Alastair's shoulder, and her golden hair rippling down her back. He, in contrast, looked strong, dark and brooding.

For a while Edward forgot about them, as he did his duty dances with the girls in his dinner party, but by then he realized it was nearly midnight, and Juliet was still on the dance floor, held tightly in the arms of her partner, their cheeks almost touching as they swayed to 'These Foolish Things'.

'Bloody hell!' he exclaimed laughingly to Charles Padmore, as they came off the floor with their respective partners. 'Alastair Slaidburn's sweet on Juliet, isn't he?'

Charles's eyes were popping and he looked quietly distraught. 'It really is *too* much, isn't it?' he fretted miserably.

Rosie had spent most of the evening in the ladies' cloakroom, too upset to join the party and not wanting anyone to see her tear-stained face. Coming out of a cubicle in which she'd been lurking, trying to blow her nose on the stiff shiny Bronco loo paper, she collected her wrap, and slipped out of the hotel.

As she crouched in the back of the taxi, she sobbed with a

mixture of anger and grief. It was the last straw. The last *bloody* final straw. And she felt like killing Juliet.

'I can't believe we haven't met before,' Alastair murmured into Juliet's ear, as they continued to dance. 'Never mind. Fate has brought us together now,' she replied, smiling wickedly. 'I hope you're not about to dash off and bury yourself in the country, like everyone else?' As she danced, she swayed her hips against his, a trick she'd learned instinctively during the summer, and it amused her to see how quickly she could arouse a man.

'I'm not going anywhere,' Alastair vowed with fervency. He looked feverish. The world had shrunk for him, and his attention had become focused, as if under a spotlight, on this girl with the rippling golden hair, reminding him of a pre-Raphaelite painting by Rossetti. Beside her, the other girls, with their short permed hair, looked artificial and contrived. Most of all, he was drawn to the wild streak he could sense in her. It made him suspect that deep passion flowed through her blood, so hot and feral it would drive him to a kind of madness if he got involved.

But involved he desperately wanted to be. He was on fire with longing. He wanted her right now, this minute. Then he felt deeply shocked at himself. What was happening to him? He'd become attached to a perfectly sweet heiress called Rosie Granville during the summer . . . but for some reason he'd hesitated to commit himself to her.

Now he knew why. Rosie had been a mere shadow of what he'd wanted. A charming but pale edition of this girl who was now in his arms, pressing herself against him in a way that was setting him on fire.

'I'd like a drink,' Juliet said, suddenly extricating herself from his arms. She could feel his reluctance to let her go.

'Let's go this way,' he said, as he collected two glasses from the champagne bar. Leading the way to an anteroom, they settled themselves at a small table in the corner.

'Why haven't I seen you before?' he asked wistfully.

Juliet gave a low chuckle. 'You obviously don't read the *Bystander* or the *Sketch*, or even *Queen* magazine,' she mocked gently. 'And why haven't I met *you*? Do you *ever* go out?'

Alastair leaned forward, his expression entranced. He loved the way she spoke, like a sophisticated woman, instead of a drippy little débutante.

'I live in Yorkshire, but I have been to quite a few parties this summer.'

'Then you're going to totally the wrong sort of parties,' she teased.

Alastair took a swig of his champagne. 'Do you live in London?'

'Some of the time.'

'Which do you like best? Town or country?'

She shrugged. 'It depends.'

'Are your parents here, tonight?'

'No. I came in a dinner party, but I haven't even seen my hostess for hours.'

Alastair smiled suddenly, as if the sun had come out. 'Not much of a chaperone, then?'

She smiled flirtatiously. 'I don't pay any attention to chaperones. They're such a bore. Have you got a gasper?'

He looked bemused for a moment, then he jumped to his feet, realizing what she was asking for. 'I'll get some right away.'

While he was gone, Juliet considered her situation. Alastair was never going to look at Rosie again, and Rosie was never going to speak to her again, either. Oh well! Juliet suddenly started laughing quietly to herself. It would serve Rosie right for being Mummy's Little Pet, and such a goody two-shoes.

At that moment Alastair returned with a packet of Craven A, and a tiny box of matches.

'Can I take you to lunch tomorrow? Or tea at Gunter's?'

Juliet took a deep drag on her cigarette and looked up at him through her eyelashes. 'Tea would be lovely.' She made it sound as if she was accepting an invitation to an orgy.

Flushing with pleasure, he squeezed her hand until it hurt. 'You're the most . . .' He drew a shuddering breath. 'The most beautiful girl I've ever met.'

Her eyes swept lazily over him. 'Thank you.'

'Let's dance again.'

'Can I finish my cigarette first?'

They danced until they realized they were almost alone in the ballroom. Stragglers were drifting through the lobby into

Park Lane, and disembodied shouts of goodbye filled the air. Over Hyde Park a full moon bathed the trees in a ghostly light and the grass was a shimmering silver carpet.

The débutante season of 1935 had come to an end.

'My darling girl,' Liza sympathized, putting her arms around Rosie as she helped her up to her room. She'd been awakened from a deep and much needed sleep shortly after midnight, when Rosie had burst into their room, sobbing hysterically.

'I could kill her,' she kept saying, between explaining what had happened.

Henry, annoyed at being disturbed on their only early night of the week, huffed and puffed, and told Rosie it was better to find out now, rather than later, what the wretched fellah was like.

'It's all Juliet's fault,' Rosie wailed. 'She went after him the minute she saw him, before I even got to the dance, and she hung on to him all night.'

'Presumably he could have desisted,' Henry retorted acidly.

'It's so unfair, Mummy,' Rosie wept. 'Juliet behaved terribly badly.' Mother and daughter shared a deep conviction that men were easily led astray, couldn't help themselves, could be duped, seduced and preyed upon by designing women, as if they had no will of their own. It was the 'other woman' they both feared, never the 'poor man'.

Liza looked grave as she sat on the edge of Rosie's bed. If Juliet started jumping the queue to the altar now, something would have to be done about it. Liza didn't know quite what, but what she did know was that Rosie must get married first.

'There's nothing you can do until the morning, sweetheart,' Liza told her. 'Try and get some sleep.'

It was nearly three o'clock in the morning when Rosie heard the landing floor creak. With a bound she was out of bed, pouncing on Juliet as she was about to go to her own room.

'How could you! That was the meanest thing . . . and what have I ever done to hurt you?' Rosie sobbed. 'I *love* Alastair.'

Juliet eyed her sister with contempt. 'It's not my fault if he prefers me. I didn't *ask* him to dance all night with me.'

'Knowing you, I bet he couldn't get *away*. You knew how

much I cared for him and you deliberately set out to take him from me. I'll never forgive you for this. Never,' Rosie stormed.

'You're so busy whispering to Mummy, how was I to know it was Alastair you were after? If you weren't so bloody secretive . . . !'

'But you *knew* . . . you knew . . . !' Rosie screamed, making a wild grab for her sister's long hair.

'Get off me.' Juliet tried to push her away.

'He was going to marry *me*. You've ruined my life . . .' Beside herself with rage and grief, Rosie pulled harder at Juliet's hair. 'I hate you . . . I hate you . . .' She lashed out, delivering a stinging clap on Juliet's cheek with her other hand.

Juliet grabbed her by the wrist, twisting her arm and forcing her down on to her knees. 'He's no longer interested in you,' she shouted harshly. 'Who would be interested in a drab creature like you, once they'd met me?'

'You bloody cow!' Rosie screeched. 'You've always been jealous of me.'

They started punching and slapping each other, rolling over and over on the landing in unabated fury.

'Jealous of *you*?' Juliet shrieked. 'I can get any man I want, while you can't even keep one.' She tried to grab Rosie's hair, but it was cut too short to get a real grip.

'You spoil everything. You always have. I wish you'd never been born,' Rosie shouted, breathless now. She crumpled up into a heap on the floor, with her knees drawn up to her chin.

'You're such a Mummy's girl,' Juliet snarled, punching Rosie on the shoulder.

They were unaware of bedroom doors being flung open, as Nanny and the rest of the staff leaned over the bannister from the top floor, open-mouthed at the spectacle of the two young ladies slugging it out like a couple of fishwives.

Then there were thunderous footsteps pounding along the corridor and a man's voice, roaring, 'Girls! Girls!'

Henry stood over them, in his silk dressing gown, his face crimson with anger. Behind him Liza stood, a study in mortification.

At first the sisters didn't hear him, so engrossed were they in trying to do damage to each other.

'*Girls!*' Henry yelled.

'Stop that at *once!*' boomed another voice, of such authority that even Henry jumped, and the girls instantly loosened their grip on each other.

'How old do you think you are?' continued Nanny, looking down on them, her hands on her hips. 'I used to smack your bottoms when you were small, and don't go thinking you're too old to be punished now. Go to your rooms at once, and in the morning you will apologize to your parents for your disgraceful behaviour.'

For a moment there was a stunned silence, broken by Ruby giving a nervous giggle.

'Sorry, Nanny,' Rosie said automatically, struggling to her feet, her dress torn and her hair awry.

'Sorry, Nanny,' muttered Juliet, picking up her evening bag and gloves.

Henry and Liza watched as their daughters stumbled into their rooms and shut the doors quietly behind them.

Nanny turned to the servants, who stood stock-still and wide-eyed. 'Never seen children having a tantrum before?' she jeered, before stomping back to her own room.

In order to avoid further confrontation, Juliet stayed in bed until quite late, telling the parlour maid who wanted to 'do' her bedroom, that she had a bad headache. In fact she'd never felt better. Alastair had kissed her goodnight. On the lips. And he'd done it so sweetly and gently, cupping her face in his hands, that she'd allowed him to kiss her again, more intimately this time.

'I'll see you later? Four o'clock at Gunter's?' he said insistently.

'Yes,' she whispered, nodding.

Now, as she snuggled under her pink satin eiderdown, she thought pleasurably about the previous night, knowing she had Alastair in the palm of her hand.

Her reverie was broken at ten thirty, by her mother marching into her room.

'I want to talk to you, young lady,' Liza said without preamble. 'How dare you go off with Alastair Slaidburn when he's Rosie's boyfriend? Don't you realize what you've done?'

Juliet drew herself up in bed, her hair tumbling around her

shoulders. 'What? They're lovers? Engaged to be married? Do let me know when the wedding's taking place, won't you?' she said sarcastically.

Liza stood at the foot of the bed, like a tragic figurehead. 'He was *about* to propose to Rosie.'

'Like it's *about* to rain? Mummy. He's a free agent. He could never have been all that keen on Rosie in the first place, or he wouldn't have kept me on the dance floor all night.'

'But you stole him from your sister,' Liza said, on a rising shrill note.

'I did not. It's not my fault if he finds me more attractive, you know. Anyway, I didn't know Rosie was really serious about him, because she'd never said a word to me. You never mentioned him either, which is very strange if you'd hoped he'd become your son-in-law.'

Liza bit her bottom lip with vexation. 'That was because . . .' she began uncertainly and then stopped.

Juliet seized the moment with relish. 'Exactly! You didn't want me to know about him, because you thought he'd make a perfect husband for your precious Rosie.'

Liza blushed and looked confused.

Juliet continued; 'So last night I saw no reason not to be friendly, did I? Edward Courtney introduced us, Alastair asked me to dance and we got on so well . . .'

'Stop! Stop . . .' Liza raised her hands as if to push Juliet's words away.

'Don't you want me to make a good marriage, Mummy?' she asked wistfully, hugging her knees with her slim arms. 'Don't you want me to make you proud of me?' She tilted her head to one side and her pale blue eyes held a look of hurt. Beneath her abrasive manner there were moments when she appeared like a four-year-old who was being scolded just for being herself.

'Of course I want you to make a good marriage, darling,' Liza said guiltily, 'but Rosie has to come first . . .'

'Why? *Why?*'

'Because, well, because she's the eldest. It would be terribly humiliating for her if her younger sister got married first.'

'No, it's because she's your favourite,' Juliet burst out, her voice thick with unshed tears. 'Don't pretend she isn't, because

40

everyone knows she is. She always has been. Everything has to be for Rosie.'

'That's not true, darling. Daddy and I want *all* of you to do well and have happy lives.'

Juliet raised her chin. 'Good. Then I'll marry first and Rosie can have my leavings.'

Alastair was already seated at a table in the window of London's most fashionable tea room.

'Juliet,' he greeted her, rising and coming forward as soon as she entered.

'Hello,' she replied, giving a low sexy chuckle. She glanced askance at the white damask-covered table, set with gilt-edged white china. 'Can we perhaps . . . ? My mother thinks I'm out shopping and the whole of London will spot us if we sit in the window.'

Alastair looked abashed. 'I never thought. Sorry.' He quickly asked for a table at the back of the restaurant, grinning sheepishly as they took their seats. 'It shows you how unaccustomed I am to taking young ladies out to tea. I live in the sticks these days; my etiquette is a bit rusty.'

She smiled beguilingly, but said nothing.

When he'd ordered China tea for both of them, and a selection of sandwiches and tiny cakes frosted with icing sugar, he said, 'It's wonderful to see you again, Juliet. I was beginning to wonder if last night had just been a marvellous dream.'

'I woke up wondering the same thing,' she admitted.

Then he frowned. 'Will your mother mind awfully, your meeting me like this?'

Juliet regarded him from under the straw brim of her hat. 'She worries about things like reputations.'

'Yours or mine?' he countered swiftly, with an engaging grin.

She laughed. 'Definitely yours!'

Their conversation continued in a bright and breezy way, as if they were dipping their toes in the water, hovering on the edge of real intimacy, which for the time being suited Juliet very well. She could tell he was fearful of plunging in, in case he got carried away, and then it crossed her mind that she'd quite like to be 'carried away' by him. And then, suddenly, it seemed to her that he decided to throw caution to the winds.

41

'I know this sounds crazy,' he began diffidently, 'and you'll probably send me packing, but . . . but I'm in love with you, Juliet.' His eyes bored into hers and she felt her insides quicken with excitement. 'I didn't even go to bed last night because I couldn't stop thinking of you. I was desperate to telephone you this morning, and then I realized I didn't know your telephone number. I don't even know your last name! Isn't that the *maddest* thing? The moment I saw you, something happened. I've never felt like this before,' he added, almost brokenly.

His face shone with a fervid intensity that shocked her, and his hands, resting on the table, were clenched into fists.

For a moment she felt overwhelmed and slightly scared. Brought up in a family where it was *de rigueur* to control one's emotions, Alastair's impassioned admissions made her feel uneasy.

'I see,' she said inadequately.

'Please say you'll come out with me tonight? We could go to the Savoy; what do you say?'

'I'm not allowed to go out at night without a chaperone,' she pointed out.

His face suddenly lit up. 'I have an idea.' He leaned forward earnestly. 'I'm staying with my cousin, Alice Heysham. I'll get her to telephone your mother, and invite you to a supper party at her house in Chelsea. I can pick you up from your house, and we can go straight to the Savoy. How about that?'

Juliet nodded. 'There's just one thing.' He looked both excited and embarrassed. 'Can I have your telephone number? And . . . erm . . . what's your mother called?' he added, blushing.

That was when Juliet realized he honestly had no idea who she was. Oh, *dear*! And she did so like intelligent men.

'My mother's Mrs Henry Granville, and I'm Juliet Granville; Rosie's sister.'

'I can't bear it . . .' wailed Rosie, when she heard Lady Heysham had telephoned, inviting Juliet to supper. 'Mummy, can't you see what's happening? Alastair is staying with her. You should have said Juliet couldn't go.'

'I was rather caught on the hop,' Liza protested, knowing Rosie was right.

'Ever since I can remember, I've dreamed of marrying a

42

man like Alastair,' she wept. 'This is breaking my heart.'

'Oh, darling. What about Charles Padmore? He's besotted with you.'

'You said that about Alastair,' Rosie shot back.

'Yes. Well, lots and lots of young men are in love with you.'

'But Alastair is the only one *I'm* in love with,' she said piteously. The absolutely worst part about the whole thing, and what made it so galling, was that her younger sister had pinched Alastair. Not one of the Duke of Rutland's two beautiful daughters, which would have been sort of *bearable*. Not Megan Hamilton, or any of her other fellow débutantes, but her own sister, who shouldn't have come out at all this year.

Alastair was fifteen minutes late, and Juliet, lingering in the hall in a beautiful silk evening coat with white fur cuffs over her evening dress, was terrified he wouldn't turn up. There was something edgy and unpredictable about him that was exciting but also nerve-wracking.

At last, the front door bell rang, and Juliet hurried to answer it.

'Thank you, Parsons,' she said lightly, whipping open the door before the butler could get to it.

Alastair was standing on the doorstep, looking flushed and harrassed. 'I'm so sorry. The traffic is at a standstill at Hyde Park Corner, because there's been a road accident. Will you forgive me?'

Juliet just wanted to get away. 'That's fine,' she replied. 'You're all right, are you? You weren't involved in the accident?'

Alastair's expression softened. 'Oh, you're so sweet. No, I wasn't anywhere near it.'

A shabby old Daimler was parked outside the house. He ushered her into the passenger seat, and then walked around the car and climbed in himself.

As it pulled away from the curb, a face at the second-floor window peered down, seeing it gather speed as it headed towards North Audley Street. Then the view became blurred, breaking up into fragments like a kaleidosope, as the tears poured down Rosie's cheeks. She knew now, without a doubt, that she'd lost her great love.

* * *

43

'I do hope your sister . . . ?' Alastair began diffidently, as they drove round Trafalgar Square. 'I do hope she doesn't think . . . I mean, I never said anything to give her the impression that I was . . .'

'Rosie has masses of young men, all mad about her,' Juliet said quickly, wanting to alleviate any feelings of guilt he might have.

'That's what I thought,' he said gratefully. 'I'd hate her to think . . .'

'Oh . . . quite.'

'She's awfully sweet, a dear girl, but . . .' He drew a deep ragged breath. 'But I feel quite differently about you.'

'I'm glad you do,' Juliet said in a small voice.

He took his eyes off the road ahead, and threw her a searching look. 'Really?'

'Yes. Really.'

'Oh, darling. I wish to God we'd met at the beginning of the season, and not the end.'

'So do I.' Compared to Edward and Archie, or James and Colin, this slightly older man had a dark, dangerous strain running through him which she found irresistible.

Seated at the best table in the restaurant, he ordered their dinner with flair; champagne and oysters, followed by ragout of lobster with a side salad, and a chocolate pudding laced with fine shreds of real gold, created by the resident chef, Gustav Escoffier, which greatly impressed Juliet.

'When can I see you again?' he kept asking obsessively, as they danced. 'Can we meet tomorrow?'

'I told you I was going away for the weekend.' Juliet gave him her catch-me-if-you-can smile.

'Is there no way you can stay in London?'

'Mummy would never allow that.'

'God, it's going to be a long weekend without you,' he groaned, pulling her closer. 'And a longer summer if you're in the country.'

'Can we have some coffee?' she asked. The intensity of his feelings slightly alarmed her.

'Of course.' Alastair led her back to the table. 'Turkish coffee?'

'Yes, please.' She'd never had Turkish coffee before, but she wanted to appear sophisticated in the face of such open passion.

'So what will you do while I'm pining, all on my own?'

She shrugged. 'Play tennis. Go for walks. Relax. Just the usual things.'

'Real family life. How sublime. Both my parents are dead and as I'm an only child, I envy you having a big family.'

Juliet sipped the thick black coffee from its tiny cup, and the bitterness made her lips shrivel, but she kept on smiling sweetly.

'It's very nice,' she remarked without enthusiasm, knowing the next three days would be spent with Rosie.

Hartley Hall was grand, but it was not a stately home. Wisteria, climbing up to the grey slate roof, softened the lines of the white-framed symmetrical windows, and Virginia creeper grew neatly around the white front door. There was also an adjoining staff wing, stables, and a coach house.

Lady Anne had been brought here as a bride, shortly after Frederick Granville had inherited the place from his father. She loved the house with its big airy elegant rooms, but most of all she loved the sixteen-acre garden. With Spence, the head gardener, and three under-gardeners, she'd created a magical place of beauty and style that was the talk of the neighbourhood.

To this comfortable and welcoming home, the Granville sisters had come every weekend since they'd been born, with or without their parents.

Hartley was special in their minds. Hartley was home. And the most special thing about it was their grandmother.

'Darling mother,' Liza said to Lady Anne when they arrived on Friday afternoon, 'will you forgive me if I have a cup of tea in my room? I still have a mass of thank-you letters to write and it's been the *most* exhausting week.'

'Of course, my dear, anything you like,' her mother-in-law replied mildly.

Although it was now Henry's house, he'd insisted his mother should stay on when he got married, telling her he needed her to run the place for him. Lady Anne knew he was being kind, because he could easily have run it himself, even if he did have to work in town, but she appreciated the gesture enormously.

Luckily Liza was more than happy to have her live there too.

45

Liza loved the metropolis and had no feel for the country. She didn't know the difference between a camellia and a hollyhock, or an oak from a silver birch, and she cared even less.

'Come along in, my darlings,' Lady Anne greeted the rest of the family. Tinker, her red setter, and Brandy and Whisky, Henry's terriers, bounded excitedly around her, overjoyed to see the children again.

'Down! Down!' Liza shrieked, worried they would jump up on her pale blue skirt.

'Mother, dear,' Henry said warmly, kissing Lady Anne on both cheeks. Then he looked up as he always did at the large mellow pink-brick Georgian house, and wished he could stay here all the time. Hartley had the ability to wrap itself around him like a warm, comforting cloak, and although he never mentioned it to Liza, he intended to retire here one day.

'How's everything, Mother?' he asked, following her into the conservatory, where Warwick, the ancient butler, had laid out tea.

'Wonderful, darling. You must have a look at the kitchen garden. Not only do we have enough vegetables to feed the whole village, but the figs are ready to eat. So are the damsons and Victoria plums; anyway, you'll be eating the produce over the weekend.'

'Can we play in the garden, Granny?' Amanda asked.

Lady Anne smiled. She thought the way Nanny dressed the children was faintly ridiculous, especially for the country. 'You might like to change out of your smart clothes and shoes first,' she suggested, careful not to catch Nanny's eye.

Up in the nursery the three younger children couldn't wait to change. Off came the white silk socks, the white buckskin strap shoes, the pastel linen coats, the smocked shantung dresses, and the neat satin hair ribbons, to be replaced by shorts and jumpers, and gym shoes or sandals.

Nanny Granville looked sadly at the rosy-cheeked dishevelled children, as they tore into the garden to go on the swing suspended from a tree, the see-saw and the climbing frame, and felt nostalgic for the days when a spotless appearance and decorum at all times were the order of the day.

After tea, Henry ambled off to his study, and Juliet offered Louise a game of tennis. Lady Anne, finding herself alone

46

with Rosie, eyed her granddaughter with concern. Rosie seemed to have slumped into a wordless depression and she looked pale and wretched.

'Are you all right, darling?' she asked gently.

Rosie promptly burst into tears, too distraught to even speak.

Her grandmother took her hand. 'Let's go to my sitting room, where we won't be disturbed.'

Lady Anne's private retreat, a small, cosy, chintzy room off the hall, with comfortable armchairs, overflowing bookshelves and a work bag of embroidery on a footstool, overlooked the rose garden, which on this late afternoon was banded by golden beams of light from the setting sun. Tinker, like a shadow, never left her side, and as she settled herself in a chair, he draped himself around her feet with a contented sigh.

'Tell me what's happened, Rosie,' she said gently.

Slowly and brokenly, she told her grandmother everything.

'I loved him so much,' she said poignantly. 'I really believed we were made for each other.'

'Oh, my dear girl,' her grandmother kept saying sympathetically, 'I'm so sorry.' She blamed Liza of course. There'd been far too much pressure on Rosie to be the débutante of the year, to get engaged to an eligible man, to be the toast of the town and the first one to get married.

Juliet had obviously been very naughty, if what Rosie said was true, but had Alastair Slaidburn really been on the point of proposing to Rosie? Mightn't he just have been an admirer? A dancing partner? A flirt? No doubt Liza had made much of him being a marquess, with a large estate, and this would have nourished Rosie's fantasies and a desire to please her mother.

'I can only say, darling,' Lady Anne said diplomatically, 'that I don't think he sounds worthy of you. If he'd given you the impression that he was going to marry you, then, of course, he's behaved appallingly.'

Rosie was instantly defensive. 'It's not his fault, Granny. Juliet stole him away from me. I don't suppose she cares for him at all, she just doesn't want me to have him.'

A pained expression flitted across Lady Anne's finely boned face. Rosie is just like her mother, she reflected; nothing is ever the man's fault. 'You talk of him as if he's so weak-willed he doesn't know his own mind,' she said carefully. 'A man who is really in love with a woman *can't* be "stolen", as if he were a pound of butter. It seems to me he's not worthy of you.'

Rosie's mouth dropped. 'But he returned my feelings. And I'd set my heart on marrying him.'

'I'm sure you had. Are you sure you didn't just fall in love with the whole idea of being a titled lady living in a fine house?'

Rosie looked taken aback. 'But that's how I've always seen myself,' she confessed.

'I wonder where you ever got that idea from?' her grandmother enquired drily.

Only the ticking of the little brass carriage clock on the mantelshelf broke the uneasy silence.

'What on earth shall I do if he marries Juliet?' Rose finally blurted out in panic.

'Now brace up, Rosie. He's probably just a flirt, but if he were to marry Juliet, you must conduct yourself with dignity and wish them both well.'

'Oh, I *couldn't* . . . !'

'Why cross bridges before you come to them, my dear? Juliet is a flirt, too. There's probably nothing in it. In any case, the season ends next week, and then you'll all be down here for August and September, and he'll go back to wherever he comes from, and that will be the end of that.' Lady Anne smiled and then rose, bringing their little chat to an end. 'Why don't you have a nice hot bath before dinner, while I get a grated raw potato from the kitchen and bring it up to you.'

'A potato?' Rosie asked blankly.

Her grandmother spoke briskly but kindly. 'If you place raw potato on your eyes and lie down for fifteen minutes, the puffiness and redness will go, and no one will know you've been crying. You must never be seen in tears in front of the servants, you know, because it embarrasses them.'

During that following week, Alastair pursued Juliet with zeal, sending her notes, telephoning her every day, and ordering extravagant bouquets of flowers to be delivered.

Liza, watching Juliet's elation and Rosie's unhappiness, found herself deeply torn between being thrilled by Juliet's conquest, but at the same time wishing fervently that Rosie was still the object of his desire. One part of her wanted to tell Juliet not to respond to this amorous onslaught, but another part of her was filled with fierce pride that at least one of her daughters looked like making a brilliant match.

'Keep out of it,' Henry warned. 'You must not interfere, and let's hope to God that once the season ends, and everyone leaves London, this young man will cool off, and leave *both* girls alone.'

That wasn't what Liza had in mind at all, but she said nothing. If only the season could have lasted another month, she was sure Juliet would have been engaged, but going to the country was inevitable. Nobody stayed in town during August, or appeared to stay in town, that is. The impoverished gentry were known to put up the shutters and draw the curtains if they couldn't afford to go away, and, like troglodytes, only crept out at night.

On the Thursday evening, Juliet told her mother she'd been invited to join a party hosted by Alastair at the Café de Paris.

This wasn't true, of course, but she knew her mother would never agree to her going out alone with a man, not even a marquess. Whether Liza believed her or not, and Juliet had a feeling they were both bluffing, she nevertheless lent her daughter a beautiful diamond necklace and matching earrings, telling her not to flaunt herself in front of poor Rosie, because it wouldn't be kind.

Liza and Juliet had entered into a secret unspoken pact, and when Alastair collected her in his old Daimler, she was in high spirits.

Three

'Nanny, is it true Juliet's getting engaged?' Charlotte asked, as she got ready for bed. It was mid-September and the Granville family had returned to London earlier that day.

'Who's been listening to tittle-tattle?' Nanny snapped, smoothing the front of her starched apron.

Amanda, sitting in the bath, turned the cake of soap round and round in her hands. 'Mummy thinks she will,' she said stoutly. 'Look at all the letters she's been getting from Alastair. He's been writing to her every day.'

'People write to each other about the weather and that sort of thing,' Louise said knowledgeably. 'It doesn't mean anything.'

'But Mummy thinks Alastair's letters mean a *lot*,' said Charlotte darkly.

Amanda made a face. 'Who wants to know about the weather? Nanny, if Juliet gets married, she can have babies, can't she?'

'There's no question of her getting married,' Nanny said severely. 'For one thing, she's much too young.'

'How will she get babies?' Charlotte asked, tugging her white cotton nightdress over her head.

'It's simple,' Louise retorted, sponging her face. 'While she's in the church, getting married, God plants a seed inside her and when she comes out of the church she can have a baby.'

Charlotte's eyes widened in wonder. 'Is that what is called a miracle?'

'It's more like a lot of nonsense to me,' countered Nanny, whose broad shoulders, Charlotte observed, were shaking for some reason. 'Now come along. Out of the bath.' You've still got to clean your teeth.'

Juliet was seeing Alastair tonight for the first time in six weeks, and she had a strong feeling he was going to propose.

Throughout her stay at Hartley, she'd been bombarded by letters, little presents, poems and flowers, which she found flattering but exhausting. At least tonight she'd know where she stood; by tomorrow . . . who knows? She might actually be engaged to be married.

Meanwhile she needed a new dress for the occasion. Both she and Rosie had been invited to this big ball at Claridge's, and she wanted something pale blue to wear, because Alastair had said it was his favourite colour. Bond Street was the place to go, so she slipped out of the house, not wanting Rosie to know what she was doing or she'd want a new dress too.

*　　*　　*

50

These days, Rosie felt like a wilting flower, fading into the background, while Juliet blossomed and grew more prominent. She was going through her wardrobe, wondering what to wear tonight, with her self-confidence at a low ebb, and her weight loss causing all her dresses to hang off her unbecomingly. There was only one man on the horizon these days, who thought she was the most perfect creature on earth, but did she really want a man who resembled a devoted bloodhound trailing around after her? Charles Padmore, or to give him his title, Lord Padmore, but 'only a baron, not an earl', according to Liza.

He was quite sweet, if weak, Rosie reflected, but when his mother had invited her to stay with them at Coldberry, in Cumbria, it had been rather a shock. Coldberry turned out to be not just a crumbling castle, but a derelict ruin with a dungeon, the main building having collapsed around 1919.

Nevertheless . . . Rosie selected a silvery-green dress that she knew Charles liked, and decided to ask Mummy if she could borrow some jewellery.

To have someone who cared, Rosie decided, was better than having no one at all; especially as Juliet had *someone*.

Juliet, having bought herself an exquisite chiffon dress that matched her eyes and clung to her body like a second skin, was walking briskly home, when a familiar figure of a young man waved at her and, risking life and limb, sprinted across the road, to say hello. It was Edward Courtney.

'Juliet!' he exclaimed, grinning engagingly at her. 'How are you?' He raised his Homburg hat. 'It's yonks since I've seen you; I've been in America. How was your summer?'

Her eyes danced mischievously. 'Over, thank God. We returned to London yesterday.'

'You certainly look well, but then you always do, sweetie.' He leaned forward to kiss her on the cheek. 'When am I going to see you again?'

'Are you going to the Buckinghams' tonight?'

'Sure thing! Let's have a dance. So what's happening in your life? Proposals by the dozen, no doubt?'

She laughed. Edward was such fun to be with, and she wished he were more eligible. 'Well . . .' She cocked her head to one side. 'Between you and me, Alastair Slaidburn is hot on the trail.'

'Alastair Slaidburn?' Edward raised his eyebrows in surprise. Then his brow furrowed. 'I introduced you, didn't I?' He hesitated for a moment before continuing, 'Lovely chap, but do be careful. He's got no money, you know. His reputation as a fortune-hunter has overshadowed every deb season for as long as I can remember.' Then he laughed. 'But you're far too shrewd to be taken in by someone like that, aren't you, sweetie? Listen, I must dash; got to meet my mother at Gunter's, but I'll see you tonight? Don't forget to save a dance for me, will you?'

Juliet walked slowly back to Green Street, feeling sick.

How could Alastair have no money? He owned Ashbourne Court for a start, and thousands of acres of surrounding land.

Edward must have got it wrong.

Once home, she rushed up to her mother's sitting room, where Liza was writing letters.

'Oh, no! That can't be right,' Liza exclaimed, when Juliet told her what she'd heard.

'Edward wouldn't lie about a thing like that.'

'But maybe he's sweet on you himself, and is trying to put you off Alastair?'

Juliet removed her hat and shook out her hair. 'No. Edward and I are just great friends. What am I going to do now?'

Liz reached for her phone. 'I'm going to ring Daddy. He has contacts everywhere who will know if it's true. The Slaidburns certainly used to be rich. I can't understand it.'

Juliet made a late entrance at the Buckinghams' dance, where the ballroom was banked by pyramids of white flowers, the band was blasting out 'Let's do It (Let's Fall in Love)' and the party was already in full swing.

She spotted Alastair at once, sitting with a group of friends. Out of the corner of her eye she saw him jump up as soon as he saw her, so, pretending she hadn't noticed him, she walked casually in the opposite direction, thankful she knew nearly everyone at the party.

As usual, she was immediately surrounded, her willowy figure enveloped by dinner-jacketed swains.

'Darling!' exclaimed Colin Armstrong.

'Darling,' she replied, clinging coquettishly to his arm. 'God, it's been a long summer without seeing you.'

'It's been *forever* without seeing *you*,' he retorted, giving her a swift kiss on the side of her neck.

'Where shall we go tonight?' she whispered provocatively.

'Are there any good parties we can crash?'

'What a girl you are!' he laughed, slipping his arm around her waist.

She cuddled into his side, whilst reaching out to greet a sandy-haired young man she knew, called Andrew Stevens. He grasped her hand with its long scarlet nails, and stroked her arm, as her wrist glittered with diamonds.

'It's been an *age*,' he burbled, happily.

'An *absolute* age, sweetie,' she replied, gazing into his eyes. She had succeeded in gathering a circle of her best men friends around her, as if she was a magnet in a box of pins.

And all the time she was aware of Alastair, circling the group like a prowling shark, his expression angry as she continued to ignore him.

'Juliet!' he called out loudly.

She looked up at Colin from under her blackened eyelashes. 'Oh, listen! They're playing my favourite tune. I simply have to dance . . . Come along . . .' She grasped his hand, and then he whisked her away across the polished floor. A moment later she was snuggled in his arms, her eyes closed and a blissful smile on her face.

'What's going on with Juliet?' Charles Padmore asked Rosie, as they sat together, having a drink and watching the dancing.

She was beginning to find his constant presence strangely comforting and reassuring. As Alastair had so obviously switched his affections from her to Juliet, it was a salve to her hurt pride to have *someone* interested in her.

'You know Juliet,' she said, trying to keep the bitterness out of her voice. 'I expect she's just trying to make Alastair Slaidburn jealous; bring him to the boil, that sort of thing.'

Charles frowned disapprovingly. 'I can't believe you're sisters. I've never met two people who are so unalike.'

Rosie beamed, taking this as a great compliment. She squeezed his hand and gave him a look of gratitude, thinking him quite dashing.

'I think perhaps I'm more like Mummy.'

'So, does Juliet take after your father, then?'

'I don't know who she takes after,' she said drily. The way her sister was cavorting around the dance floor with such supreme confidence made her wince. Juliet was behaving in a fast fashion, and if she went on like this, she'd get a bad name. Rosie bit her bottom lip, feeling jealous because she knew she'd never get a bad name or anything else, because she wasn't exciting enough.

'Rosie, would you like to dance?'

She was on her feet before he'd finished speaking, and to counteract her too obvious eagerness, she then said languidly, 'Yes, why not.'

She could feel his bony knees knocking against her legs and wondered if he would feel bony all over, without his clothes. The thought made her feel queasy and at the same time excited.

Embarrassed by her own thoughts, she averted her eyes as they danced.

'Juliet!' Alastair spoke despairingly. He'd managed to corner her as she re-emerged from the powder room. His face was flushed and red. He gripped her wrist fiercely. 'What's the matter with you? Why do you keep avoiding me? Where's the corsage of orchids I sent you? Why aren't you wearing it?'

Juliet stood quite still, her small features like carved marble, her pale blue, cat-like eyes cold and watchful.

Alastair started haranguing her vehemently again, his voice loud and hysterical. 'Why have you been ignoring me ever since you got here?'

She tried to quench her own rising temper. 'I do have other friends, you know. And the flowers didn't go with this dress.'

'What do you mean, you've got other friends?' His eyes glittered strangely. A group was forming around them now, of people who loved nothing more than watching others quarrel.

Alastair continued, his voice rising. 'We *all* have friends! What about *us*? You and me, goddammit! Why have you been cutting me dead? Dancing with everyone else? Why won't you answer me *now*?' Sweat gleamed on his face, his body was rigid with rage.

Something started to unravel in Juliet's brain. 'I've been enjoying myself,' she said icily.

'Yes, with every Tom, Dick and Harry.' His grip tightened, hurting her.

'Alastair . . . !'

He stood over her, almost menacingly. 'We were meant for each other. You know that. What's wrong? I was going to ask you to marry me tonight.'

There was an electrified silence. People shuffled closer.

Juliet's temper rose. 'Well, I don't want to marry you, so will you please let go of me . . . ?' she retorted shrilly.

'But you said you loved me!' He dropped her wrist abruptly and ran his hands through his hair in frenzied anguish. 'You *told* me . . . You said you felt the same . . .'

She'd regained her poise, and her anger was calculated now, fine-edged and savage. 'I didn't know then you were a well-known fortune-hunter and that you're on the brink of bank-ruptcy. I actually thought you loved me for myself. Silly me! Now that I know it was my family's money you were after, I want nothing more to do with you.'

Then she turned and walked away along the corridor and vanished from sight.

'Poor old chap! Did you see his face?' Colin Armstrong whispered to Archie Hipwood, as they made their way to the bar, in need of strong drinks.

Colin nodded, shaken. 'He was actually crying. He must be devastated.'

'I feel very sorry for him, but it was a bit silly of him to think Juliet would actually marry him, as he's penniless, wasn't it?'

Colin sipped his drink, and lit a cigarette. 'I blame his cousin, Lady Heysham. I hear she told him that there are lots of girls from very rich families who would marry him for his title.'

Archie looked doubtful. 'Lots of *American* girls, perhaps, or industrialists' daughters, but one look at Juliet should have told him she'd never marry someone who was poor.'

Edward Courtney strolled up to them, looking worried. 'I feel awful, you know. I warned Juliet earlier today that Alastair was broke, because I had a feeling she didn't realize it.'

'Probably just as well you told her,' Archie said reassuringly, 'but I'm surprised she didn't know. Two lots of death duties have clobbered him. A shame, really. Basically, he's a decent chap, desperate to save his estates.'

'He's always been very neurotic, though,' Colin pointed out. 'I mean, the way he was going on! Rather bad form, all that hysteria.'

'I tell you one thing,' Edward mused, drawing deeply on his cigarette.

'What's that, old fellah?'

'I'd hate to get on the wrong side of Juliet Granville.'

The three men gulped their whiskies and puffed away and thought about the responsibility of having a strong wife who would expect them to provide a lavish style of living.

'I'm not getting—' began Edward.

'Neither am I,' said Colin with feeling.

'Nor me. Let's have another drink,' Archie added.

'Is it true?' Rosie hissed. She'd cornered Juliet in the cloak-room and she was looking deeply shocked. Having missed the altercation because she and Charles were dancing, she'd heard, to her mortification, rumours of what had happened.

'Is what true?' Juliet asked loftily, as she collected her furs from the attendant.

'You know perfectly well.' Rosie was hunched forward, her arms held across her front as if she had stomach-ache. 'Everyone's talking about you,' she whispered, white with anger. 'They're saying you behaved like a virago. How *could* you, Juliet? How could you treat Alastair like that?'

'If that's what they're saying about me then it must be true,' Juliet flashed back, shrugging.

'Where do you think you're going?'

'Mind your own business.'

Rosie protested in panic, 'I can't go back to the ballroom on my own. People are *talking*.'

Juliet had had enough. She turned recklessly away, five foot six and eight stone of champagne-fuelled venom. 'Let them bloody talk! I've done you a favour; you're so stupid you'd have married him if he'd asked you, and *then* found out he was after your money.'

*   *   *

56

Tears of rage and disappointment streamed down Juliet's face as the taxi rattled through Mayfair towards Green Street. Like Rosie, she'd set her heart on marrying Alastair, and she'd convinced herself so thoroughly that she cared for him, that she no longer knew now whether it was actually true or not. But how differently she and her sister had regarded him. To Rosie, Alastair had been a knight in shining armour, brave, kind, true and of course eminently eligible. To Juliet, he'd been someone who was dangerously exciting, possessed of dark forces, a wild stallion whose love-making would be thrilling and feverish. Tonight she'd been almost scared by his uncontrollable emotions, but at the same time horribly enthralled.

But would he, if he'd been rich, have been the right man for either of them? She wondered.

'I'm afraid there's no question of it; you can't possibly marry Alastair Slaidburn,' Liza had told her fretfully, earlier in the day. With Henry's help she'd found out what she should have already known; Alastair was broke, and his cousin was trying to find him a rich bride.

'He didn't know I had money when he first met me,' Juliet had pointed out swiftly. It was true. He'd known from the beginning Rosie was a Granville, because Lady Heysham had made a point of introducing him to her, but that first magical night when Juliet met him, he hadn't even known her name.

'You may be right,' Liza agreed, reluctantly, 'but please don't say that to Rosie. He's hurt her enough as it is.'

'And you don't think I'm hurt? And disappointed?' Juliet had retorted. And so she'd gone to the ball, deciding to ignore Alastair whilst flirting with all the other young men, so she'd at least have the pleasure of being the one to end their relationship.

It was still only midnight, and to her annoyance Parsons was lurking in passageways and landings, checking locks and switching off lights.

'Miss Juliet?' he said in surprise at seeing her arrive home so early and unchaperoned.

'Good night, Parsons,' she said coldly, averting her face so he wouldn't see her tears.

On the second floor landing she ran into Miss Ashley, Liza's lady's maid, who was about to put Liza's jewels back in the safe after their return, a few minutes before, from another party.

Juliet nodded to her silently, before tapping on her mother's bedroom door. 'Can I come in, Mummy?'

Liza was taking off her make-up at her dressing table. She called out, 'Come in,' at the sound of Juliet's tear-thickened voice. 'What happened, darling?'

'I told him I couldn't marry him.' Juliet slumped on to her parents' large bed, her beautiful face woebegone.

Liza spoke anxiously. 'Nicely, I hope?'

'How can one do it nicely? He used me, and I'll never forgive him for that.'

'Does Rosie know?'

'I think you'll find the whole of London knows by now.'

Liza jumped to her feet, her face covered with Pond's cream, her blue satin and lace negligee slipping off her bare shoulders.

'Surely you were discreet? You didn't let anyone know you were turning him down, did you?'

Juliet rose, suddenly tired, sickened and defeated. 'He got what was coming to him,' she muttered, marching out of the room, and slamming the door behind her.

'What's going on?' Henry demanded, emerging from his dressing room wearing dark blue silk pyjamas.

'Leave her alone, Henry,' Liza said firmly, as she quickly averted her face so he wouldn't see the cold cream. 'Juliet's overtired. We're *all* overtired.' Her bottom lip trembled. Really, it was all too heartbreaking. She'd worked so hard to bring out the girls, and give them every opportunity, and now everything had been ruined.

It didn't end there. Two days later Juliet received a letter from Alastair. His small writing, like mouse scratchings, was difficult to decipher at first, but eventually she was able to make out his rambling exhortations as to why they were meant for each other.

Phrases such as 'We belong together. I can't imagine a life without you . . .' and 'How can you think I'm only interested in your money? You *must* know I love you more than life itself. I *adore* you' caused Juliet to have doubts about rejecting him, for all of ten minutes. But her mother was right. There was no way she could marry a blatant fortune-hunter. On the other hand, would she ever find another man who cared about her so passionately?

In the end, Liza helped Juliet compose a polite but simple letter, saying they had no future together, and under the circumstances she didn't want to see him again.

Two days later, Rosie and Juliet left London for a weekend house party given by Sir George and Lady Frobisher, in Gloucestershire. Around a dozen of their friends had also been invited.

The Frobishers had a grand country house, much more formal than Hartley, and with many more staff. When they arrived, Lady Frobisher greeted them in the main hall. Here, heraldic armorial bearings and insignias abounded, and they were told that tea would be served in the library in fifteen minutes.

'You will find an itinerary of the weekend arrangements in your rooms,' a housekeeper in a black dress informed the sisters, as she led the way up a broad sweeping staircase.

As Rosie and Juliet weren't talking to each other, this announcement didn't garner much response.

Having made sure everyone had been introduced, Lady Frobisher, a vague-looking woman with a rictus grin and eyes so blank she might have been comatose, retired to her throne-like chair by the fire, while Sir George held forth to the group of his own friends who were also staying.

Juliet's heart sank. Especially when she found herself trying to balance a cup and saucer and small plate with a cucumber sandwich, as she sat perched on a chair, amid her hosts' friends. Colin, Archie, Edward, and all her other chums had formed a group in a bay window on the far side of the room, and there was no way she could join them without appearing rude.

'It's to be hoped the Prime Minister's attitude will soften if the Conservatives are returned to power,' Sir George was pontificating.

'I don't think Stanley Baldwin's the right man for the job,' a retired colonel opined. 'We need someone like Winston Churchill at the helm.'

'But he's a warmonger,' quavered an elderly dowager, whose sagging neck was contained by a choker of pearls almost up to her ears.

Ignoring this boring discussion, which she'd heard a hundred times, Juliet was surreptitiously trying to attract

Colin's attention. At last he caught her eye, smiled and then tilted his head towards the door. 'Later,' he mouthed.

Juliet raised plucked eyebrows, and gave the hint of a nod. Suddenly the room seemed to have gone quiet. She looked around wonderingly, and found Sir George staring at her with a pained expression.

'I'm sorry . . . ?' She had no idea what for, but it seemed expected of her.

'I was asking if your father is still a keen supporter of the League of Nations,' Sir George repeated testily.

Juliet's eyes flew open, like glistening aquamarines. 'I'm so sorry . . . I've had a bad ear infection and it's left me slightly deaf, but yes, Daddy is certainly still a supporter. A strong one, actually.'

She was aware of Colin's suppressed laughter from the far corner, and Rosie's nervous stare of astonishment.

'Jolly good,' Sir George muttered, but he turned away with a sneer on his face, as if he had a bad taste in his mouth.

Into the stuffy and old-fashioned formality of this house party, there was much worse to come.

Juliet deliberately waited to come down from her room until everyone, including some of the guests invited to dinner before the ball, had gathered in the hall for drinks.

Earlier in the evening, Colin had managed to secure two glasses of gin and tonic from one of the footmen, and he'd sneaked one to Juliet, to drink while she was getting ready.

The alcohol gave her a lift, brought a slight flush to her cheeks and made her feel exultant. As soon as the dancing started, she intended to enjoy herself in spite of being in this great unfriendly mausoleum of a mansion.

Descending the stairs slowly, she knew her appearance was making an impact. Her ice-blue chiffon dress clung to her body before floating out around her feet.

People looked up, caught sight of her, and were hooked, fascinated. Others turned to see what they were looking at and, seeing her, were unable to turn away either, mesmerized by the strong sexual chemistry that emanated from her.

The men felt lust pulse through their veins, while the women, with sinking hearts, knew that Juliet Granville would be the centre of attraction for the rest of the night.

'I might as well go home now,' one débutante murmured in depressed tones.

Rosie, whose features were more perfect, whose hair was a purer gold and whose eyes were a heart-stopping shade of blue, had faded into insignificance by comparison.

'Bitch!' Rosie thought, as Juliet came down the last few steps. Bitch for stealing her thunder, for luring Alastair away, for ruining her whole year. A bitch she wished had never been born.

Then a curious thing happened. Four guests who had driven down from London arrived at that moment, and Lady Frobisher stepped forward to greet them. A moment later, after whispered words, she gave a little gasping shriek and then threw her hands up in the air.

They were telling her something in low voices, and apologizing for being late. 'We didn't know what to do when he didn't turn up to join us,' a white-faced young man was explaining in urgent tones.

A girl near the group was in tears. Beside her a young man covered his face with his hands. The guests who had just arrived stood huddled together as if they'd endured the most terrible experience.

Something was dreadfully wrong.

'What's happened?' Juliet asked someone.

One of the older women guests stepped forward and put her arm around the weeping girl's shoulders. There were cries of 'Oh! My God!' Lady Frobisher stood transfixed. Then Sir George rallied, and took charge, ordering brandy and a quiet room in which the new arrivals could collect themselves. The rest of the guests had broken up into little groups, muttering quietly, looking shocked.

Everyone had forgotten Juliet, who stood alone and ignored.

Then she noticed Rosie, rushing out of the front door into the garden, her hand clamped over her mouth as if she was going to be sick.

'What's *happened*?' Juliet repeated, her heart contracting with fear.

'And so young!' a woman was saying shrilly. 'It's too tragic for words.'

Juliet pushed her way across the crowded hall to where Edward stood. He looked shattered.

'What's going on?' she demanded, feeling suddenly very frightened.

Edward's face was like candle wax. 'Haven't you heard?' he said almost accusingly. 'Alastair Slaidburn's dead.'

Her blood seemed to freeze into tiny particles that surged through her veins, leaving her feeling numb and faint.

'Dead?' she repeated stupidly. 'Was he driving?'

'What do you mean?'

'On his way here, tonight . . . was he in a car accident?'

Edward turned wild and bloodshot eyes on her. 'For Christ's sake . . . don't you understand? Alastair has committed suicide. Your letter was in his hand when they found him.'

Rosie and Juliet left the Frobishers early the next morning, before anyone was up and about. Throughout the journey Rosie's eyes continued to brim with tears, and on the rare occasions she looked in Juliet's direction, her expression filled with hostility and loathing.

Juliet ignored her as she watched the countryside slip past, seeing humble cottages and shabby terraced houses, back yards hung with washing, or carefully tended flower beds, while envying the people who lived in them for their simple blameless lives.

Nothing would ever be the same again for her; for ever branded as the girl who caused a man's suicide, she'd become a notorious figure of curiosity, with a reputation of being a heartbreaker. Infamy would stalk her from now on, ready to pounce from the shadows no matter what she did.

'Christ Almighty!' Henry exclaimed, appalled, as he picked up the newspapers Parsons had arranged on the hall table.

There were pictures on the front page of Juliet looking stunning in an evening dress, her eyes cat-like and seductive, her mouth luscious. There were ones of Alastair, too, glass in hand, looking handsome and jovial.

According to the style of the newspaper, the headlines ran from MARQUESS COMMITS SUICIDE to DEB'S JILTED SUICIDE SUITOR!

Henry's eyes skimmed the text with growing horror. 'The tragic suicide of the Marquess of Slaidburn, aged twenty-eight, who fell from the roof of his ancestral home . . .' and further on, 'It is believed he was depressed at having been turned down by Miss Juliet Granville, the most beautiful débutante of the year, whose letter of rejection was found in his hand when his body was discovered in the early hours of Friday morning . . .'

Henry sank into his chair at the end of the dining-room table, too shocked to do anything but sit and stare into space.

Breakfast was the one meal when the family helped themselves to what they wanted from the range of silver dishes kept warm on the side. But today, Parsons, who had already scanned the newspapers and passed on the juicier bits to Mrs Fowler, took it upon himself to stay in the dining room, hovering helpfully, with offers to serve Henry.

'Just coffee, please,' Henry said, in a dazed voice. This was awful. Worse than awful. Nothing Juliet had said had prepared him for the exposure of his family in such a common, vulgar way, and in the national press, too.

Despairingly, he glanced at the papers again. Ghastly sentences seemed to jump out of the print to assault him with their mortifying purple prose: '. . . rich society débutante who has already left a trail of broken hearts', who was '. . . a great party-goer.'

'He was in love with her and wanted to marry her,' a member of Alastair's staff had apparently vouchsafed. Asked if Lord Slaidburn's suicide could have been caused by recent financial problems arising out of death duties, the servant was dismissive. 'It was the young lady's rejection what killed him,' he stated.

Even Rosie hadn't been left out of the scandal. One newspaper observed that the marquess had previously been seen in the company of Juliet's sister, Rosie, and that 'Society nobs had thought *she* would get engaged to him.' Which made it clear to even the most dumb-witted, that Juliet had stolen Alastair from her sister, only to discard him cruelly when she'd grown bored of him.

Henry sat brooding over his coffee, trying to take in the enormity of what had happened and the effect it would have on the whole family. The Granvilles, in their four hundred years of being part of the landed gentry, had never appeared in the press, except when announcing a birth, a death, an engagement or a marriage, and *that* only in the court circular.

Juliet was done for, that was certain. But what of his own position as chairman of Hammerton's Merchant Bank? His memberships of White's, Brooks's, the MCC?

The fact was, he, Liza and the five girls were all going to be stigmatized by this tragedy. It was a situation that, even if he'd had foreknowledge of it, could not have been hushed up, in spite of his money. They'd all be sitting targets for the gossips of London and the gutter press, whether he liked it or not.

They'd been shouting at each other for the past hour in the privacy, but not the sound-proofing, of Liza's sitting room.

While Nanny was out and the younger ones at school, Ruby was practically hanging by her toes from the top floor bannister to hear what was being said. Even Miss Ashley's workroom door was ajar as she went through the motions of ironing Liza's lingerie.

'How could you have handled it all so badly, Juliet?' Liza wailed with distraction.

Juliet's voice was harsh. 'You told me to refuse his proposal . . .'

'But *discreetly*, for God's sake! You should have let him down gently, even perhaps given him a tiny bit of hope so he wouldn't feel so humiliated . . .'

Rosie broke in, ashen with self-righteousness. 'You turned him down in public, Juliet. In front of everyone. Oh, God, he must have felt terrible.'

'Why are you all blaming me?' Juliet shouted. 'I never asked him to fall in love with me.'

'He was in love with *me* until you stole him from me,' Rosie exploded, bursting into tears.

'He was unbalanced,' Juliet retorted. 'No normal man behaves the way he did.'

Henry intervened. 'That's probably true.' He felt deeply sorry for Juliet at that moment, with both her mother and sister berating her, their criticism charged with a lot of what might have beens. She may well have handled the situation rather badly, but she was only seventeen, far too young to have been put in this position in the first place. Juliet was right. Alastair must have already been unbalanced, and, tragically, she had been the catalyst that had driven his already disturbed mind over the edge.

Rosie was crying hysterically now. 'It's all your fault he killed himself.'

Juliet was enraged. 'It's not my fault.'

'Mummy, she's lying.'

'I'm *not* lying.' The sheer injustice of it all was driving Juliet crazy. She turned appealingly to her father. 'Alastair did all the chasing, not me.'

'You encouraged him,' interjected Rosie.

'And you didn't?' Juliet shot back.

'Girls, for God's sake, stop it,' Henry said heavily. 'This is getting us nowhere.'

'But I'll never forgive Juliet. She never wanted him for herself; she just didn't want me to have him.'

'Well, it's a great pity you became so friendly with him, Juliet,' Liza sighed.

She stared at her mother, open-mouthed. 'But you wanted one of us to marry him, because he was supposedly eligible.'

Rosie cut in, aggressively, 'But you never loved him like I did. You were just after the title and the position.'

Henry rose abruptly. 'I'm going out,' he announced in clipped tones. 'I will think of a *modus vivendi* and tell you what I've decided this evening. In the meantime, none of you is to leave the house or take any telephone calls. Let's try to keep what little dignity we've got left.'

At six o'clock that evening Henry called Rosie and Juliet into the morning room.

'Mummy and I have been talking,' he began, which they both knew meant he'd been doing the talking and making the decisions, while Liza had been forced to be acquiescent.

'As a family, we must lie low for several months, until the dust settles,' he continued.

'What does that mean?' Juliet asked sharply.

'Mummy is taking the girls down to Hartley, where we will live until next spring, and I will stay in London and go home at weekends.'

'I don't have to go to the country, do I?' Rosie asked anxiously. 'The Little Season has just begun, I've got parties every night . . .'

'You will go with Mummy. No . . . Don't argue, Rosie. I

65

will be closing up the house as a mark of respect to the rest of Alastair's family, and I will stay at my club.'

Juliet raised her chin. Her eyes looked strong and defiant, but her beautiful mouth was vulnerable. 'And me, Daddy?' she asked in a small voice.

Henry cleared his throat and studied the carpet at his feet for a few seconds. His blue eyes were overbright when he spoke.

'We're sending you to Italy for six months, Juliet. Sadly, your reputation is in shreds. I'm afraid you're being blamed for what's happened, which is unfair, but the sooner you get away from here the better, for your own sake.'

'Daddy . . . !' She looked stricken, like a little girl about to receive a terrible punishment.

'I'm sorry, darling,' he said more softly. 'But it is for the best. I have an old friend, the Principessa Silviane Borghini, who told me over the telephone today that you can stay with her. She takes in students since her husband died, and I've arranged for you to study Italian while you're there.'

'That's *so* unfair, Daddy,' Juliet said in a small unprotesting voice.

Henry's nod of agreement was almost imperceptible.

'It's *me* you're being unfair to,' Rosie burst out childishly. 'Why should I be made to suffer for something that is all Juliet's fault?'

He looked at her severely, his expressiom suddenly stern.

'I expect you to conduct yourself with dignity, Rosie, and stop behaving like a hysterical housemaid. Remember you're a Granville, for goodness' sake.'

PART TWO

Far-Reaching Consequences

1936–1939

Four

The engagement has been announced between ...
Rosie read *The Times* with a sense of disbelief. Was it really true? *Charles, son of the late Lord Padmore and Elsbeth, Lady Padmore, of Coldberry Castle, Cumbria, and ...*

Here her heart lurched every time she read it ... *and Rosemary Helen, eldest daughter of Mr and Mrs Henry Granville ...*

She was actually engaged and she wasn't sure which of her feelings was uppermost, happiness, sheer relief or mild terror.

Mummy was thrilled to bits, of course, promising her the most marvellous wedding dress from Norman Hartnell and the loan of her best diamond tiara. Charles was going to buy a house just off Berkeley Square; *so* fashionable! And she'd get some visiting cards and at home cards printed by Frank Smythson's. *Lady Padmore At Home ...* How good it would look!

Then another delightful thought struck Rosie. Juliet, who was still stuck in Rome, was going to be *maddened* with jealousy. What an utterly gratifying thought that was! Not that it had been plain sailing. Daddy had been fearfully against her marrying Charles. All that rubbish about him being poor and not good enough for her. In the end Mummy had lost her temper.

'Henry, you don't seem to realize I've got to find five husbands in all before I'm finished. We've *got* to be sensible about this. What's wrong with Charles Padmore? He's a baron, good-looking, works in Lloyd's of London, adores Rosie, and has a family seat in a beautiful part of Cumbria.'

'You don't know that. You've never been there,' Henry retorted.

'What?' Liza looked flustered, patting her permed curls nervously. Why didn't he understand that she wanted the girls to do as well as she had, or even better?

'Nonsense, Henry. You're just trying to put difficulties in the way. You should be happy for Rosie. Charles is a catch in his own way, and I, for one, would be delighted if they got married.' But in the end it wasn't really up to Henry. Liza had brushed his fears aside, and assured Charles, when he proposed to Rosie, that he was welcomed by the family, but suggested they wait until the following week before actually announcing their engagement.

'To let Henry get used to the idea of losing his first daughter, which is always a wrench for a father,' she said gushingly.

To Henry, Liza had said gently that 'Rosie is considering Charles's proposal.'

'Is she merely considering it? Or is she using her brains for once?' he replied acerbicly.

'Henry! What is the matter with you?' Liza exploded angrily.

'I hate the idea of Rosie being pushed into marriage when she's only just nineteen. What the hell's the rush? Why can't she have a few years just finding her feet?'

'I met you and married you when I was still eighteen,' she shot back.

Kindness, good manners and good nature forbade him remarking that she'd actually been lucky to have met him in the first place. If he was honest, she wasn't from the same background, but his great-aunt had told him she had a lovely nature, and would make an excellent wife, because she was prepared to learn the ways of the upper classes. If he was *completely* honest, would he have married her if the Great War hadn't just started? If the fear of being killed in the trenches in France hadn't overshadowed his every thought?

Her blonde prettiness and willingness to please had swayed him, and he'd promised, when she said anxiously that she'd never be able to keep up with his family, that he'd never let the difference in their backgrounds come between them.

'That's true, darling,' he said gently now, 'but fate brought us together, and I believe we were meant for each other.'

Mollified, Liza gave him a quick smile, but her eyes were still troubled. 'You don't understand, Henry. There are always more girls than there are young men. If a girl doesn't make a good match when she first comes out, she's lost her best chance. The following year there'll be a whole batch of new girls, all after the same available young men. We don't want our daughters ending up as *spinsters*.' The very word sent a cold shudder of horror through her.

'But do you really want Rosie to end up with a young man who will never make anything of himself?'

'She won't. For one thing she'll have a title, which is always useful.'

For the life of him, Henry couldn't think how. Having a title had never made any difference to his mother.

'I'll see you at lunch, darling,' he said, leaving her in the book-lined library.

Liza returned to writing letters to her London friends, fearful their absence from Green Street would make her lose contact with everyone who mattered. Meanwhile, Henry went for a walk with the dogs in the countryside he so loved.

The constant chatter of voices and the endless stir of activity created by Liza drove him mad when he was at home, and he felt guilty when he realized how his mother's normally tranquil existence had been upset by their extended stay.

When he returned, he went straight to Lady Anne's sitting room, to which she seemed to have withdrawn since they'd all descended on Hartley.

'Are you all right, Mama?' he asked anxiously. 'I'm worried that our all being here for so long is too much for you.'

'Of course I'm all right, Henry, and this is *your* home, anyway, darling,' she replied sturdily. 'I love seeing so much of the little ones, and it's so good for them being in the countryside. Gives them true values,' she added rather pointedly.

'I think we will be returning to London in a few days now,' Henry continued. 'Liza and Rosie seem determined to go ahead with her engagement to Charles Padmore, and anyway, I want to get Juliet back from Italy.'

'Very well, my dear.' Her expression was non-committal. Privately she wished Henry wouldn't let Liza bully him so. He looked so tired at times and she worried about him.

As it turned out, the family returned to London the following week, Nanny declaring she'd missed Lyons Corner House something dreadful, while Louise, Amanda and Charlotte protested that they hated London and why couldn't they stay with Granny in the country? Liza and Rosie, of course, were elated. *Things*, at last, were about to happen.

The announcement of the engagement appeared in *The Times* and the *Telegraph* two days later, and Charles presented Rosie with a family ring of diamonds and sapphires.

'Need's cleaning,' Liza said out of the side of her mouth when she saw it. 'Take it to Asprey, Rosie. There's *nothing* worse than dirty diamonds. It looks as if his mother wore it to peel potatoes.'

Rosie was delighted, however, and took to leaving off her left glove whenever she went out, so everyone could see she was engaged. There was only one disappointment; she seemed to be more heavily chaperoned than ever.

When Charles came to dinner, they were only allowed fifteen minutes alone in the drawing room, before he returned to his bachelor flat, with Parsons patrolling up and down the hall, like a prison warder, while Liza and Henry retired to their own room.

'Never mind, my sweet,' Charles whispered, kissing her rather sloppily. 'Once we're married . . .' Then he pressed himself up against her, and Rosie suddenly felt like a really grown-up woman.

In the face of Henry's disapproval, Liza's loyalty to Charles was fierce.

When people sounded surprised by Rosie's choice of husband, Liza backed their relationship totally. Charles might not be a marquess, like Alastair, or even an earl, but she approved of his gentleness and mild manners. He was not the straying type, either. Rosie would be able to trust him.

And if Rosie seemed less ecstatic than expected, Liza knew she would come in time to appreciate the solid support of a kind man.

It would have been nice, of course, Liza reflected, if Rosie had been able to marry Alastair Slaidburn, but it had been revealed at the inquest after his death that he'd had a history of manic depression, which could be triggered by any deep emotional upset, so really she'd had a lucky escape.

'I think Juliet should return to London now,' Henry announced that evening.

'But we did tell her Easter, at the earliest,' Liza pointed out.

71

She feared Juliet's arrival might upset the applecart.

Henry was determined. 'I know we did, but January is a quiet time of year. She can slip back into town without any fuss.'

'But she'll try and steal the limelight again. I do think this is Rosie's big moment, and I don't want her to be over-shadowed,' Liza fretted.

As it turned out, Juliet's return coincided with an event which shocked the country and drove everything else from people's minds, including Rosie's engagement.

The announcement on the wireless was simple and moving. 'The King's life is moving peacefully towards its close.' It was 9.35 p.m. on January 20th. Liza wept silently at the announcer's words and Henry looked wretchedly sad. The King, a shy and retiring man, had nevertheless been a popular king, and his devoted wife, Mary, had captured the admiration of the nation with her elegance, dignity, and strong sense of duty.

Early the next morning, Henry turned on the wireless to hear it confirmed that George V, King, and Emperor of the British Empire, had died at five minutes past midnight, surrounded by his family.

A great era, part Victorian but overlaid with the elegance and stylishness of the Edwardians, had come to an end.

The Granville household instantly went into mourning, the adults in black from top to toe, with a minimum of discreet jewellery, and the children and servants with wide black armbands, in lieu of black clothes. Parsons wore a stern and sad expression.

'God help us all, now that David is King,' Henry remarked as they all dined quietly at home that evening. 'I heard today that Mrs Simpson was sitting up all night, by her telephone, waiting for the Prince of Wales to phone her to give her the news. Like a bloody vulture, waiting for the pickings, if you ask me,' he added in disgust.

'Will he marry her now he's the King?' Juliet asked. 'They've been together for several years, haven't they?'

'I don't see how we can have a woman who has been divorced *twice* as our Queen,' Liza pointed out scathingly.

Henry sighed deeply. 'I don't think the Prime Minister will allow him to marry her.'

'What happens if he insists?' Rosie asked, filled with sympathy for the couple whose love affair she'd always viewed as romantic.

'Surely he can refuse to be King?' Juliet protested.

Henry looked haunted. 'It would mean he'd have to abdicate, and that could bring the whole royal family down.'

Rosie darted a nervous look at her mother. She was longing to ask, but simply didn't dare, whether it meant she'd have to postpone her wedding.

Up in the nursery, Nanny and Ruby were red-eyed, but it didn't stop Nanny from giving the children a rundown of what would happen next.

'The Prince of Wales, who is called David by the royal family, will be crowned King Edward VIII next year . . .'

'Why is he called David if his name is Edward?' Louise asked.

'He's got several Christian names, and I suppose he prefers David,' Nanny responded. 'The old King will lie in state in Westminster Hall . . .'

'The . . . *dead* King?' Charlotte asked.

'Of *course* the dead King, you silly girl, and then he'll be buried at St George's Chapel, in Windsor Castle.'

Charlotte looked eager. 'Can we go? Like we did to the Jubilee?'

Nanny looked severe. 'Certainly not. Funerals are no place for children.' Nanny didn't even know if she'd be able to listen to the proceedings herself on the wireless. Some things were just too painful to bear.

'He'll *have* to get rid of her now,' Liza said indignantly.

The Granvilles were holding a quiet dinner party two weeks after the King's death. Quiet it may have been, with all the women in black and pearls, but dull it certainly wasn't, with starry guests like Lady Diana Cooper and her diplomat husband, Duff Cooper, and, from America, the millionaire novelist and socialite, 'Chips' Channon and his wife, the former Lady Honor Guinness, of the Guinness beer family, whose personal fortune almost matched his. Henry's lifelong friend, Ian Cavendish, and his wife had also been invited, together with a few couples to whom they owed hospitality.

In the past few days, Wallis Simpson, and her future as the new King's mistress, was the topic of conversation throughout the land, from humble dwelling house to royal palace.

Chips spoke. 'David will never give her up. She's his ideal. That woman –' there was a mixture of admiration and wonderment in his voice – 'that woman can do things for him that other women can't . . .' He flashed a knowing look around the table. Everyone leaned forward, intrigued.

Lady Diana spoke with the sanguine bluntness of the aristocracy. 'People think she was taught by prostitutes in the brothels of Shanghai, but that's nonsense. She had a Chinese ayah as a little girl, and *she* taught her, by using ivory rods.'

Liza flushed and looked embarrassed.

'So *that's* her secret,' Juliet said with genuine interest.

Liza shot her a horrified look. The fact that Parsons was hovering around with more wine, listening to every word whilst pretending not to, made her want to *die*.

'Wallis has certainly got a hold over him,' Henry said calmly. 'I hear they're talking of a morganatic marriage, but I don't think this country would wear that either.'

'But they're in love, aren't they?' Rosie reasoned, her eyes tender as she glanced at Charles to support her view.

Charles picked at his lobster, and said nothing.

Duff spoke briskly, his intelligent eyes darting around the dining table. 'If Mrs Simpson *really* loved him, she'd go abroad and get out of his life now, and stay out of it for ever.'

'I agree,' said Juliet. 'She's being utterly selfish, but then I've heard she's an adventuress, so she'd obviously be all out for herself.'

There was a stunned silence. The adults turned to look at her, surprised by the maturity of her manner, while Liza eyed her nervously. Juliet had grown up a lot during her incarceration with the Principessa. She'd learned sophistication, and a degree of worldliness. Tonight she even looked much older than her age. Her simple black velvet evening dress, with two long ropes of pearls, gave her a regal air.

Rosie bristled, seeing her sister take centre stage again, but she said nothing, because she lacked the confidence to air her opinion in front of her parents' friends.

Henry's eyes narrowed speculatively as he studied Juliet for a long moment.

Juliet's gaze was level as she looked back at him. 'Mrs

Simpson must be stupid, or ignorant, to think she could become Queen in the first place.'

'Exactly,' agreed Lady Diana. 'What an adorable girl you are, Juliet, and so beautiful with it.'

Juliet flushed with pleasure. They were indeed flattering words coming from this renowned beauty of the past two decades.

'I think they should be given a chance,' Chips persisted. 'In the States we don't take divorce so seriously. Wallis makes him very happy. She's good for him. Bosses him around in a teasing way that no one else has ever dared do.'

'That's the trouble,' Duff cut in, drily. 'David's weak. He'll listen to whoever talked to him last, and he dithers all the time, and can't make up his mind about anything . . .'

'Except about Wallis, evidently, and he's sure fixed on her,' Chips chortled.

'Except for Wallis,' Lady Diana agreed diplomatically.

'And,' continued Chips, getting heated, 'I don't know why you people want to get rid of *him*! There's a suggestion that the Duke of York should take over . . . I ask you!'

Liza smiled. This was a dangerous topic, especially in front of the servants. 'It doesn't quite work like that in this country,' she simpered.

At that moment, Parsons led six footmen into the dining room. They were all bearing silver platters containing the meat and vegetables for the main course.

'I hope you all like venison?' she continued, desperate to divert the conversation into safer waters. 'Have you been stalking recently, Duff?'

'So what *will* happen?' Lady Honor asked, ignoring Liza completely. 'Chips and I entertained David and Wallis to dinner last week . . .'

'Such dreadful social climbing,' Lady Diana murmured *sotto voce*, casting her large blue eyes up to the ceiling.

Henry spoke. 'The King will lose the respect of the people if he doesn't make an honest woman of Mrs Simpson, and he'll incur the fury of the people if he does.'

Charles, feeling he'd been silent for too long, spoke. 'Fancy her going to watch the official proclamation at St James's Palace! Peering out of a window at the ceremony, so all the photographers could see her.'

'Dreadfully common,' agreed Lady Diana. 'Like a suburban housewife, twitching the net curtains.'

Duff nodded. 'Have you heard what she said about having to wear mourning?'

Everyone leaned forward, enjoying the gossip.

'Tell us!' Ian Cavendish asked. He was an old gossip himself, and hated the fact that most of his work at the Foreign Office was subject to the Official Secrets Act.

'Wallis said –' Duff paused, looking around the table, timing it for effect – 'that she "hadn't worn black stockings since she gave up doing the cancan!"'

'No . . . !' Gasps of titillated amusement combined with self-righteous shock ebbed and flowed around the table.

The chatter continued. Liza felt she should take the ladies upstairs, and leave the men to their port and cigars, but every time she caught Henry's eye, he demurred with a tiny shake of his head.

The topic of conversation had shifted to darker matters that affected them all, and everyone sat listening as Duff spoke with the voice of experience.

'I saw the writing on the wall back in 1933,' he said gravely. 'Diana and I attended the first Nuremberg rally. When Adolf Hitler, an insignificant little man who'd been a plumber, appeared in uniform, I knew we could be doomed.'

'It was dreadful,' agreed Lady Diana, whose acute intelligence matched her husband's. 'Four hundred *thousand* supporters went wild. Mass hysteria, of course. Then Hitler started an impassioned oration, yelling and gesticulating like a raving lunatic. It was the most horrible and frightening display of egomania I've ever seen.'

The others sat still, chilled by her words.

'Then Duff did something incredibly stupid,' she continued. 'I don't know how he wasn't arrested on the spot.'

The dapper diplomat's eyes twinkled, as everyone turned to look at him. He gave a nonchalant little shrug. 'I walked out,' he said simply. 'I realized that Hitler wouldn't let anything stand in his way. The Nazis are going to overrun Europe before long, like a plague of rabid rats. I had no wish to stay and listen to how he was galvanizing the Germans into action.'

'Do you *really* think they'll attack the rest of Europe, sir?'

Charles asked. 'I believe we have nothing to worry about.'

Duff gave Charles a brief glance, as if dismissing the yelps of a puppy. 'I *know* we have,' he said coldly. 'Both Britain and France are being too timid to recognize the danger signals, and Hitler's using a softly-softly policy. Churchill told me that German munitions are being manufactured as never before. The German Army is growing in size, thanks to thousands of ardent volunteers. The Rhineland, or the "west wall" as he's calling it, is growing apace. Heavy fortifications are being built. Air-raid shelters have been constructed.' He looked at Charles, coolly. 'Do you want me to continue?'

Charles turned red. 'It doesn't mean they're going to invade England,' he said, weakly.

Duff's face was also flushed. 'Wake up, young man. Hitler is winding up the people of Germany, preparing them for war. It's inevitable.'

There was silence around the table. The candles burned down. Parsons produced more decanters of wine.

Ian, who knew more about what was going on than anyone in the room, spoke. 'We mustn't forget Mussolini either. His conquest of Ethiopia has been brutal. There's no doubt he'll join forces with Hiter before long, posing a desperate threat to us all.'

'I can tell you all one thing,' Chips cut in, authoritatively. 'Our President is very worried about the deterioration of the European situation.'

'Do you think Roosevelt will aid Britain in a war?' Henry asked.

'Churchill's mother was American. If *only* Churchill was in power, I bet you he would pull every string imaginable to get Roosevelt on board.'

'We'd have to get rid of Neville Chamberlain first,' Charles observed, desperate to keep up with the older and wiser men.

Juliet, who had been following the discussion with close interest, turned to her father, while Rosie fiddled with a lock of her hair, and Liza kept giving Parsons fussy whispered instructions.

'I thought you said, Daddy, that thanks to the League of Nations, a peace treaty was signed at Versailles, which would end hostilities between Britain and Germany for ever.'

For the second time, everyone looked at Juliet in surprise.

Not many girls of seventeen would even take an interest in the situation, far less ask pertinent questions.

Henry smiled at her with a look of tender pride. 'You're quite right, darling. But now it seems it was not so much a peace treaty, as a declaration of a twenty-year armistice.'

'My dear Duff, won't you have some grapes?' Liza gushed, in a desperate effort to lighten the sombre mood.

'And it's only a matter of time before the Germans ignore the treaty completely,' Duff said, ignoring Liza. 'Then you can expect the worst. Civilians will be affected this time, too. Cities will be bombed. London in particular will be targeted. I've heard the Luftwaffe have sufficient bombs to flatten the city in the first few days.'

As everyone took in the enormity of what had been said, and the consequences another war would bring, there was an atmosphere of almost palpable apprehension in the room.

Liza decided to make a last desperate bid to jolly up the party. 'Diana, have you ordered your outfits for Ascot yet?' she trilled, without missing a beat.

For a long moment Henry stared at her, appalled. Then, with an effort, he recovered himself. 'Liza, is that a signal for our lovely lady guests to retire,' he asked gallantly, his smile strained, 'while we men set the world to rights?'

Liza flushed. He'd called her by her name instead of 'darling'.

'I'm . . . I'm sure that's what they'd like,' she said, falteringly. 'Shall we . . . ?' She glanced distractedly around the table at the women guests. 'Shall we . . . ?' she repeated.

Rosie leapt to her feet, glad not to have to listen any more to such depressing opinions, but Juliet stared at her mother coldly.

'*Such* a gloomy discussion,' Liza prattled nervously, as she led the way upstairs to her bedroom.

'But a very interesting one,' Lady Diana observed darkly, wondering why on earth Henry Granville had married such a silly little woman.

Juliet regarded Rosie's wedding preparations with quiet amusement, as opposed to jealousy. Charles was no great catch. She was determined to do better. But her sister had become obsessed with every tiny detail of the Great Day.

'What does it matter what colour knickers you have in your

trousseau?' Juliet demanded. 'Only Charlie is going to see them, and he'd probably prefer you didn't wear any at all.'

Rosie blushed violently. 'His name's Charles, not Charlie,' she corrected, 'and I've always heard that white underwear represents love; other colours are for sex,' she added with pursed lips.

Juliet threw back her head, screaming with laughter. 'Where on earth did you hear that? When I was in Rome, I managed to sneak down to the shops in the Corso, where I bought the most heavenly black satin brassieres and knickers. And a couple of black nightdresses. They're too divine for words.'

'Well, that just about says it all, doesn't it?' Rosie retorted, pettishly. 'I must say you've changed a lot since you've been in Rome.'

'The world has moved on; you've just stayed still.'

'How can you say that? I'm engaged to be married, and there's *nothing* more grown-up than that.'

'That depends who you're marrying.'

Rosie looked indignant. 'What do you mean?'

'You and Charlie are a couple of inexperienced children beside the people I met at the Principessa's. She may have been strict, but she did include me in her dinner parties. And her friends were *fascinating*.'

'But . . . weren't they all very old? Like her?'

'They were all in their fifties, I suppose. But both the men and the women were sophisticated and stylish. Much travelled and well read. Knowledgeable about the arts. About politics. About *life*. All you and Mummy ever think about is clothes, and who'll be at the next party. Mummy only likes going to the opera because it's smart. These people know all about opera, ballet, *and* music. They all speak perfect English, which was very polite, because they knew I hardly understood any Italian. I'm going to take more lessons, though. And brush up my French.'

'Quite the little intellect,' Rosie bitched peevishly. Then she picked up a swatch of different shades of blue silk. 'I'm not sure which to have for the bridesmaids' dresses.'

'I hope you're not expecting me to be a bridesmaid.'

'I'm having my six best friends, and Louise, Amanda and Charlotte, of course.'

'Of course,' Juliet sniped sarcastically. She'd have quite liked to have been asked, if only to have the satisfaction of refusing, but instead, to her secret surprise, she felt quite hurt at not being included. She was at a loose end these days. Liza was submerged in Rosie's wedding plans, the younger ones had their own nursery and school life. Henry was working hard at Hammerton's, and in the evenings going to various political meetings.

It was time, she decided, to get back into the swing of things, even if her contemporaries were going to seem a bit juvenile compared to the Principessa's friends.

First she telephoned Archie Hipwood.

'Hello,' he responded, coolly.

'What are you up to these days?' she asked breezily. 'Any good parties we can gatecrash?'

'I don't think . . . there aren't many parties, because of the King's death.'

She knew it was an excuse. Archie had been particularly shocked by the way she'd dropped Alastair Slaidburn, and his subsequent suicide.

'Oh, well . . . I'm back from Italy and catching up with friends . . . See you soon.'

'Perhaps.' Archie sounded cautious.

Juliet phoned Colin Armstrong next. He was another one who had been at the Frobishers' ball when they'd all heard about Alastair's death.

'Are you back from Italy already?' he said, in surprise. He didn't sound welcoming.

'I returned a couple of weeks ago. What are you doing with yourself these days?'

They'd had such a laugh last summer, she and Colin. Creeping into parties through the kitchens, drinking and talking into the night, sharing a last cigarette as dawn crept stealthily over the chimney pots.

'I'm very busy,' he replied briskly. 'Working in a law firm. No time for partying these days.'

'Poor old you. How about the weekend? Why don't you come down to Hartley?'

'No can do,' he said with finality. 'Got to rush. 'Bye, Juliet.'

She replaced the receiver very slowly, and felt immensely hurt and shocked. She'd thought Archie and Colin were real friends, but it appeared that was no longer the case. Should she risk one more snub and telephone Edward Courtney?

She picked up the receiver and dialled his number, KNI 3467. 'I'm afraid Mr Courtney is out,' a housekeeper informed her when she got through. 'Can I tell him who called?'

'It's Juliet Granville. He has my number. Could you ask him to telephone me when he returns?'

'Certainly, madam.'

She trawled through her address book. It was not pleasant to be *persona non grata*. What she wanted was an amusing young man who would take her out; give her lunch at Simpson's-in-the-Strand, tea at Gunter's, cocktails at the Berkeley, dinner at the Ritz, then on to a nightclub like the 400 or the Orchid Room. She wanted some *fun*. Now she was no longer a débutante, she wanted to get out and live a little.

Ten minutes later she'd compiled a list of young men she'd met, but didn't know as well as the others. She decided to give a small cocktail party, adding a few plain girls to the mix. Surely one or two of them would ask her out? The thought that they might not was too scaring for words.

It did the trick. Within weeks, Juliet had collected a coterie of eager young men, and quickly gained the reputation of being a man's woman, rather than a woman's woman.

Other girls bitched about her, jealous of her beauty, her money, and her success with the opposite sex.

They criticized her clothes for being 'too showy', and said she looked 'too actressy', which she took to be a huge compliment. Other young women were becoming afraid of her. She took that as a compliment too.

As a result, and just to tease, she flirted with their boyfriends, flirted with their fathers, and flirted with other women's husbands. If the wives were stupid enough to think she would actually want to *go off* with their husbands, they were bigger fools than she'd imagined.

Once, when challenged by an irate hostess, whose best friend had locked herself in the bathroom because her husband seemed to have forgotten he had a wife, Juliet retorted frankly, 'I don't go to bed with other people's husbands – I don't even kiss them; but I know how to keep them on the dance floor all night.'

Which in many cases was more than even their wives could achieve, and they knew it. Her secret lay in her innate sex appeal and her lively and intelligent conversation.

One man told her, stressing it was the greatest compliment he could pay any woman, that what he'd really like would be to spend a night with her – just talking.

It was true. She dazzled, she was witty and articulate, she looked stunning, and she made men adore her – and all without losing her virginity.

She wasn't stupid enough to throw *that* away on a meaningless relationship.

Then she met Daniel Lawrence.

The jazz club was dark and smoky, dense with people and loud with music.

'Who have we got here?' The man's voice was as deep as a mineshaft.

Juliet turned around with curiosity. He was looking straight at her. Over six feet tall, and in his early thirties, he had a strong jawline, thick black eyebrows and hair, and quizzical eyes. The thought that sprang to mind as she took in his full-lipped mouth and quirky smile was, *My God, this is an homme fatal.*

The aura of energy and power that emanated from him was almost palpable.

'I haven't seen you here before. What's your name?' he asked, although she hadn't said anything.

Juliet gave her wicked smile, liking him a lot. 'Juliet,' she said simply.

It was two o'clock in the morning, and after an evening of dining and dancing at Ciro's, she and several friends had gone on to the Black Cat in Soho.

'Mine's Daniel Lawrence. What are you drinking?' He'd moved closer, cutting her off from her friends.

She raised her glass. 'Pernod.'

He screwed up his face. 'Ugh! I hate aniseed. Let me get you a decent drink.' He gently but firmly removed the glass from her hand. 'A White Lady, please,' he asked the barman. Then he took her elbow and gently pushed her away from the bar to a small table in a dark corner. 'It's quieter here.'

Juliet sipped the gin, cointreau and lemon juice cocktail, and reached for a black Sobranie in the gold cigarette case she'd secretly borrowed from her mother.

'I know your face,' Daniel said, producing a lighter. 'I've seen your picture somewhere.'

'I very much doubt it,' Juliet replied, raising her chin defiantly, showing her long neck and jawline to perfection.

Enlightenment suddenly filled his eyes. 'You're one of the Granville sisters, aren't you? A débutante. And that young man . . .' He stopped, embarrassed. 'Sorry, that must have been awful for you.'

Juliet nodded, glad in a way he knew everything without her having to explain herself, but also realizing, with a pang, that she was probably always going to be associated in people's minds with Alastair's suicide.

'One wishes there was a nice way of saying no,' Juliet remarked, as if to explain the situation. 'But there isn't. And there's never a right time either.'

'You're right.' He spoke with feeling and Juliet imagined that, with his looks and charm, there was probably a string of wrecked relationships and broken hearts in his wake.

'What are you doing with yourself now?'

Juliet shrugged. 'Trying to free myself from parental claustrophobia.'

The quirky grin deepened, crookedly. 'Sounds interesting.'

'I can assure you, it's not.'

'Kicking over the traces, are you?'

She drew deeply on her cigarette. 'Something like that.'

'Isn't your sister getting married soon?'

'Yes, God help her.'

Daniel chuckled, his dark eyes sparking with amusement. 'I gather you don't like her intended?'

'It isn't me who's marrying him, so it really doesn't matter.'

He raised one dark eyebrow quizzically. 'So who do you plan to marry?'

She stubbed out her cigarette. 'No one I've met so far,' she replied firmly, rising as she spoke. 'You must excuse me, I must go back to my friends. Thank you for the drink.'

'I hope I'll see you again.' He'd risen also, and seemed about to follow her.

'Who knows?' Her tone was amused and careless. A moment later she vanished into the dimly lit club, swallowed up by the crowds and the smoky atmosphere.

83

Daniel Lawrence looked thoughtfully after her. He always got what he wanted, and he didn't intend to fail this time.

'What is wrong with the Granville family?' Edward Courtney remarked, as he and Colin Armstrong wandered around the Chelsea Flower Show one afternoon, looking at the magnificent displays of roses in one of the marquees.

They'd just bumped into Liza Granville, with Rosie and Charles in tow, and all she'd talked about was the forthcoming wedding, and all the parties leading up to it, and how exciting it was that the London season had come round again so quickly, and were they going to the Eton and Harrow match at Lord's on Saturday?

'They're English,' Colin replied, as if that explained everything, overlooking the fact that he and Edward were also English, as English as roast beef and Yorkshire pudding, or eggs and bacon, in fact. 'Mrs Granville's in complete denial about *anything* unpleasant. Alastair's suicide, Juliet's current wild behaviour, even the goddamn way Hitler has sent thirty-five thousand troops to invade the Rhineland . . . she simply doesn't want to face reality. I've heard it drives Henry Granville mad; nothing but yatter-yatter-yatter about meaningless trivialities. I don't know how he stands it.'

'He's very loyal,' Edward pointed out, raising his hat to a passing lady he knew. 'And he does spend a lot of time at White's, and at meetings of the League of Nations.'

'And the fact she thinks Charles Padmore has a brilliant future is enough to scare anyone. God, the man's a moron.'

Edward laughed. A lazy bumble bee drifted past him to settle in the centre of a pink cabbage rose. He gave the stem a gentle tap, and the bee rose indignanly from its resting place, and droned off, heading for a bower of tiny rambler roses.

'That's what I'd like to do to Rosie,' he remarked thoughtfully. 'Give her a good shaking up. Get her to open her eyes to the real world. What the hell is she going to *do* with a loser like Padmore?'

Colin looked at him askance. 'You're not sweet on her, are you?'

'God, no. I just think she's heading for a very dreary future. Why, are *you* sweet on her?'

Colin shook his head. 'I was rather smitten with Juliet for a while, but she's too hot to handle. Too heartless, as well. She needs someone who can tame her.'

'Like the shrew, you mean?' Edward chuckled at the comparison. 'I quite envy the man who finally does . . . tame her, I mean.'

'I hear she's seeing someone called Daniel Lawrence.'

Edward looked thoughtful. 'Daniel Lawrence, eh? Dear God!' He turned to Colin. 'I say, old chap, do you think she's a masochist?'

It was the third bouquet in a week. The first one, a large bouquet of white roses, had come with a card bearing the words, *You're the tops, you're the tower of piza* . . . It was unsigned.

The next morning, pink roses arrived in a basket. *You're the tops, you're the Mona Liza* was written on a note, and again there was no signature, but Juliet began to guess who might be sending them.

This morning, an arrangement of dark crimson roses, lavishly tied with red velvet ribbon, was delivered. Intrigued, she ripped open the little envelope, and drew out the card. Then burst out laughing.

Cole Porter can say it better than I can . . . Daniel.

Juliet was still laughing with delight when the phone rang a few minutes later.

'There's a call for you, Miss Juliet,' Parsons announced primly. 'A Mr Lawrence.'

'I'll take it in the morning room,' she said lightly, as she sashayed out of the dining room.

'Who's Mr Lawrence?' Rosie asked, agog with curiosity.

'No one you know,' Juliet replied lazily over her shoulder.

Daniel's first words surprised her. 'I thought we'd go out to dinner tonight, Juliet.'

Not – *When can I see you?* Not – *Can I take you out?*

'That depends,' she parried.

'Do oysters and champagne appeal?'

'They're so *passé.*'

'Caviar and vodka?'

'*Ordinaire.*'

'The lady is difficult to please.'

'It's *who* I dine with, not what I eat, that I'm choosy about.'

'Not where?' he queried.

'Mostly who.'

'How about this, then. I'll pick you up at eight o'clock and we'll dine somewhere you've never been before.'

'I've dined everywhere.'

'Not in this place.'

'How can you be sure of that?'

'As sure as I am that you'll be looking ravishing. And very, very sexy.'

Giggling to herself, Juliet went to finish her breakfast.

'Why are you looking so pleased with yourself?' Rosie bristled, putting down her newspaper.

'Wouldn't you like to know,' Juliet replied with maddening evasiveness.

That evening a scarlet sports car drew up outside 48 Green Street and a moment later Daniel was standing on the front doorstep, filling the space with his presence.

Thankful that both Rosie and her parents were out, Juliet hurried forward, and after saying hello, slipped into the passenger seat, her white fox furs pulled close against the chill of the evening. Then Daniel jumped into the driving seat and they were off, roaring towards Hyde Park Corner.

'Where are we going?' Juliet asked curiously.

'Not far,' Daniel replied, 'and you *do* look very, very sexy.'

So does he, she thought, looking covertly at his strong profile. He intrigued her. No other man would dare take command of a situation, with a comparative stranger, the way Daniel was doing. Yet at the same time his manner suggested great intimacy, as if they'd known each other for years.

What am I getting into? she thought, with a mixture of excitement and wariness, as he drove speedily towards the Embankment.

In the darkness, the river glinted with sinister stillness and the gas lamps threw patches of mellow light on the old paved streets. A pang of alarm shot through her. She knew nothing about this man. She was taking an impossible risk going off with him, without even telling her family where she was going.

Then he stopped the car and, getting out, came round to open her door.

'What *is* this place?' she asked, standing very upright, her head raised, as if she were sniffing the air.

'Come with me,' he said softly, cupping her elbow in the palm of his hand.

For a wild moment she felt like running away . . . hailing a passing taxi, shouting for help . . . but how far would she get in high heels, and her long tight skirt? Visions of rape flashed through her mind. She started to tremble.

'It's all right, Juliet.' His deep voice rumbled like the growl of a gentle lion, as if he sensed her perturbation.

'I'm fine,' she retorted sharply, raising her chin, determined to look more confident than she felt.

He led her along the Embankment, until he stopped by a gangplank, its handrails hung with lanterns.

She stopped dead in her tracks. 'A *boat*?' she exclaimed, in alarm. 'I don't understand . . .'

'This way, darling.' Calmly taking her hand, he led her down the steep incline of the wooden planking, until they reached the deck of a houseboat.

'Welcome aboard,' he said, ushering her into a large cabin, with windows all around, overlooking the river. Candles glowed on a table set for dinner. Through the large windows the Thames flowed past, carrying dimly lit river boats.

A waiter stepped from the shadows, holding a silver tray with two glasses of champagne.

'Thank you. You can go now,' Daniel told him, taking the glasses and handing one to Juliet.

In silence the waiter withdrew. A minute later they heard him walking up the gangplank.

'To you, Juliet,' Daniel said, raising his glass. 'Come and sit down.'

The waiter had left dressed crab, lobster and crayfish on a fish platter, surrounded by sliced lemons. There were different salads, Italian bread studded with dark fruit, and piles of grapes in a basket, beside a cheese board.

'This is fun,' Juliet remarked with brittle lightness, determined to sound sophisticated, as if she was used to dining on boats with strange men every night of the week.

'So tell me about yourself,' he asked softly, topping up her glass.

'There's so little to tell,' she replied, shrugging.

'But I don't know anything about the real you; only what I've read in the magazines and newspapers.'

'That's all there is to know. Very boring, really.' She sipped her champagne, and smiled her wicked smile.

'What about your time in Rome? Surely, away from your parents, you had a good time?' He looked deeply into her eyes, probing, searching.

As if mesmerized, the saying *like a lamb to the slaughter* flitted through her mind. Juliet couldn't help speaking with painful honesty, such was his effect on her.

'The Principessa was as strict as a prison warder. I managed to slip out on my own occasionally, to do some shopping, but mostly she chaperoned me. And what's the use of going to the Spanish Steps if all one does is look at Keats's house?'

Daniel looked at her sadly. 'Rome is such a romantic city too. Didn't you meet anyone . . . ?'

'I met lots of really divine people, but they were all the same age as my parents. It was very educational, though, in more ways than one.'

He looked at her intently. 'What sort of ways?'

Juliet shrugged again, tilting her head to one side. 'I'd never been away from home before,' she admitted. 'I think it made me grow up fast. I had intelligent, worldly people to talk to, and that rather opened my eyes.'

Daniel's smile made the corners of his mouth tip up attractively. 'Which you don't get at home?' he quipped swiftly.

'Daddy's very clever,' she replied defensively. 'Mummy . . . well, she's had five children, and a big house to run . . . She doesn't have much time for anything else.'

'What do you enjoy doing most?' Daniel persisted, never taking his eyes off her face.

Juliet found that a hard question to answer. She didn't want Daniel to think she was a shallow party-loving ex-débutante, and yet what else *did* she like doing? 'All sorts of things,' she replied lightly.

He looked at her with tenderness. 'You're a rebel, my darling, and I love you for it. And you're holding something back from me; I can feel it. What is it? What keeps you awake at night? What gives you nightmares?'

Juliet felt her cheeks flushing red. 'Nothing!' she retorted hotly. And too swiftly.

'But you have bad dreams?'

'What are you? A psychiatrist?' He was crossing the boundary line, getting into forbidden territory, and it made her angry.

Daniel immediately looked contrite. 'I'm so sorry. I really didn't mean to pry, and why should you tell me anything, anyway? It's just that I think you're the most . . . the most fascinating and beautiful girl I've ever met; and I want to get closer to you,' he added, his voice soft and low.

Juliet looked at him warily. 'Then let's talk about something else,' she suggested crisply.

'Of shoes and ships and sealing wax, of cabbages and kings? How about the new King and Wallis Simpson, then?' Daniel teased, laughingly.

'Yes, indeed. What about her?' Juliet replied. For the first time since she'd been a small child, she'd found someone she wanted to confide in; she wanted to tell Daniel all about herself, although she barely knew him. The desire was almost overwhelming, but she drew back, not daring.

To tell him everything would be like opening Pandora's box, and God knows what would come flying out, to beset her and make her nightmares worse.

'Talking of the new King,' he said easily, realizing she was not going to open up to him, 'I can't help thinking it was a bad omen when the jewelled Maltese Cross on the Crown of England came crashing down from his father's coffin and rolled into the gutter as it was paraded through the streets.'

'Did it? I didn't know that,' she said, intrigued, glad to talk about something else.

'Are there lots of things you don't know?' He reached for her hand, and held it tenderly.

'That depends.'

'You've been to Paris, I suppose?'

She shook her head.

'Then *I'll* take you,' he said in delight. 'We'll stay at the Ritz, dine at Maxim's, go shopping in the Rue de Rivoli, have lunch in Montmartre, go to l'Opera, and end up being real tourists by going up to the top of the Eiffel Tower, to see the whole city spread out at our feet. What do you say?'

89

The look in his eyes sent a shiver down her spine.

'I don't see how I can . . .' Tantalizing visions of a week-end in Paris with this incredible man seemed thrilling but impossible.

'If you think your parents would make a fuss, I'll get my mother to invite you for the weekend to our place in Kent. In reality, we'll drive to Dover, and cross on the ferry to Calais. Then we'll drive to Paris.'

He leaned across and took her other hand, as he gazed intently into her eyes. 'You'll come with me, won't you?'

Juliet felt momentarily dizzy. It was one thing sneaking off to a houseboat whilst pretending to be at a girls' supper party in Chelsea, but to go *abroad* . . . ! She gazed back into his eyes and met the challenge.

'Why not?' she replied boldly, after only a moment's hesitation. His audacity at inviting her away for a weekend was stunning but terribly exciting. 'But only as a friend,' she added quickly, in case he thought she was fast.

'Of course,' he agreed, with equal speed, and seeming understanding, which then made Juliet feel immoral for even suggesting he might have had other ideas.

Daniel spoke reassuringly. 'So when would you like to go?'

She looked into his eyes and felt a thrilling sort of terror. No matter what she'd just said, she knew without a shadow of a doubt that this man was going to be her first lover. An experienced lover, too. She started trembling, unable to meet his gaze.

'Let's go in a couple of weeks,' he said, without waiting for her answer. Then he leaned closer, so she could feel his breath on her cheek. 'We'll have a never-to-be-forgotten time, I can promise you that.'

She smiled. 'Paris in the spring,' she said, putting on a grand society voice, as if she'd just said *Shopping in Bond Street*. 'What fun!'

'Who is she?' Liza asked. 'It's very kind of her to invite you for the weekend, but who else is going to be there? Is she having a house party?'

'I think so,' Juliet lied. She'd shown her mother the letter from Sonia Lawrence, handwritten on pale blue stationery, with the address in Kent printed at the top.

'Then you'd better accept,' Liza said vaguely. She was having a dreadful time working out the seating plan for the church for Rosie's wedding, and Henry wasn't helping her at all.

'I'll do it right away,' Juliet replied. In reality, she thought dreamily, I'll really be accepting . . . being wined and dined at all the best places in Paris, before Daniel . . . She gave a quick intake of breath, visualizing a large double bed, with snowy white sheets and soft pillows, and Daniel carrying her to it, and then lying down beside her . . . she replayed that bit over and over in her mind, because the anticipation of that moment was so delicious . . . Then he would reach for her . . . The rest of her reverie was hot and hazy; she could hardly wait.

'How do you like it?' Charles asked Rosie. He'd taken her to see the small house in Farm Street where they were going to live when they were married.

Rosie was stunned by the tiny rooms, and hurt because he'd bought the house without consulting her first. She decided, however, it would be best to make appreciative sounds at this stage. Anyway, it would do for a start, but of course they'd have to get a bigger place within the next year or so.

'It's *sweet*!' she exclaimed, tucking her hand through his arm. 'And it's lovely being just a few minutes' walk from Green Street too.'

'I thought you'd like that.' He looked satisfied with himself, walking around the empty rooms, which were so small he could actually cover them in four or five strides.

'Where will the staff go?' Rosie asked, mystified. On the ground floor there was a small hall, a dining room and the kitchen; an L-shaped drawing room took up the first floor, and on the floor above, there was a bedroom, a dressing room and a tiny bathroom. Two more very small bedrooms took up the top floor.

'Staff?' Charles queried, taken aback. 'Well, I suppose, if you want a maid, she could sleep in the attic, except there's no bathroom up there.'

Rosie turned her drenched bluebell-coloured eyes on him; they were filled with anguish.

'A *maid*? Darling, we'll have to have a cook, a housemaid, and a parlour maid, and who is going to open the front door? My mother says . . .'

Charles was to hear a lot more of what her mother said in the months ahead.

'A lot of people have dailies now,' he urged, an edge of panic in his voice at the thought of how much all this was going to cost. 'When we're married, do we really want a lot of living-in servants hovering around, so we never have any privacy? I want to be alone with you, my darling,' he wheedled, slipping his arm around her waist. 'I want us to live here as a honeymoon couple, so we can make love whenever we want to, wherever we want to, night and day.' He pressed himself against her, his hand lightly stroking her stomach so that her insides quickened with desire. 'We'll move to a bigger house, of course, in due course, but this will do for the time being, won't it?'

Rosie gave an inward sigh of relief. For a ghastly moment she thought Charles had expected her to live like this for ever. Instantly mollified, she wound her arms around his neck, and kissed him warmly. Charles was right, and so romantic. This was just a love nest. A place where they could indulge in all sorts of decadent things, like drinking champagne in bed after they'd . . . She blushed in anticipation.

'It's perfect, darling. So cosy,' she whispered. 'I wish we were married now.'

'So do I . . .' There was a catch in his voice. 'Shall we . . . ?'

'Oh no, we mustn't.' Rosie pulled away, slightly shocked. 'We must wait until our wedding night.'

Reluctantly, he started talking about the furniture they'd need, in order to distract himself.

On their first night in Paris, Daniel took Juliet to Maxim's. 'Shall I order for both of us?' he asked.

'Why not?' she said, smiling. She was beginning to like being taken care of by this powerfully charismatic man.

Daniel signalled to the waiter. 'We'll start with *foie gras*, please. Then the salmon.' He reached for the wine list and studied it closely.

Sitting beside him on the banquette, which was covered in crimson plush, Juliet looked around with interest. Her reflection was repeated again and again in the art deco mirrors that were hung on the walls. The lighting was dim and discreet. The place had an air of dignified opulence.

For the first time, Juliet felt confident in a way she'd never felt before. She was free of family shackles and disapproval and she was with a man she felt deeply attracted to, relishing the thought of wielding her sexual power over him, because although he was an even more controlling person than she was, she felt she would ultimately hold the ace card. After all, she was a woman.

Daniel had arranged for a hairdresser to come to their hotel suite, and she was thrilled by the way her hair had been caught back into a chignon, and decorated with a spray of black osprey feathers. No one in London had ever made her look so chic. She was also wearing a low-cut black evening dress she'd secretly bought the previous week. Diamond drop earrings shimmered in the dim light. She knew she'd never looked so good. Or so grown-up.

Daniel had even presented her with a corsage of intoxicatingly perfumed gardenias, when they'd had champagne in their *petit salon*, before leaving for Maxim's.

'You're so beautiful,' Daniel had said when she'd emerged from her room. 'I've never seen anyone as exquisite as you.'

Then he'd leaned forward and very slowly and carefully kissed her white throat.

All this is happening to someone else, she thought. Green Street is a million miles away. Juliet Granville, ex-débutante, no longer exists. The smell of the roses in the *salon*, combined with the clinging sweetness of the gardenias, suddenly assailed her, making her take a deep breath. She wanted to fill her lungs with the potent perfume until she drowned in it. This was paradise. She wanted to stay here for ever, where all her earthly desires were about to be satisfied.

Later, a small orchestra started playing, and the small dance floor quickly became crowded, as rich and fashionable couples foxtrotted and quickstepped their way around. Juliet spotted Douglas Fairbanks, over from Hollywood, and Barbara Hutton, the Woolworth millionairess, wearing diamonds as big as quail eggs, but with eyes as dull and listless as grey pebbles on a beach.

'Shall we dance?' Daniel asked softly.

Juliet nodded, rising and slipping into his arms as if that was where she belonged. Soon she became oblivious of

93

everyone else, letting the music and the feel of Daniel's body carry her into a world of magic. She played her old trick of swaying her hips against his, wondering how quickly she could arouse him.

He pulled apart from her suddenly. 'Stop that,' he said sternly. 'I do the leading in this relationship.'

For a moment anger flaired up in her, and her aquamarine eyes flashed. She was not used to being talked to like that, but then she remembered she'd only danced with young men in the past, some of them mere boys.

For a moment she held herself stiffly, her shoulders squared, her chin raised in defiance. Suddenly she wasn't sure if she really wanted to be dominated like this.

'I'd like a drink,' she said coolly, extricating herself from his arms, and walking back to the table.

They sat in silence for a few minutes, and she refused to look at him, although she knew he was staring at her profile.

Not being in control . . . that's when the demons returned. Mocking her, giving her nightmares, frightening her terribly. She *had* to feel in charge of a situation, and she had no intention of relinquishing that position.

Then she felt his hand close over hers. It was warm, powerful and strong. He spoke, softly but firmly, as if she were a nervous, highly strung filly.

'This is only going to work if you trust me, Juliet.'

She flicked a quick, tentative look in his direction, and saw only tenderness and kindness in his expression. Her eyes suddenly brimmed with tears, and she gave a shaky smile.

He spoke again. 'I promise you I won't hurt you, darling.'

'I know you won't,' she said in a small voice.

'You'll be quite safe with me.'

She nodded, unable to speak. This was all going to be much more difficult than she'd imagined. And difficult in a way he'd never understand.

'Can I have a brandy, please?'

'We'll *both* have brandies, and then we'll go back to the hotel, shall we?'

Juliet nodded again, hoping the waiter would bring very large brandies.

* * *

94

They strolled the short distance from Maxim's to the Ritz in the Place Vendôme under a soft starry sky. A drift of Gitanes smoke filled the air. The sound of traffic was a distant hum.

Back in their suite, Daniel led her by the hand into her luxuriously furnished bedroom, with its gold satin draperies and dark mirrors. Then he took her in his arms and kissed her, gently at first and then with growing passion. She started to say something between his kisses, but he placed his forefinger against her lips to hush her, before gently unpinning her hair, until it rippled down her back, like ripe corn.

Unresisting, she let him remove her earrings, one by one. She tried to catch his strong hands, and hold them in her own small ones, but he brushed her softly aside. Then, with infinite patience, he started undoing the row of tiny buttons down the side of her dress, tantalizing her by making her stand still when all she wanted to do was to fling herself into his arms.

At last the dress slid to the floor, and lay around her feet in pools of black chiffon.

'Oh God, you're beautiful,' he groaned, as he carefully undid her suspenders, his hands stroking the insides of her thighs as he did so, before he eased off her black satin shoes and silk stockings. Shaking now, with frustration and longing, she let him remove the black lace and satin underclothes she'd secretly bought in Rome.

'Take off your clothes,' she urged, tremulously, reaching for his black bow tie.

His voice was thick with yearning. 'Not until I've kissed you all over.' Then he trailed his fingertips over the marble whiteness of her body, kissing her where his hands had been, stroking her until she shivered violently.

Even when she whispered brokenly that she wanted him, he still didn't hurry. Murmuring tender words of love between his kisses, he continued soothing her, stroking her as if she'd been a cat, wanting her to be completely relaxed.

'You're so desirable,' he murmured, his voice husky.

Juliet felt a rising tide of passion within herself, a need she'd never known before, a desperate wanting to belong to this man, and be his, for ever.

Her hands were seeking him out now, trying to unbutton his trousers, searching feverishly for him. Wanting him more than she'd ever wanted anything in her whole life.

He looked directly into her face, his eyes drilled hers. 'Are you sure?' he whispered, his hands stilled.

'Oh, yes, yes. Absolutely sure.'

And she was. Ripe for picking, he reflected, as he tore off his own clothes.

Juliet gasped at the full revelation of his ardour, crying out with a mixture of fear and desire.

Without a word, he carried her to the bed and lay down beside her, but even then he held back, whispering to her softly until she became submissive.

Then his kisses became rough and urgent, as he slowly, so slowly she thought she would scream with frustration, began to enter her. He was very gentle at first, as he tentatively pressed against the resistance of her virginity. Then, with a sudden cry of joy, she was all his, letting the moment ride on a tide of passion, so that their cries became mingled. The waves became deeper, more violent, more desperate, as she strained to make him all hers, crying out, 'Don't stop . . . ! Oh, never stop. I want you, I want you, I want . . .'

Juliet was sobbing when it was over, as they lay still locked together, wanting it to happen again. And again. And again.

'Did you have a nice weekend, darling?' Liza asked brightly, looking at Juliet with curiosity. Something was different about her, but she couldn't quite put her finger on it. Her eyes seemed a paler shade, and her skin had a luminous glow that had nothing to do with make-up. She also seemed very preoccupied.

'Is Mrs Lawrence nice?' Liza continued. 'What's their house like? Who else was staying?'

'I had a lovely time,' Juliet replied vaguely.

'Good.' Liza didn't press her for details, knowing Juliet would clam up even more; she was becoming very secretive these days. Anyway, Liza's mind was full of Rosie's wedding arrangements, apart from all the social engagements the London season brings with it. That evening she and Henry were guests at a dinner party given by Chips Channon and his wife, in their new home at 5 Belgrave Square.

Liza dressed with care, and wore her best sapphire and diamond necklace. She'd heard the new King and Wallis

Simpson were expected, as well as Winston and Clemmie Churchill.

As soon as they arrived, Chips drew Liza to one side. He looked concerned and embarrassed.

'My dear Liza, forgive me if I'm speaking out of turn, but was it really Juliet I saw at Maxim's last Friday night?'

Liza blinked. 'Maxim's? In Paris?' Then she smiled at the absurdity of the suggestion. 'Absolutely not, Chips. She was staying with friends in Kent.'

Chips frowned. 'Are you sure? She was too preoccupied to see me, but I would swear on my life it was her. I must say she looked much older in a black dress and feathers in her hair, but her face is so distinctive. It couldn't have been anyone else.'

Liza remembered how strangely different Juliet had seemed since she'd returned. Her heart gave an uncomfortable lurch.

'Was she in a party of young people?' she asked, hopefully.

'That's the point,' Chips said, agitated. 'I wouldn't have even mentioned it if that had been the case, but she was with a nasty piece of work called Daniel Lawrence.'

The blood drained away from Liza's face. She felt cold and sick. 'Juliet received a letter from a Mrs Lawrence to go and stay with them. Is Daniel her son?'

Chips raised his eyebrows, quizzically. 'Sonia Lawrence is his wife. She stays at home in Kent, with their three young children, while Daniel seeks out beautiful young women, who he seduces.'

'Oh! My God . . . !'

Seeing her expression, Chips took her hand and held it firmly. 'Oh, my dear Liza. I'm sorry. I've had sleepless nights. Worrying about whether I should tell you or not . . .'

'You were right to do so,' she said, faintly. 'Henry will be devastated. But why did his mother write to Juliet? I saw the letter myself,' she added, dazed into stupidity.

'His mother died years ago. Knowing him, he probably wrote the letter himself . . .'

'Oh, my God,' Liza said again, swaying slightly. A footman came up with a tray of drinks, and she took a glass of champagne, her hand trembling. 'I've been so busy with Rosie . . . I never thought to check who Juliet was staying with . . .' Her voice trailed off, and she bit her lower lip.

'You'll have to put a stop to it, Liza. If it gets around that Juliet and Daniel Lawrence have been . . .' He paused, delicately. 'I know. I know.' Liza shut her eyes for a brief moment. 'My dear, I'm so sorry. I should have telephoned you tomorrow, but I was just so anxious about Juliet. She was so involved . . . well, she didn't see me the other night, but she's such a beauty, and she's so young and so obviously being led astray by this bounder,' Chips said contritely. 'Why don't you sit down for a moment?'

Liza straightened her back and raised her chin. Her lips parted in a much practised smile, which never reached her eyes. Since she'd married Henry, she'd learned that ladies never display their emotions in public; it was such a common thing to do, as Lady Anne had once said.

'I'm fine, my dear Chips,' she replied, brightly. 'You were quite right to tell me, and thank you. I will deal with it tomorrow. Oh, is that Lady Londonderry over there? I *must* go and say hello to her.' And, with a gracious hand briefly touching his arm, and another smile, she glided away as if she hadn't a care in the world.

Liza decided to say nothing to Henry until they got home; the question was, what were they going to do with Juliet now? Supposing she refused to stop seeing this married man? This wanton womanizer? Who preyed on young girls? Supposing his wife found out about the weekend in Paris? Worse, much, much worse, supposing she asked Daniel for a divorce, citing Juliet as the co-respondent?

Hot and cold waves of horror and anguish swept over Liza, as she tried to make polite conversation, whilst her mind was in turmoil. She couldn't eat a *thing*. Even vintage champagne tasted sour.

For the second time, it looked as if Juliet was on the brink of social ruin.

'So, how was Paris?' Liza asked Juliet the next morning, as they sat in her study, opening the morning mail.

Juliet started, and her face reddened.

'Paris?' she asked, questioningly. 'I don't know anything about Paris.'

Her mother looked steely, her eyes piercing and angry.

'There's no point in lying, Juliet. You were seen at Maxim's, with a person called Daniel Lawrence.' She spoke his name as if it were a dirty word. Then she repeated everything Chips Channon had told her. 'I'll get Daddy to tell him you can't see him again,' she concluded. 'You can't afford the scandal of it getting out that you've been with a married man.'

Juliet looked stunned. For a long moment she stared down at the carpet. Then she rose, pain etched on her face, her eyes dulled by disillusion and deep disappointment.

'No,' she said at last, her voice firm. '*I'll* bloody do it.'

It wasn't as easy as that. To her consternation and amazement, Juliet realized she knew absolutely nothing about Daniel. She'd spent four days in Paris with a man whose telephone number she didn't even have.

Daniel had been so busy asking her all about herself that she'd barely had a chance to find out about him; except that she loved him. Loved him more than she thought it was possible to love anyone.

Then she remembered she still had his mother's . . . no! Not his mother, his *wife's* letter, for God's sake! Her heart physically ached and felt bruised as the enormity of his deception hit her. How dare he treat her like this . . . ? Make her a party to his adultery. Seduce her because she was young and . . . well, fairly innocent.

Did he really think she was so stupid that she'd never find out he was married with three . . . *three* children?

Sonia Lawrence's letter was in a drawer of the bedside table. Juliet read it again. The handwriting was large and scrawly; so who had written it? The signature was almost illegible, but because she'd been expecting a letter from Daniel's mother, she hadn't questioned it.

Should she phone him? And risk his wife answering? Or did he live on the houseboat? Juliet threw down the letter as if it might sting her. She couldn't even bear to begin to think about his children.

'The rotten, *rotten* bastard!' she exclaimed aloud, tears of rage and grief storming her eyes.

There was nothing for it but to take a taxi to the houseboat on the Embankment, and have it out with him, face to face.

* * *

Rosie was now having doubts about marrying Charles.

'I don't know why,' she wept, 'I love him, and I know he loves me, but . . .' She gulped on a sob. 'It's such a terribly big step, isn't it?' She turned to Liza, her eyes bloodshot and her nose red. 'I'm going to miss being at home,' she confessed.

Liza quelled a stab of panic. St Margaret's, Westminster had been booked and a thousand guests had accepted to come. Banks of white flowers had been ordered from Constance Spry, cars had been hired, and Claridge's had taken their order for food and champagne for the reception. Hundreds of arrangements had been made.

They were *past* the point of no return, so far past it that they'd already hit the Titanic's iceburg. Liza put up her hands to cover her eyes at the thought of cancelling the biggest wedding of the year. Then she was struck by an even worse thought. Think of the public humiliation, mortification and embarrassment that would be caused. Think how badly it would affect Rosie's marital future too.

Liza's mind worked quickly. 'You've just got wedding nerves, my darling,' she gushed nervously. 'I don't know a *single* bride who hasn't suffered like this before their wedding. I was actually *sick* just before I married your father. It's a sign of good luck, like actors getting stage fright before a first night.'

At the mention of a first night, Rosie wept harder than ever. 'I don't think I can bear it,' she sobbed.

'Darling, you're going to be *all right*,' Liza commanded fiercely. 'Is there anything you want to know about . . . ?' But she simply couldn't say the word; hopefully Rosie had grasped the facts of life from the dogs down at Hartley. 'Anyway,' she blundered on, 'you'll only be living five minutes walk away from here, so we can see each other every day. Won't that be fun? Supposing you'd married an American, and had to live in New York? Or worse, an Australian . . . ?' Liza gave a little shudder. 'Now, that *would* be heartbreaking.'

An elderly man, carrying a shopping basket, was making his way slowly up the gangplank when Juliet alighted from the taxi.

'Exuse me,' she said politely, 'is Mr Lawrence in?'

His face creased into a good-natured smile. 'Dan? You want Dan?' he asked.

100

'Yes. Is he in?'

'He doesn't live here, my dear.' He'd reached the pavement, panting and wheezing from the effort, for the tide was out and the gangplank was steeply raked.

'But I'm sure this is the houseboat where . . .' Juliet glanced at the other vessels that were moored on either side of it.

'Oh, yes,' the old man followed her gaze. 'this is the *Four Winds* all right, but it's my boat. I rent it out to him on occasions. Been to dinner here, have you?'

Juliet flushed, humiliated, and ignored the question. 'Where can I find him?'

He shook his head. 'Moves around, does Dan. I don't know where he is, right now.'

Juliet thanked him, and, trying to be gracious with gritted teeth, stalked off along the Embankment.

There was nothing for it but to wait until the bastard telephoned her; which she knew he would.

Charles invited Henry to have dinner with him one evening at White's, to which he also belonged. 'Get to know the future father-in-law a bit better before the big day sort of thing,' he said jovially.

'Certainly, old boy,' Henry replied, rather touched. After all, Charles would soon be a part of the family, and if he was going to make Rosie happy, that was all that mattered.

Conversation was rather stilted at first, as they took their seats in the formal dining room. Once they'd ordered, Henry tried to help it along by asking Charles about his late father.

'He was in the army, and was so badly wounded at Mons that he never fully recovered,' Charles replied. 'I was ten when he died.'

'And came into your inheritance?'

Charles hesitated. 'Well, I suppose you could call it that.'

Henry frowned, puzzled. 'And there's just your sister?'

'That's right. It was hard for Mother to have to bring us up on her own.'

'I can understand that.'

The waiter filled their glasses with wine and, to Henry's surprise, Charles picked up his glass, drank deeply and then signalled for more. Perhaps, he reflected, the young man was nervous at having to entertain his bride's father. He set about trying to put him at his ease.

'How are you enjoying Lloyd's, old fellah? Bit like a big club, isn't it?' He chuckled. 'Friend of mine manages to squeeze in four games of chess during the day, between meetings, and if he's not playing chess, he's having a three-hour luncheon with friends.'

Charles didn't smile. He took another gulp of wine and seemed preoccupied. 'Actually, sir, I was wondering . . .' He paused and seemed nervous. 'Umm . . . I was wondering when you would be settling Rosie's dowry? I mean, will you be waiting until after the wedding?'

'A *dowry*?' Henry repeated, shocked. 'My dear fellah, girls don't get dowries these days.'

Charles shot him a haunted look. His hands were shaking. 'You mean . . . ?'

Something at the back of Henry's blue eyes hardened. 'I sincerely hope you weren't expecting my daughter to come with a dowry,' he said coldly. 'She has a dress allowance, and that is all I intend to give her.'

'I see.' It was obvious Charles was struggling with an inner turmoil which he was trying hard to hide. 'Well, that's fine. I only mentioned it because my father left a dowry in his will for Henrietta when she gets married . . . but no matter. My prospects at Lloyd's are so good that we'll do very well on our own.' His smile was strained on his pale face.

'I'm afraid you'll have to,' Henry replied crisply.

Back at home, he told Liza what had happened.

'Oh!' she said, horrified. 'For God's sake don't let Rosie know. We can't cancel the wedding now, because people would suspect something.'

'I'm not going to help him financially, though,' Henry said firmly. 'He's going to have to stand on his own feet and make his own way in the world.'

'He *will*, Henry. He will. He's such a bright young man. I know everything's going to turn out all right.'

'How are you today, my love?' The deep, intimate voice sent a thrilling tremor through Juliet. It was two days later, days in which her hurt and anger had grown deeper and more bitter.

'I'm very well, thank you. How are you?' She kept her voice steady.

'Are you all right?' he asked, puzzled.

'Why on earth shouldn't I be?'

'I just wondered . . . I can't wait to see you, darling.'

'I can't wait to see you either,' she replied. 'Where do you live, by the way?'

'Live?'

She might have asked how often he flew to the moon, from his surprised tone.

'Yes. Or do you come up and go down to Kent every day?' she added, innocently.

'Lord, no! I've just sold my flat in Albany, and until I buy another one, I stay with various friends. Listen, my darling, I've booked a suite at the Dorchester for tonight. We'll get room service to bring us dinner and . . . Oh, God, I can't wait to be with you again.' His voice trailed away huskily.

'Eight o'clock?' she asked, pertly.

There was a moment's silence on the line. Had he guessed she'd found out about him? But then he said, 'Marvellous, darling,' and Juliet realized he had no idea at all.

She wore black again; a dramatic, clinging, halter-necked dress, with a long trailing scarf around her throat that fell to the ground. Her only jewellery was a pair of dazzling emerald and diamond earrings; real ones, borrowed from her mother, who thought she was going in a party to a smart charity ball at the Savoy.

Daniel was waiting for her in the lobby.

'Juliet . . . !' His eyes swept over her as if they were stripping her, making her feel naked. She suddenly felt horribly cheap. He kissed her cheek and slipped his arm around her waist. 'Let's go up to my room,' he whispered, leading her towards the lifts.

Out of the corner of her eye, she saw the concierge give her a contemptuous look, and her cheeks flushed with shame. How many women had that concierge seen Daniel escort up to his room?

His suite was opulent in a glamorous Hollywood style. The obligatory bottle of champagne stood in an ice bucket. Juliet

threw her ermine cape on to a sofa, and looked at him coquettishly.

Her tone was brittle. 'Are we going to eat now . . . or afterwards?'

Daniel looked startled. Then he frowned. 'Whenever you
like . . .' he said slowly.

'Then let me do the leading this time,' Juliet said, reaching
for the lapels of his dinner jacket. 'Let *me* seduce you. That
will be quite a novelty for you, won't it, sweetheart?'

He looked puzzled, and she thought she detected a glint of
disappointment in his almost black eyes.

'I can't think of anything more exciting,' he said drily.

Without another word, she undid his bow tie, and ripped
open his evening shirt, exposing his muscular tanned chest.

Leaning forward, she kissed him hungrily on the mouth,
while her hands feverishly unbuttoned the flies of his trousers.

'A-h-h-h!' he gasped, as her hands found him, held him,
arousing him instantly. Automatically, he put his arms around
her hips, trying to pull her closer.

'Hands off,' she said crisply, breaking away.

'I want you, darling, I want you so much,' he implored. He
made a grab for her, thrusting his thigh between her legs.

She wished his voice wasn't so wonderfully deep and sexy;
it was almost her undoing. She wished with all her heart she
didn't have to do this, but nobody, *nobody* used her for their
own ends.

Breaking away, she snatched up her wrap and walked briskly
to the door, leaving him standing with his trousers around his
ankles, and his ardour clearly visible.

'Go back to your wife, Daniel,' she said icily. 'And your
three children. I'm not some silly little débutante, you know.
And I don't appreciate being treated like a hooker, sneaking
around hotel corridors. I never want to see you again.'

Then the door slammed and she was gone.

Juliet breezed into the morning room the next day, where Rosie
was supposed to be writing thank-you letters for the latest
batch of wedding presents. She sat crouched, a damp handkerchief in her hand, her shoulders slouched. Juliet, taking in
the situation, dropped into an armchair.

'You're disappointed, aren't you?'

Rosie looked up through tear-blurred eyes. Then she nodded, slowly. 'I thought it would all be like a fairy tale,' she admitted. 'Like in the movies.'

Juliet smiled briskly but kindly. 'Believe me, real life isn't a Hollywood movie. If it turns out to be all too dreadful, you can always get a divorce, you know.'

Rosie perked up and gave a watery grin. 'I suppose marriage needn't be a life sentence; it's not like being sent to prison, is it?'

Juliet shot her an amused look. 'Not unless you want it to be, but it can always be a comfortable padded cell.'

Rosie blew her nose. 'Mummy says it's only wedding nerves, and I'll be all right on the day.'

'Of course you will,' Juliet said robustly, sounding rather like her grandmother.

Five

Hearing the excited roar of the crowds outside St Margaret's, Westminster, the congregation of a thousand guests wondered what the commotion was all about.

Surely the bride and her father couldn't have arrived so early? Heads turned to look down the aisle, the pretty flowers on the women's hats trembling like a herbaceous border in a gust of wind. Who was arriving? A member of the royal family? The Prime Minister? Flashlights popped and another cheer went up.

Then Juliet made her entrance, and everyone knew what the furore was about. Dressed in pale aquamarine silk, which exactly matched her eyes, and with a saucy concoction of matching feathers and veiling tipped over one eyebrow, she looked straight ahead as she sashayed up the aisle, ignoring the stares of other guests, who were stunned by the sheer beauty of her exquisite face.

'It's the younger sister . . .' people whispered, then turned to each other with knowing looks. Once again Juliet was stealing the limelight.

'I, Charles Douglas Hugo, take thee, Rosemary Helen . . .' Charles's voice was high and tinny, tight with nerves.

Rosie stood trembling beside him, her ivory satin wedding dress gleaming in the light that streamed through the stained-glass windows. A diamond and pearl tiara held her tulle veil in place, and from her shoulders trailed a thirty-foot satin train, embroidered with tiny crystal beads. Liza had insisted that Norman Hartnell, who had designed a twenty-eight foot train for the famous beauty, Margaret Sweeny, in 1933, should make Rosie's just that much longer.

Liza watched, dazzled with pride, and relieved there had been no more from Charles about a dowry, and that Rosie was unaware of his talk with Henry.

Henry looked grave, moved by the occasion, yet worried about his daughter's future.

Juliet watched Rosie with pity. If Charles had been the last man on earth, she wouldn't have wanted to marry him. After her experience with Daniel, she wasn't sure she trusted any man now.

Lady Anne, sitting very upright in lilac chiffon and a waterfall of pearls, felt a mixture of concern and disapproval. The former because she thought Rosie was too young to be tying herself down for the rest of her life, the latter because Liza was to blame; for pushing her daughter into marriage, and for arranging this ostentatious and vulgar display of wealth.

'. . . for better for worse, for richer for poorer, in sickness and in health . . .'

Rosie listened to the marriage vows, while Charles repeated them in his rather reedy voice, and in her head she was packing a small suitcase. Filled with necessities. Doubt about marrying him swept through her again; but there was nothing to stop her running away if the whole thing became too unbearable, was there?

The terrible solemnity of the vows was hitting her like hammer blows. They were even more profound than she'd realized. Making promises to God she wasn't sure she could keep.

'. . . to love, cherish and obey, till death us do part . . .'

The thought of that little case helped Rosie keep her composure as the marriage service continued. She was promising her life away to this young man, who, in the excitement of arriving at the church, the centre of attention and in a whirl of cheering and photographer's flashes, *she'd forgotten would be there*.

Her surprise at seeing him, waiting for her by the chancel steps, was like bumping into an old friend at a cocktail party, safe in the knowledge she could move on to talk to someone else after a few minutes.

And now these life-binding vows . . . ! How could she possibly promise to love, cherish, for richer for *poorer* . . . ! Oh, God, what have I done, she thought in panic.

Then it was her turn. 'I, Rosemary Helen . . .' The rest was a blurr. All that mattered was the thought that if the worst came to the worst she could run back to Granny at Hartley at any time.

The reception passed in a jolly haze of shaking hands and cutting the cake, listening to the speeches, whilst vaguely aware that, even though this was *her* day, people were saying how beautiful Juliet looked.

At last it was over. In a flurry of goodbyes, showers of rose petals and Henry saying to Charles, with an intimate man-to-man look, 'I've popped a couple of bottles of champagne into your luggage, old chap,' as they drove off and the guests piled into Bruton Street to wave and cheer.

They were to spend the first night of their honeymoon at the Ritz, before setting off the next day for a three-week driving excursion through France, Italy and Switzerland.

'How nice of Daddy to give us that champagne,' Rosie remarked, cheering up, as the car edged neared the hotel.

Charles nodded, looking serious. 'Yes, but we should keep it for a special occasion, don't you think?'

'Aren't you going to take off that silly hat?'

They'd been shown to their suite. Still in her sapphire blue dress and coat, with a hat trimmed with matching feathers, she was relaxing on a sofa, admiring the welcoming flowers her mother had ordered to be put in their sitting room.

She flushed, startled by the rebuke, and looked hurt.

'Don't you like it?'

'I hate feathers.' Charles sounded sulky, as he unpacked his overnight case. Ignoring her, and remaining silent, he pottered around in an aimless sort of way.

A block of ice seemed to form itself in Rosie's stomach and she started trembling. It seemed as if she'd married a complete stranger, with whom she had absolutely nothing in common. Who was this truculent young man, fidding with his wash bag? Wandering, looking bored, from their bedroom into the sitting room, and then back to the bedroom again?

For the first time in her life, Rosie had no idea what to say. *Well, here we are, married at last!* sounded too hearty. *Darling . . . at last we're alone* sounded rather forward to someone who'd suddenly become a stranger. On the other hand, *What's the matter with you, Charles?* were the words of a nagging wife.

She removed her beautiful hat very slowly, and laid it on the table. She felt cold and miserable and homesick. She wanted to run back to Mummy and sit with her in her cosy sitting room, so they could gossip about the wedding and who'd been there. She wanted Daddy to tell her everything would be all right, and then she wanted to slip up to the nursery, to see if Nanny had any aspirins.

But instead she sat in numb silence, experiencing the terrible feeling that, now Charles had secured her as his wife, he no longer intended to show her he cared for her, or to reassure her they were going to be happy together.

'Shall I order room service, or do you want to go down to the restaurant for dinner?' was all he asked, breaking into her bleak thoughts.

'Dinner in the restaurant would be nice,' she replied, in a small voice. Whether Charles liked her or not, she'd order champagne, and in front of a lot of people he wouldn't be able to stop her. Getting tipsy might be the only way she was going to get through the rest of the evening. And the night ahead.

The pain was excruciating. She felt as if an iron spear was being thrust inside her. Charles was trying to be gentle, she was sure of that, but nevertheless, why hadn't her mother told her the first time would be so painful? There was absolutely none of that 'pleasure in pain' that people talked about, either.

'Oh-h-h!' she gasped again and again, shrinking back from the steely probing. 'Wait . . . please.'

But Charles did not intend to wait indefinitely. With a final impatient thrust he completed the act, and then lay, spent, on top of her, panting. Without having said a word.

Later, while he slept heavily beside her, she lay awake, gazing into the darkness.

She'd always been jealous of Juliet, but never more so than at this moment. To be home, and safe, and feel loved was all she wanted, she thought, as hot tears scalded her cheeks and dampened her pillow.

'It's *such* an amusing little doll's house,' Juliet mocked, when Rosie invited her to cocktails in her new home, after she'd returned from honeymoon. 'I suppose it's all Charlie could afford.'

'Charles,' Rosie corrected automatically, 'and we'll be moving somewhere bigger in due course, but we just wanted a tiny place to begin with, where we could be on our own.'

'How cosy.' Juliet sounded unconvinced.

'Come and sit down.' Rosie patted the new two-seater sofa, and then went over to a side table, where there was a small selection of drinks on a tray with a hunting scene, which they'd been given as a wedding present. 'Sherry?'

'Sherry?' Juliet repeated. 'Haven't you any gin?'

Rosie nodded. She did not look happy. 'I've only got lime juice to go with it, I'm afraid.'

'The tart's drink,' Juliet remarked, amused. 'That'll do, but go easy on the lime.'

Sitting in uncomfortable silence, the sisters looked at each other. Juliet was amazed by how different everything was, now that Rosie was married. She seemed to have taken a great leap into another world, to which Juliet did not belong, and it was a strange feeling.

'So tell me, Lady Padmore, how was the honeymoon?' she asked in desperation, trying to sound flippant and jokey. 'Did you see Nice and Die? Did you break the bank at Monte Carlo? Was the Tower of Piza really leaning?

Rosie tried to laugh, but then her face crumpled and she burst into tears.

Juliet looked at her in astonishment. 'Rosie? What's the matter?'

'I . . . I don't think I like being m-married,' her sister sobbed.

'You mean you're not enjoying sex?' Juliet asked bluntly.

Rosie turned red with embarrassment, and blew her nose on a tiny handkerchief.

'Go on. You can tell me, for God's sake!'

'It's just that . . .' she began tentatively, 'I should warn you, because no one warned me, that it's . . . difficult. Terribly painful at first. And then . . .' Rosie's voice drifted away, and she dabbed her eyes.

'And then . . . what?'

'Then . . . nothing,' she said lamely.

'How do you mean . . . *nothing*?'

Rosie shrugged her thin shoulders. She'd lost a lot of weight in the three weeks she'd been away, and her pretty red and white summer dress hung limply on her.

Juliet leaned forward. 'Do you really mean you don't enjoy it?' She could hardly keep the amazement out of her voice.

Rosie nodded slowly. 'It's very nice to be loved, of course,' she added awkwardly. She and Juliet had never indulged in intimate talk, and making love with Charles was a very private matter, something she'd be reluctant to discuss even with a doctor.

'If you don't enjoy it, it's because you've never been properly aroused,' Juliet said knowledgeably. 'And if you had been, it wouldn't really have hurt, even the first time. At least, only a tiny bit . . . and in a very exciting way.'

Rosie's mouth fell open. 'How do you . . . ? You *haven't*, have you?' she asked, shocked.

Juliet suddenly smiled, a really warm, happy smile that lit up her eyes and made her face glow. No matter that Daniel Lawrence had turned out to be an adulterous rogue, she'd never forget how happy he'd made her during that weekend in Paris.

'Yes. I have,' she admitted, proudly. 'It was the most marvellous experience. Sex is so important, Rosie. It's so fulfilling . . . and wonderful for the skin.'

'But . . . who? When . . . ? Are you going to get married?'

There was an immediate edge of jealousy in Rosie's voice, and frustrated longing in her eyes. Trust everything to be 'wonderful' and 'marvellous' for Juliet, she thought.

Juliet took out a cigarette and fitted it into a long green holder. 'He's already married and an utter rotter,' she said, matter-of-factly, as she lit up. 'I'll never see him again, nor have anything to do with him, but I'll be for ever grateful. He showed me how it *should* be done . . . I'll probably never have such a wonderful lover again,' she added, laughing wrily, 'but it was worth it.'

'How do you mean? There is only one way it *can* be done,' Rosie said irritably. 'What was so special about it?'

Juliet looked thoughtful, and drew deeply on her cigarette. 'He was older than me, and very experienced. I think one's first lover should always be experienced. These boys we meet at parties are fumbling amateurs by comparison. They're only out for their own pleasure, and to hell with what the woman wants. It's very important for a lover to have good bedroom *manners* too.'

'You mean like saying thank you afterwards?' Rosie looked bewildered and dazed. That her younger sister seemed to know such a lot about what had always been a taboo subject in the Granville household shocked her.

Juliet burst out laughing. 'He's not holding a door open for you, or offering you a seat on a train, Rosie.' She held out her glass. 'I say, could you top up this drink, with more gin?'

Rosie got to her feet, as if in a dream. 'Yes. I think I'll have another one, too.' She tottered over to the drinks tray, suddenly feeling deeply envious. That her younger sister should have had an obviously marvellous time in bed with an experienced man, while she'd been struggling to enjoy herself with Charles, filled her with chagrin.

Charles had recently suggested that in future they should only make love on Tuesdays and Thursdays . . . what had happened to staying in bed, consumed by lust night and day, whilst drinking champagne? It felt as if her sex life had been committed to a calendar.

'If I were you, Rosie,' Juliet observed, tapping the ash of her cigarette into a hideous ashtray, obviously another wedding present, 'I'd be a good little wifey until after you've had your children, and then I'd get a divine lover, and meet him in the afternoon, when Charlie is at Lloyd's. That's what they do in France.'

Rosie looked stunned. 'But I'm not French,' she bleated.

111

'Then your only other option, if the whole thing gets too ghastly, sweetie, is to leave him.'

'I missed you all so much,' Rosie exclaimed, hugging her little sisters and kissing their soft plump cheeks. 'But I've brought each of you a present from France.'

She'd bought presents for Nanny and Ruby, too, and as she joined them all for tea round the nursery table, she could have wept with joy at being home in her old nursery again.

'Are you Lady Padmore, now?' Charlotte asked. 'And did God put a baby in your tummy in the church?'

Rosie blushed. 'We'll have to wait and see,' she said hastily, avoiding Nanny's eye.

'Tell us about the places you visited,' Louise begged. 'I'm longing to go to Italy to see the ruins of the Coliseum, where they threw the Christians to the lions.'

Charlotte's eyes widened. 'Real lions?'

Louise nodded, importantly. 'They ripped the people to pieces with their teeth. We're learning all about it at school.'

'Cor blimey!' muttered Ruby into her cup of sweet tea. Nanny shot her a look of disapproval. Cockney slang wasn't allowed in the nursery.

'Did you go up the Eiffel Tower?' Amanda asked. She needed glasses more than ever now, but in spite of Nanny's protestations, Liza wouldn't hear of it. Who looked at girls in glasses? It would ruin her appearance, she declared.

'Yes, we went up the Eiffel Tower. It rattled and shook in the wind, so I didn't like it much.' Rosie helped herself to one of Mrs Fowler's fairy cakes, and then remembered she'd bought nothing for dinner tonight. Their daily cleaner didn't cook, so this was another daily horror she had to face, having no idea how to even boil an egg.

Rosie glanced at her diamond-studded wristwatch, a wedding present from her grandmother. 'Oh! I'm going to have to go,' she said sadly. 'I haven't bought tonight's dinner yet.'

'You haven't *bought* it yet?' Nanny echoed, disapprovingly. 'Well, I expect Mrs Fowler could rustle up something for you to take home. Why don't you pop down to the kitchen after tea, and ask her?'

A wonderful smell of cooking greeted Rosie when she sailed

into the kitchen, making her wish, even more fervently, that she still lived at home.

'My, you look thin, m'lady,' Mrs Fowler exclaimed in a shocked voice, 'if you'll pardon me for saying so,' she added hastily. She'd known Rosie since she'd been born, but you didn't take liberties with a titled married lady.

'I'm fine, Mrs Fowler,' Rosie replied, trying to sound breezy. 'I wondered if there was any cold meat you could spare? I've completely forgotten to buy anything for dinner tonight, and I'm afraid Fortnums will be closed by the time I get there.'

'Very expensive they are too,' Mrs Fowler observed. 'Wicked what they charge for a cooked chicken, and as for a piece of salmon . . .' For once words failed her as she thought of the extravagance of shopping at Fortnum & Mason. She pressed her thin lips together. 'Let me see what's in the larder, m'lady.'

She returned a few moments later with a steak and kidney pudding, the bowl covered with a piece of white cloth tied around the rim with string. 'You just stand this in a big pan of boiling water for thirty minutes, and it will hot up nicely,' she explained.

'How shall I know when the water's boiling?' Rosie asked, mystified. She'd been buying ready-cooked food for dinner, with biscuits, cheese and fruit to follow.

'When it bubbles,' Mrs Fowler replied hollowly, after a deadly, shocked silence. 'Have you got some veg?'

'I don't think so.'

'Then I'll put a few spuds and some runner beans in a bag. You have to peel the potatoes, and chop up the beans, and boil them in separate pans,' she enunciated slowly. Cor blimey! It was like talking to a child of six, she thought. 'Would you like a summer pudding for dessert? I made an extra one this morning, and I can give you some cream to go with it.'

Mrs Fowler's summer puddings were legendary. The proportions she used of strawberries, raspberries, redcurrants and blackberries were sweet yet sharp, gentle on the palate, yet pungent. Once again Rosie was transported back to her childhood, and she was engulfed in a fresh wave of acute homesickness.

'Thank you, Mrs Fowler,' she said, blinking away her tears. 'That would be wonderful.'

'Doing the cooking yourself, are you?' she remarked in a voice charged with pity. It really was a shame that Miss Rosie had married someone who couldn't even provide her with a cook.

'Yes, for the time being. Of course, I'll have someone to help me when we move to a bigger house.'

'She's not eating,' Mrs Fowler informed Parsons, as they sat drinking tea in the servants' hall that night. 'Looks like the scrag end of a piece of mutton, she does. Gone right down, in my opinion. Trouble is, them girls have never been taught how to do anything.'

'That's right, Mrs Fowler. They were brought up as proper young ladies.'

'If you ask me, I don't think Lord Padmore has got tuppence to rub together. Imagine, they've only got someone who comes in to clean in the mornings! That's not what Mrs Granville wanted for Miss Rosie, now, is it?'

Parsons nodded gravely. 'I'd say,' he replied heavily, 'that she's never got over the death of the young marquess.'

'But he had no money either.' Mrs Fowler sounded scandalized. 'They attract fortune-hunters, that's the problem with them young ladies. I wouldn't wonder if Lord Padmore wasn't after her money. Probably hoped Mr Granville would give Miss Rosie a big dowry when they got married.'

'Mr Granville would have expected her husband to keep her in style,' Parsons opined.

'She'll be lucky,' Mrs Fowler joked, baring her teeth like a grinning greyhound.

The long hot days of August, filled with the sound of children's laughter, the *pluck-pluck* of tennis matches, the whirr of the lawn-mower, and the song thrush in the old oak tree near the house, gave way to the golden month of September, and the warm days waned in a flurry of falling leaves and cooler nights.

After the rest of the family returned to London for the little season, Juliet finally began to recover her spirits, after the shock of finding Daniel was married. Like a fern, with its tightly rolled new leaves slowly unfurling and stretching towards the light, so did she regain a sense of purpose, energy, and a feeling of rebellion. She was no longer going to be pushed into going to parties, to see and be seen. Nor was she going to be made to feel guilty for going her own way.

'It's all thanks to you, Granny,' she said when she announced she was returning to London at the end of the month. They were strolling through the garden with the dogs one balmy evening, and the setting sun glowed red in the west.

'Darling, I haven't done anything,' Lady Anne laughed. She stopped to dead-head one of the last roses of summer. 'Hartley is a healing place. I felt it the first time your grandfather brought me here.'

'It's more than that.' Juliet looked directly at her grandmother. 'You handle me so much better than Mummy. I sometimes think that some of the things I do are just done to annoy her.' Her wicked smile had returned.

'How honest of you to admit it.'

Juliet looked thoughtful. 'Mummy and Rosie are so . . . so . . .' She paused, searching for the right description.

'Anxious to do the right thing?' Lady Anne suggested.

'Yes. We always seem to have to go to the right place to meet the right people, wearing the right clothes and saying the right thing; it really *does* make me want to kick over the traces, you know.'

They looked at each other, Juliet as much startled by her admission as her grandmother.

Then they both started laughing, laughing so much that Lady Anne had to sit down on the nearest bench, throwing her head back like a young woman. Juliet sank down beside her, wiping the tears of mirth that were gathering in her eyes. The sheer relief of admitting, even to herself, why she behaved as she did was cathartic.

'My darling girl, you are a scream,' Lady Anne said, when she could speak, 'but try not to hurt your mother. She has your best interests at heart. She just wants you to be happy.'

'Yes,' Juliet said, serious again, wondering how she was ever going to be happy without Daniel, who still filled her thoughts all the time. 'I know I wanted to come out at the same time as Rosie, because I didn't want to be left behind, but it was Rosie who made such an issue of it. Like she was scared I'd take something away from her. Of course that made me all the more determined, and that's when we started competing with each other. She takes everything so seriously.'

'Some girls don't have your confidence, Juliet. I hope you're not being unkind to Rosie, sweetheart?' she added gently.

Juliet sat in silence for a few moments, deep in thought, her brow furrowed. 'Some women make me *want* to be unkind to them, including Rosie. She's so – so perfect.'

'No one's perfect.'

'I know, but she's so damned immaculate.'

Lady Anne looked up sharply. 'That's an odd word to use, isn't it?' she observed lightly.

Juliet shrugged. 'Rosie's always been immaculate. Pure as the driven snow; Mummy's favourite.'

'Your mother loves every one of you equally. I've never seen any sign of favouritism. Are you sure, darling, that it isn't because you don't regard *yourself* very highly, that you want to hit out at other women? Including Rosie? And the way you know best is by being more attractive to men than they are?'

'I don't know.' Juliet sounded despondent again, thinking how she hated the very existence of Daniel's wife. 'Granny, I think I'll go and have a rest for a while.'

'You do that, sweetheart. And I'll see you later.' Lady Anne watched as Juliet wandered slowly towards the house.

What raw nerve had she touched that accounted for that remark of Juliet's? And why had she chosen a word that meant 'without sin' to describe Rosie?

'Darling, how thrilling! I'm so excited for you!' Liza clapped her hands in delight, while a very pale and sickly looking Rosie sat in a heap in the drawing room of Green Street.

'No one told me I'd be sick every morning,' Rosie complained. 'How long will it last?'

'It varies, sweetheart,' her mother replied, blithely.

'Oh, God!' Rosie slumped deeper into the chair, her arms folded across her front. 'I hope it's a boy then, because I don't want to go through all this again.'

'Is Charles pleased?'

'A bit shocked, actually.' She didn't tell her mother that Charles' first reaction had been: 'I say, old girl, that's a bit of a disaster, isn't it?'

'Are you going to buy a bigger house now?'

'No, we can manage where we are, with just one baby.'

Liza looked fussed. 'So you'll turn the top floor into a nursery suite, will you? It'll mean the nanny will have to sleep with the baby, if there's to be a day nursery. Oh! But you don't have a bathroom up there, do you?' she added, aghast.

'I'm not going to have a nanny.'

'No *nanny!*' Liza's mouth opened; she looked like a stunned fish.

Rosie reflected they'd be lucky if they were still solvent by the time the baby was born. Her first shock had been when she'd accidentally opened a letter addressed to Charles. It was a final demand for the rent. Fifty pounds a quarter was owing, the letter said. Those were the terms of the agreement. Would Lord Padmore kindly forward his cheque for that amount, immediately.

'I don't understand,' she told Charles when he returned from Lloyd's that evening. 'I thought the house was ours. I thought you'd *bought* it.'

Charles turned bright red. 'I was going to . . . but the owners decided at the very last moment they wanted to rent it out, not sell, and by then it was too late for us to find somewhere else.'

Rosie knew him well enough by now to know he was lying.

'Then why don't we buy somewhere else now?' she suggested craftily. 'This place is too small for a baby and a nanny.'

He looked sullen. 'I don't want our children brought up by nannies. It's a mother's job.'

She eyed him with suspicion. 'Did your mother look after you and Henrietta?'

'Things were different in those days,' he blustered. 'We've got a daily as it is. We can ask her to come a bit more often, perhaps.'

Rosie couldn't believe this was happening. Charles had never warned her they'd be living like a working-class couple, in a tiny rented house, with no proper staff.

'You'd better pay this before we get evicted,' she remarked coldly, handing him the rent demand.

He shook his head. 'I can't.'

'What do you mean, you can't?'

'Stop going on at me, will you? I haven't got the money. You know Lloyd's don't pay me until the end of the month.'

'But the rent was due on September twenty-fifth. That's four weeks ago. Why didn't you pay it with your September cheque?'

'Oh, for God's sake . . . ! What is this? You're turning into a bloody nag. The trouble is you're so extravagant, Rosie. The food bills are enormous. Then there's the daily: six pence an hour, I ask you! And you keep inviting people to drinks. We're not rich like your parents, you know.'

'But I didn't think we were *destitute*.' She twisted her second-hand engagement ring – for that was how she now thought of it – round and round on her finger. 'Does this mean that we can't buy a house of our own?'

He raised his chin arrogantly. 'I never promised to buy a house. I said we'd get a house, I'd provide a house. I never said I'd buy one.'

Something cold and hard moved in her chest, gripping her heart, cutting off her supply of love, as if an artery had been severed. Did he hope her father would buy one for them? She dismissed the thought instantly; it was too terrible to think he'd married her for her money.

'Give me that bill.' Her manner was imperious. '*I'll* pay the rent out of my dress allowance. We can't risk being thrown into the street, especially now I'm going to have a baby.'

Charles groaned theatrically. 'For Christ's sake . . . ! Now you're playing the martyr. Look, I work jolly hard at Lloyd's, in spite of the fact I hate the bloody place . . .'

'I'm not being a martyr. I just wish . . .' Rosie felt like saying that she wished he'd told her he had no money before they got married; but what would she have done if he had? Broken off their engagement? How would that have made her look?

'I just wish,' she repeated, 'that you'd told me the rent needed paying. If it helps, I'll pay it in future. And I'll try and cut the food and drink bills as well.'

Charles didn't look as pleased as she'd expected. 'Now you're trying to make me feel I've let you down. I hope you're not going to tell anyone we can't manage on my salary.'

He needn't worry, Rosie reflected angrily. Pride would prevent her from telling anyone for as long as she lived.

Even her family, especially Juliet, must remain unaware that, after all her mother's efforts, she'd ended up with a penniless peer.

'But you'll never be able to go out in the evenings if you don't have a nanny,' Liza was saying in shocked tones.

'Charles doesn't like going out much, now that we're married,' Rosie said casually. 'Anyway, I don't feel up to it at the moment.'

Liza's eyes narrowed. 'Is everything all right, darling?'

'Fine, Mummy. Fine.' What was her mother going to say when she found out that she probably wasn't ever going to be able to socialize on a grand scale again? No Royal Ascot. No Eton and Harrow match at Lord's? No racing at Goodwood. No cocktail parties, dinner parties, or dances? And no money to buy clothes, because she'd promised Charles she'd pay the rent for the horrid little house in future.

Whirlpools of laughter kept coming from the table in a corner of the Café de Paris. People craned their necks to see who was among the glamorous diners, and saw Juliet Granville, in the white halter-neck dress.

It was December 3rd, 1936 and she was celebrating her nineteenth birthday. Old friends, like Colin Armstrong and Edward Courtney, had come back into her life again, unable to resist being in her company. Andrew Stevens sat next to her, and someone she'd met the previous week, called Luke Harmon, was on her other side. Three girls, of no importance to Juliet, but who were necessary to make up the numbers, had also been invited.

'Here's to the Birthday Girl!' Andrew said, holding his glass of champagne aloft.

'The Birthday Girl!' everyone chorused.

'I think I'll stay nineteen for the next ten years,' Juliet announced, waving her cigarette about in its long holder. Her slender arms, bronzed from the long summer at Hartley, moved with the grace of a ballet dancer. 'Then when I'm twenty-nine, I'll start going backwards!'

'And your *derrière* will still enchant us all!' cried her new friend, Luke.

'Here's to Juliet's *derrière*!' Edward chortled, raising his glass.

The group drank another toast, and fell about laughing.

'Here's to . . .' Colin began, a wicked twinkle in his eyes.

'That's enough,' Juliet commanded, thoroughly enjoying herself. The other girls in the party looked at her enviously, mesmerized by her wit and confidence, and the way the men were obviously fascinated by her.

In between courses, she danced with each of the young men, teasing them, flirting with them, making them feel so good about themselves that they became half in love with her. The champagne flowed. It was the first time she'd had a party that wasn't shared with Rosie, and she revelled in it.

Shortly after midnight, for no apparent reason, the atmosphere in the restaurant changed. It became charged with tension, as if something extraordinary had happened. The younger groups started chattering excitedly, the older ones looked grave and shocked.

'What's going on?' Juliet asked. 'What's happening?'

A man came running down the stairs from the balcony, brandishing the first edition of the *Daily Mail*. He rushed over to the rest of his party, and they all made a grab for it. A middle-aged woman burst into tears. A man swore loudly, his face purple with rage.

'Colin, quickly! Go and buy a newspaper,' Juliet urged him nervously. She'd begun to fear the gossip columns, in case she was mentioned again. These days journalists who dealt in the depravity of the rich upper classes watched her closely. She'd managed to rise above two scandals, but her name was already tarnished; she couldn't afford another debacle.

The band played quietly, almost drowned out by the cacophony of voices raised in a mixture of shocked titillation and absolute horror, as more newspapers appeared and were snatched up and devoured.

Juliet heard a man exclaim, 'This is a tragedy!'

'That dreadful woman,' an elderly lady sobbed.

Colin came hurrying back, breathless. 'I got the last copy. It's mayhem in Leicester Square.'

The headlines were black and heavy.

THE KING TO MARRY WALLIS SIMPSON. A photograph of her in evening dress was on the centre of the front page.

'So at last the press has broken the story,' Juliet observed.

'Did you know about it?' asked one of the girls, looking impressed.

Juliet gave her a quick smile. 'It's been going on for years, but the British press, out of respect for the monarchy, have kept quiet. Until now.'

'Good God!' Edward exclaimed. 'Are we to have Queen Wallis on the throne? What is this country coming to?'

Juliet shrugged calmly. 'By the sound of her, she'll make a good job of being the King's wife,' she remarked. 'She's a very modern woman. No doubt she'll regard her marriage as a career. And one thing is certain; they'll have to stick together for ever.'

A man at the next table, who had been intrigued by Juliet throughout the evening, heard what she'd said. He watched her now with renewed interest, as she scanned the news-sheet. Of course, he'd immediately recognized her from photographs in the glossy magazines. His interest quickened.

She could be just the woman he'd been looking for.

The man was a Scottish lawyer called Hector Mackenzie. Small, thin and with sparse grey hair, he had the manner of an inquisitive little bird. His wire-framed glasses were always perched on his beaky nose. He had a habit of tilting his head to the side, when pontificating with a slight Scottish accent.

The day after he'd spotted Juliet at the Café de Paris, where he'd been dining with clients, he took the train up to Inverness, where he was met by a car which drove him to Glenmally Castle.

His most important client lived here, and his duties to Cameron Kincardine stretched far beyond the usual brief of a lawyer. He was also his financial advisor, mentor, and had originally been a close friend of Cameron's father.

On arrival, a manservant showed him into the study, where Cameron was writing letters. After the usual exchange of greetings, Hector described Juliet, and repeated what he'd overheard her say about Wallis Simpson.

'The girl's got her head screwed on, Cameron,' he said. 'She's not the usual type of shallow débutante. She's also very beautiful.'

'You think she'd be interested?' Cameron asked.

'I tell you, if the new King had only been fifteen years younger, she'd have made a perfect royal bride for him. Instead of the shameless hussy he's gone after,' he added heatedly. 'The Granvilles are a good family. They have wealth and breeding. I've read that Juliet's been a bit of a naughty wee girl . . . but mightn't that be a good thing, in the circumstances? I could tell she liked the good things in life, too. I think . . .' He paused, small head cocked to one side. 'I think she'd understand the meaning of *quid pro quo* . . . which, let's face it, most society girls wouldn't.'

Cameron's piercing brown eyes skewered Hector's. 'To begin with, we let her think . . . ?'

'Of course. Of course,' Hector tutted gently.

Cameron rose from the desk, and went to the window, gazing at the rugged wildness of the surrounding mountains. Tall, thickly built, and with a thatch of dark hair, he remained standing there, deep in thought. There was something wild about him too, this son of the Scottish soil; this man who hated towns, was distrustful of foreigners, and preferred to have a very private existence.

Eventually, and with a certain reluctance, he turned round to face Hector. 'So how do I get to meet this girl?'

'On her own territory,' Hector replied instantly.

'You mean . . . ?'

'You should give a cocktail party at a smart London hotel, and invite her and her parents. I'll make up a guest list for you, and it must include people she knows. You should also invite some of your late father's more distinguished friends, to set the right tone.'

Cameron sank wearily into the chair behind his desk again. His bland but kindly face was puckered anxiously. 'I suppose I have to go through with this?'

'Absolutely. It's essential.'

In due course, invitations arrived at 48 Green Street for Henry and Liza, and one for Juliet. A few streets away, another arrived for Rosie and Charles.

Juliet looked blankly at the stiff white engraved card. 'Why have we been invited? I've never heard of him, have you?' she asked her mother.

Liza was flushed with pleasure. 'Yes, of course I've heard of him, but I don't know why we've been asked; we've never met.'

Juliet read again. 'The Duke of Kincardine, At Home. Tuesday, twenty-eighth January, 1937. At Claridge's.

Cocktails: six thirty – eight thirty p.m. RSVP Glenmally Castle. The Highlands. Scotland.'

Liza had already reached for *Debrett's Peerage*. Her expression was serious, as if she was researching a grave matter of state. Finally she spoke. 'He's the fifth Duke, Juliet. He's thirty-three, and unmarried. The title will become extinct if he doesn't produce an heir. I've heard he owns nearly as much land as the Duke of Buccleuch.' She looked into Juliet's face, while her mind spun in circles. 'I wonder if he's invited any other young women to this party.'

'I don't know who the hell he is, and I've no intention of going, looking like this,' Rosie grumbled, throwing the invitation down on the breakfast table.

Charles picked it up and studied it. 'It might be a good party,' he pointed out.

'Then you go.'

'But you'd enjoy it. I thought you loved socializing.'

'Not any more.' She knew she'd become a slattern, using the discomfort of her pregnancy as an excuse for lounging around the house in her dressing gown all day, nursing her unhappiness as if it was a tangible presence. She was tired, disillusioned and longed to be back in the luxurious surroundings of Green Street, yet was too proud to admit it.

'I'm suffering from terrible sickness,' she'd say, if even her mother invited her to lunch. 'My back's killing me,' or, 'I keep getting dizzy spells,' were her other reasons for avoiding seeing other people.

'Please yourself,' Charles snapped nastily. 'I'm going. Anything for a bit of fun.'

'You might even meet another heiress,' she taunted, slamming out of the dining room.

The thought of that little packed suitcase was never far from Rosie's mind. But how could she possibly walk away from her marriage after only five months? And pregnant at that? What a fool she'd look, apart from anything else. And how humiliating; everyone would guess Charles had married her for her money.

But was she going to ruin the rest of her life, married to someone who made her deeply unhappy?

A week ago something had happened that had rocked the establishment, shaken Britain to its roots, and sent a message around the world that personal happiness comes before responsibility, and romantic love is all.

King Edward VIII, as yet uncrowned, and determined to marry Mrs Simpson, had been forced to abdicate because of the government's objections to a twice-divorced woman taking her place beside him as his Queen. So he'd given up his throne, his family, his country, and his duty, for 'the woman he loved', as he described her.

Unlike the rest of her family, Rosie was inspired, and felt deep sympathy for the King, as she'd listened to his speech on the wireless. Edward VIII hated his life, and wasn't afraid to run away from all his obligations. If a King could do it – why couldn't she? Who would really care if she did? Only Charles, her family, and a bunch of shallow socialites. She'd actually started composing a letter to Charles when Liza phoned. Rosie could tell her mother was crying.

'Isn't this a terrible calamity? Did you hear his farewell speech?' Liza wept.

'He didn't want to be King, Mummy. He's in love with Mrs Simpson.'

'*Love?*' Liza stopped crying, she was so horrified. 'What's love got to do with it? It was his duty to stay. Rosie, don't be so naive, darling. That woman is a dominatrix, and their's is a sadomasochistic relationship. No good can come of it.'

But Rosie wasn't listening. The way her mother put it did make the new King's action seem very selfish; but does anyone deserve to be unhappy? Even if it is in the line of duty?

Later though, Rosie started reading about the new King and his sweet Scottish wife, and how they were going to have to leave their own lovely home and move into Buckingham Palace for a life devoted to the country.

Gradually Rosie began to see that there was something very noble in doing one's duty. She felt inspired. As much as it was their duty to take their places on the throne, so was it her duty to stand by Charles, and bring up their child.

Like the new King and Queen, she must somehow make the best of it, she told herself.

*   *   *

Juliet arrived at Claridge's with her parents for the Duke of Kincardine's cocktail party. The lobby leading to the ballroom, where it was being held, was already filled with people, milling around and talking to each other, whilst a long line of guests waited to be received.

'*Everyone's* here,' Liza murmured, adjusting the folds of her sable-edged wrap.

Henry nodded. He'd already seen several members of parliament and the lords that he knew, and some of his old cronies from White's.

At that moment, Colin Armstrong came rushing up to Juliet.

'What are *you* doing here?' she asked laughingly. She leaned forward, her cheek pressed to his while she whispered, 'Have you gatecrashed?'

He shook his head. 'Have you . . . ? Oh, I suppose not, if you're with your parents. Who *is* this duke? I've no idea why I was invited.'

'I've no idea why any of us were invited,' she replied, succinctly. 'It looks as if he's invited a very motley crowd, of all ages.'

They joined Henry and Liza in the line to be received.

Colin continued, 'Maybe he wants to launch himself as a politician?'

'But what good would people like us be to him?'

'I haven't the faintest. Let's just enjoy the champagne; what are you doing afterwards?'

'Nothing, actually.'

'Fancy supper at the Berkeley?'

'Divine idea! Yes, please.'

The master of ceremonies was announcing the names in a loud voice. 'Lord and Lady Lonsdale. Sir Geoffrey and Lady Armstrong. Mr and Mrs William Wakeley. Lord Doughty. Lord and Lady Eastham . . .'

In a moment her parents would be announced. Suddenly Juliet's heart gave a great lurch as she saw the back view of their host, as he turned to have another word with the Easthams. It was Daniel . . . ! She'd recognize that thick dark hair anywhere, those broad shoulders . . . but something was wrong. Daniel was taller than this man, with longer legs. Her spirits swooped down in disappointment as she realized she'd been mistaken.

'Mr and Mrs Henry Granville, and Miss Juliet Granville,' boomed a sonorous voice.

The man she'd thought was Daniel was greeting her parents with delight, almost as if they'd been old friends. Then he turned to her, his brown eyes sharp and drilling, the only features in an otherwise bland face.

'Thank you so much for coming,' he said, his voice filled with sincerity; not the wonderfully deep voice of Daniel, she thought, but pleasant enough. She liked his firm handshake. His appearance was immaculate.

'Thank you for inviting me.' She smiled, looking up into his face. 'We haven't met before, have we?' she asked bluntly.

Cameron Kincardine smiled back, showing even white teeth. 'No, we haven't, but I've heard a lot about you; all nice things, I have to say.'

'Well, that's lucky, isn't it?' she joked.

A waiter holding a tray offered her a glass of champagne. She moved forward to join the melee, as more guests were announced.

'May I introduce myself?' A small white-haired man had popped up by her elbow. 'My name's Hector Mackenzie. I'm a neighbour of the duke's, and an old friend. It's very nice to meet you.'

Juliet sipped her drink. Her parents had been swallowed up by the crowds, and Colin had also vanished.

'It's nice to meet you, too.' She moved closer to Hector Mackenzie. 'Can you tell me something?' Her voice was low and confidential. 'Is this a special occasion? Is it the duke's birthday or something?'

Hector's bird-like head tilted to one side. He rose on his toes, as if to take flight. 'Cameron is thinking of spending more time in London. He's been so busy looking after his estate since his father died that he feels he's rather neglected his social life. This party is to ... well, help him get back into circulation,' he added with a chuckle.

'I don't think he'll have a problem,' Juliet remarked drily, eyeing the large dishes of Beluga caviar, resting on crushed ice, being offered to guests.

'The duke is probably going to buy a house in Park Lane. There are still a few nice ones left which haven't been pulled

126

down to make way for new hotels like the Dorchester,' Hector Mackenzie continued, in a chatty voice.

'We live just off Park Lane, in Green Street.'

'Is that so?' The tone was surprised, the Scottish accent soft, as if he didn't know; but hadn't it been he who'd drawn up the invitation list, after doing some assiduous research? 'A very nice part of London,' he added.

He continued to keep Juliet in conversation, and bored. She looked around, and saw several of her friends bunched together in a corner, as if they were having a private party of their own.

Just as she was about to make her excuses and join them, her mother came up to her. 'Ah, there you are, Juliet!' She looked questioningly at the Scottish lawyer.

'Mummy,' she said, seeing a way of escape, 'You must meet this delightful gentleman. This is Mr Mackenzie.' She turned to Hector. 'And this is my mother, Mrs Granville.'

They shook hands and started talking, and Juliet slipped away, bumping into Edward Courtney, who was tucking into *foie gras* canapes.

'This is *the* strangest party I've ever been to,' she whispered.

He grinned. 'It's the first time I've ever been to a party where no one knows the host,' he chortled. 'And no one knows why they've been invited. Do *you* know why you're here?'

'No idea at all,' Juliet replied. 'At least we all seem to know each other, and the champagne is flowing, so who the hell cares?' She helped herself to another glass from a passing waiter.

'Have you noticed there aren't many girls, though?' he sounded disconsolate.

'That's true,' she agreed, looking around, suddenly consumed with a longing for Daniel to be here. Shocked to realize he still had the power to arouse her, even though she hadn't seen him in weeks. A wave of sick desire shot through her at the memory of his love-making. 'I think I'm going to leave,' she murmured, Suddenly feeling miserable.

'But you've only just arrived! Colin told me you're having supper with him afterwards.'

Her brow wrinkled. 'I've got a headache coming on.'

Edward looked at her strangely. 'I thought you'd be setting your cap at this duke none of us have ever heard of,' he whispered, drawing her behind one of the square pillars that stood in the four corners of the ballroom. 'He's single, you know. And fearfully rich. He'd be perfect for you, Juliet.'

She leaned against the pillar, and looked up at one of the art deco chandeliers. There was a long pause before she spoke.

'I'm in love with someone else,' she said slowly, as if the thought had just occurred to her.

Edward's eyes widened. 'Not that married chap you went to Paris with?'

'Oh, God, does *everyone* know about that?' she groaned.

'Gossip travels, sweetie. You're a star turn on the social scene, you know. Everyone wants to know what you're up to.'

'Have you got a gasper?' As she spoke, she reached for the long jade holder in her handbag. Edward snapped open his cigarette case and held it out to her.

'Thanks. If only he hadn't been married. I was so angry with him when I found out, but . . .'

'He was good under the covers, was he?' Edward gave her a knowing wink as he struck a match.

Juliet looked at him, brazening it out. 'Don't be so vulgar, Edward,' she chided, crossly.

'But you regret chucking him now?'

She shrugged, appalled at this sudden rush of emotion that was edging towards tears.

'It might make you feel better to know he'd never have married you even if he'd been single,' Edward suggested.

She straightened up, eyes flashing, their pale blueness cold as ice. 'Why do you say that?' she asked sharply.

Seeing her hurt, Edward immediately said, 'Oh, darling, not because he wouldn't think you were marvellous. Not because he wouldn't be attracted to you; but because he's a Jew. They can never marry Gentiles. You know that, don't you?'

Juliet shook her head, astonished. 'I never thought about that. I just know he's the sexiest man I've ever met. You've no idea . . . and he had so much *soul*. So much feeling, and yet a wonderful vibrancy and zest for life.'

'You sound like my eldest sister.' Edward looked rueful. 'The love of her life was a Jewish man. She told me all her girlfriends found Jewish men more attractive.' He shrugged. 'She's thirty-five now, and I don't think she'll ever marry.'

'That's terrible.' The colour had drained from Juliet's face now and she looked drawn.

'Sorry, sweetheart. But isn't it better to know that, apart from being married, Daniel's unattainable? And through no fault of yours?'

Juliet drew a last drag on her cigarette, before stubbing it out. 'I'm off, Edward. God knows where Colin is, but could you give him a message, please? Tell him I've gone home because I'm feeling rotten.'

Edward kissed her gently on the cheek. 'Yes, I'll tell him. And try to forget all about Daniel Lawrence. You could have anyone you wanted, you know.'

'Thanks.' She nodded, her eyes cast down and her mouth tight. Anyone; except the one man she loved.

At that moment her mother came trotting up to her, eyes blazing with excitement. 'The duke has invited us to stay on for dinner,' she whispered, as Edward slipped away. 'You, me and Daddy.' Her manner was conspiratorial. 'Don't tell anyone; I don't believe he's invited many other people.'

'I'm on my way home, Mummy,' Juliet protested, wearily. 'I've got a headache.'

'Don't be ridiculous, Juliet.' Liza spoke sharply. 'You *must* stay.' The unspoken implication hung over them, like a tantalizing prize.

'All right,' she said reluctantly. If she couldn't have what she really wanted, and at that moment wanted desperately, then she might as well go back to her original plan of making a brilliant marriage.

They dined in the high-ceilinged restaurant of Claridge's. Cameron had invited two other couples, but Liza was very gratified by the seating plan. He'd placed her on his right side, and Juliet on his left. Henry had been seated beside Cameron Kincardine's mother, the dowager duchess, a strange-looking woman with a mass of black hair, a white face, and the dark, darting eyes of a knowing child. Dressed in a long white floaty dress, like an elderly Ophelia, there was a doomed whimsicality about her that jarred with the modern world. And yet, beneath this ingenious manner, Henry detected a steely core.

Cameron engaged Liza in affable conversation during the

first course, as etiquette required, and then turned to talk to Juliet during the main course.

'So tell me about yourself,' he asked, his manner easy and relaxed. 'Do you spend all your time in London? Or are you mostly in the country?'

'Weekends and the summer in the country, but I need London, during the week, like an anaemic person needs a blood transfusion,' she replied crisply, determined to lay her cards on the table from the start.

Cameron laughed as if she'd said something amusing. 'And what do you do when you're in town?'

She raised her plucked eyebrows provocatively. Her eyes smouldered. She felt so unhappy she didn't care if she appeared fast and reckless. 'That depends. What do *you* do?'

'That's the problem,' he confided, as if he wasn't aware of her flirting. 'It's so long since I've been down here, I'm out of touch. That's why I'm looking for a house to buy.'

'Near where I live, I believe?' Her body was turned towards him, her elbow resting on the arm of her chair, her hand cupping her chin in a kittenish fashion. Her dress revealed a perfect cleavage, her crossed thighs looked slim beneath her dress. Leaning forward, her face was close to his as she gazed into his eyes.

'Park Lane,' he replied. 'Are you near Park Lane?' He dabbed his mouth with the damask napkin. 'That's where I'm looking.'

'*Very* near,' she breathed in a low voice.

'Right! Well then, we shall no doubt see a lot of each other,' he replied, gazing down at his plate.

Juliet smiled her sweetest scarlet smile. 'Oh, I do hope so.'

Iona Kincardine was watching Juliet closely, through narrowed eyes. 'What makes you think she's suitable?' she mouthed to Hector, who was sitting on her left.

'She's sophisticated,' he replied, *sotto voce*. 'Worldly. We don't want some romantic little fool. That girl has her head screwed on, and I'd say her head rules her heart.'

Iona nodded, in silent approval.

'It's my belief,' Hector continued in a whisper, 'she also knows which side her bread is buttered. Look how thrilled her mother is that Cameron is paying her attention. She'll encourage this match, I'm certain.'

'Her mother looks a fool to me.'

'So much the better, don't you think?' He gave a sly smile.

'What do you make of the father?'

'A nice man. Straight as a die. Very honorable. The less he knows the better, though.'

'Deal with the mother then, Hector. I think she rules the roost in that family. Funny how stupid women can have such a hold over intelligent men.' Iona Kincardine gave a puckish smile.

'Yes.' But Hector wasn't looking at Liza, he was studying Juliet, as she directed her charms towards Cameron. There was nothing stupid about Juliet, though, he reflected. She knew exactly what she was doing.

As the dinner party broke up shortly before midnight, Iona Kincardine went to say goodbye to Juliet, her arms outstretched as if to embrace her.

'It's been lovely to meet you,' she gushed, sounding like a young girl who had just made a new chum. 'You will come and stay with us, won't you? Do you fish? Never mind,' she continued swiftly, seeing Juliet's look of surprise, 'there are lots of other things to do.'

'Thank you,' Juliet replied with a radiant smile. She'd drunk far too much, and at that moment she was prepared to go anywhere, meet anyone, do anything, as long as this warm floaty feeling continued.

Iona was holding both her hands now, in a firm grip. Much shorter than Juliet, she gazed up into her face. 'You are so beautiful, my dear, but I expect everyone tells you that. And such a lovely dress.' She held Juliet's hands out to the sides, to see more clearly what she was wearing. 'Exquisite, my dear,' she said with satisfaction, as if she was studying a great work of art.

'What a success!' Liza chirruped, as they were leaving Claridge's. She was a bit tipsy too, but her elation came mostly from the heady realization that Cameron was seriously interested in Juliet.

'He seems a nice enough man,' Henry remarked cautiously, helping Liza into their waiting car. 'Odd mother, though,' he added.

Juliet, sitting in the back, said nothing. She was tired and sleepy, filled with alcohol and wanting only Daniel. Tomorrow, she would wake up sober, knowing she had to try and get through another day without him, and wondering if she'd be able to.

'He's *perfect*, Juliet. In every way,' her mother murmured. 'Ummmm . . .'

'There is something I can't make out about him, though,' Henry observed.

'I think he's shy,' Liza pointed out in a hushed voice, as if it were a sad disability.

'Juliet probably frightened him to death, then.' He turned to look at his daughter in the semi-darkness of the car; her profile was as expressionless as a marble bust. 'You overdo it, you know, Juliet. It's not seemly. No man's going to be interested in a girl if she throws herself at him.'

Juliet didn't answer, but gazed out of the window sadly.

'Didn't I throw myself at you?' Liza asked with champagne-fuelled coquetry, as she placed her hand on Henry's arm.

'I flung myself at you first, darling, so you were only responding,' he said with swift *faux* gallantry.

'I didn't throw myself at Cameron,' Juliet retorted, stung. 'I don't even *care* for him. What with Mummy on one side, encouraging me to go after every eligible man in Britain, and you on the other side, practically accusing me of acting like a tart . . . what am I supposed to do?' Her voice broke angrily, and she was near to tears.

Henry spoke calmly. 'Don't exaggerate, Juliet. I merely think you were a bit forward.'

'Most men like it,' she replied sulkily.

'Not those who are looking for a wife,' Henry pointed out mildly.

'Rosie would have enjoyed the party tonight,' Liza said peaceably. 'I saw Charles, and he said she didn't feel well enough to go out.'

Juliet gave an impatient sigh. 'God, who would want to be pregnant? It's a ghastly thought.'

'I might ask them to dinner next week to meet Cameron,' Liza chattered on, as if she was thinking aloud.

Juliet shot her mother a dark look. 'I wouldn't if I were you. If she's in one of her moods, she's bound to bring up something that will ruin my chances of becoming a duchess.'

*   *   *

When all the guests had gone, and he'd thanked Liza for her kind invitation to dinner the following week, Cameron Kincardine turned to Hector.

'As Mother's gone to bed, let's have a nightcap,' he suggested.

'Aye, fine, man,' Hector replied, slipping into the informal father-and-son casualness that typified their relationship when no one else was about.

They'd retired to the 'drawing room' of the hotel, which was empty at this hour, and ordered whiskies.

'Well?' Hector asked, his expression hopeful, as they settled themselves in two easy chairs.

Cameron rubbed his hand across his brow, not answering.

Hector continued, 'What's the problem? She's beautiful, aristocratic, dresses well and seems accomplished – what does she lack?'

'Nothing. I think it's me that's lacking.'

Rosie couldn't find a comfortable position in bed. To lie on her back made her spine hurt. To lie on her side made the bump seem heavier. She hated being pregnant. She hated this poky little house. She hated her life.

It was after midnight, and Charles still hadn't returned from the Duke of Kincardine's cocktail party, and all sorts of thoughts were preventing her from falling asleep. Had he gone out to dinner with her parents? Had he gone out to dinner with someone else? Not that she feared he might be interested in another woman; it was his heavy drinking that disturbed her. Something he'd never done before they married.

She eventually fell into an uneasy slumber, and was awakened at dawn by the sound of Charles snoring. Worse, he smelled strongly of drink, and as he was taking up the centre of the bed, she found herself clinging to the edge of the mattress.

'Charles . . . ! Move over,' she exclaimed irritably.

'Wha'? Whatch t'matter?' he slurred.

'You smell of drink, and you're taking up all the bed.' She clutched at the sheet and blankets and pulled them towards herself. 'I'm freezing, too.'

'Go to hell!' He rolled on to his side, and instantly fell into a deep sleep again.

'Oh, God ... !' Her back ached and so did her hips. Struggling to her feet, she got out of bed, dragged on her dressing down, reached for a lacy shawl, and padded down to the kitchen. Tears stung her eyes as she filled the kettle with water and lit the gas stove.

Her life was becoming unbearable. She knew she'd been spoilt by her parents, knew she'd always been waited on by servants, and given money to spend on what ever she wanted, but losing those privileges wasn't the main source of her misery. What was causing her sense of desolation was the knowledge she'd fallen out of love with her husband, knew he cared nothing for her either, and into this hellish mess she was bringing a child.

'I want us to move to the country,' she told Charles, when he returned from Lloyd's the following evening. She'd been thinking about it all day, planning what they should do, and how much less expensive it would be.

He looked shocked. 'The *country*?' he repeated, as if she'd suggested the Moon or Mars.

'It would be cheaper. And better for the baby.'

'What's brought this on?'

Rosie ignored the question. 'We're living beyond our means, Charles. We could rent a cottage for a fraction of the cost of this house; a bigger place too. Food would be cheaper, everything would cost less. And you could come up to London by train every day, like Daddy did when we all stayed at Hartley last autumn.'

Charles flushed angrily. 'But I don't want to live in the country. I hate the country. I never even stay up in Cumbria, which is my *home*, if I can help it. Why on earth do you want to bury yourself in some corny little village in the country, for God's sake?'

'Because it's easier and less humiliating to be poor in the country than it is in a smart part of London, where one's friends are soon going to cotton on to the fact we've got no money,' she replied heatedly.

'Oh, come on, Rosie, we won't be poor for ever,' he reasoned in a coaxing voice.

'Why? What are you waiting for? My inheritance when Daddy dies?'

He looked at her, shocked, wondering if Henry had told her he'd asked about a dowry.

Rosie's deep blue eyes were filled with anguish. Somehow she was going to have to make this marriage work, because she could never get divorced. No one in her family had ever been divorced.

'Sorry, I didn't mean that,' she said, her fighting spirit wilting.

'It sounds very like it to me.'

'No, really . . . you don't understand. I'm pregnant and it makes me nervous and jittery. If we had a nice little cottage, perhaps on the outskirts of Shere, life would be much simpler. For one thing, I wouldn't keep running into my friends, who all seem to be rich, and have big houses and lots of servants.'

'So you're saying you're fed up because I'm not rich? God knows, I work myself to death at Lloyd's, in an effort to—'

'That's not what I'm saying, Charles,' she cut in, though of course she knew it was true. 'But we might even be able to afford to *buy* a cottage in the country. Maybe the bank would lend us the money. It would be a good investment,' she added.

'Who have you been discussing this with? Your father? Since when did you know about investments?' he demanded, furiously.

She looked distressed. 'I haven't discussed it with anyone. My parents still think you own this house, and we're comfortably off, and that's what I want them to think. We'd be better off in the country, Charles, we really would.'

Charles looked uncomfortable. 'It might suit *you*, but what about me? I like meeting my friends for a drink at the club. Having the odd game of cards. What in damnation am I supposed to do in the country? The next thing you'll be suggesting is that we grow our own vegetables or something,' he scoffed derisively.

Rosie blanched. She'd never heard him swear before, and the ugly word hovered like a stain in the atmosphere.

'Charles,' she said, carefully drawing a deep breath. 'I want, more than anything, for us to be a happy family. It will be so much better for the baby if we're in the country. We can have a little garden for him to play in—'

'Him?'

'Your son and heir, if it's a boy,' she continued smoothly. 'And we can have a much higher standard of living. If we have a spare room, you can invite friends down for the weekend.

Please, Charles, it really would be better for us all.'

'I don't know if I can get a bank loan,' he muttered, sulkily.

Rosie smiled at last. 'No, but I'm sure I can.'

In a thinly disguised manoeuvre, Liza invited several single people to the dinner party, as well as two couples, so Cameron Kincardine wouldn't think she was matchmaking. And in spite of Juliet's warning, Rosie and Charles were one of the couples.

'I don't know why you think it's a good idea,' Juliet protested. 'Rosie feels sick half the time, and Charles is a crashing bore.'

Liza frowned; any criticism of Rosie annoyed her. 'It will give Cameron the message that your sister, who is only a year older than you, is already happily married and having a baby. Then he'll realize you're ready to make the same commitment.'

'I'd have thought the sight of Rosie, all fat and bulging, is enough to put him off marriage altogether,' Juliet retorted. 'He'll probably take to the hills and we'll never see him again.'

'Don't be silly, darling.' Liza went off to discuss menus with Mrs Fowler. Forget minor members of the royal family, foreign ambassadors and the cream of London society; this was probably the most important dinner party she had ever given.

Henry, returning from the city, found Liza in a fever of nervous agitation. 'What on earth's the matter, darling?' he asked in alarm.

She was pacing up and down their bedroom, trying on different necklaces to go with her long new lime-green dinner dress.

'I just want everything to be perfect tonight,' she replied reproachfully, as if he ought to know. 'Juliet's whole future, the rest of her life, could depend on tonight.'

Henry tried not to laugh at the absurdity of her remark, but at the same time, he felt annoyed.

'For goodness' sake, Liza . . . !' he burst out crossly.

'What . . . ?' She suddenly looked scared, tears welling in her eyes. He was calling her Liza again. He seemed to be calling her Liza more and more these days, whilst he used to use loving pet names for her. Being called plain 'Liza' made her feel very insecure, and once again the impoverished daughter of a village seamstress, desperate to be accepted by the upper classes.

She'd been frightened that she wouldn't be able to keep up with Henry and his family, and now she felt scared all over again; was the fact that she was an *arriviste* showing?

'Well, I . . .' she floundered, dashing the tears away. 'I want to do the best for all the girls.'

'Sweetheart,' Henry said, going to her, remembering how sensitive she still was about her background, 'you're going to be a wreck by the time you've brought out five daughters at this rate! By the time Charlotte's eighteen, you'll be an invalid, and I'll be pushing you around in a Bath chair,' he teased laughingly, putting his arms around her, and smiling into her face. 'Now, we can't have that, can we? The beautiful Mrs Granville in a wheelchair?' He kissed her gently on the lips, and he could feel her relax against him with the sheer relief of knowing he still loved her.

'Now, my darling,' he continued brightly, reaching for her jewel case, 'I think this is the one to go with your dress tonight.' He picked up a Cleopatra collar, made of pale-green aventurine stones linked by Asian pearls. He'd bought it for her on a business trip to Hong Kong years ago and it would go well with her dress tonight.

'Thank you, darling.' Liza stood still while he fastened the clasp at the back of her neck.

'You'll look marvellous, as you always do,' he told her firmly.

'Thank you,' she repeated, grateful for his support. Sometimes she envied Rosie and Juliet their *laissez-faire*.

As the result of a stiff brandy and soda, however, Liza presided over the evening with aplomb. The friends she'd invited were what Henry referred to as lightweight – 'Because I don't want any horrid talk of war,' she'd told him. 'Let's keep off the subject of the King's abdication and Mrs Simpson, too. It's *so* depressing, and I want it to be a jolly evening.'

Juliet listened to her mother with amusement. 'You mean we should only talk about things like the latest Noel Coward play, and is he really having an affair with Gertrude Lawrence?' she mocked. Then she took a quick sip of champagne, the name Lawrence reminding her of Daniel again. I wonder where he is tonight? she reflected, painfully. In Paris with another gullible young woman? Maybe staying at the

Ritz again? Her heart hurt as if it had been bruised, aching for the man she'd been forced to reject.

Everyone seemed to arrive at once, and amongst them was Cameron Kincardine. Juliet studied him surreptitiously across the room, while he chatted to her parents and a friend of theirs. He looked more attractive in a dinner jacket than he had in a suit, she reflected. And he laughed a lot, which she liked. And he was very pleasant-looking. If she narrowed her eyes, so his outline was blurred, and his back view was turned to her, he could *almost* be mistaken for Daniel. This realization was suddenly comforting.

'So what's all this about?' a voice said in her ear. Juliet turned round and there was Rosie, her expression quizzical.

'Mummy's matchmaking, isn't she? Who's the victim tonight? Or is it you, being thrust into the arms of another fortune-hunter?'

'Oh, shut up!' Juliet snapped.

'There's no need to be nasty!' Rosie averted her face, her jawline now white and bony, whereas before there'd been soft rounded curves. Yet her drawn face and hollowed eyes made her more beautiful, in a remote way.

'So, how are you feeling?' Juliet asked.

'We're thinking of moving to the country.'

Juliet nearly choked on her dry Martini. 'The country? You've always hated the country, Rosie. You've always complained there's nothing to *do* . . . you don't play tennis, or golf, or even croquet; so what on earth *are* you going to do?'

'It'll be much better for the baby.' Rosie tried to sound superior, grown-up. 'Fresh air is what a baby needs. And a garden to play in.'

Juliet still looked dumbfounded. 'So you're going to live among the ruins, in Cumbria? With Charles's mother and sister?'

'Of course not! How could Charles travel to the city every day from there? Granny is looking around Shere for us, to see if there are any pretty cottages on the market.'

'What's that Granny's doing?' Liza said brightly, coming up to greet Rosie at that moment.

Juliet slid away. It was a conversation she didn't want to hear. Her mother was going to be fearfully disappointed that Rosie was opting out of London to bury herself in the wilds of Surrey.

'How are you, Juliet?' Cameron greeted her, when he saw her.

'Very well, thank you. How's the house-hunting going?'

His dark eyes lit up. 'I think I've found a perfect place. It's about three minutes walk from here, in Park Lane.' He sounded like a child with a new toy.

Juliet smiled, amused by his obvious pleasure. 'Welcome to the delights of the neighbourhood,' she said drily.

'Thank you,' he replied seriously. 'It's got to be redecorated. It faces Hyde Park, but I'm sure I'll get used to the noise of the traffic in time.'

'What are you going to do with yourself when you're down here?'

'Oh . . . go to the theatre, I suppose. Concerts, exhibitions . . . and I'll probably do some entertaining.'

'How exciting.'

He looked at her quizzically, not sure whether she was being sardonic or not.

'Are those the sort of things you like doing?' he asked hopefully.

She played with her long rope of pearls. 'I like going to restaurants, cocktail bars, nightclubs. Then there's the cinema in the afternoons, and shopping, of course . . .' She pretended to sound exhausted by her round of activity. 'One just never *stops!*' she drawled, wondering how far she could push him.

Cameron looked at her earnestly. 'What . . . you and a group of friends, I suppose?'

Juliet nodded. 'Close friends.'

His dark eyes scrutinized her face almost analytically for a long moment, and she had the uncomfortable feeling that she was a specimen, being examined under a microscope.

'I see.' His voice was expressionless. Then he reached for his glass, and drank his champagne as if he was actually thirsty.

'So *he's* the reason for this dinner party.' Rosie cornered Juliet in her bedroom when she'd rushed up after dinner to touch up her make-up.

'Who?' Juliet unfolded a square of pink chiffon, to the centre of which a swansdown powder puff was stitched. Gazing at her reflection in the mirror, she calmly patted her nose and chin with it.

139

'*Who*?' Rosie echoed crossly. 'Who do you think? The Duke of What's-his-name! God, you and Mummy are so unsubtle. You get asked to his cocktail party, and the next thing, Mummy is cultivating him as a suitable husband for you.'

'It's not quite like that.' Juliet renewed her scarlet lipstick, which made her mouth fuller and more voluptuous than ever. 'I've heard he's actually looking for a wife.'

Rosie dropped heavily on to the side of Juliet's bed. Her face was taut with barely controlled rage. 'So of course you instantly imagined that you're the only girl in London he will look at.'

Juliet turned to look at her sister mockingly. 'What's it to you? You're already married to a titled man, fulfilling all Mummy's wildest dreams; it's my turn now. You surely can't begrudge me that?'

'To hell with Mummy's dreams,' Rosie said bitterly. 'Is he rich?'

Juliet nodded. 'Yes, definitely. He owns a quarter of Scotland from what I've heard. The family seat is Glenmally Castle, and now he's buying one of those houses in Park Lane.'

'And, knowing you, you'll marry him, whether you care tuppence for him or not, I suppose.'

Juliet frowned, and looked more closely at her sister. Rosie looked awful. Her skin had a greenish tinge, and her soft mouth seemed to have vanished into a thin line. Pregnancy did not suit it. 'What's the matter, Rosie? You've *got* everything, why do you resent my wanting a good position in life?'

'Everything?' Rosie scoffed, her voice harsh. 'Oh yes, I've got everything, all right.' Then she heaved herself off the bed, and stumbled out of the room.

When Juliet rejoined the ladies for coffee in the drawing room, there was no sign of Rosie.

'Where is she?' Juliet whispered to her mother.

'Feeling ill,' Liza murmured with a beaming smile, so the guests wouldn't know anything was wrong.

When the men came up from the dining room, smelling of cigar smoke and fortified by port, Cameron came straight over to where Juliet was sitting.

They started talking and, to Juliet's surprise, their conversation was easy and relaxed. Thanks to her father, she always read the newspapers, so her general knowledge of current affairs was up to date on a range of subjects.

Cameron looked delighted by her responses, something he had not expected in so young a girl.

Suddenly Juliet realized she was no longer flirting with Cameron. No longer flaunting her looks or her ability to charm coquettishly.

This was because she was beginning to see him as a friend more than anything else. It was almost as if Cameron was becoming the brother she'd longed for, and never had.

Six

'My God, you'd think this was 1837, not 1937!' Juliet exclaimed, drawing deeply on her cigarette.

Cameron was closeted in the study with Henry, while Juliet and her mother waited in the drawing room.

'I didn't think arranged marriages happened any more, except in the royal family,' Juliet added.

'This isn't an arranged marriage, Cameron adores you,' Liza protested. She was a nervous wreck but at the same time, terribly excited. The decision had already been made. The rituals were merely being observed now. Henry was not going to put up any objections.

'It's not what I'd call a love match either,' Juliet observed pragmatically. 'Cameron and I have become good friends in the past three months. We get on well. I don't think either of us is in love, though.' She certainly knew she wasn't. Her feelings for Cameron bore no resemblence to the way she still felt about Daniel. There were no sleepless nights spent fantasizing, no palpitations when she saw him, no breathless desire to be in his arms, giving herself to him, body and soul.

On the other hand, she was getting exactly what she'd set out to achieve, and she felt a certain satisfaction at having reached her goal.

As the Duchess of Kincardine, wife of an extremely rich Scottish landowner, with a house in Park Lane, she was made. No matter what happened, nothing could diminish this moment, or deprive her of having succeeded in attaining her ambitions.

At last she would have her mother's approval. At last she was doing the Right Thing. Yet she was desperately missing the chase and the challenge of falling in love. Of being pursued romantically, thrillingly, then of surrender, whispered promises, and finally total commitment.

Her forthcoming engagement to Cameron held all the excitement of opening a new bank account.

Liza spoke. 'Friendship is the best basis for marriage. Look at Daddy and me. We're the best of friends.'

'But you told me you were madly in love when you first met,' Juliet pointed out, not daring to ponder on how marvellous that must be; to actually marry the person you were in love with.

Liza smiled coyly. 'Well . . . yes, we were,' she admitted, 'but good friends, too. It's talking the same language that matters. Having things in common. Cameron has even let you help him with the decorating at his house round the corner.'

At that, Juliet's eyes did sparkle. When he'd asked for her advice, he hadn't mentioned marriage, because there was really no need. They both knew they were heading towards a future as predictable as the setting sun. And knowing all along that the house would one day be hers, she'd insisted on the latest art deco furniture and fittings, in rooms almost exclusively decorated black, white and silver . . . She'd even persuaded him to buy a large silver bed with a canopy, which had been designed for a maharaja.

'Yes, I think he was a bit bemused by my taste,' Juliet agreed, smiling. 'But as Glenmally is all tartan hangings, floral carpets and the heads of dead beasts stuck on the walls, I told him we needed something different down here.'

Remembering when she and her parents had been invited to stay at Glenmally a few weeks ago, she cast her eyes up in horror, knowing she'd never be allowed to change a thing, because his mother still lived there, and it was she who had done it up forty years ago.

'Wasn't it ghastly?' she remarked.

But Liza looked alarmed. 'For heaven's sake, don't tell him that! Men hate it if you try to change their ancestral homes.' There was a pause. 'That's why I've never so much as changed a cushion at Hartley. Especially while Granny's still alive.'

'I'm sure Granny wouldn't mind.'

'I still wouldn't like to tread on her toes. You'll have no trouble with the duchess, though. She's sweet and she adores you already.'

Juliet's fine pencil-line eyebrows shot up. 'How sweet is a viper?' she retorted. 'Wandering around in long robes clutching a posy of herbs and listening outside doors. She's so possessive of her only son, I'm surprised she doesn't want to marry him herself,' she added acidly.

Liza frowned. Juliet had never talked like this about Iona before. 'Don't get on the wrong side of her, whatever you do,' she warned.

'Don't worry. Once we're married, I don't intend to spend much time in Scotland. That's why I'm encouraging Cameron to take to the joys of living in London. I want to entertain on a grand scale, and I want our house to become a talking point; the most fashionably decorated house in town.'

A few minutes later, Henry came into the room. He was smiling but his blue eyes held a glint of sadness.

'Where's Cameron?' Juliet asked.

'Is everything all right?' demanded Liza, nervously fiddling with her pearls.

Henry went over to Juliet and, putting his arms around her, kissed her on the cheek. 'Cameron and I have spoken; if this is what you want, darling, then I'll give you both my blessing. I am going to miss you though, when you leave home.'

'Then it's all settled!' Liza exclaimed, laughing and crying with relief.

'I still have to accept him formally,' Juliet pointed out, scarlet mouth teasing. 'When he proposes, I might say no.'

Liza drew in her breath sharply. 'You wouldn't . . . !'

Juliet laughed. 'No, Mummy. Don't worry. I shall enjoy being the Duchess of Kincardine, and all that goes with it.' Her tone was brittle, and Henry spotted a hardness in her expression he hadn't seen before.

'Juliet . . . ? Are you sure?' he asked suddenly, looking

at her intently. 'For God's sake, if you've got the slightest reservation . . .'

She flung her arms around his neck, as she'd done as a small child, and pressed her cheek against his. 'Daddy, you're the best man in the world, but as you're married to Mummy, I'll have to make do with someone else,' she teased.

Henry looked tenderly into her eyes, knowing he shouldn't, but unable to stop himself loving her the most, while Liza breathed a sigh of relief.

'So when . . . ?' she began, but Henry was still looking at his daughter closely.

'You're sure you love him? This is not a game, Juliet. This is a lifetime commitment. If you have any doubts, you mustn't go ahead with it.'

'I have no doubts, Daddy. This is what I want.' *And I'm not lying*, she thought. I can never have Daniel; so I'm going to enjoy what I can have.

Henry looked relieved. 'Then so be it. Cameron is taking you out to dinner tonight. He said he'll pick you up at eight o'clock.'

Juliet turned to take a cigarette out of the silver box on the table. This is all so strange, she thought, knowing she must keep these feelings to herself. Cameron hadn't even kissed her properly, yet. It was not a bit like how she imagined getting engaged would be. There should be rejoicing, excitement, the pop of champagne corks, everyone hugging and kissing; like it was when Rosie got engaged.

But then Rosie had been intoxicated with love, dizzy with blind passion, and so, it had seemed, had Charles been. But Juliet felt flat, and a chilly sense of disappointment swept through her, leaving her with a stomach-ache and a feeling of anxiety. Was she really doing the right thing? Almost immediately a voice in her head told her that of course she was; everything would be fine as soon as she saw Cameron tonight. She'd get things into perspective and realize how happy she really was. He would surely tell her now how much he cared for her, cared enough to want to marry her . . . but it wouldn't be like Daniel telling her that, would it?

But then no man, she realized, would ever make her feel like that again.

*   *   *

They dined at the Savoy Grill, the only young couple in a restaurant filled with elderly businessmen, foreign potentates and public figures. Earlier, when Cameron had arrived at Green Street, he'd presented her with a corsage of slipper orchids, before producing a ring set with a large square emerald, surrounded by diamonds.

'I hope you'll accept this,' he said awkwardly, his face red, as if he was finding it difficult to express himself, 'as a token of my ... erm ... esteem, and that ... erm ... that you'll agree to our getting married.'

The last three words came tumbling out in a rush, like the last flush of wine from a bottle.

'I'd love to,' she replied simply, looking into his eyes. He showed no visible sign of emotion, except perhaps slight relief.

'I'm so glad,' he replied. Then he leaned forward and kissed her on the lips, a dry puckered kiss that left her totally unmoved.

It was the most clinical moment in any relationship Juliet had ever experienced, and she realized Cameron was hopelessly shy and unused to dealing with women. The thought of showing him, of being perhaps the first woman he'd ever had, excited her for a moment. Maybe she could do for him what Daniel had done for her? Guide him to finding out how simply marvellous sex was; and give him the biggest thrill of his life?

And if she thought it strange that a man of thirty-two might still be a virgin, the faint alarm bells that rang in the back of her head were quickly dismissed. He was just shy. He lived in a remote area and had met few girls. He had strong morals.

It was only later, sitting in the staid and elderly atmosphere of the restaurant, that she began to realize the rules of an arranged marriage.

With Daniel, she'd known what was expected of her. Right from the beginning. Their whole relationship had been set alight by a driving passion that was impossible to resist. The instant attraction between them had crackled like a firework display, so that they lost themselves in each other, never wanting to become separate entities again. Sheer instinct told her what to do, what to expect, and Daniel had been the perfect teacher.

Juliet told herself she must stop thinking of Daniel, and stop comparing Cameron to him. That way lay eternal anguish.

'Here's to us, Juliet ...'

She realized Cameron was smiling at her across the table, his glass raised.

'Yes . . . of course,' she said quickly, collecting her thoughts. 'Here's to us.'

Everything went very smoothly and very quickly after that. Their engagement was formally announced, photographs were taken for the society magazines, and the wedding set for June. Like Rosie's, it was to be held at St Margaret's, Westminster, with the reception at the Hyde Park Hotel, where, if it was fine, guests could spill out from the ballroom into the garden overlooking the park.

All the arrangements seemed to have been taken out of Juliet's hands and she wondered what she was supposed to be doing. Most of the time she felt totally detached, as if it was someone else's wedding that was being arranged. Even when Cameron produced the magnificent Kincardine diamond tiara for her to be married in, her reaction was: Yes. Very nice. Nothing more.

However, Louise, Amanda and Charlotte, having fittings for their bridesmaids' dresses, could hardly contain themselves.

'Aren't you excited?' Louise asked Juliet wonderingly, when the imposing invitations arrived from Smythson's.

Henry had arranged for one of his secretaries to spend a week at Green Street helping Liza to send them out.

'Not really,' Juliet replied, 'I always expected to have this sort of wedding.'

In truth she didn't understand her own impassivity. Her heart seemed numb, a dead unfeeling organ. It had happened the moment her ambitious dreams had turned to reality, leaving her with an intense sense of anti-climax. She was joining the adult world at ninteen, and a part of her grieved for the crashing down of the fantasy world that her tender years had conjured up with such vivid desire. What could she dream about now that all her wishes had been supposedly granted?

While all around her people were boiling up into a frenzy of excitement, Juliet felt no more than if she'd secured a good, steady occupation for life. Daniel she had put firmly out of her mind. He belonged to her giddy youth, a treasured memory to be tucked away with her newspaper cuttings of her coming out.

'It's a good thing the coronation will be over before the

wedding,' Liza said dismissively, as if the marriage of Juliet and Cameron were more important than the crowning of George VI and Queen Elizabeth. 'It will give people something to look forward to.'

Rosie didn't bother to get out of bed these days. She lay there, dozing, reading, eating packets of biscuits, and listening to her beloved wireless.

The move to Speedwell Cottage had been a success; it was fifteen minutes walk from Hartley Hall, had three bedrooms, a delightfully ramshackle overgrown little garden, but the best thing, as far as Rosie was concerned, was that Charles went up to London from Monday to Friday, because he described the daily train journey from Victoria Station to Guildford as 'utter hell'.

When they'd first moved in, Rosie had loved arranging all their belongings in the sweet little rooms. The cottage felt more like home than Farm Street had ever done. Lady Anne helped out by producing side tables, lamps, a bookcase and a long looking glass, from amongst the stuff stored in the attic at Hartley. She also found some rugs, a rocking chair and a small desk.

'Thank you, Granny,' Rosie said gratefully. 'Isn't this cosy?'

Lady Anne smiled. 'It's lovely, darling. Very peaceful. Much better for you at the moment than living in London.' She had more diplomacy than to mention the absence of Charles during the week; in her opinion, some marriages benefited from the couple being away from each other from time to time.

'Isn't the garden heavenly?' Rosie continued enthusiastically. 'Look at the sweet peas. I want to grow roses too. And lavender. Do you think I could grow lavender on either side of the path up to the front door?'

'Most certainly.' An experienced gardener, Lady Anne studied the tiny front patch of moth-eaten grass. 'As a house-warming present I'll get Spence to plant half-a-dozen *lavantera* on either side for you. You won't be sitting out here, will you? Then may I suggest you get rid of that grass, and plant some shrubs? Maybe *hydrangea macrophylla*? And *camellia japonica*? The flowers are such a lovely shade of pink.'

'Yes, if you'll tell me how,' Rosie replied with delight. She slipped her arm through her grandmother's, and, hugging her to her side, kissed her cheek.

Dear God, thought Lady Anne, hugging her back affectionately, Rosie still *is* a child. Far too young to be married. Far too young to be having a baby.

But everything was going well, with Rosie beginning to even enjoy her pregnancy, when the shock of Juliet's engagement exploded in her face, stripping her in that instant of self-confidence and self-esteem. *She* was supposed to be the golden girl in the family, not Juliet. She was the one who was meant to have made a brilliant match, not her wild and wayward sister.

It was a blow to her heart to realize she hadn't lived up to the expectations of her mother.

Liza, almost hysterical with excitement, had telephoned to impart the thrilling news. Rosie realized in that instant the shift in Liza's approval from herself to Juliet.

'Isn't it the most marvellous thing in the world?' Liza crowed. 'Daddy and I are *simply* delighted. The wedding's going to be . . .'

It didn't help Rosie that by some dark demonic coincidence, the date chosen was that of her own wedding anniversary.

'. . . and you'll have had the baby by then,' Liza was gabbling on, 'so you must get Hartnell to make you a beautiful outfit.'

Rosie lowered her bulky body on to the little chair by the telephone, feeling stunned and sickened. For a start, how was she going to tell her mother that she had taken out a bank loan to buy Speedwell Cottage, which she was paying back month by month out of her generous dress allowance? How could she explain that Charles hardly gave her enough for food and the household bills, because he said staying in London during the week was expensive, for which he blamed her?

Appearances meant so much to Liza; she'd be mortified if it got out that, after all her effort, Rosie was reduced to doing all her own housework and cooking, like an ordinary working-class woman.

The full impact of what Juliet's impending marriage really meant, compared with her own, hit Rosie when, unable to sleep, she went down to the little kitchen to make a warm drink at three o'clock one morning. The milk was stored each day in a slate box, chilled by cold water, and kept outside on the window sill. When she poured some into a pan, she realized it had gone off. Congealed, sour lumps splashed on to the stove, making her feel nauseous.

Resentment, envy, anger, and sorrow for what might have been, welled up in a surging mass of sheer misery, sweeping away all sense of proportion and reducing her to a weeping wreck.

Speedwell Cottage suddenly seemed, not sweet and cosy, but cramped and poverty-stricken. How had everything gone so wrong? Why was it that Juliet, badly behaved and unscrupulous, was going to be living in the lap of luxury for the rest of her life, and a duchess at that . . . while she scraped together the little money she had to keep a roof over their heads? She'd done everything Mummy had wanted; played by the rules of her class and upbringing, and yet everything seemed to have gone wrong. Her marriage had become insufferable, and she couldn't rid herself of unhappiness.

Rosie didn't even have the courage to tell Lady Anne how bad things were, because her pride wouldn't let her. After a while, she blew her nose, poured herself a glass of water, and, going back to bed, decided to stay there until the baby arrived in six weeks time. Sleeping would blot out how hideous her life had become. As for going to Juliet's wedding . . . In one of her old outfits . . . ? Like bloody hell! she reflected, with unaccustomed spirit.

'Henry, I'm sorry to ring you at the bank, but I wanted to have a –' Lady Anne paused pointedly – 'a word with you in private. I'm worried about Rosie. She's not looking after herself. And she seems very depressed.'

'In what way, Mother? Is she ill?'

'I don't think she's physically ill, so far, but she will be unless something is done. Charles only comes down at weekends, and not even every weekend, and I think she's lonely. She also seems to be living in poverty. When I dropped in unexpectedly this morning, the cottage was filthy and there was only a stale loaf and some cheese in the house. She's so proud, you know, she'd never complain, but I was shocked by the state of things. The poor child made some excuse about not feeling up to doing any shopping, but it's more than that. I sense a feeling of *despair* about her life.'

'Mother, I'll drive down this evening. Do you think I should bring her back to Green Street?'

Again Lady Anne hesitated. 'I think she'd be better here, at Hartley, you know. It's peaceful, and I can look after her and see that she eats properly,' she added carefully.

'You're right,' he said immediately. 'It's a madhouse at home, with the wedding preparations and everything. Thanks for letting me know, and I'll pop in and see you too this evening.'

'That would be delightful, Henry.'

Rosie fell into a deep dreamless sleep as soon as her head touched the pillow. Back in her old room at Hartley, her sense of relief at admitting her circumstances to her shocked father was so great, she felt instantly relaxed and content again.

She would only stay at Hartley until the baby was born, she said firmly, not wanting to be a burden to her grandmother, and everyone agreed; yes, of course, it was only until she had the baby, but no one believed it.

'Poor child,' Lady Anne said to Henry, who stayed to have supper with his mother before returning to London. 'She's been most awfully badly let down by Charles. I can't bear to think how miserable she must have been.'

'I said all along she was too young to rush into marriage,' Henry said testily, as he helped himself to another glass of Burgundy.

Warwick, creaking more than ever, had served lamb chops, creamed potatoes and brussel sprouts, before retiring to the kitchen, so they could talk.

'Rosie's baby can be born here, as you were, Henry. The local family doctor is excellent, and there's a splendid midwife in the village.'

'Are you sure it won't be too much for you?'

'My dear, Rosie will be no trouble; neither will the baby. And I won't have to worry about her if she's living here. What are you going to do about Charles?'

Henry sighed heavily. 'I'll have to talk to him. I honestly don't feel like giving him any money under the circumstances, but I may be forced to make some arrangement, so that Rosie has a decent home, with staff. As long as Charles isn't made to feel like a kept man.'

Lady Anne gave her son a pitying look. 'My dear Henry, don't delude yourself. That's *exactly* what Charles Padmore is longing to be.'

The next morning Henry phoned Rodwell, Singer and Brett, insurance brokers in Leadenhall Street.

'I'd like to speak to Lord Padmore, please,' he said, when he got through.

There was a pause before the girl on the switchboard answered. 'Lord Charles Padmore?' she queried.

Henry had a nasty feeling he knew what she was going to say next. 'That's right. Charles Padmore,' he repeated.

'I'm afraid he doesn't work here any more, sir.'

Henry's heart sank. 'When did he leave?'

'A couple of months ago. Would you like to speak to Mr Parish?'

Henry knew Theodore Parish, and knew he'd been Charles's boss. 'I think I'll leave it,' he replied. He could guess what Parish would say. There was no point in their both being embarrassed.

Thanking the girl on the switchboard, he rang off. Then he phoned White's. Rosie had told him Charles stayed at the club during the week.

Henry spoke commandingly when he got through. 'I'd like to leave a message for Lord Padmore, please. Will you ask him to phone Henry Granville as soon as possible?'

So what the hell was Charles doing? Henry wondered angrily. No wonder Rosie was having to pay for everything. And supposing Charles was not actually staying at White's? Suppose . . . ? Henry shut his mind to the possibility of there being a mistress in the background; it just didn't bear thinking about.

As soon as he got home that evening, Liza knew he had something on his mind. She also had some worrying news for him.

'Henry, there was no answer when I phoned Rosie today. I tried three times. Where can she be? Do you suppose the baby has arrived prematurely? That she's in hospital . . . ?'

Henry raised a reassuring hand. 'She's staying at Hartley. I helped her move there last night. I didn't tell you because you were asleep when I got back.'

'You went to Hartley? Last night? I thought you were dining with Ian Cavendish?'

'That's tonight, darling. My mother phoned me yesterday, and suggested Rosie stay with her until the baby arrives.' Henry was used to giving Liza an edited version of events to avoid her getting into a state, suffering from her 'what will people think' syndrome.

'So I just popped down to see Rosie settled in. She sent you her love, by the way.'

Liza still looked disgruntled at being left out of a family decision.

'So, is Charles staying at Hartley too?'

'He'll probably go down at weekends, as he's been doing,' Henry replied with deliberate vagueness.

'Why didn't Mama phone me if she was worried about Rosie?'

'She phoned me because she actually wanted to discuss getting another gardener,' he lied, glib with long practice at spinning white lies for the sake of peace, 'and the topic of Rosie came up.'

He walked abruptly over to the drinks tray and helped himself to a whisky and soda, without the soda. 'How are the wedding plans going, darling?'

It did the trick. Liza prattled on for the next half hour, and he caught something about the page boy's trousers, Juliet's shoes being embroidered with crystal beads, and forty more acceptances, while his mind dwelled on more serious matters. Such as, if Charles really had lost his job, what was he doing for money?

It was two days before Charles returned his call.

'I've been frantically busy,' he muttered vaguely. 'Was there something you wanted?'

Henry felt incensed by his attitude. 'Have you been staying down at the cottage with Rosie?'

Charles fell into the trap. 'That's right. Jolly nice weather it's been too.'

'Then you must have had a very lonely time, because Rosie's moved out,' Henry said coldly.

'Er . . . what was that?'

'You haven't been down to Shere, have you? And you haven't been to work, either. The truth is, you've been sacked from Lloyd's and you haven't got a job, have you?'

'No, I mean . . . I've left Rodwell, Singer and Brett because

152

I've had a better offer.' Charles sounded flustered, and Henry could tell he was lying.

'That's good,' Henry said genially. 'Which firm has made you an offer?'

'I'm not in a position to say at the moment, but as soon as it's confirmed, I'll be able to tell you.'

'Charles, why are you lying like this? Rosie has been paying for everything. Before you got married you asked me if I was giving her a dowry, and I repeat, I'm not. She's not an heiress, you know. It is a husband's job to look after his wife, and not depend on the little money she has.'

There was a stunned silence on the line.

Henry continued tersely, 'You gave my wife and I the impression you were able to support Rosie. When I questioned you about your finances, you lied to me by saying you had a private income, as well as a good future as a name at Lloyd's. You led me to believe you were in a position to *buy* a house in Farm Street. Don't think I'm going to support you now,' he added heatedly, inwardly cursing himself for not seeking more proof of Charles's financial position before the wedding.

'I've had a lot of bad luck, and your daughter really is very demanding. And extravagant,' Charles said defensively in a self-pitying voice. 'She wants to go on living in the style of *your* house, although she knew I was just starting out on my career.'

'And now she can't even afford a woman from the village to do the washing,' Henry cut in angrily.

'Well, what am I supposed to do about it?' Charles demanded sulkily.

'Are you staying at the club?'

'I can't afford to. I'm staying with a friend in Ebury Street.'

'Which friend?'

'Guy Douglas. You know, he was my best man at the wedding.'

Henry remembered him well; a twenty-five-year-old rake, whose interests seemed to consist of drinking, gambling and chasing girls.

'I want to see you tomorrow,' Henry said grimly. 'Be at my office by ten o'clock.'

Charles sounded appalled. '*Ten* o'clock?'

'Ten o'clock. And don't be late.'

*   *   *

Henry phoned Lady Anne at eleven o'clock the next morning.

'Mother, I hate to do this to you, but . . .'

He'd arranged for Charles to stay at Hartley, where he must try and patch up his marriage. He knew his mother could keep an eye on him, at least until Rosie had the baby. The other condition was that Charles must come up to London for job interviews; Henry would even buy him a season ticket, so there'd be no excuse.

'After the baby arrives we can review the situation,' Henry had told him. 'You've got to face up to your responsibilities. I'm only doing this to spare Rosie's feelings. She's vulnerable at the moment and she needs you. But mind you behave yourself.'

Lady Anne took the news with her usual sanguineness. 'That's fine, Henry. Rosie needs her husband at a time like this.'

'I hate to lumber you with this, Mother.'

'My dear Henry,' she replied calmly, 'with Mrs Dobbs, Warwick, who's still working in spite of his bad feet, and three able-bodied young women who clean and do the laundry, why should it be too much?' She gave a chuckle. 'I've a good mind to get Charles to help Spence with the garden at weekends. A bit of exercise and fresh air might be good for him.'

It was the proudest day of Liza's life. The sight of Juliet coming down the aisle with her new husband so overwhelmed her that tears sprang to her eyes. For a moment she wished her parents were still alive, so she could turn to them and say, Look how far I've come, Mum! And look how far your granddaughter's come!

Every dream, every wish, and all her life's ambitions had now culminated in this glorious moment. Liza slipped her hand through Henry's arm. Sheer gratitude for what he'd given her over the years amounted to a kind of devoted love she'd never felt before.

'All right, darling?' There was a hint of surprise in his voice, especially when he saw the tears glistening on her rouged cheeks.

'*More* than all right,' she whispered back, her voice catching.

Outside St Margaret's, Westminster, crowds of people and photographers had gathered to see the high-society bride and groom emerge through the stone portals into the sunlight.

There was cheering and clapping, and even the passing traffic ground to a halt as people craned their necks from the top of buses to have a look.

Juliet was in her element. She loved the crowds who gazed in awe, she loved the photographers whose shutters clicked like dozens of snapping insects, she loved being the centre of attention; this, it flashed through her mind, is almost better than sex.

As she stood in the sunshine in a long white dress with medieval sleeves moulded to her body, and the Kincardine tiara blazing brilliantly on her head, she wished this exact moment could last for ever.

Cameron, standing stiffly by her side, might not have existed at that moment. This was *her* wedding, *her* day, and she gloried in this moment.

Then the dowager duchess came out of the church, wearing a white muslin Empire-style dress, with a white toque, supporting a pearl and diamond tiara and a clutch of grubby white ostrich feathers. Clutching a white ermine muff, she slid up to take her place on her son's other side, so that for a bewildering moment it looked as if Cameron had two brides.

Henry, seeing what was happening, gently pulled the duchess to one side, so that she stood with him, Liza, and Lady Anne, while the child bridesmaids and pages completed the group.

But Iona Kincardine was a determined woman. As Cameron and Juliet moved forward to step into the waiting Daimler to take them to the reception, his mother began to follow, as if she expected to go with them.

'This is our car, my dear,' Lady Anne said, taking the dowager's arm, and leading her firmly to the second car. 'We're going with Henry and Liza.'

Henry flashed his mother a grateful look. Liza felt alarmed. Was Iona suffering from dementia? Did she believe this was her wedding day too? Or was she just plain possessive of her son?

The fact that she'd come so eccentrically dressed was worrying enough, but if she was going to hang on to Cameron all the time, Liza began to understand why Juliet had been so keen to have a house in London.

Rosie, looking suspiciously thin, in spite of giving birth to a premature daughter six weeks before, climbed into the third car with Charles and her three younger sisters, who were all dressed in their pale pink *broderie anglaise* bridesmaid's dresses.

'I've just remembered,' Louise said suddenly, as the car swept round Parliament Square, 'that you were married a year ago today, weren't you, Rosie?'

Charles looked startled. 'Were we?' He glanced at Rosie, who had flushed red, and was blinking hard.

She nodded, turning to look out of the car window, too upset to speak.

'Are you going to celebrate?' Amanda piped up.

'We *are* celebrating,' Charles pointed out with forced joviality. He reached for Rosie's hand and squeezed it.

Charlotte, clutching her posy of white sweet peas and pale blue love-in-a-mist, peered into Rosie's face with the instinctive perception of the very young.

'Why are you crying? Are you missing your baby?'

Rosie gave a wobbly smile. 'That's right.'

'Shall we pick her up from Green Street and take her to the reception?' Louise suggested helpfully. Sophia had been left with the monthly nurse, thanks to the generosity of Henry, who could see Rosie was in no state to look after her tiny daughter by herself.

Charles looked at Rosie again, anxious to steer her away from one of her ever more frequent crying jags, especially today of all days. 'What do you think, darling?' he asked.

With a tremendous effort, Rosie had pulled herself together. 'It's a sweet idea, Louise,' she said, 'but she mustn't go to crowded places until she's bigger, in case she picks up germs.'

'That's true,' Charles confirmed, smiling at Rosie again.

These days their marriage was as fragile as eggshell; and already so fractured it would take very little to crush it into sharp little particles. He had to watch what he said and did if he wanted to avoid a row with Rosie. He also hoped that at some point Henry would make over a large sum to his daughter, which would solve their financial problems.

But gone was the beautiful, cheerful and loving girl he'd married. Gone was the sex life he'd greatly enjoyed. Instead he had a cold and brittle wife, who always seemed to be miserable, tired and withdrawn.

Meanwhile, Lady Anne was insisting they both stay on at

Hartley for the time being, as Rosie hadn't yet recovered and there wasn't room for a nurse at Speedwell Cottage.

Not that Charles had any objection to this. Life at Hartley was comfortable. There was just one snag. He felt Lady Anne was watching him all the time. Making sure he came back from London to be with Rosie and the baby, and questioning him about his interviews for jobs. Monitoring his movements at weekends.

He missed living in London. He missed his drinking sessions with his friends. But most of all, he missed gambling at the Mall Casino; not that he could now, even if he'd wanted to. The bank, to whom he owed a lot of money, had refused to lend him any more.

He was, in fact, penniless, and now totally dependent on the Granvilles.

Like flocks of brightly coloured birds, guests were spilling into the garden from the overcrowded ballroom of the Hyde Park Hotel. The fluttering feathers, squawking voices and tottering high heels reminded Daniel Lawrence, as he drove slowly past, of the exotic flamingoes he'd seen in Africa, pecking at their food, high-stepping daintily, mingling with each other with great amiability.

Then he spotted Juliet. He pressed hard on the brakes, nearly causing the car behind to crash into him.

She was standing just inside one of the open French windows of the ballroom, talking to a group of guests. Her beautiful face and hands seemed to rise out of a cloud of white silk tulle, crowned by a blaze of glittering diamonds. She was talking and laughing, a glass of champagne in one hand, which she waved about as she gesticulated, and a bouquet of white orchids in the other.

Daniel had forgotten he'd read somewhere that she would be getting married today. Forgotten? Or had he pushed it to the back of his mind in an effort not to remember? He parked the car a few yards further on, and walked back to where, standing half-hidden under the trees, he could watch her through the windows.

She dazzled, of course. Vivacious and sparkling, she drifted from group to group, always surrounded by admiring friends, kissing and being kissed, holding out her glass for a waiter to fill again, before moving on to talk to other admirers.

Daniel had been mesmerized by her when he'd first spotted her in that dark and smoky jazz club, and she mesmerized him still. He stood, his eyes straining to catch glimpses of her in the chandelier-lit ballroom, no longer caring if anyone saw him. She was the most fascinating woman he'd ever known, and whilst his head told him they had no future and never would have, his heart seemed to fold in half in his chest, as if a door was closing for ever.

At that moment he saw a tall older man with grey hair put his arm around Juliet's shoulders, and smile down into her face. She nodded, as if she agreed with what he'd said, and reached up to pat his shoulder. Daniel caught the bright glint of gold on her left hand. Her father was obviously urging her away from the window, pointing to something . . . were they about to cut the wedding cake?

Juliet was laughing, and then, suddenly, as if she'd felt someone was watching her, she turned sharply, and looked out at the Park.

Their eyes met across the narrow stretch of grass and road. Juliet's face registered shock. A second later, her expression became reproachful, her eyes blazed, as if it was all his fault.

Daniel felt his own heart stop mid-beat, stop so suddenly and painfully he was afraid it would never start again. Then she turned abruptly away, her back view hidden by the mist of white tulle. A moment later she'd vanished into the crowd.

He walked slowly back to his car, wishing he'd driven along Knightsbridge instead of through Hyde Park. Too many memories had been stirred, too many uncomfortable emotions that were best forgotten had been aroused.

Those damned dark eyes were still haunting her. Of all the people in the whole of London, why had it been Daniel Lawrence she'd seen, standing in the park, looking into the hotel ballroom? Had he come on purpose? To taunt her with memories of what she'd lost?

Shaken by the split-second encounter, Juliet could now not think of anything else. She was barely aware of helping Cameron cut their three-tiered cake with a sword; of listening to the speeches, of going up to change before kissing her family goodbye and leaving in a shower of confetti.

Damn Daniel for appearing today, of all days. Damn him to hell. All she could see in her mind's eye was his face, and those black, black eyes. All she wanted to think about was the touch of his hands, his mouth, the whole virile strength of his body as he'd guided her to heights of ecstacy.

Glancing at the gentle, polite face of Cameron, she thought, Oh, God, what have I done?

An hour later, they arrived at Croydon Airport, where the private plane Cameron had chartered awaited them, ready to fly them to Nice.

Juliet smiled brightly as she climbed on board, and settled herself in the luxuriously upholstered interior, where a steward was ready to serve them with drinks.

In the last few hours Juliet had achieved what she'd set out to, and she didn't intent to be miserable now. Three glorious weeks lay ahead, staying in the best hotels, cruising around the Greek islands on a yacht, dining at the finest restaurants, and shopping for things she didn't really want.

It was all going to be marvellous. *Wasn't it?* she asked herself. Yes, it was going to be wonderful – as long as she stopped thinking about Daniel.

Henry and Liza held a large dinner party in Green Street that evening.

'Cameron will be telephoning me when they arrive in Nice,' Iona Kincardine announced as soon as she arrived. She'd changed into a replica of a Mary Queen of Scots black velvet gown, with a great mass of pearls, and a posy of myrtle, this time, clutched in her bejewelled hands.

'Won't that be rather late to phone?' Henry remarked in astonishment.

Liza was getting the measure of this old dowager. She was stark raving mad. A demented figure, obsessed by her son, and by dressing up as romantic characters from a bygone age.

'Far too late to be phoning anyone,' Liza observed firmly. 'Anyway, they're on honeymoon. They've better things to do than ring home.'

'Oh, Cameron will ring *me*,' Iona said with a whimsical

smile, and tilting her head to one side. 'He always does when he goes away.'

Hector Mackenzie, who had been escorting Iona Kincardine all day, spoke now. 'Whisht now, my dear,' he said, his Scottish accent soft and melodious, 'you can't expect the wee man to be ringing you on his honeymoon.'

Iona turned, wide-eyed, and looked at him with an expression of innocence. 'But he knows I'd never sleep if I didn't hear from him.'

Hector glanced at Liza, smiling and laughing as if a small child had said something amusing. Then he turned to Iona. 'I think you'll have to forgo that privilege this evening. It is his wedding night, you know.'

Something in the way he spoke made Liza feel uneasy. His tone was licentious, and the knowing way he looked at the dowager was as if they shared a private secret. For some reason she couldn't explain, Liza felt soiled from overhearing his remark.

More guests arrived, then Rosie and Charles appeared from upstairs, and Liza forgot about the matter until much, much later.

The Negresco Hotel reminded Juliet of a giant white iced cake. The car bringing them from Nice airport had dropped them off just before midnight, and they were quickly shown to the Presidential Suite, which overlooked the Mediterranean.

'I'm going to have a quick shower,' Juliet said, still in her going-away outfit.

'Good idea,' Cameron replied.

To her delight, she saw the suite had two bedrooms, each with its own bathroom, on either side of a large reception room. After her shower, she returned to the bedroom she'd chosen to be hers, wearing only a bathrobe. In the salon next door, she heard Cameron's voice. Then she heard a click as he replaced the phone.

'Who are you phoning?' she called out idly, as she brushed her hair. 'If you're ringing room service, I could do with some coffee.'

Cameron appeared in the bedroom doorway, looking bashful and still wearing the dark suit in which he'd travelled.

'Coffee? At this time of night? All right, dear. I'll order you

160

some.' He vanished again. Juliet followed him into the salon, her robe falling seductivly open as she moved.

He glanced up at her exposed breasts and then turned quickly away to pick up the phone.

'Don't you think you should have some coffee too?' she asked provocatively. 'It's been a long day . . . and I hope it's going to be a long night.'

'I – I think I'm going to have to call it a day, as they say! If you'll forgive the pun,' he added, with forced joviality. 'The truth is, dear, I've got the most awful headache. It's been coming on for the last hour. I was ordering aspirins on the phone a minute ago. I think I'll have to go straight to sleep.'

Juliet, to her surprise, felt neither disappointment nor delight. She'd had a feeling all along that Cameron was not going to be a great lover; though she hadn't expected to sleep alone on her wedding night. She shrugged. 'I'm sorry you don't feel well. Probably too much champagne,' she added lightly, as if to spare his feelings. 'Actually, I'm rather exhausted myself. Why don't you get a good night's sleep in the other bedroom, and we'll meet for breakfast?'

Relief seemed to pour off him like stale sweat. 'You wouldn't mind?'

'Of course not,' she said with seeming generosity. 'Sleep well, Cameron. I hope you'll be better in the morning.'

As she slid between the smooth sheets of her own bed, her body ached restlessly. Not for her new husband. But for another tall, dark-haired man with black eyes, who dominated her thoughts, aroused her emotions, and fuelled her desire.

Only by fantasizing he was making love to her could she assuage her violent longing.

'How about it?' Charles suggested, as Rosie sat at her dressing table, cleansing her face with Pond's cream. His pale, lean, stringy body was naked as he came to stand behind her, and seeing his reflection in the looking glass, she felt only revulsion.

'Oh, I don't think so, Charles,' she replied wearily. 'It's late – I never thought the dinner party would come to an end, and I can hardly keep awake.'

'What's the matter with you?' he demanded petulantly. 'It's weeks since you had the baby. It can't *still* hurt you to be touched.'

161

It wasn't her body that hurt any more, she reflected bitterly. 'Well, it *does*,' she snapped.

'I have my rights, you know. You're not even feeding Sophia. You're just making excuses. It's not fair, Rosie.' He sounded like a spoilt boy who'd been denied some sort of treat. Turning away from her, he flopped on to his side of the bed, huddling himself under the blankets, his face to the wall.

Rosie finished creaming her face slowly, hating the fact she was having to share her old bedroom in Green Street with him.

This room was where she had dreamed of a fairy-tale future ever since she'd been a little girl. Mummy's constant assurances of 'when you're grown up . . .' had indeed seemed like a promise of some future paradise.

The reality was so different. Her marriage to Charles was bleak and loveless. She didn't even feel a sisterly affection for him. Did she even like him any more? she asked herself. They had no money, no nice house to live in, and no staff. And no matter how much she adored living at Hartley, she couldn't help feeling like the poor relation the rest of the family were having to support.

How could this have happened to her? Why hadn't she made a brilliant marriage like Juliet, who now had *everything*.

She thought about her sister at this moment, revelling in luxury in the south of France, with cars and private planes and a yacht at her disposal, and everything she could ever want in life, hers for the taking.

Rosie fought back sobs of anger and bitterness, stuffing the sheet into her mouth because the last thing she wanted was to awaken Charles. *Why* should everything have gone to her younger sister? Juliet had spoilt everything from the moment she'd been born. Always there. Always grabbing the attention, in spite of not being Mummy's favourite. Always getting in the way, just when Rosie wanted to shine. Just when she wanted to be The One. And always, *always* a step ahead, damn her.

Iona Kincardine ran forward on tippy-toes to fling her arms around Cameron's neck as soon as he got out of the car.

'Welcome home, my darling boy! You're looking so well. It's so good to have you back.'

Today she was draped in tartan shawls, pinned to her left

162

shoulder by a large silver brooch, engraved with the Kincardine crest. No doubt, Juliet reflected, climbing out of the car, she was playing Flora MacDonald and Cameron was her Bonnie Prince Charlie.

Three black labradors and a clutch of West Highland terriers came swarming over to them, with equally joyous greetings.

Cameron turned to Juliet, who was being ignored by his mother, and spoke. 'Well, here we are. Home at last.' His voice was resonant with relief.

Home indeed, Juliet reflected drily, as staff appeared to welcome them, and a piper played his bagpipes.

She looked up at Glenmally Castle, which was silhouetted against the sunset, and it reminded her of a dramatic illustration in a fairy tale, with its mass of sinister towers and turrets, crenellated ramparts and battlements and long slitty windows. This was where the wicked witch resided, ready to put a curse on anyone who crossed her.

'Tea's almost ready,' Iona said gleefully, hanging on to Cameron's arm as she led the way through a deep stone portico, above which was carved the Kincardine coat of arms.

Inside, blazingly bright carpets, curtains and colourful cretonne sofa covers fought for attention with gilt clocks, brass bowls of heather, stuffed birds in glass domes, and stags' heads peering down at them from the high dark panelled walls.

Mrs Maxwell, the housekeeper, appeared at that moment. She was small and washed-out-looking, with thin sandy hair and a dour expression. Her eyes narrowed in close scrutiny as she looked at Juliet.

'Your Grace, would you like me to show you to your rooms?' she asked in an Edinburgh accent.

'Thank you,' Juliet replied. She had to admit she rather enjoyed the deferential way servants spoke to her these days.

Mrs Maxwell showed her to a bedroom as big as a small ballroom, with an adjacent bathroom and sitting room, as well as a dressing room, furnished with several wardrobes and a large chest of drawers. The decorations were restrained to the point of being beige and bland, but the rooms were light and commanded a spectacular view of the distant mountains of Invergordon. In the foreground, reddish-brown shaggy-looking Highland cattle roamed, as did sheep, with their sweet black faces and legs that looked as if they were wearing black stockings.

'If there is anything you want, Your Grace, please ring,' Mrs Maxwell said, indicating a bell by the fireplace. 'Duncan will be bringing up your cases in a few minutes, and Flora, your personal maid, will do your unpacking.'

Juliet smiled with gracious insincerity and thanked her again.

Mrs Maxwell continued, 'His Grace's suite of rooms is at the other end of the corridor.'

Juliet had the uncomfortable feeling the housekeeper was watching her closely for some reaction.

'Good,' Juliet remarked lightly. Her heart sank at the sad bleakness of it all. Separate suites. Just like the royal family. It wasn't that she wanted Cameron in her bed, or even in her room, and perhaps that was the saddest part of all, but what sort of relationship was this going to be?

Juliet's marriage had finally been consummated on the third night of their honeymoon, and whilst Cameron, technically, knew what to do, it struck Juliet that his mind was elsewhere, because he was certainly not thinking about her. He kept his eyes tightly shut throughout the quick, perfunctory act, and seemed almost surprised to see her lying beside him when it was all over.

Juliet quickly learned that if she was to get any pleasure from making love to him, she had to play tricks with her own mind, mixing self-deception with denial.

It was several days after they'd arrived at Glenmally before Cameron appeared in her bedroom. She was lying in bed, reading.

'Hello there,' he said gruffly.

'Hello,' she replied softly, putting down her book.

'Would you like to . . . ?' He climbed into the bed, still in his striped flannel pyjamas.

'Yes, of course,' she said politely, and she hoped encouragingly. 'I've hardly seen you all day.'

'There's always a lot to do on the estate.' It was obvious he didn't want to talk. Reaching for her bedside light, he turned it off, plunging them into darkness. Then he climbed clumsily on top of her, fiddling with the flies of his pyjamas as he did so.

Through the open curtains a moon as bright as a street lamp

164

shone on them, revealing that Cameron had his eyes tightly shut. Moulding her legs around him, she held him close, so she could delude herself into believing it was Daniel's dark hair she was seeing through half-closed eyes. That it was Daniel's cheek pressed to hers, that it was Daniel who was entering her needy body, satisfying her desire, giving her his love.

When it was over she rolled away, her own eyes now tightly shut too, so as not to break the spell.

'Sleep well,' she heard Cameron say in a kindly voice, as he slipped quietly out of the room.

When she'd first seen Glenmally, knowing that one day Cameron would ask her to marry him, she'd imagined how she'd redecorate the place.

By the end of that first stay however, it was made very clear that Cameron and his mother liked things just the way they were.

But she decided that at least she could brighten up the atmosphere of the castle by entertaining her friends. There were eighteen spare bedrooms, and an enormous staff. They could give wonderful weekend house parties.

At the first opportunity to talk to Cameron without his mother being there, she suggested they send out some invitations.

Cameron's face froze. 'I think we should do that sort of thing in London,' he replied stiffly. 'The only time we have people to stay here is during the shooting season. Old friends of my parents, who come every year. Of course, we have a dance for the staff in the servants' hall at Christmas, but that's the only entertaining we do.'

'Why?' Juliet's eyes widened with bewilderment. 'You've got the money and the staff, and this great –' she was about to say *edifice*, but quickly changed it to – 'castle, so why wouldn't you want to entertain?'

'My mother and I like a quiet life, without ostentation,' he said gravely.

'You had a house party when you invited me and my parents to stay.'

'That was different.' His smile was kind though rather rigid. 'It was important to see whether you would fit in here if we got married.'

'So I passed muster, did I?' she asked coldly.

'You know that. It'll soon be the shooting season, Juliet. If you want to, you could ask a few of your friends up for that, I suppose.'

She thought of her best chums; Archie, Edward, Colin and all the others. They were more at home in a nightclub than they'd ever be on the grouse moors. Her mouth tightened.

'So I have to go to London if I want to see all my friends?' she asked coldly.

'That's why I bought the town house, isn't it?' Seeing the angry expression in her eyes, he continued in conciliatory tones, 'Don't be cross, Juliet. You have to realize this is my mother's home, too. She's getting on now, and lots of strangers staying here fluster her. Especially if they're all young and quite . . . erm . . . boisterous.'

'*Boisterous?*' Juliet echoed.

Cameron nodded, eyes dull and bleak. 'I don't really like parties, Juliet. I thought you realized that. I'm prepared to socialize when we go to London, for your sake, so I hope, in return, you'll respect my wishes by not entertaining when we're up here.'

Juliet sat in silence, staring at him, and a lot of things were beginning to make sense. 'I didn't realize you were so shy,' she said slowly, almost sympathetically. She couldn't imagine anything worse than suffering from shyness.

Cameron shrugged. 'Probably being an only child didn't help,' he said. 'I find having to mix with a lot of people really painful.'

'I had no idea,' she admitted, shaking her head. 'You don't have any friends of your own age, do you?'

'Running the estate keeps me busy, and I had tutors as a boy, so I've not really had much of an opportunity to make friends.'

'I can ask my family to stay, I suppose?'

'Of course you can,' he said quickly. 'And if you want to pop down to London for a few days now and then, to do some shopping, then I've got no objection.'

'Thank you,' she replied formally. She was stunned by the irony of the position in which she now found herself. Here she was, one of London's most avid socialities, the toast of the town, accustomed to going to several parties a night, married to a man who was so shy he prefered solitude and the company of his mother to that of her and her friends.

166

Seven

'You ask her, Mother,' Cameron implored. 'I've asked her several times, but she always says no.'

'Are you sure she's not doing something to prevent it happening?'

'How should I know?' he asked incredulously. 'That sort of thing's not up my street.'

Iona Kincardine gave her son a sideways glance; fond, understanding, coveting the knowledge they shared, which was all the sweeter because it was a secret. It gave Iona a feeling of one-upmanship over Juliet, the mere wife.

'I don't want to make her suspicious,' Iona said, frowning, and biting her lower lip. 'You're getting on all right? I mean, you know?'

Cameron nodded manfully. 'Yes. Maybe I should go to her room more often . . .' His voice trailed off.

Iona hitched her plaid shawl closer around her narrow shoulders, and leaned forward to be closer. They mustn't be overheard. Her dark eyes glistened in her small white face, enjoying the power she had over her son.

'Why don't you wait until the next time she's indisposed – you know what I mean? And then afterwards, go to her room every night for the next month.'

Cameron's mouth tightened. 'Oh, God,' he groaned.

'Every night,' she repeated. 'That should do the trick. It's not a hit-and-miss affair, my darling boy. You can't leave it to chance.'

'So, will you ask her now? I mean, she might already be pregnant,' he said hopefully, 'and then I needn't . . . you know.'

The dowager's eyes narrowed. Hadn't she watched Juliet every day to see if there was a change in her? It usually showed around the eyes, but she also scanned her figure to see if her

167

breasts were swollen. But Juliet, always looking slim and exquisite, flitted about the castle like a visitor, not belonging, not a part of the place.

It would soon be Christmas, and six months since she and Cameron had married. Surely she should be pregnant by now?

Juliet turned on the brass taps of the old-fashioned cast-iron Victorian bath with its claw-and-ball feet, and then tipped some sweet-smelling oil into the warm water. This was where she relaxed before she went to bed, for the room was large and comfortably furnished with a *chaise longue*, a dressing table, side table, and an oak linen press, in which were stored stacks of fluffy white towels.

Large mirrors faced each other on either side of the room, reflecting the bright candle flames in an endless galaxy which glowed gently into infinity. Watching herself undress, she couldn't help revelling in the beauty of her perfect body.

When she was naked, she stepped into the bath, and taking some oil from another bottle, smoothed it on to her breasts and arms, across her stomach and down her thighs. The rising steam misted the mirrors, so that the reflection of the flames became crystallized, and her body a pale wraith that echoed itself again, and again, into the distance.

The perfume of the oils was heady and seductive. She felt herself becoming aroused as she lay back in the warm water, so she closed her eyes and began to fantasize. Cameron was her husband. She must try to love him, and show him that making love could be wonderful; not a miserable snatched few minutes, like animals mating, but something that could lift your soul, and fill your heart with joy.

He'd looked at her after dinner tonight in a way that suggested he might come to her room later on. She wanted to be ready for him.

As she lay there, in the warm scented water, her desire became unbearable.

'Daniel . . . Oh God, Daniel . . .' Juliet soaped herself gently, imagining him there, kissing her, stroking her . . . telling her he wanted her . . . With a shudder, the exquisite moment passed.

Then she got out of the bath to dry herself.

When Cameron came to her room shortly after, she pretended to be asleep.

'Duchess,' said Juliet, who refused to call Iona *Mother* or even *Mama*. 'Where's Cameron? I haven't seen him all day.'

The dowager looked up from the book she was reading, her expression bright, like a little bird who has caught the early worm. Her smile was impish. Around her on the library floor, the labradors and Highland terriers raised their heads and wagged their tails lazily at Juliet.

'He'll be somewhere on the estate,' she proffered unhelpfully.

'He's always "somewhere on the estate",' Juliet retorted impatiently. Cameron seemed to vanish, without a word of explanation, shortly after breakfast every morning and often didn't reappear until the late afternoon.

'Is there anything I can do, my dear?' It was the wolf speaking, disguised as Granny.

'I want to go to London next week. There are people I want to see.' She'd only been south once since their marriage, and that had been to see her family, fleetingly, before Christmas, to give them their presents. Now she wanted to go again, but it wasn't her parents she wanted to see this time. She was desperate to see Daniel, tell him she was sorry she'd ended their affair, and now that she was also married . . . did it matter that he was too?

'So, there are people you want to see in London?' Iona asked, curiously.

'Yes, and I have some shopping to do as well.'

'Ah!' Her dark eyes flashed with meddlesomeness. 'I suppose you'll want to see your doctor?'

Juliet looked genuinely surprised. 'No. Why should I?'

Iona's smile was arch. 'Are you not *enceinte* then?'

'Not that I know of. Anyway, Cameron would be the first person I'd tell if I was.'

'Yes, of course, my dear.' Iona folded herself into her mass of tartan rugs as she sat curled up by a smoking log fire, and went back to her book.

Glenmally Castle and its inhabitants were driving Juliet mad, making her feel claustrophobic and imprisoned. Ever

169

since they'd been married, Cameron's attitude towards her had changed. Always shy and awkard, he was now becoming remote. At times Juliet could hardly believe she was actually married to this polite stranger, with whom she had less and less in common.

What a heavy price she'd paid, she realized, for becoming a duchess. Her original hope that they could at least be good friends had now faded away. It seemed Cameron didn't even want her companionship. Instead it was his mother who hung around, listening to and spying on everything she did.

'You don't seem to realize,' Cameron said to her one day when she complained he was never there, even to talk to her, 'this is an enormous estate. I have work to do, tenants to visit, foresters to see, a hundred and one things . . .' His voice had risen in agitation.

Juliet shrugged, unconvinced.

As a result she now craved to swap burns for Bond Street, mountains for Mayfair, and lochs for Leicester Square. She was sick of wearing tweed instead of tulle, and sheepskin instead of satin. And although the castle crawled with people who ran her bath, lit fires in her bedroom, laid out her clothes and kept the old gloomy place, with its long dark corridors, spick and span, she missed the buzz of the metropolis.

It was almost dark, and there was a high wind whistling through the tall pine trees. Juliet stood with her arms folded protectively across her midriff as the dogs snuffled around, their paws making little crunching noises on the gravel. How ironic, she reflected, that, with all her worldy goods, her only companions right now were a lovable collection of dogs.

She braced her shoulders and took a deep breath of the icy air. This was not going to do. She was only twenty and she did not intend to spend the rest of her life with a frigid husband, and a nightmare mother-in-law, in a remote part of Scotland.

When she returned from her walk, she picked up the smallest terrier, Molly, and carried her up to her bedroom.

At least the company of the sweetest of all the dogs would be better than nothing, she thought, placing Molly on the satin eiderdown. Cameron and his mother were going to be furious, for the dogs had to sleep in the gun room at night. This thought made the presence of Molly, curled up against the small of her back as she settled down to sleep alone once again, all the more delightful.

'You're in town, darling?' Liza exclaimed with excitement, when Juliet phoned her two days later. 'How perfectly lovely. We're all going down to Hartley tomorrow; you will come for the weekend, won't you?'

'Yes, I'd love that. It seems like years since I last saw you all.'

'How's Cameron? We might give a luncheon party on Sunday; several people down in Surrey haven't met him yet.'

'I'm on my own, Mummy. I want to see all my friends, and do some shopping, and . . . well, catch up on everything.'

Liza's voice was sharp with anxiety. 'There's nothing wrong, is there, Juliet?'

'Why should anything be wrong?'

'Then . . . then . . .' Liza faltered, embarrassed.

'No, Mummy,' Juliet broke in impatiently, 'I'm not pregnant. I've already had this conversation with the old witch. I just wanted to come down to London to have a bit of fun, for God's sake.'

'All right, Juliet. There's no need to get angry. I just wondered . . . so, would you like Daddy and I to give you a lift to Hartley?'

'No, thanks. I'll drive myself down on Saturday morning.'

Liza didn't like to say any more. Juliet had always had a mind of her own. Anyway, now that the two eldest girls were off her hands, Liza's thoughts constantly turned to Louise, Amanda and Charlotte's futures. They must be given the same opportunities as their elder sisters. The thought of three more débutante seasons filled her with excitement too. Oh, the parties she'd arrange! The eligible young men she'd cultivate! The fun it was going to be, once again.

Henry's mind was on other things. He'd been talking to his old friend from the Foreign Office, Ian Cavendish, and he was deeply concerned about the ever-growing prospect of war. Only that morning he'd read in *The Times* that Winston Churchill was quoted as saying: 'Hitler and the forces of darkness are preparing for an onslaught on Europe.'

In the reassuringly solid English masculinity of White's the previous evening, Henry had dined with Ian. They were given a discreet table in a corner, where they could not be overheard.

Friends since they'd been at Eton, their relationship had always been based on total trust. They could confide in each other without fear of betrayal.

'The American President is extremely concerned at what's happening,' Ian told Henry, after they'd given their order.

'So I've heard, but what can Roosevelt do about it? I can't see the Americans wanting to get involved,' Henry replied.

Ian lowered his voice. 'When Hitler invaded Austria in February, Roosevelt realized the lengths the Third Reich will go to, to get what they want. He was especially shocked when it got out that Hitler had informed the chief of his armed forces that Germany needed more *Lebensraum*, adding that they must go on to capture Poland, White Russia and the Ukraine.'

'I never thought I'd live to see another war in Europe,' Henry said sadly.

'Did you know that the British Ambassador in Washington has been contacted by the White House?'

'I heard a rumour to that effect. I know that MI6 are trying to find out exactly when Hitler plans to strike.'

Ian leaned closer. 'Churchill says it's vital we meet with Roosevelt. We're going to need the Americans when things hot up. We can't fight this war alone, especially as our government has dragged its feet about rearmament.'

'But we've got to do something about the situation, before it deteriorates further.' Henry crumbled his bread roll as if he wanted to destroy it. 'You do know that the Duke of Windsor and Wallis have met Hitler?'

'So I believe. Thank God he's no longer our king. If it was up to him and Wallis, I think they'd welcome Hitler . . . because I gather he had promised to overthrow our present King, and reinstate David and Wallis when, not *if*, he conquers Britain.' Ian's busy little dark eyes flashed at the thought.

Henry spoke. 'Nothing is going to stop Hitler rampaging through the whole of Europe, is it? Germany is armed to the hilt. Only last week I heard that the Nazis have trained six thousand pilots for the Luftwaffe.'

'It doesn't help, either,' Ian remarked forcefully, 'that Britain has been selling bloody Rolls-Royce aircraft engines *to* the Germans for some time.'

'I know. Sometimes I despair of this government. The Prime Minister was crazy to trust Hitler when he signed that peace treaty in 1937.'

Ian glanced around to make sure he couldn't be overheard.

'There's going to be something different about the way we fight this war if it happens,' he murmured.

'Such as?'

'Apart from the usual armed forces there are plans to create a secret organization, led by a British Army Officer, which will train suitable people to be dropped behind the enemy lines; not only to spy on the Germans and transmit the information back to England, but also to carry out acts of sabotage.'

'That's interesting,' Henry said thoughtfully. 'I suppose they could recruit the members of any resistance movement in whichever country they will operate in.'

'Better than that,' Ian whispered. 'In this country they plan to recruit the cream of the criminal world. Safe-breakers, cat burglars, pickpockets – they've all got skills that will be invaluable for a saboteur. The regular Army are furious of course; think it's an underhand way of fighting a war.'

'To hell with that,' Henry agreed.

'Churchill has been having secret talks . . . he backs the idea to the hilt.'

'All we're really waiting for now is for Hitler to make a move towards European domination, isn't it? Before we do anything?'

'We'll intervene before that happens,' Ian said quietly.

Henry raised his blonde eyebrows, his blue eyes sharp with anxiety. 'When?'

Ian nodded, and drank deeply of his Burgundy. 'What will happen is we'll issue the German government with an ultimatum.'

'When?'

Ian gave a slight shrug. 'When the time comes. Where are we now? July . . . I'd say, if things continue like this, we'll be at war in just over a year's time.'

Although Henry already knew it was an inevitable outcome, he didn't think it could happen as soon as 1939. Confirmation from someone in Ian's position was like a blow to the heart.

'Dear God,' he murmured, appalled. 'How can we? We're not equipped for war. We won't be ready by next year, even if we started to re-arm right now. Why the hell didn't the government listen to Churchill back in '35? Instead of calling him a warmonger?'

They'd sat talking until they were the last to leave White's imposing dining room.

Henry slept badly that night, dreaming of the men in his regiment who hadn't returned from the Great War. Dreaming of the shell fire, the bloodied and broken bodies of his comrades, the hideous pungent stink of latrines, sulphur, and of death. Wondering all the time, guiltily, why he was still alive.

When he awoke, he realized for the first time that he was glad he'd only had daughters.

'Henry? . . . Did you hear what I said?' Liza asked.

They were entering Guildford, busy with people doing their weekend shopping.

'Sorry, darling. I was concentrating on the traffic,' Henry apologized glibly. 'What did you say?'

'I *said*,' Liza repeated, with martyred patience, 'that I'd never make the mistake I made last time . . . by bringing out two of the girls together. It blighted Rosie's year; that's why she lost her confidence. I wish we'd done it differently. Given them each a season; things might have worked out better, mightn't they? Anyway, now that Charles has got a job in an art gallery, and there's another baby on the way, Rosie seems quite happy again. And coming out that year was certainly very good for Juliet. What a wonderful life she's living now! I wonder when *she'll* have a baby. Cameron must want an heir. Anyway, as I was saying, how far ahead do you think we should book the Hyde Park Hotel for Louise's coming-out ball? On the other hand, there's nothing as nice as a ball in a private house, is there? Henry! Henry, what are you doing?'

Gripping the steering wheel with both hands, Henry swerved the car violently up a side turning into a quiet little street. Then he slammed on the brakes so hard, Liza was thrown forward, her face missing the windscreen by inches.

174

She turned on him, enraged. 'Have you gone out of your mind?' she screamed. 'What are we doing? You could have killed us both!'

'Attempting to get you to face reality! That's what I'm doing,' he shouted back. It was the first time in twenty-four years he'd raised his voice to her.

'What . . . what do you mean?' she quavered, about to burst into tears.

'Liza, do you never read a bloody newspaper? Or listen to the wireless? Unless it's the weather forecast so you'll know what sort of bloody hat to put on your head? How can you be so bloody stupid?' Henry thumped the steering wheel with the heel of his hand, his face scarlet with anger. 'Don't you realize there's going to be a war? Possibly next year? You've got to stop behaving like an ostrich. It's going to happen, and it's no good pretending it isn't! Forget about bringing Louise out in three years' time. Remember how long the Great War lasted?'

'Of c-course I remember.' She was sobbing now, her face buried in her hands. 'I prayed *every night* for four years that you'd return safely. It was the worst four years of my l-life . . .'

Henry looked at his pretty, vapid little wife, whose worst fear was that the splendid life she'd acquired through marrying him might all come to an end. He sighed inwardly, wishing sometimes that he'd married an intellectual equal; a woman with whom he could share a real life, not a roundabout of parties.

'Darling, don't cry,' he said wearily. 'You were such a brave girl during the last war. Such a brave little bride . . . waving me off at Waterloo Station.' He knew he ought to put his arms around her, but the chill of anxiety paralysed him, and he was unable to offer her comfort beyond the reassurance of his words.

'But what are we going to *do*, Henry?' Liza felt soggy and shaken. 'You won't have to go to the front again, will you?'

'Of course not. Much too old,' he replied with false jocularity. 'They wouldn't want an old timer like me. In truth, I don't know what will happen. But we'll manage, like we did last time. We'll get through it, Liza, because we're Granvilles.'

'What's wrong with Mummy?' Louise asked. The sisters had come down earlier by train, with Nanny and Ruby in attendance.

Liza had slipped up to her room as soon as she and Henry had arrived, avoiding seeing anyone, including Lady Anne.

'She's got a headache,' Henry said lightly.

'She *always* has headaches when she comes here,' Charlotte remarked. Now seven, and acutely observant in the same way Juliet had been at that age, she was also inclined to ask awkward questions and make blunt remarks. 'I don't think she likes being in the country. It's too quiet,' she added sagely.

'The reason Mummy doesn't like it here,' Amanda pointed out bossily, 'is because there aren't enough parties.' She'd been forced to wear glasses during the past year at Henry's insistence, not that she cared. If wearing glasses prevented her from making 'a good match', so what? She hated parties anyway and thought they were a dreadful waste of money.

Amanda had become a ten-year-old rebel, who, to her father's amusement, disapproved of most of her family's activities.

'I thought we'd have tea in the conservatory,' Lady Anne said.

'A lovely idea,' Henry agreed. 'Come along, girls.'

'Shall I be mother, then?' Lady Anne asked gaily, picking up the silver teapot.

Smiling with relief at being back in the peaceful haven of Hartley, Henry sank into one of the cane chairs. 'That would be marvellous, Mother.' He surveyed the table, set with cucumber sandwiches, scones and jam, and a rich Dundee cake. 'I see Mrs Dobbs has been busy.'

His mother smiled. 'I don't know what I'd do without her.' Her bright eyes looked at him closely. 'You look tired, Henry.'

He made a little grimace. 'It's been a long week.'

Louise sat down beside him. 'You work too hard, Daddy.' She was approaching the borders of puberty with serenity and there was a gentle stillness about her that attracted people, as if they felt safe in her company. Slightly plumper than her elder sisters, and with freckles scattered across her nose, she was the calm one. The placid one.

'It's half term, Daddy. Can't you stay for the rest of the week with us?' she asked.

'I wish I could, pet,' he said ruefully. 'But everything is . . . well, very unsettled.'

'Can't you take a holiday? Everyone has holidays, even if they are chairman of a bank.'

Henry looked at her tenderly. She had a great nurturing streak, always rescuing motherless kittens, or birds that had fallen out of the nest. One day she would make a wonderful mother, he reflected.

'Daddy,' Amanda asked. 'I want to start collecting money for the poor children of the village. I don't think they have enough to eat. And why don't we give them some of our clothes? And *someone*,' she continued darkly, 'someone should be raising the money to get a new school built. And cottages with loos *inside* the house and not in the back yard. Couldn't you give some money to help?' she suggested.

Henry and Lady Anne exchanged looks.

'Could it be,' Lady Anne asked Henry, when the children had gone out to play, 'that we have a budding Socialist in our midst?'

They both started to laugh. Neither mentioned Liza, reclining upstairs on her *chaise longue*, but both could imagine the uproar it would cause if Amanda were to grow up and betray her own background.

'Oh! Is that your car?' Charlotte exclaimed excitedly, rushing out of the house as Juliet parked her new Rolls Royce coupé next to her father's Bentley.

'Yes, darling. Cameron gave it to me for Christmas.' She started gathering up all her parcels. 'These are presents for you all. I had a shopping spree in Harrods yesterday.'

'But it's not Christmas,' Charlotte pointed out.

'Who cares about Christmas?' Juliet joked, as Warwick helped her with her luggage.

Louise and Amanda came running up. 'How much did that car cost?' Amanda asked immediately.

'I haven't the faintest,' Juliet replied merrily. 'Lots and lots, I expect, but then Cameron has lots and lots.'

Charlotte looked impressed. 'As much as the King?'

'Maybe more,' Juliet teased, amused.

'More? *More?*' Her little sister's mouth dropped open.

'Does he give any to poor people?' Amanda enquired.

Juliet had no time to reply, as the whole family, led by Henry, came out to greet her.

'You look well, darling,' Lady Anne told her. 'How is life in the Highlands?'

'Not as much fun as life in the Lowlands,' Juliet quipped drily.

'Don't be silly, darling,' Liza exclaimed dismissively. 'You have a lovely time up there.'

Lady Anne looked closely at Juliet, recognizing the signs of boredom. In spite of everything, she could tell Cameron Kincardine was obviously not enough for Juliet. She needs a real man, Lady Anne reflected, and then immediately wondered why she'd used that phrase.

In fact, Juliet was inwardly feeling desperate. She'd found Daniel's telephone number in Kent, through directory inquiries, and, plucking up courage, she'd actually dialled it, only to have it answered by a servant, who informed her that Mr and Mrs Lawrence were away. Juliet had hurriedly hung up, without having to leave her name. But how long was he going to be away? Did she dare telephone him again in a few days? A week? Cursing herself for not having got more information, she'd decided to go back to the houseboat on the Embankment. Maybe the old man who owned it could help. But there was no one on the boat and it had a depressingly deserted air.

On Friday evening she'd phone Cameron to say she'd have to stay down in London longer than she'd expected, because she'd need several fittings for the clothes she'd ordered.

Letting Hartley work its magic on her, Juliet felt much calmer and happier by Sunday morning. She *would* find Daniel somehow, and meanwhile it was wonderful to be back with all her family.

Dressed in elegant cream slacks and a silk shirt, she decided to walk to the village to see Rosie, once more living at Speedwell Cottage, whilst trying to make a go of her marriage.

She found Sophia, who had just turned one, in her playpen on the tiny back lawn, while Rosie kept an eye on her through the open kitchen window, as she did the washing-up.

'Hello, there!' Juliet called out gaily, walking round to the back door.

Rosie, furious at being caught unawares, and wearing an old cotton dress covered by a grubby apron, with her hair a mess, was less gracious. 'What on earth are you doing down here?'

The stark contrasts between their lives hit Juliet like a thunderbolt. She hadn't made a bed in her life; hadn't washed even a teacup; didn't know how to work one of those modern vacuum cleaners, and didn't even know how to boil an egg. And she had more money than she knew what to do with.

'Don't overdo the warm welcome, will you,' she remarked sarcastically.

'You might have warned me you were coming,' fumed Rosie. She jerked the plug out of the sink by its chain, and the soapy water glugged noisily down the drain. 'I thought you were still in Scotland.'

'Would you prefer it if I went back?'

'Do as you like,' Rosie snapped sulkily. She glanced round the small cluttered kitchen, seeing it through Juliet's eyes. The charwoman didn't come on a Saturday, so there was a pile of saucepans still to be cleaned; dirty nappies in a bucket of water, waiting to be washed, and a dustbin brimming to the top, so that the lid was placed at a precarious angle. Even Rosie, accustomed to the mess, realized it looked like a slum dwelling, and the rest of the cottage wasn't much better.

'I'm having to do everything myself today. Mrs Black doesn't come at the weekend,' she said defensively.

'Get Charles to help,' Juliet said, looking round, wondering where she could sit.

'How *can* he?' Rosie replied with savage fury, throwing a damp tea towel over the back of a chair. She hated Juliet for barging in like this, uninvited. She felt humiliated by the squalor of her home, and bitterly jealous of the fact that her sister, looking fresh and elegant and rich, had never had to do a single menial task in her life.

'He's still spending the week in London, is he?' Juliet asked, to make conversation. 'I heard he was working in a gallery in Duke Street. I brought you a little present, by the way.' From her crocodile handbag, she produced a small gift-wrapped box.

Rosie, who felt like weeping with aggravation, filled the kettle at the sink, and then plonked it down, with a resentful bang, on the stove. 'You needn't have bothered.'

'No, I needn't, but I wanted to.' The sisters looked icily at each other. Rosie picked up the box, and unwrapped a bottle of Shocking perfume, by Schiaparelli.

'Oh ... !' Her breath seemed to have been sucked out of her body, and her face turned scarlet.

'I remembered it was your favourite.' Juliet spoke with sudden gentleness. 'There's nothing like a good squirt of scent to cheer a girl up.'

Without saying anything, Rosie put the bottle down, and turned away, so Juliet wouldn't see her face.

'Sophia's growing fast, isn't she?' Juliet remarked, to fill the awkward silence. 'She'll be walking before long, I imagine. Does she sleep through the night, yet?'

'Mostly,' Rosie murmured, her voice choked.

Juliet reached into her handbag for her gold cigarette case. For the life of her, she didn't know what to say or do. The gap between them was too wide, too serious, to be bridged by a flippant remark.

We're both so proud, Juliet thought, as she drew on her cigarette, and watched Sophia playing in the garden. Neither of us will even admit we made a mistake, and are unhappy.

'I hear you're having another baby?'

'Yes.'

'That'll be nice for Sophia.'

'Providing it's a *boy*,' Rosie snapped.

At that moment, Charles arrived, carrying some shopping bags.

'Hello there, Juliet,' he said, brightening when he saw her. 'What a nice surprise. And how is Your Grace?' he teased.

Compared to Rosie, he looked good in his casual country tweeds, which disguised the gangling thinness of his body.

'Terribly well,' Juliet said with brittle lightness, sounding like a parody of a witless débutante. 'Thriving, in fact.'

'Good.' He looked her up and down, approvingly. 'And have you brought His Grace with you?'

'Poor Cameron has so much to do on the estate, he simply couldn't get away,' she trilled. 'So I've popped down on my own.'

Rosie filled the sink with fresh hot water. 'Did you get all the shopping, Charles?'

He'd ignored Rosie up to now, but as he plonked his shopping on the kitchen table he remarked casually, 'They didn't have any cucumbers. Or beetroot. Do we really have to have another bloody salad for lunch?'

Rosie grabbed the brown paper bags, accidentally splitting

one of them, and there was a series of thuds as the potatoes fell to the ground and rolled away.

'Damn!' she swore, her face scarlet with misery and embarrassment.

'Don't fuss,' Charles remonstrated in a weary voice. 'They're only potatoes, for God's sake.'

'But they're covered in earth! I've *already* washed this floor this morning.' She looked so vexed, Juliet didn't know whether to laugh or cry.

Charles had scooped up the offending potatoes by now. He chucked them in the sink.

'*Now* look what you've done!' Rosie screamed. 'I was about to wash those dishes, and now the water's all muddy.'

He looked askance at Juliet, and made a grimace. 'As you can see, I can't do anything right.'

Juliet ignored the look, and rose to her feet. 'I must be off, or I'll be late for lunch. Why don't you both come to dinner tonight? And bring Sophia. Nanny can look after her.'

'Thanks, we'd love to,' Charles replied with alacrity.

Rosie said nothing. Not even goodbye.

Henry's sister, Candida Montgomery, who lived ten miles away at Whitchurch, in Hampshire, also joined the family for dinner that night, arriving late and bringing her son Sebastian.

'Sorry, Marina couldn't come,' Candida said bluntly. 'These young things are always making their own arrangements and only telling you at the last moment,' she added cheerfully.

Her portly figure was encased in a maroon dinner dress that Liza privately reflected must have been designed by a tent manufacturer. But ropes of pearls made Candida a regal figure, dignified and commanding in her own way.

Sherry was offered.

'Sherry?' she repeated, appalled. 'My dear Henry, who drinks sherry these days? It's a filthy drink. Too liverish. I'll have a dry Martini, please.'

Henry grinned. 'Right-o! A dry Martini coming up.'

Liza smiled bravely. Part of her envied Candida's nonchalant cheek; she'd never have dared ask for anything different, not even in a relative's house. Candida's self-assurance was awesome, and she had a habit, although Liza didn't think she realized it, of making Liza feel very small and very provincial.

'So, how are you, old thing?' Henry asked with equal breeziness.

'Plodding on, you know. Plodding on. I've bought a new hunter. Grey Ghost, sired by The Siren out of Grey Mist; great dam, that Grey Mist. Goes like the clappers. Can't wait for the hunting season to start again,' Candida boomed.

Liza twisted her diamond rings. The only hunting she was planning to do was to look for a new mink coat for the winter.

'Good for you.' Henry looked at his sister affectionately. She was indomitable; strong, brave, and determined not to mope since the death of Marcus, her husband, five years ago.

Candida moved closer to Henry and spoke, her low rumbling voice like a motor mower just about to peter out. 'What's the matter with Rosie? She looks terrible.' She glanced over to the far side of the room, where her niece sat, huddled and frail-looking.

'She's having another baby.'

'That's not what I mean, Henry. She's changed. She used to be sweet and gentle; a really lovely girl. Now, she looks so –' Candida paused, frowning in her search for the right word – 'so hard-bitten! Sort of . . . cold and ruthless.'

Henry's eyes widened in surprise. 'I hadn't noticed. I suppose, seeing her every weekend . . . but has she changed so much?' he added, looking distressed. He glanced at Rosie, who was talking to his mother. She'd become very gaunt in the past couple of years, but Candida was right. Her face seemed to have frozen into hard lines, and her eyes no longer reminded him of bluebells, but of cold steel.

'She's not happy with that drip, is she?' Candida continued, undaunted. 'Damn shame she got married so young. What was she ever going to do with a loser like that?'

By the fireplace, Liza was now trying to make small talk with Charles. 'Bond Street is a nice place to work; all those lovely shops,' she gushed. 'Is it very busy in the gallery?'

Charles shrugged, one hand holding his drink, the other in his trouser pocket, while he lounged against the mantelshelf.

'Fairly busy. This is not the best time of year, though.' He looked beyond her, bored.

'It must be very interesting work, though,' she persisted.

182

'It's always nice to be surrounded by beautiful things.'

Juliet came up to them at that moment, relieving him of having to reply to his mother-in-law.

'When are you and Rosie coming back to live in London, Charles?' Juliet asked.

'It was never my idea to leave London,' he retorted, offended. 'I hate the country. I don't know how you manage, stuck up in Scotland, or perhaps you don't? Perhaps that's why you've come south, is it?' he added slyly.

Juliet ignored the taunt.

A shrill voice spoke, just behind her.

'If you'd *bought* the house in Farm Street, Charles, instead of just renting it, and then not paying the rent, we'd still be in London,' snarled Rosie. Her eyes were flashing furiously, while her hand was held protectively over her stomach.

An uneasy hush fell over the room. Lady Anne looked deeply troubled. Liza had turned scarlet with embarrassment and shock, and Henry, looking grave, went and put his arm around Rosie's shoulders.

'I don't think, my darling, that everyone wants to hear about our troubles, do you?' he whispered in her ear. 'Let's talk about it in private, tomorrow.'

'What good is that going to do?' Rosie retorted loudly.

'Dirty linen is always better washed in private,' Candida boomed cheerfully. 'Henry, are we going to eat soon? I don't know about you, but I'm starving.'

'I'm sick to death of protecting Charles,' Rosie said to her grandmother, as she went upstairs after dinner to collect Sophia, to take her home. 'He may have a job, but I don't see any of the money, except for the bits and pieces of food he buys at the weekend. Even then he says the shops don't have the things I want.'

'Darling, in public one must always stand by one's husband,' Lady Anne said firmly. 'Of course I sympathize with you for the position you're in, but is it really necessary to humiliate Charles in front of the rest of your family?'

'I simply couldn't help myself,' Rosie admitted. 'Maybe the sherry went to my head. I bet it gave Juliet a kick to know that while she's married to a multi-millionaire, I'm married to a pauper.'

'I'm sure it gave Juliet no pleasure at all. You let yourself down tonight, darling. More than you actually let Charles down. I'm not taking his side for one minute,' Lady Anne said quickly, as Rosie was about to protest, 'but whatever happens, you've got to keep your dignity. At least, thank God, it was only a family party, because if you'd done that in front of outsiders, it would have been really embarrassing.'

'I don't care.' Rosie spoke rashly and with desperation in her voice. 'Daddy's increased my dress allowance – which has been turned into money to support the three of us, and soon there'll be four mouths to feed, but he refuses to subsidize Charles.'

Lady Anne spoke firmly. 'It wouldn't be good for Charles if your father did. He must learn about responsibility. Do you want to turn him into a kept man?'

'He's a kept man, already,' Rosie flashed back. 'I don't think I can stand much more, Granny. I'm at the end of my tether. Mummy never brought me up to be a domestic drudge.'

That's the root of the trouble, Lady Anne thought. *She brought you up to be a duchess . . .*

'Divorce is out of the question, Rosie.' Liza looked aghast.

The previous night, Henry had made Liza face the facts about Rosie's unhappiness.

'Everything will be fine, once Charles gets a better job. That gallery ought to pay him more.'

'Charles is never going to have any money,' Henry said severely. 'He's a penniless waster, who spends what he's got on drink and gambling.'

'But we can't let Rosie starve, if they're as poor as you say; especially as she's having another baby.' Liza clasped her hands, fingers interlaced in anguish. 'We've got to help her more, Henry. If it gets out that . . .' She closed her eyes, unable to continue.

Liza decided to go and see Rosie the next day, to try and persuade her to make a go of her marriage.

'It's not just the money, Mummy,' she explained fretfully, 'it's *everything*. I can't bear Charles now; he's weak and self-ish and hopeless. I certainly didn't want this other baby, but he got very drunk one weekend, and he . . . he forced himself on me. I couldn't stop him. The only answer is to get a divorce.'

Liza spoke harshly to her daughter, for the first time in her life. 'The scandal of a divorce will ruin you,' she raged. 'Even a separation is out of the question. Pull yourself together, Rosie, for God's sake! Other people have unhappy marriages, too, but they just get on with it. Don't you realize you'll be marked for life if you split up with Charles?'

Rosie sat very upright, her face stony. 'To be rid of Charles would be worth it.'

'Don't be silly, darling,' Liza said, looking frightened at the prospect of such a family scandal. 'You're just feeling low because you're tired, and you're pregnant, and everything's got on top of you. Why don't you come and stay with us in London, for a bit? Nanny would adore to look after Sophia again; she really misses not having a baby to care for. Do come, sweetheart,' she coaxed more gently now. 'We can go shopping; I'll get you some lovely clothes. We can meet friends for lunch at the Choiserie, give some little parties, get you back in the swing of things among your old friends. Then it won't be nearly so hard, being married to Charles.'

Rosie's body slumped, as if the fight was going out of her. 'If I stay at Green Street, Charles will stay also. That will be worse; I'll be forced to be with him during the week, as well as at weekends.'

Liza crumpled, too. 'Oh, dear. Apart from giving you some money, what can I do?'

'Hope he drops dead?' Rosie shot back harshly.

Liza looked at her in horror. '*Rosie!* That's the most terrible thing to say.'

'Shall I invite Rosie and Sophia up to Glenmally?' Juliet suggested, as she walked around the gardens of Hartley with her father on the Sunday afternoon.

'That could exacerbate the situation, sweetheart,' he replied. 'She already sees you as having everything, while she's got nothing. Don't offer her money either.'

'What a mess.' There was genuine sympathy in Juliet's voice.

'At least you're happily married, to a very nice man,' Henry remarked, putting his arm around her shoulders. 'I'm really happy you've made such a success of your life.'

Juliet, longing to tell him how barren and loveless her marriage really was, and how unhappy she felt at Glenmally, looked up at him, and knew she couldn't. He'd be so disappointed by her failure, on top of Rosie's.

Instead, she said lightly, 'Then you and Mummy must come to stay again. Very soon. I do miss you, you know.'

Henry hugged her to his side. 'We miss you too, sweetheart.'

'Rosie will be all right, you know. She's really quite tough under that wilting appearance.'

He was silent for a moment, but then he said, grimly: 'I hope you're right, but I think she's being held back from the edge by the finest of threads.'

Something happened a few days later that made Juliet realize how right her father was.

As she was walking down Duke Street, in Mayfair, she stopped to look into the window of a jewellery shop. Jewels had always been her passion, and although Cameron had produced a dozen cases from his safe, each containing a king's ransom in diamonds, sapphires, rubies and emeralds, it didn't stop Juliet hankering for more. Like a magpie, she was attracted to anything that glittered.

Her eyes scanned the display and noticed an exquisite art deco diamond brooch, in the shape of a bow, tied with a knot. She sighed with pleasure. It was so fashionable, so modern, so different from anything she had.

On impulse she went into the shop; there was no harm in having a closer look, was there? The cheque book in her handbag seemed to be shouting out that it wanted to be used.

A loud bell clanged as she opened the door. The shop hadn't changed since the Edwardian era. The elderly assistant, in pinstriped trousers and a black coat, who emerged from behind dusty red plush curtains, looked like he'd been there since 1900 too.

'I'd like to see the art deco brooch in the window, please,' she told him.

'Certainly, Your Grace.'

How pleasurable to be recognized, Juliet thought, trying not to look pleased. While he unlocked the glass screen and slid it back so he could pick up the broach, Juliet gazed at the jewellery displayed under the glass-topped counter. Then she suddenly started, unable to believe her eyes. Surely not! It couldn't be . . . and yet, she was certain it was.

'I'd also like to have a look at that diamond and sapphire ring,' she said, pointing to it.

Juliet examined the ring closely. 'Did a tall young man, with light-brown hair and blue eyes, sell it to you? Quite recently?'

'We never reveal where our antique jewels come from, Your Grace.' There was a sudden note of suspicion in his gravelly voice. 'This ring was made around 1887, that's all I can tell you. The stones are very fine. Especially the centre sapphire.'

'Lord Padmore sold it to you, didn't he? It originally belonged to his mother.'

He turned pale. 'I – I really cannot comment . . .' he stuttered with obvious discomfort.

'How much is it?' Juliet asked.

He told her the price.

'I'll buy it.' She fished out her cheque book.

'And the brooch, Your Grace?' he asked hopefully.

'I've rather gone off the brooch,' she said politely. She wanted to get out of this little shop, which had suddenly become claustrophobic, with the rottenness of Charles sickening her.

That evening, Juliet dropped in to Green Street, managing to get her father on his own for a few minutes.

'Should I give it back to her now?' Juliet asked Henry that evening, showing him the ring. 'She may be upset and think she's lost it.'

Henry's mouth tightened. 'What a bastard!' he muttered, under his breath. 'She *does* think she's lost it; she admitted it to me the other day. She said she didn't dare tell Charles, because he would be so angry. And all the time . . . Oh, my God,' he groaned. 'I never thought he'd sink so low.'

'I think I'll play a little game with Charles,' Juliet said, with her wicked smile. 'I'll be down at the weekend. And I'll go over and see them.' She gave a throaty chuckle. 'This could be quite amusing.'

Henry looked worried. 'You won't humiliate Rosie, will you? I know what you two can be like; anything to score points off each other.'

Juliet's pale blue eyes widened in mock innocence. 'Me?' Then she burst out laughing. 'Oh, Daddy, you know me so well, don't you? But I promise you . . . not this time.'

When she'd been a child, Juliet had been told that if someone stood long enough by Eros, at Piccadilly Circus, they'd eventually meet everyone they knew.

It was bound to happen, she told herself, sooner or later, because the rich and privileged area of London was little more than a village, a one-mile radius from Hyde Park Corner, but when she saw him, walking towards her up South Audley Street, it was as if a miracle had happened.

He was wearing a dark suit, a trilby, and he was carrying a rolled umbrella as he swung along. Looking at him, her legs felt suddenly weak, too weak to take another step.

Then he spotted her. For a moment he stood still, gazing at her, a shocked look on his face. His dark eyes were wary, sizing her up. Juliet, hardly able to breath, stared back.

'Hello, Juliet.' His deep, rich voice sent an icy sensation down her backbone.

'Hello, Daniel,' she croaked. *How different he is from Cameron*, she thought, her mind whirling in a confusion of thoughts.

He raised his hat. 'How are you?' He was standing close to her now, looking down into her face, blotting out everything from her mind, except that this was the man who filled her thoughts, day and night. The man whose body she craved, her memories of their weekend in Paris still vivid, the man she had come down to London to find again, no matter what.

'Very well, thank you,' she heard herself murmur.

'You looked beautiful at your wedding.'

'Most brides do,' she quipped crisply, gathering strength. 'White can be very becoming.' She was beginning to feel sick with shock and desire.

'You married the wrong man, you know.'

'I married the man I wanted to marry,' she said defensively.

'Because I *couldn't* marry you, there was no need to rush off and marry someone else.'

She looked away sharply, gazing with unseeing eyes into the distance. The pain in her heart was physical.

Daniel spoke. 'I deeply regret not telling you I was married.

It was wrong of me and I'm really sorry. I should never have led you to believe I was single.' He paused, drilling her with his eyes. 'But there's nothing to stop us being together . . . when we can.'

Juliet's face became suffused with colour. 'I know,' she said in a small voice, because there was nothing else to say.

'Being married needn't stop us *loving* each other.'

'I know,' she repeated.

Daniel held out his hand to take hers. 'I knew if I told you the truth you'd have had nothing to do with me.' His hands tightened their grip. 'Juliet, you've no idea how much I love you. And want you. I thought I'd lost you for ever – and when I saw you just now . . .'

'I live in Scotland,' she said, dazed.

'You're not in Scotland now.'

She couldn't trust herself to speak.

'Are you in love with your husband?' he asked harshly.

She looked up quickly then. 'Not at all.'

'And I'm no longer in love with Rachel. I'll never leave her and the children. But if you can accept that, then you will always have the best of me. And the best of my love.'

Juliet nodded slowly. As long as no one ever found out, what was the harm?

'You're looking very well, darling,' Lady Anne remarked, when Juliet drove down to Hartley for the weekend.

'I *am* very well, Granny. I've bought you some of your favourite chocolates, violet cream.'

'Darling, that's so sweet of you.' Lady Anne looked closely at her granddaughter. She was glowing, eyes sparkling, a lightness in her step.

Something's happened, Lady Anne reflected. Perhaps Juliet is pregnant, but I don't think it's that. She remembered how she'd been herself, in her youth, when she'd fallen in love. Juliet had the same rapturous aura of happiness she remembered having, the same secret excitement that had made her glow, unaware of everything around her, thoughts fixed only on the object of her love.

Lady Anne didn't need to be told. Instinctively, she knew Juliet's radiance had nothing to do with Cameron.

*   *   *

189

'Are you still here?' Rosie ungraciously led the way into the kitchen. 'I thought you'd have returned to Scotland by now. I suppose you want a cup of coffee or something?'

Juliet followed, picking her way over floor mops and brooms that Rosie had abandoned in the doorway.

'So when are you going back?' Waddling now, in her advanced state of pregnancy, Rosie filled the kettle and put it on the gas stove.

'Next week, probably. How are you feeling?'

Rosie's shoulders were bent, and, from the back view, she resembled an old lady. 'Never get pregnant if you can help it,' she murmured. 'I can't find a comfortable position to sleep in, my back aches all the time, my ankles are swollen, and I feel lousy.'

'You poor old thing.' Juliet looked around the little cluttered kitchen, seeing it as a nightmare of disorganization and mess. As before, dirty dishes had been chucked into the sink, where they lay half-submerged in grey soapy water. Bits of cabbage leaf lay on the floor, and there was spilt sugar on the only narrow work surface. She thought about her own kitchen at Glenmally, which she'd visited twice. Even if it was old-fashioned, with its big black stove, and rows of copper pans hanging from the ceiling, it was immaculate. And big enough to hold a party for a hundred people.

'Shall we have our coffee next door, in the drawing room?' she suggested.

Rosie threw her a poisoned glance. 'You know perfectly well it's not a drawing room,' she snapped, 'so don't patronize me. We're only here until after I've had the baby. Then we'll get a place in London again.'

It was on the tip of Juliet's tongue to ask sarcastically who was going to pay for a town house, but she held herself in check, instead smiling broadly, and nodding. 'That'll be nice. Mummy will be glad to have you near again.'

Rosie carried the coffee tray into the front room, and set it on a low table, between two armchairs.

Once again Juliet found it difficult to think of anything to say. Pointless to ask *Have you seen so-and-so?* or *Have you seen such-and-such a film?* because the answer could only be in the negative. Not diplomatic, either, to talk about the shopping she'd done since she'd come down to London. And she could hardly confide in her sister about her affair with Daniel, and the wonderful four nights when he'd stayed at Park Lane, coming late, after the skeleton staff had gone to bed, and slipping away before dawn.

'What's up? Why are you looking so pleased with yourself?' Rosie asked crossly, and she pushed a cushion into the small of her back.

Juliet frowned. Trying to hide her happiness. 'I was thinking about Granny,' she lied, swiftly. 'She's wonderful for her age, isn't she? Whenever I see her I'm amazed at how active she is. I don't know what this family would do without her.'

Rosie's face softened. 'She's so kind and sweet,' she agreed.

The front door opened at that moment, and then slammed shut again. Charles, looking disgruntled, put his head round the living-room door.

'Oh, hello, Juliet. What are you up to?'

Juliet burst out laughing. 'You two really know how to make a person feel welcome, don't you? How are *you*, Charles?'

He sighed wearily, casting an irritable look at his wife.

'Oh, this and that . . . what's the matter, Juliet?'

She was wriggling in the armchair, her brows gathered in perplexity, one of her hands down the side of the padded chair.

'What the . . . ?' she began, pulling her hand out again. She was gripping the sapphire and diamond engagement ring with her fingertips.

'My *ring!*' exclaimed Rosie, flushing with pleasure. 'Oh, how wonderful.' She grabbed it from Juliet, and put it on the fourth finger of her left hand.

Charles's eyes seemed to be popping out of their sockets. He turned scarlet, shot Juliet a bewildered and suspicious look, and immediately set about berating Rosie.

'Do you mean to say you *lost* your ring?' he demanded furiously. 'For Christ's sake, Rosie, it's a valuable family heirloom. How could you be so bloody careless? You're always losing things!'

Rosie's eyes brimmed, and she looked scared. 'It must have slipped off when I was plumping up the cushions. I'm sorry, Charles. I'll be more careful . . .' Then she fled from the room, and they could hear her footsteps, hurrying up the stairs to

191

the bedroom, her breath coming in gasping sobs.

Juliet rose and faced Charles, shaking with anger. 'You loath-some rat,' she said in a low voice. 'We both know where it was, don't we?' she demanded grimly. 'God, Charles, you're the scum of the earth. I know you sold Rosie's ring, so don't deny it. You also guessed she'd be too frightened to admit she'd lost it – and then when I appeared to find it, you have the sheer bloody gall to have a go at her for being careless. Is there no end to the depths to which you'll sink, to get money?'

Charles shuffled his feet, his face flaming with anger and embarrassment. For a moment Juliet thought he was going to deny the whole thing, but then he burst out savagely, 'I'm *sick* of not having enough money.' Like a petulant boy, he kicked a small footstool, so that it shot off and hit the skirting board.

Juliet stood her ground, her beautiful face filled with disgust. 'I'm warning you, Charles, I'll tell the whole family what you did, unless you apologize to Rosie. Have you any idea how unhappy she is? You're making her life hell.'

'It's not my fault we've got no money,' he said angrily.

'It's your fault my parents gave their consent. You misled them by giving the impression you had enough to support her,' Juliet said tartly. 'But, as you obviously hadn't, you thought you'd marry money instead, didn't you?'

There was raw hatred in his eyes as he looked at her. 'It's easy for you to talk,' he slammed back. 'Your father's rich and so is your husband. Now get out of my house, Juliet, and stay away. You make Rosie discontented, coming here in your expen-sive clothes, driving a Rolls coupé, having everything you want.'

'Not everything,' she replied evenly, thinking of Cameron. 'But I'm working at it,' she added, remembering Daniel.

'I'd give anything not to have to go back,' Juliet confessed, 'but I've had both Cameron and my mother-in-law on the tele-phone, practically demanding my return; I have been away for three weeks, you know.'

She was lying with Daniel in her art deco silver bed, with its parma violet velvet hangings and silk sheets. A pale misty dawn filtered through the window, revealing the plane trees in Hyde Park, their trunks dappled, their green leaves strongly veined.

'I don't think I can bear to let you go,' Daniel said, his face buried in her neck. 'You're never going to find this bliss with Cameron.'

'I know,' she said sadly. 'But I'm married to him, so what can I do?'

'He's expecting you to give him an heir, isn't he?'

She put her hands behind her head, and gazed up at the canopy of the bed.

'I believe that's the only reason he married me.'

Daniel sat up, his bronzed chest broad and bare. He looked down at her. 'Juliet,' he said seriously. 'I want you to make me a promise.'

Her pale blue eyes shifted their gaze to his face; a face that was now as familiar to her as her own. His full mouth was set in a serious line.

'What is it, Daniel?'

'I want to be the one to give you a baby. I want it to be my seed, growing inside you. My baby you will hold in your arms. No one else's.'

Her eyes widened, startled at first, and then filled with wonder, as the strongest sensation of desire she'd ever felt in her life swept through her.

'Your baby?' she said huskily, reaching for him. 'Oh, Daniel, could we really?'

'Why not? I can't bear to think of you having Cameron's child. Have my baby, darling. Let me love you and give you a child.' he added, his voice thick with emotion. 'I'm in your blood, Juliet. I'm a part of you now, and for ever.'

'When will I see you again?' he asked later, as he got dressed, ready to slip out of the house before the servants were up and about.

She slid out of the bed and pulled on her black chiffon negligee. 'I'll try and get away as soon as I can,' she promised.

He gave her a last kiss. 'You'll be careful not to get pregnant by Cameron, won't you?' he urged.

'I'll make sure of that,' Juliet whispered, giving him a last kiss, 'as I have, ever since we got married.'

Juliet looked at herself in the mirror as she got ready to leave for Euston. This would never do, she decided. Her face glowed and her eyes shone with happiness. She looked exactly what she'd become; a woman in love, who was having a sublime and fulfilling sex life.

The old witch would spot the change in her immediately, she thought, even if Cameron didn't. Although she'd booked a first-class sleeper for the overnight journey to Inverness, she decided to stay awake, reading and drinking coffee. This, coupled with a lack of make-up, would assure her looking wan and exhausted on arrival. A perfect excuse, too, for going straight to bed, thereby avoiding any questions about her stay in London.

'Where's Cameron?' Juliet asked her mother-in-law as she pulled off her gloves and hat, and threw them down on the oak chest in the baronial hall.

Iona looked nervous, clutching her plaid shawl around her narrow shoulders with her bony hands. 'He had to go out,' she said quickly. 'You looked tired, Juliet.'

'I am. I think I'll go up for a rest. Can you tell Cameron I'm back?'

'Yes.' Iona Kincardine's face was very pale, and her dark eyes flickered anxiously towards the front door, as if she was expecting someone.

'Is everything all right?'

'Perfectly all right,' Iona replied firmly.

The chauffeur appeared, carrying Juliet's overnight case. He put it down, and turned to the dowager. 'Your Grace, shall I go back to Inverness? To fetch His Grace? Do you think he'll be ready by now?'

'Go back . . . ?' Juliet queried. 'Why? Is my husband in Inverness? Why didn't we bring him with us?'

Iona and the chauffeur exchanged nervous glances.

'What's going on?' Juliet demanded.

'Cameron . . .' Iona began hesitatingly, 'Cameron's had a slight accident. Nothing to worry about, Juliet. He had to go the hospital yesterday, but he'll be home today.' She turned back to the chauffeur. 'I'll telephone the hospital. I'll let you know when it's time to fetch him.'

'What *sort* of accident?' Juliet persisted, when she and Iona were alone again.

Iona fixed her with her beady eyes and spoke harshly. 'Oh,

194

you know what it's like. It's no one's fault, and we want to be very discreet about this. We don't want to get anyone into trouble, so please do not talk about it. Not to anyone.'

Juliet frowned. 'What are you talking about? I don't understand.'

The old dowager came closer. She stank of moth balls, as if she'd been shut away in a cupboard for months. Her whispered breath was fetid. 'There was a shooting accident yesterday. One of the . . . one of the people on the estate. He tripped, and his gun went off. A bullet accidentally caught Cameron on the thigh. Only a flesh wound. Nothing more. Nothing to worry about. But we want to keep it quiet, because it was an *accident*, you understand. Nothing more.'

Bemused, Juliet stared at her mother-in-law. 'Is Cameron all right?'

'He's fine.' Iona laid her hand on Juliet's arm. 'Remember. Not a word. Don't even ask Cameron about it, because he's . . . well, he's upset.'

Juliet nodded silently, and then turned to go up to her quarters. Something was wrong. For a moment her mind wrestled with some shadowy doubt, trying to catch hold of it and face it, but it kept slipping elusively away.

Then she remembered; after years of Nanny's coaching about the dos and don'ts, how could she have forgotten?

It was May, May 8th, to be exact. The shooting season didn't start until August 12th. If someone had been shooting, it certainly wasn't after wildlife.

PART THREE

As Darkness Closes In

1939

Eight

'When are you coming to London again?' Daniel asked in desperation. It was six weeks since Juliet's last visit, but they spoke on the telephone as often as they could.

'I'm a virtual prisoner here,' Juliet whispered back, in case Iona, given to lurking around corners, should overhear her.

Since Juliet had got back from her trip to town, Cameron and Iona had put heavy pressure on her to remain at Glenmally.

'Why do you want to keep running off to London?' they both asked, whenever she suggested she might like to pop down to see her family again. If she said she had shopping to do, Cameron said airily that if she made a list, he'd get Harrods or the Army & Navy Stores to send her what she wanted. Even when she said she wanted to be with Rosie, who was having a baby any moment, Cameron tut-tutted, and became very bad-tempered, saying if she didn't like Scotland, she shouldn't have married him in the first place.

'I miss you so much,' she told Daniel repeatedly. 'I daren't even write to you because we have to leave our letters for posting on the hall table, for the butler to post.'

'Oh, God . . . why don't you invent a reason for getting away they can't oppose?' Daniel suggested. 'I'm going crazy . . . not seeing you, not being with you.'

'Me too,' Juliet whispered. 'I'll think of something.'

'Don't take too long.'

'I'll let you know as soon as I can get away,' she promised.

The answer was so obvious she couldn't think why she hadn't thought of it before.

'I've got to have a check-up with my doctor,' she announced at breakfast, the next morning, 'so tomorrow I'm catching the overnight train to London.'

'Are you ill?' asked the dowager hopefully.

Juliet hesitated long enough to get both Cameron and Iona interested. 'Not exactly.' She smiled sweetly. 'But I want to make sure everything's all right,' she added, giving Cameron an intimate look.

His expression brightened and his relief was marked. He'd taken his mother's advice, and since he'd recovered from his injury, he'd been to Juliet's room every night. It seemed now he was to be rewarded for his efforts.

'Oh, I see,' he said. 'Right then. How long will you be away?'

'Not long,' she assured him, 'unless, of course, I have to have tests or something.'

The dowager looked from one to the other, not wanting to be left out. 'What sort of tests?'

Juliet shrugged and looked enigmatic. 'We'll have to wait and see.'

Daniel was waiting at Euston station when she arrived, and they went straight to a flat in Belgrave Square, which he'd borrowed from a friend.

'I've been counting the hours,' she told him excitedly, as he tore off her clothes. They made love all afternoon, and it was nearly six o'clock when Juliet said, 'I must go to the house now. Cameron will have been phoning to ask if I've arrived safely. I'll have to say I've been in Harley Street all afternoon.'

'I'll pick you up at eight o'clock, then. We'll dine at a discreet little restaurant I know in Soho.'

'I'll tell the servants not to wait up for me,' she murmured, giving him a last kiss.

Over a dinner of *foie gras*, lemon sole, and a tender fillet of beef, Daniel pointed out she couldn't use the excuse of a visit to the doctor very frequently.

'If Cameron begins to think there's something really wrong with you, he'll start bringing in his own doctors. I know I would, if I was married to you.'

Juliet closed her eyes for a moment, to savour the thought. Married to him. God, she'd give everything – her way of life, her money, her jewels and furs, everything – if she could only marry Daniel.

'What shall I say, then?' she asked.

'Why don't you get involved in charity work, down here?'

Startled, she raised her eyebrows. 'That doesn't sound like me. I've never done charity work in my life.'

'I'm not suggesting you take blankets and baskets of food to the slums in the East End.' He grinned. 'With your title, there are charitable organizations that would give anything just to have your name on their headed paper. All you'd have to do is attend the occasional meeting, and maybe take tickets for charity balls or concerts: that wouldn't be difficult, would it? And what a perfect excuse to come down to London.'

A glow of delight spread across Juliet's face. 'It's a brilliant idea.'

'Be sure to tell your husband –' Daniel could never bring himself to call Cameron by name – 'that he'll be highly thought of if his name is involved in supporting various good causes.'

'You're right. He needs to be seen to lead a normal life, he's far too reclusive. I think that's one of the reasons he married me. That and his desperate need for an heir.'

'So he married someone who wanted a title?' Daniel asked slyly.

Juliet flushed. 'Don't,' she begged, miserably. 'It was the worst mistake of my life. If I could have married you, I would have . . .'

'I know.' There was a flicker of guilt in Daniel's eyes. 'I should never have pursued you. I should never have fallen in love with you. It was unfair of me . . .'

'I'm glad you did.'

He held her gaze. 'So am I.'

There were two letters for Juliet on the breakfast table, a week after she'd returned from London.

'Your family keeping in touch with you, are they?' the dowager remarked, nearly screwing her head off to see what the postmarks were.

Juliet opened the first with caution. It was from the Red Cross asking her if she would become a patron of their fundraising committee, the first event being a ball at the Dorchester in October. The second was a similar letter from the Family in Need charity, which provided accomodation for widows with children, asking if she'd be president of their fundraising committee.

Flushing with pleasure, knowing Daniel was behind this, Juliet handed the letters to Cameron. 'Isn't this nice? What an honour! They obviously think a lot of you, to have invited me.'

'Charities?' snapped Iona, seeing the letterheads. 'They're only after your money. All that flannel about it being an honour to have you is pure flattery.'

A wash of anxiety swept away some of Juliet's hopes that she'd found the perfect way to take frequent trips to London.

'Times have changed, though,' she said hurriedly. 'I think people like Cameron and I, a rich and very privileged couple, should be seen to be helping those less fortunate, don't you, Cameron?'

After re-reading the letters, and studying them, Cameron spoke. 'Isn't it rather strange that you suddenly get invited by two charities on the same day?'

Juliet smiled sweetly. 'Not really. When I was in London I was lunching with Hermione Ridsdale. Do you remember her? She's the wife of the Conservative MP, Lansdowne Ridsdale. She asked me if I'd help her with her charity work. I couldn't very well say no, so I suppose she's put my name forward.'

The ease with which she could lie amazed Juliet. And only Cameron would be so gullible as to believe her, she reflected. His mother was another matter. She'd have to be careful. It was obvious Iona didn't like her, and probably wouldn't care what happened to her once she'd produced a son; in the meantime, she must somehow allay her suspicions.

Juliet continued, 'It would be so nice, Cameron, if you could come down to London with me when there's a big fundraising do, like this ball,' she suggested, smiling at him across the breakfast table.

'Cameron hasn't said whether you can go gallivanting off to London in the first place,' Iona said with poisonous venom. 'It's time you started a family. Like your sister.'

'Of course it's up to Cameron,' Juliet replied smoothly.

Cameron spoke. 'These are highly regarded charities, but Mother's right. It is time we started a family. On the other hand, it would look churlish to turn down their requests.' He paused, reaching for a piece of toast. The only sound in the dining room was the ticking of a hideous purple marble clock on the mantelpiece, while he ponderously made up his mind. 'Tell them you accept, Juliet,' he said eventually. 'But don't take on any more. Two charities is quite enough,' he added firmly.

'I agree,' she said brightly.

In spite of Cameron's caution and Iona's downright misgivings, it was the start of a new pattern in Juliet's life.

Travelling on the overnight sleeper from Inverness every couple of weeks, sometimes for only forty-eight hours, she managed to fit in a couple of genuine fundraising committee meetings, have lunch or tea with her mother, for the sake of an alibi, and spend the rest of the time with Daniel, usually in someone's borrowed flat and occasionally on the houseboat, which held such romantic memories.

'I live for the time we can be together,' Juliet told him, as they lay in bed together, wrapped in each other's arms. 'I wish it could always be like this.'

'You could always leave Cameron.'

'And would you leave your wife?'

There was a long pause before he spoke. 'There are the children. I can't upset their lives.'

Juliet never knew how much time he spent with his family in Kent. Never knew where he stayed in London when she wasn't with him. Never knew how he managed for money, but presumed he was a man of independent means. And as long as she could go on seeing him, she didn't want to know. But nothing assuaged the pain when they had to part. Something inside her seemed to die when they said goodbye, never sure when they'd see each other again. And she knew she'd never get used to the agony of separation.

'I can't bear this,' Juliet said one morning, sitting up in bed. They'd spent the night on the houseboat, but now she had to slip back to Park Lane, so as to be found in her bed when her breakfast tray was brought up to her. She sat gazing at the river through the large windows. Daylight was beginning to break up the night sky with pale streaks of yellow, and there was a stillness at this hour of the morning she found deeply melancholic.

'It gets harder every time,' she admitted, a tear rolling down her cheek and plopping on to her naked breasts. 'What are we going to *do*, darling?'

'I'll have a surprise for you, next time you're down,' he said, watching her get out of bed, her legs long and lean, her stomach perfectly flat as she reached for her discarded evening clothes.

'What sort of a surprise?'

He clambered quickly out of the bed, and took her in his arms.

'Tell me?' she asked, resting her head on his shoulder. He smelled of fresh sweat and musk and she felt weak with desire again.

'Wait and see,' he teased, holding her tightly, raising his thigh and thrusting it between her legs, so he could lift her slightly off the ground. She clung around his neck, pressing herself against him.

'Tell me,' she implored. 'Oh, if only we could be together all the time. You've *no* idea how much I hate leaving you.'

'I know, my darling. We'll just have to make do with for ever,' he whispered. 'I'll love you for ever. I'll want you for ever. We're a part of each other for ever. That will never stop, even when we're apart.'

She knew in her heart it would always have to be like this; snatched nights and somehow more partings than greetings; or did it just feel that way?

'Next time you're down you'll see my surprise,' he continued, looking into her eyes.

'A new car?'

'Better than that. Now, no more guessing.' As he lowered her to the ground, he placed his hand on her flat stomach. 'Don't forget, we've yet to make our baby.'

Two weeks later, because she couldn't bear being away from him any longer, Juliet phoned Daniel.

'I'm coming down to London tomorrow,' she said. 'Can you meet me at the station?'

There was a pause. He hesitated before saying, 'Could you make it the next day? I'm a bit tied up tomorrow.'

Darts of panic shot through her. Daniel sounded odd, wary.

'Why?' she asked sharply, knowing it was unreasonable of her to expect him to drop everything at a moment's notice, but nevertheless, she felt dashed with disappointment. 'What are you doing?' Her mind was spinning. Had his wife found out about them? Or perhaps she was also coming up to London tomorrow? Bringing their children with her?

Jealousy seeped through her brain like a feverish poison.

'What's so special about tomorrow, that you don't want to see me?' she snapped recklessly, not caring whether anyone overheard her or not. Supposing he'd met someone else? That was when it hit her that she knew nothing about him.

'Calm down, Juliet.' Daniel's deep rich voice was authoritative and commanding. 'I do have to make a living, you know.'

'Why can't you get the day off,' she shot back, edging towards hysteria. He'd *never* been too busy to see her in the past.

'What's wrong with Wednesday?' he asked, calmly. 'I'll meet your train and we can—'

'Perhaps you'd rather I didn't come at all?' she raged. Then she slammed down the receiver, shaking all over. If he left her . . . But the idea was too terrible to even think about. Tears of frustration and vexation rushed to her eyes. She could hear the servants in the next room, laying the table for luncheon. In a few minutes, Iona would come drifting out of her room, trailing one of her many strange outfits, carrying a posy of herbs and surrounded by all the dogs, who padded in her wake as if they were attached to her by invisible leads. Juliet turned and hurried upstairs to compose herself, wondering what the hell she was doing with her life in a place like this.

Later that day, there was a telephone call for Juliet.

'The gentleman said he was the treasurer of the Red Cross Ball,' the butler informed her.

Glowing with exultation, Juliet picked up the receiver as a warm flood of relief surged into her heart.

'I'm afraid it's very short notice but is it possible for you to come to London tomorrow, Duchess?' Daniel said carefully, in case anyone was listening on the line. 'We have . . . erm . . . figures we should look at. Things to go through. We urgently need to convene a meeting; that is, if you can mangage it, Duchess?'

'If I change a few things around, I could possibly manage it,' she replied, her voice cool and businesslike. 'Could you arrange for a car to meet me at the station and take me straight to your headquarters?'

'Of course, Duchess. It would be our pleasure.'

'Where are we going?' Juliet asked curiously. 'To the house-boat?'

Daniel was heading west, along the banks of the Thames.

'Have you forgotten I have a surprise for you?' he asked, his dark eyes sweeping over her body as they stopped at the red lights. One look at him had banished her fears; he was as much in love with her as ever.

'I hadn't forgotten.'

'Well then,' he teased, reaching for her hand.

'I want to *know* what it is . . .' she begged.

'Sit still and keep quiet,' he commanded, but his lips tipped up at the corners with amusement.

'Oh, Daniel. Don't torture me.' Her hand slid up his thigh.

'It won't be long now.'

'What won't?' she asked.

'Until you see my surprise.'

She was like a restless child, maddened with impatience. 'Can't you give me a *clue* . . . ? Can I try guessing?'

'No guessing. No clues.'

'Beast. I hate you.'

'You'll love me when you see it.'

'See *what*?'

They were in Chelsea now, and he drove along the King's Road for a short distance, before turning up a small side street. Halfway along, he slowed down, and parked his car on the left.

Juliet looked around, bewildered. 'What am I supposed to be looking at?'

A slow smile spread across his face. 'Come with me.'

They got out of the car, and he took her hand, leading her twenty yards along the narrow pavement.

'There you are,' he said, stopping suddenly. 'Do you like it?'

'What are you looking . . . ? Oh! My God! It's *yours*? Since when? I can't believe it!'

'It's *ours*,' he said softly.

They were facing an adorable doll's house of a cottage, with little windows with pale blue shutters, and a pale blue front door. There were even roses in the tiny front garden.

'Ours?' she repeated stupidly.

'I've just bought it, for us. I didn't think I'd have the keys until tomorrow, which is why I wanted you to come to London a day later, but I managed to exchange contracts, and here we are.' He threw out his arm with an expansive gesture, before pushing open the small blue gate.

'It's perfect! The *most* enchanting house I've ever seen!' Juliet exclaimed, entranced. 'I can't believe you've bought it.'

Daniel nodded. 'It's ours,' he repeated. 'A place of our own, where we can do as we like,' he added, drawing her to his side as they entered the tiny square hall.

'Oh, darling . . .' She flung her arms around his neck and kissed him. 'This is the most marvellous surprise I've *ever* had. We must christen every room by making love in it!'

'There are only three rooms, so we'll have to christen them several times,' he laughed.

'Surely the hall makes a fourth? And the bathroom? What are we waiting for?'

'Juliet?' Liza looked at Juliet with surprised curiosity.

'Oh! Hello, Mama.' Juliet blushed, the front door key of her house in her hand, and although it was ten o'clock in the morning, she was wearing a black cocktail dress and a sable wrap. Liza's eyes followed the car that had dropped Juliet off, as it sped away down Park Lane.

'What on earth are you doing?' Liza asked suspiciously. 'Where's Cameron?'

'I stayed over at a friend's house last night. They gave a dinner party that went on for *hours* . . . and they wouldn't let me come home alone,' Juliet replied lightly, slipping her key into the front door lock.

The lies were getting bigger and deeper and more complicated, like strands which were dependant on each other; if she forgot her story and made a mistake, the whole lot would get hideously knotted.

'Oh.' Liza looked unconvinced. 'Isn't Cameron down here, then?' She followed her daughter into the black and white and silver art deco hall.

'You know he hates London, Mama. I just popped down

for a couple of days. Fundraising committe, you know.' Juliet lingered at the bottom of the stairs, which were carpeted in black, hoping her mother wasn't going to stay, asking awkward questions. She'd spent the night with Daniel, after they'd been out to dinner, and she was exhausted. All she wanted now was to be on her own, so she could relive in her mind the wonders of his love-making. It amazed her that one moment he could be utterly tender, and the next masterfully passionate, leading her to heights of ecstacy she had never thought possible.

'Mummy, I have to catch a train . . .' she began, but it was no use.

'I'll talk to you while you change. How's Glenmally? Any chance of you and Cameron coming to Ascot with us?'

Sighing inwardly, Juliet ordered coffee to be brought up to her bedroom. While she slipped into a hot scented bath, Liza sat in the dressing room, giving a monologue that required no answers.

'In spite of what Daddy says about the prospect of war – I do wish Ian wouldn't tell him so much, he gets so depressed – there are more parties than ever this year! My dear, I've got luncheon parties, tea parties, cocktails, dinners, dances . . .'

His hands drive me crazy, Juliet thought, as she lay in the fragrant water. They're so strong and yet gentle . . . Was there ever a lover like him? I'd *die* if he ever tired of me. I wish I could stay longer . . . Does his wife miss him? Does he still sleep with her? I can't bear to think of that; them being together.

'Juliet? Did you hear what I said?'

'Sorry. What was that?'

'I asked whether you'd heard about Harrods?'

'*Harrods*?' Juliet stepped out of the bath, and wrapped herself in a soft white towel.

'Yes, darling. Richard Burbridge – you know, his family own the store – has asked for Territorial recruits, in case there is a war. Apparently the Harrods staff have rallied magnificently, providing volunteers for all three services.'

Juliet emerged from the bathroom and started dressing, putting on exquisite cream satin and lace lingerie that was part of her trousseau.

Liza continued, 'I find the situation so *blurred*, don't you, darling?' She held up a small mirror from her handbag, and touched up her bright red lipstick. 'I mean ... did Czechoslovakia and Austria *originally* belong to Germany? Daddy says a treaty that was signed after the Great War has been overturned. But who by? Oh! The whole thing is an absolute *nightmare*. Just when everything was getting back to normal after the Depression, and we all had lots of money, and such a good time. Daddy says it may all come crashing down again, later on this year! Do you believe that? What does Cameron say?'

Sitting at her new dressing table, which was entirely made of mirror, Juliet looked at the reflection of her mother's face.

'As long as Cameron can kill every living creature he sees in the Highlands, he couldn't care less about the Germans,' she replied acidly.

'Do you think you should come down to London so often, without him?' Liza dabbed her nose with a scrap of swansdown and a little pink cloud of powder hung in the air. 'I'm surprised he doesn't mind.'

Juliet shrugged. 'He's been *hors de combat*; someone took a pot-shot at him a little while ago.'

'Who? Cameron? Someone shot at him?' Liza's mouth fell open.

'He said it was an accident.'

'What do you mean – he *said* it was an accident? What else could it have been. Is he all right?'

'I'm afraid so,' Juliet murmured in a low voice.

'What? What did you say?'

'He's fine.'

'He doesn't mind your trips to London? It's gorgeous to see you, sweetheart, but are you sure Cameron doesn't feel neglected? It's very, very important to put your husband's feelings before everything else, you know. And he's so good to you. Look at the jewels he's given you. And that car. You're a very lucky girl to have such a kind and generous husband.' Liza was thinking of Charles as she spoke; poor Rosie was lucky if he gave her a box of chocolates for her birthday.

'Cameron's fine,' Juliet insisted wearily.

Liza started gathering up her gloves and handbag, as she rose to leave. 'I suppose you might as well run around, until you have a baby ... there's no sign of one yet, I presume?'

Juliet's smiled secretly at her reflection. 'Not yet,' she replied lightly, 'but hopefully, soon.'

'You're such a *pessimist*, Henry,' his sister exclaimed. They were all staying at Hartley Hall for the weekend, and Candida had put forward what she called a 'spiffing idea'.

'Are you out of your mind?' Henry exclaimed incredulously. 'It's bad enough with Liza, but I didn't expect you to put your head in the sand too.'

'This is different,' Candida retorted. 'I know there's going to be a war, but don't tell me it's going to happen within the next three months. All I plan to do is take Marina to St Malo, which is just the other side of the Channel, for God's sake. She's been really ill with glandular fever and the doctor says she needs a change of air. I thought it would be fun if Louise came with us. They're both fourteen now and they've always got on. They can keep each other company.'

Henry rubbed his hand across his head. His face was creased with anxiety. 'To go abroad right now, and to Europe, of all places, is crazy. Why don't you take Marina to Cornwall?'

'The weather is too dicey in England. Even in July. We don't want to be cooped up in a hotel, looking at a rainswept beach, Henry.'

'What about Scotland, then? Stay with Juliet and Cameron? Or the Norfolk Broads?'

'Henry,' Candida groaned good-humouredly. 'Why are you always such a stick-in-the-mud? We'll be perfectly safe. If the worst comes to the worst,' she added in her booming voice, 'we can hop on the ferry and be back at Southampton in a few hours.'

'It seems safe enough to me,' Liza intervened. 'It would be fun for Louise too.'

Henry sighed heavily. It would soon be August. The situation was very unsettled, with Hitler whipping up a patriotic fever amongst the Germans.

'They'll invade Poland, Norway and Denmark,' Henry said. 'France will be next. Then England. Hitler is unstoppable. It was just a matter of time.'

'Rubbish!' Candida scoffed. 'Nothing's going to happen that fast.'

'Only for two weeks, then,' Henry agreed reluctantly. 'And come back at once, if there's the faintest sign of trouble.'

'We will, old boy.' Candida smiled affectionately at him. Since the death of her husband, Henry had been very supportive, not only of her, but of Marina and Sebastian, but there were times when he drove her mad with his caution. 'That's settled then. We'll be off next week,' she said before he changed his mind.

'Liza, I suppose you'd better tell Louise,' Henry said wearily.

'She'll be so excited, Henry. I'd better get her some nice beach clothes. And a hat with a brim. She mustn't get the sun on her face.'

On Sunday, Rosie and Charles, pushing Sophia and baby Jonathan in the big smart pram that had been hers, walked over to Hartley for lunch.

'How he's grown,' remarked Lady Anne in delight, when she saw the new baby.

Rosie plonked Jonathan in her arms, and he looked up at her, gurgling and waving his tiny hands around.

'He likes *you*, Ma,' Candida observed tactlessly, and then, too late, saw Liza wince. 'But then, I suppose,' she continued, without missing a beat, 'that you see him almost every day; and the rest of us only see him occasionally.'

Lady Anne gave her daughter the hint of a conspiratorial smile. They never talked about it, but they both felt Liza was only interested in children when they became social-climbing fodder.

'That's right, Candida,' Lady Anne agreed. 'I can hardly keep away from Speedwell Cottage, so I can see Rosie and her lovely babies. I'm probably the most awful bore,' she added, knowing perfectly well she wasn't.

'You can come as often as you like, Granny,' Rosie said warmly. She looked wan and strained. Two children had done nothing to bring back the bloom of her late teens. Her blue eyes held a dull look, and her skin was dingy. Painfully thin again, her summer dress hung loosely on her frame. She was only twenty-two now, but she felt like forty.

'I'm going to Brittany, with Aunt Candida and Marina,' Louise told Rosie, as Henry offered everyone a drink before lunch, and Amanda handed round a silver dish of home-made cheese straws.

209

'Lucky you.'

Sophia clambered up on to Louise's lap. "Tory,' she begged. 'Tell 'tory.'

'I'll read you a story after lunch,' Louise promised.

'Louise has a way with children,' Lady Anne observed, watching them together. At weekends she was always running down to Speedwell Cottage, offering to help Rosie with the babies.

'I want lots of my own, one day,' Louise said now, hugging her little niece tightly.

After lunch, Rosie walked in the garden with Henry, as she pushed Jonathan in his pram. 'Daddy, I hate to ask, but . . .' she drew in a long shuddering breath.

'How much do you need?' Henry asked in a low voice, so the others, sitting on the terrace having coffee, wouldn't hear.

'It's worse than that.'

'What do you mean? You're not pregnant again?'

She shook her head, her blonde hair hanging limply to her shoulders. 'Charles has lost his job at the gallery.'

'Oh, God, I'm sorry, darling. What happened?'

'They sacked him because he was fiddling his expenses. The usual thing; he didn't tell me, stayed in London, gambling, and getting into debt, before I found out.'

'Why doesn't he sell his place in Cumbria? Of course, he'd have to find alternative accomodation for his mother and sister. Nevertheless . . .'

'You and Mummy have never seen his so-called castle, have you? It's a ruin, Daddy. His mother and Henrietta live in four rooms in the only part that's still standing.' Despair filled her eyes. 'I don't know *what* to do with him.'

Henry put his arm around her shoulders. 'I'll draft some money into your personal account at Child's Bank, first thing in the morning. As long as Charles doesn't know about it.'

'Oh, Daddy, I'm so sorry.' Rosie bit her lip, trying not to cry. She grabbed his arm as he turned to stroll back to the house. 'Why did it all go so wrong, Daddy? Look at Juliet. Everything's gone right for her, and yet she behaved so *badly*. And everything has gone so wrong for me. I feel trapped. Two children. No money. And a hopeless husband. I don't even love him any more. I wonder now if I ever did . . .'

210

'Life's a lucky dip in some ways, sweetheart. You'll find that eventually everything resolves itself, though.'

'I don't see how it can. I'm so *tired*, Daddy. All the time.'

'Why don't you leave Sophia and Jonathan with Nanny, and take yourself off for a few days? I'll stand you a nice hotel, where you can enjoy a bit of luxury.'

It was more than she could bear; his kindness, his sympathetic understanding. Tears streamed down her face.

'I – I don't want to leave the children,' she sobbed. 'I can't bear to be without them. They're a-all I've got.'

There was no point, Henry reflected, in discussing with Liza what should be done about Rosie. As long as there was no public loss of face, as long as everyone pretended Rosie and Charles were happy, Liza was unlikely to want to get involved, because she didn't like to think about unpleasant things.

Awestruck, Louise stood beside her cousin on the quayside, gazing up at the massive grey stone ramparts and battlements.

'Is this where we're staying, Aunt Candida?'

'Good gracious, no,' Candida boomed, standing, feet planted wide, surrounded by several suitcases. 'This is St Malo. It's a fortress town; we'll go round it in a few days. Now, where's a porter? We need to get this lot into a taxi.'

Louise continued to gaze around her, entranced. There was hustle and bustle everywhere. Market women in stiff white lace Breton caps were selling fruit and vegetables, while fishermen pushed their catch on long narrow wheelbarrows. The smell of fish, garlic and French tobacco hung in the atmosphere like a tangible veil. Shrill voices drowned each other out. Droves of tourists, tottering down the gangplank of the Isle of Thanet, found themselves instantly immersed in a bygone medieval age.

'Where are we staying, Mummy?' Marina asked, a touch of anxiety in her voice. Tall, very thin and sallow-looking, and still recovering from her illness, she was already exhausted by the crossing.

'Ah! Here we are. Come along, girls. At the double,' Candida exclaimed robustly, as a porter heaved their luggage on to his cart. 'Jolly good show,' she told him. He stank of cognac and sweat. *Un taxi-auto* was found, and he tossed their cases on to the roof rack.

211

Candida heaved herself in first, her wide girth in a pink dress reminding Louise of a squashy marshmallow. Marina and Louise squeezed in on either side of her.

She shouted at the driver as if she feared he was deaf.

'*Rue des Ecoles, Paramé, s'il vous plait. L'Hotel Château Forêt.*'

Grinding the gears, he started the vehicle, which spluttered and shuddered its way out of the old fortified city, heading north.

Suddenly Marina gave a piercing scream. 'Look!' she gasped.

A train, with two carriages behind, came chugging along the middle of the road.

Louise's heart flipped with fear. It was heading straight for them. At that moment, the taxi swerved to the right, the train trundled past them, and they continued along the tree-lined boulevard, as if nothing had happened.

'Oh, my goodness . . . !' gasped Marina, shaken. 'I thought we were all going to be killed.'

'Nonsense!' retorted Candida. 'Those trains run at regular intervals. They're like our trams.'

'Is it far?' Louise asked. The sea was on their left now, and they could see a golden sandy beach.

'I don't think so. The reason I chose this hotel is because your grandfather recommended it to me, years ago. He said I should bring Marina and Sebastian here for a holiday. I gather the food is first-rate,' Candida told them cheerfully.

Ten minutes later they arrived on the outskirts of Paramé, a small seaside town where rows of shuttered houses, sleepy-eyed in the warm afternoon sun, stood slumbering in the shade of tall lime trees. They saw a sign saying Rue des Ecoles, and at that moment the taxi rattled to a halt, causing them to lurch forward in their seats.

Candida looked puzzled. 'We want L'Hotel Châ—' she began and then she stopped. They could see the figure of an old man watering a dusty bed of geraniums in a neglected and derelict garden. Tired palm trees and a gravel path surrounded a patch of sun-bleached lawn. At the far end stood a villa with peeling paint and broken shutters. The place had the desolate air of having been abandoned several years ago.

'Is this right?' Louise asked, doubtfully.

'*Je vais à Château Forêt* . . .' Candida told the driver, as if it was all his fault.

The driver spat out of the window on to the road, and pointed to a broken sign hanging at an angle on the ten-foot-high, rusting wrought-iron gate.

'Mummy, it *is* the Château Forêt,' Marina said, appalled.

Candida swiftly recovered her poise. 'Well, it's certainly not what I expected, but you can never tell a book by its cover,' she remarked undaunted. 'Never mind. Come along, girls. Chop-chop! If we want a swim before dinner, we'd better get on with it.'

An aroma of linseed oil and onions hung over the vestibule, which was deserted. Candida, spying a brass bell on the desk, gave it a hearty thump with her fist.

Marina looked pained. Louise got a fit of the giggles. This was *much* more fun than the occasional holiday she'd had with her parents, where they checked into very smart hotels with people bowing and scraping around them.

At that moment, a short, rotund figure, encased in shining black cloth, emerged from the nether regions. She had grey hair and her only jewellery was a wide gold wedding ring which dug into her plump fingers.

Candida stared at her, and the elderly woman stared back. 'I know your face . . .' Candida said uncertainly. 'We've met before, haven't we?'

The woman smiled. 'Yes, we have met, Madame.' Her English was fluent. 'You were with your father, Madame, walking down Pall Mall, in London. I used to know your father in the old days, and he very kindly invited me to join you for luncheon. Do you remember? We went to Wheeler's.'

For a moment Candida was taken aback by this torrent of information. 'Goodness, you *do* have a good memory! It must have been . . .'

'It was fifteen years ago, *exactement*, Madame.'

'Was it really?' Then Candida remembered. They'd met this woman in the street and she'd been so annoyed at her father inviting her to join them, when she'd been looking forward to having him to herself for a couple of hours. They'd been forced to keep the conversation general, of course, and then he'd had to rush back to Hartley, so they'd never had their lunch *à deux*, because he'd died not long afterwards.

213

'Well, I never ... ! So this is *your* hotel?' Candida said, forcing the remembered resentment to the back of her mind. 'Forgive me, but can you tell me your name?'

The rosy-faced woman smiled. How typically English Candida was; so like her late father. 'I don't think I told you my name in the first place,' she said merrily. 'I'm Margaux St Jean Brevelay.'

'I suppose you met my father during the Great War; were you in England then?'

There was a fractional pause before Margaux replied. 'A little before the war,' she said quietly. 'Now, if you would like to register, Madame?' She placed a form on the counter, and Candida noticed her hands were as rough and worn as a servant, with broken nails and reddened skin.

Margaux saw her looking. '*Voilà, Madame*. I hope you will find the rooms to your satisfaction. You must ask for anything you need.' She began counting on her fingers. 'I have a staff of ten. There are two scullery maids, a chambermaid, an odd-job man who also tends the garden –' she rolled her eyes despairingly towards the moth-eaten lawn – 'and I am the other six!' she chortled, her vast bosom heaving, her arms gesticulating wildly. '*Alors!* I hope your stay will be happy.'

'Fancy her knowing Grandpa,' Louise remarked, when they'd been shown to their clean if shabby rooms on the first floor, with balconies overlooking the beach and the sea. Candida had been given a room with a double bed, and in the next room there were twin beds for the girls.

Candida agreed. 'That must be why he recommeded this place to me. It's sad you and Marina never knew him.'

Louise nodded. 'I almost feel as if I knew him, because Granny often talks about him, and she has lots of photographs of him in her sitting room.'

'Do you think Madame Brevelay really does most of the work here?' Marina asked, bemused. 'Or was she teasing?'

'I don't think she was teasing,' Candida replied. 'From the looks of this place she's penniless, but it is nice and relaxing; better than some chichi modern hotel.'

Louise thought of her mother, and nodded sagely. Mummy would have had a blue fit if she had to stay here, she reckoned, and that made it all the more fun.

'Let's grab our bathing things and go for a swim, while there's still some heat in the sun,' Candida suggested in a brisk manner, which Louise quite liked.

Between the château and the beach there was a dusty coastal road, along which a few cyclists were pedalling lazily. A rusting Citroën shuddered past, honking its horn, going in the direction of St Malo.

Crossing the road, they walked on to the beach, where the sand was so perfectly rippled it looked as if it had been done by a machine. The only sounds were the swishing of the ever-tumbling waves and the cries of the seagulls as they swooped fitfully above the water's edge.

'Come on, girls,' said Candida. 'Last one in the sea's a ninny.'

'You can't be away for the twelfth!' Cameron exclaimed hotly. 'It's the biggest day of the year at Glenmally. You've got to be here, Juliet.'

'Don't you think I've practically got the twelfth *tattooed* all over my body, to remind me of your bloody shoot?' Juliet retorted angrily. 'Only, this year things are going to be different. I let you and your mother organize it all last time, while I found my feet. But I do happen to be your wife, and this does happen to be my house, not your mother's, and in future things are going to be done my way.'

Cameron looked at her nervously. This was a new Juliet, and he wasn't sure how to cope with her.

'But Mother has always made all the arrangements,' he said fretfully.

Juliet's smile was razor sharp. 'That was before you were married, Cameron. Don't worry, I'll make sure all your shooting cronies are invited, but they will be diluted by some amusing friends of mine, so the topic of conversation at dinner won't only be about how many brace you've bagged. We'll have music, and dancing too, in the evenings, and for those who don't want to follow the guns, such as myself, there will be alternative entertainment.'

'I don't want all the usual arrangements messed up,' he complained. 'The shooting season is so important up here.'

'Which one?' She raised her eyebrows and glared at him.

'Last year's shooting season? Or the little impromptu one in May? Which landed you in hospital.'

Cameron flushed an ugly shade of red. 'That was an *accident*,' he said furiously. 'And keep your voice down. I do not want to talk about it.'

'So I've noticed. I wonder why? You might have been killed. Nevertheless, the greatest crime seemed to be that someone was shooting before the twelfth!' She shook her head in mock scolding. 'Terrible *faux pas*, Cameron. Unforgivable. What would the rest of the country say, if they knew? How would we have explained your unexpected demise?' She tut-tutted mockingly.

'It was an unfortunate incident,' he replied haughtily, trying to look dignified in spite of his obvious discomfort. 'Nothing more. It won't happen again. The subject is closed. I merely wanted to ascertain that *you'll* be up here on the twelfth.'

'You assume correctly,' she said grandly. 'I've come to realize one thing, though.' Was it fear she suddenly saw flash in his eyes? She couldn't be sure.

'I hate blood sports,' she continued. 'Beautiful creatures flying through the air one minute, then brought crashing down the next. For what purpose? It's just for the fun of killing and I can't bear it.'

He gave a quick nervous smile, seemed relieved. 'You were brought up in a town. That's why ...'

'I was also brought up at Hartley,' she retorted, walking out of the library, closing the door noisily behind her, and then going into the garden for a breath of fresh air.

It was time, she reflected, that she asserted herself. If she'd taken on the role of being a duchess, she might as well start behaving like one, at least at Glenmally. She'd been so wrapped up in Daniel, thinking only of him in the past few months, that she hadn't cared what Cameron did, as long as she was allowed her trips to London.

That had changed, after dinner the previous evening.

Cameron and his mother had chatted to each other throughout the soup, the Angus beef steaks, and the chocolate soufflé, as if she hadn't been there.

They took a veritable trip up Memory Lane: 'Remember your first birthday party, and you wore the kilt ... ? Wasn't that exciting, the day you caught that ten-pound salmon . . . ? We must have a big Christmas tree this year. Remember the time the candles caught fire . . . ?' And on and on it went, as Juliet sat, drinking Burgundy, while they ignored her.

She hadn't said anything at first, but a growing rage was welling up inside her as she listened to their reminiscing. Cameron and Iona's cloying devotion to each other was some- how sickening, their conversation intimate, their secret smiles and shared laughter almost disgusting. They were like old lovers, sharing tender memories.

At last she could bear it no longer. Taking another swig of wine, Juliet thumped her glass heavily on the polished table, and glared at them.

'I don't know why you didn't marry your mother, Cameron,' she said bitterly. 'However, you do happen to have a wife, or perhaps you'd forgotten? Perhaps you'd rather remain a mummy's boy for the rest of your life? You and Mummy seem so devoted to each other, I'm beginning to feel rather *de trop*.'

Her hand, with its long scarlet nails and emerald and diamond engagement ring, was pressed to her chest, as if protecting her wounded heart, but her aquamarine eyes were flashing dangerously. 'If you continue to ignore me, I just might go to London one day – and not bother to return to this hotbed of incestuousness.'

Cameron sprang to his feet, face crimson with rage. He was shaking all over. 'How dare you! Apologize to my mother at once!' he shouted.

'The girl's drunk,' Iona pointed out in a cold hard voice. 'Go to bed, Juliet,' she commanded loudly. 'You're drunk and talking nonsense.'

'I am not talking nonsense. I'm sick to death of being ignored in my own house.'

'The trouble is, you haven't had a child,' Cameron said accusingly. 'That would give you something else to think about.'

'And whose fault is that?' Juliet turned to Cameron, who was still standing, looking as if he'd been winded. 'If you spent more time in my bed, and less on your estate, I might actually *get* pregnant!'

* * *

217

Nanny's mouth was as tight as a drawstring purse. 'Louise should never have been allowed to go,' she fumed, with self-righteous disapproval. 'I don't know what they were thinking of. France indeed! It's asking for trouble.'

Ruby smoothed her starched apron nervously. Nanny in a rage was not a pretty sight. 'I thought Louise was in Brittany?' she ventured.

'Brittany! France! It's all the same. Haven't you seen the newsreels at the Odeon? Or listened to the wireless? The war's going to start at any *moment*. London will be flattened by bombs in no time at all. Me? I can't wait to get to Surrey. Not that we'll be safe there. Mark my words, Ruby, the Germans will be invading England by the end of the year. Landing on the white cliffs of Dover and all.' Nanny thumped her fist on the nursery table, where they sat, having their elevenses. The cups and saucers rattled in sympathy.

Ruby had turned pale. 'What will happen to Louise?'

Nanny snorted. 'Most likely be made a prisoner of war, poor little thing. It was irresponsible of her parents to have let her go. Mind you, I'm surprised at Mrs Montgomery taking Marina. A sensible woman like her should know better.'

'We'll be off to Hartley Hall soon, won't we?' Ruby said, hoping to soothe Nanny.

'Where are we now? July twenty-seventh. Yes, we'll be off by the first. Can't be in London in August, whatever happens. Think yourself lucky you work for a rich, posh family, Ruby,' Nanny remarked severely.

'Yes, Nanny.'

'My father was right about one thing,' Candida said at supper one evening. 'The food here is excellent. I think we should stay another week, don't you?' She tucked into her plate of grilled sea bass, having demolished a first course of chicken-liver paté with crusty bread.

Her waist had expanded alarmingly during the past ten days, but she didn't care. The days here were too perfect to be spoilt by something as stupid as not being able to do up her skirts.

It was mid-August, and it was warm and sunny, with just a gentle breeze coming off the sea. They had the beach to

218

themselves, and the château was empty except for a young couple with their baby.

In the evenings, Marina and Louise went to the deserted lounge to play games of Halma, Monopoly or *vingt-et-un*, while Margaux invited Candida into her private quarters, to share a bottle of wine; the remains of a once superb cellar.

Alone in the faded plush and worn rococo gilt plasterwork of the *petit salon*, the two women began to talk, because there was no one else with whom they could have an adult conversation.

They could not be overheard, either, and soon the wine stripped them of their natural polite reticence, and Candida, never a snob, insisted that they call each other by their first names.

'Did you know my father had died thirteen years ago?' she asked Margaux, who was opening a bottle of Veuve Clicquot, saying she thought they deserved a little treat.

'I read about it in the newspapers,' Margaux replied. 'Your mother must have missed him very much. Is she still alive?'

Candida laughed. 'Alive and kicking! She's still living at Hartley, on Henry's insistence.'

'You too are a widow? Do you miss having a man in your life?' Margaux settled her bolster-shaped body on the *chaise longue* and she put up her swollen feet, which bulged between the buttoned straps of her black shoes.

Candida nodded, glass in hand. 'Not that I was ever the clinging, needy type,' she retorted robustly. 'Mark was a great chap. We were chums. Never went in for all that romantic rubbish. Bit of a blow when he died. Stroke. First time he'd had a day's illness in his life.'

'You were left with your son and daughter to bring up? That's never easy on your own.'

'Have 'em, love 'em, and leave 'em be. That's my motto. They've been very good. Sebastian has a great seat on a horse. Goes like the clappers. Marina is more artistic.' Candida guffawed. 'God knows where she gets that from.'

'Children can be a great comfort.' Margaux's voice took on a dreamy quality. She reached for the bottle on the table beside her, and topped up their glasses.

'You've got children?' Candida asked. 'What . . . boys? Girls?'

'A son.'

'And what does he do?'

'He's a writer. He lives in Amiens. He was brought up by my mother.' She shrugged with continental exaggeration. 'Now he is a man of forty. He has no family. He lives on his own.'

'Do you see much of him?'

Again the shrug. 'He blames me for a lot of things. Including handing him over to my mother when he was a baby.'

Margaux's voice had dropped to a pained whisper. She emptied her glass, and poured herself another drink.

'Were you working?'

'I was not married at the time.'

'Ah . . .' Candida drew out the word. 'But later . . . surely his father wanted to have him with you . . .'

'The man I eventually married was not Gaston's father.'

'I see.' Candida digested this interesting fact. 'Jolly bad luck for you, getting preggers out of wedlock,' she said, more stoutly than she'd meant. 'I was lucky, myself,' she confessed, after her drink had been topped up. 'I had quite a few flings before I met Mark, but I never got caught.' She leaned forward, confidentially, enjoying this woman-to-woman talk. 'Thank God for a small sponge on a string, dipped in vinegar!' she chortled.

Then she leaned back and asked briskly, 'So, what happened to, um . . . erm . . . Gaston's father?'

Margaux's face turned a deep shade of red, and she looked down into her wine glass. 'I do not think you want to know that,' she said quietly.

'Oh, come on,' Candida urged. 'You might as well tell me the whole story now.'

'It might upset you.'

'Upset *me*? Why, for God's sake . . . ?'

Margaux raised her face, and looked steadily into Candida's frank blue eyes. 'I suppose we are all getting old. It does not seem to matter so much now. At the time it was a calamity.'

Candida frowned. Something flashed through her mind, a recollection of how her father had insisted Margaux join them for lunch that day. The look in his eyes when he'd smiled and raised his glass to drink her health.

'*Oui*,' Margaux said softly, seeing from Candida's expression that she'd guessed. 'Your father was my lover. Just for one brief *magnifique* summer, in 1909.'

'1909?' Candida repeated. 'I'd have been twenty-two at the time. Intent on travelling to far-off places . . . the war put a stop to all that, of course. I didn't meet Mark until I was thirty. So you and my father had an affair? How extraordinary.'

'Gaston was born in 1910,' Margaux continued as if Candida hadn't spoken. 'I was teaching French at a girls' school in Guildford when I met your father.'

That fitted, Candida reflected. Aloud she said, 'Our home, Hartley Hall, is near Guildford.' How had she not been aware what was going on? Too wrapped up in her own life to notice, she supposed.

'I know,' replied Margaux. 'I was never inside, but I saw it from the road. A very beautiful old house. How I wished at the time it was mine.' She sighed and then rubbed her forehead distractedly.

'Did my mother know about you?'

'*Mais non!* When I told your father I was expecting a baby, he was terrified your mother would find out. That would have been a tragedy. I was desperate to go home to my mother. Your father wanted to give me money for my fare home, and for the baby, but I was proud. We'd manage without the Granville money. And we did for a while. Then my father died. We could no longer manage. That was when your father bought this place for me to run as a hotel. He said it would secure both Gaston's and my future . . .' She shrugged. 'And it did, for a while. I married the chef I'd hired, and we were a good partnership until he died six years ago. But business has been very bad this year because of the threat of war.' Then her face softened as she looked at Candida, and her tone changed. 'Your father was a true gentleman, you know. An aristocrat.'

And a very dark horse too, Candida thought, feeling a great sense of disillusion. She'd always thought her parents' marriage had been perfect, her father's behaviour beyond reproach.

'Well,' she said at last, finding the facts hard to accept, 'I have a half-brother, then.'

'He is a nice man. A very talented writer,' Margaux said quietly.

Candida wondered what Henry would say if he knew? He wouldn't like it. He'd huff and puff, and say let's not talk about it; it's water under the bridge, and should be swept under the carpet, and every other cliché he could think of.

Margaux continued: 'I was surprised when your father invited me to join you for lunch that day, but I was pleased too.'

'You never talked about . . . anything, of course.'

'We did talk,' Margaux replied, 'when you went to powder your nose.' She smiled at the memory. 'Just a quick word, you know. I told him Gaston was all right. I also told him my husband had accepted Gaston as his son and was good to him.'

It crossed Candida's mind to suggest that surely Gaston should be helping his mother run this place now, but with unusual forbearance, she refrained.

'You have no other children?' she asked instead.

'*Non*. Just Gaston.' Fleetingly her eyes brimmed with tears.

'I'm so sorry. I had no idea. You've had a tough time.'

Once more the shrug. 'Life is difficult at the moment. No one comes here any more.'

'Except for us. No one's going to let the bloody Nazis stop us from going on holiday,' Candida retorted.

Margaux gave a wistful smile. 'You are so much like your father. So strong. So stubborn.'

'What are you going to do if there is a war?'

'I cannot afford to stay here, but I cannot afford to leave, either. Anyway, this is Gaston's inheritance. Perhaps they'll use it as an army billet.' She gave a dry laugh and topped up her drink again.

'Come on, Louise. It's your go,' Marina said impatiently.

'Sorry.' Louise rattled the dice and got two sixes.

'Go on, then. Move your boot.'

Louise was finding it hard to concentrate, and she'd lost her interest in this stupid game of Monopoly. She hadn't meant to eavesdrop, knew it was wrong, but on her way back from the loo next to the lobby, she'd heard most of what Aunt Candida and Madame Brevelay had been saying, as they sat in the *petit salon*.

To think that Grandpa had had a secret son shocked Louise to the core. What would Granny do, if she ever found out? How would her father feel if he knew he had a half-brother? Even more importantly, how was she going to act naturally in front of her aunt without this new terrible knowledge showing in her face?

'Are you going to play this game or not?' Marina asked impatiently. 'Shall we have a game of *vingt-et-un* instead?'

'If you like.'

While Louise shuffled the playing cards, Marina put the board game back in its box. 'What's the matter?' she asked suddenly, looking at her cousin.

Louise started. 'Nothing,' she said hastily. 'I think I've got a bit of a headache coming on.'

'You've either got a headache or you haven't.'

'Yes. Well, I have.' Was she going to have to keep this terrible secret to herself for the rest of her life?

'I think I'll go to bed,' she said, desperate to be alone so she could think things over.

'Shall I ask Mummy to give you an aspirin?' Marina said more gently, seeing how pale Louise looked.

'No, don't disturb her. I'm sure I'll feel better when I lie down.'

Louise slept fitfully. The next morning she looked washed out.

'Are you all right?' Candida asked, watching her niece toy uninterestedly with her breakfast.

'I'm fine, thank you. Aunt Candida, when are we going home?'

Candida stared at her in astonishment. 'Home? But it's so lovely here. I thought you were enjoying yourself.'

Louise spoke quickly. 'Oh, I am.'

'Good. I'm glad to hear it, because I've said we'll stay for another week. The weather's wonderful, and Marina is getting stronger by the day. More orange juice, Louise?'

'No thank you. So, there's not going to be a war?' she asked, brightening.

Candida shook her head. 'I don't know about that, but it certainly isn't going to happen for ages. We're quite safe here. Margaux listens to the wireless every day. If there's the slightest sign of trouble, she'll let us know.'

Privately, Louise thought that Madame Brevelay had probably persuaded her aunt to stay on because she needed the money.

The Glorious Twelfth had come and gone, and Liza had been thrilled by the splendour and hospitality provided by Juliet and

223

Cameron. They had arranged a perfectly balanced house party, with a mixture of his friends and hers, and Liza was filled with pride at how brilliantly her daughter had organized everything.

Not that she liked blood sports any more than Juliet, but she relished the aristocratic way of life, and pretended that following the guns was 'great fun, darling'.

Each morning the sight of the ghillies and beaters, standing in the drive surrounded by the gamekeeper's gun dogs (not to be confused with the eight pet dogs, who, being gun-shy, stayed indoors) made Liza's heart swell with satisfaction at how well Juliet had achieved her own ambitions.

Back in London, Liza started to plan several dinner parties for the coming months. It was good to be on home ground again, though. This was where she felt most confident, in control of her life and her household.

That evening, Henry returned from the city, distraught.

'Would you believe it?' he exclaimed incredulously. 'Candida insists on staying another week in Brittany. She said everything's very quiet, and the proprietress of their hotel is listening to the radio, and will tell them if anything happens! Have you ever heard such madness? I've a good mind to go over there and fetch them back myself.'

'Darling, I'm sure they'll be all right,' Liza replied mildly. 'Candida is sensible if nothing else. Why are you so worried?'

Henry threw her a despairing look. What was the point of having this argument again? He strode over to the drinks tray, and poured himself a neat whisky. He'd been keeping in touch with Ian Cavendish. In spite of warnings from the Prime Minister, the Germans were on the brink of invading Poland. If that happened, Britain would have no alternative but to declare war on the Third Reich.

'It's very nearly September,' Liza said soothingly. 'Then Candida will *have* to bring the girls back, because of school.'

It was, in fact, now August the twenty-ninth. 'If they're not back by the thirty-first,' Henry said heavily, 'I'm going over to fetch them.'

Lady Anne was worried too. What on earth was inducing Candida to stay on in Brittany, under the circumstances? The

224

situation was becoming dangerous. She phoned Henry at the bank, to express her concern.

'You should shut up the house and come down here, Henry,' she said. 'Thank God the rest of the girls are down here, but you and Liza are in danger. Everyone is saying the Germans will start bombing London the moment war is declared.' Her voice, usually so controlled, wobbled with emotion.

'I know, Mother. I know.' Henry felt dazed by the rapid escalations of his worst fears. 'But Candida is absolutely refusing to take the situation seriously. So is Liza! I'm at the end of my tether.'

'Henry dear, you're being too soft with Liza. Shut up Green Street, bring all the servants with you – we'll fit them in somehow; some can sleep in the flat above the coach house – and you can commute to the bank every day, for the time being.'

'You're right, Mother.'

When Henry told Liza of his decision, she exploded with chagrin.

'How can we possibly shut up the house, Henry? We've got people coming to drinks on Monday and we're giving several dinner parties during the next two weeks. It's impossible for us to go to Hartley at the moment.'

'Cancel everything, Liza,' he said angrily, ignoring her protestations. 'I'm going to tell Parsons to start packing up the house. Miss Ashley can pack up our clothes, and I'll arrange for the silver and your jewellery to be put in the bank vault.'

'Stop being such an alarmist!' she retorted, shrilly. 'We're *not* going to run away, like rats deserting a ship; why should we? We'll look complete fools if nothing happens, and worse than that, cowards.'

'I'm not having an argument about this,' he said with unaccustomed force. It was the first time he'd stood up to Liza in all their married life, and he felt slightly light-headed with shock. 'We'll all leave for Hartley tomorrow afternoon. Is that clear?'

Sobbing, her hand covering her mouth, Liza fled the drawing room, hurrying up to her bedroom and slamming the door behind her. Her beautiful, comfortable, lovely, *lovely* life that she'd worked so hard to achieve, was in *ruins*. She'd miss London terribly. She'd miss her friends, she'd miss the delightful social events, around which her whole life had revolved

225

for the past twenty-three years. What the *hell* was she going to do with herself, buried in the country? Not being able to have her hair done several times a week by Mr Reek? Her facials at Elizabeth Arden? Her manicures? Her pedicures? Turkish baths at the Dorchester? Lunch at the Ritz? A little shopping at Asprey's?

Everything she loved about her life was being forcibly wrenched from her, and she lay on her bed, crying her heart out for the losses that lay ahead.

During the last days of August, the sun had grown paler and the sea colder. Candida and the girls still went for their morning swim, but the chill in the air marked the end of a glorious summer.

Sated by good food and fine wine, Candida had become lulled by a false sense of security. Every time she thought she ought to take Marina and Louise back to England, another beautiful day dawned, and she couldn't resist telling the girls, 'We'll stay for another couple of days, shall we?'

She dismissed Henry as a 'fuddy-duddy' whenever he phoned to demand she return to England.

Of the three of them, only Louise was beginning to feel anxious. By now she had a strong, gut-wrenching presentiment that something awful was about to happen. They were now the only people staying in the hotel. Paramé was deserted. It was Margaux who was pressing Candida to stay.

'There's nothing to worry about,' Margaux told them airily. 'I listen to the radio several times a day. There is no news of an imminent war.'

Louise was waiting for Marina in the hotel lobby, when she heard voices coming from the kitchen.

Margaux was loud in her welcome to someone who seemed to have arrived by the rear entrance. Louise didn't know much French, but she could pick out certain words, and Margaux's tone of delight. Almost of relief, as if she'd been waiting for her visitor for some time.

Marina came running down the stairs at that moment, followed by her mother. 'Come on. We're off to the beach,' she said.

At that moment, Margaux rushed into the lobby. She

226

sounded agitated. 'Candida, you must depart this minute! I have just heard the last passenger steamer for England is leaving St Malo in one hour. You haven't a moment to lose!'

'The *last* passenger boat?' Candida queried, her face flushed with anger and distress. 'How do you know? This can't have happened so suddenly. There must have been an indication there was an emergency. Why didn't you tell us before?'

Margaux was also red in the face but it was a look of guilt that filled her eyes. She shrugged. '*Alors!* I did my best to find out what was happening,' she argued. 'It seems we may be at war within hours.'

At that moment a tall man, who looked exactly like Henry, emerged from the darkness of the old kitchen. He was roughly dressed, unkempt, and with dark stubble and unruly hair.

Candida drew in her breath sharply, and Louise knew exactly who he was.

'This is Gaston,' Margaux said in a low voice. 'He's just arrived from Amiens. I beg you to take him to England with you, Candida. He has his passport and enough money until he finds work, but if he stays . . .' She drew a shuddering breath and the tears streamed down her face. 'If he is with you and the girls, he'll be allowed into the country. You can tell them . . . You know.'

Stunned, Candida stared at her half-brother, and felt great anger and resentment. 'This is an imposition,' she said coldly, realizing Margaux had been persuading her to stay on for her own ends. Now, not only were they lumbered with him, they were all in danger of being stranded in Brittany.

'Please, Candida. Do this for me, for . . .' Margaux begged, her cheeks awash. 'I am an old woman and I must stay to look after this place, but he will be made a prisoner of war . . .' She broke down, sobbing now, her fat fingers covering her face.

'You have put us in danger by not warning me sooner,' Candida exploded. She glanced at Gaston, who was regarding her with narrowed eyes. 'What happens when we get to England? He can't stay with me.'

Margaux looked stricken. 'For the love of God, just take him with you, where he will be safe. He is a young man. He will find work. And somewhere to live.'

Gaston put his arm around her shoulders, whispering something in her ear. She straightened up, her expression fearful.

'*Mon Dieu*! You must hurry or you'll miss the boat. Already, Gaston says, there are many people trying to get on board.'

'What a pity you didn't think of that a week ago,' Candida retorted icily, angry with herself for being such a fool as to prolong their departure.

Then she turned to Marina and Louise. 'Go and pack now. This moment,' she ordered. 'Just grab what you can. I'll be up in a sec.'

As Louise and Marina tore up the stairs, taking them two at a time, Candida turned to Margaux, ignoring Gaston. 'Please order us a taxi.'

'This is the end of everything,' Margaux sobbed, ignoring her request. 'I'm losing my son, my livelihood and soon my country.'

'A *taxi*, Margaux!' Candida ordered, fiercely. Then she too hurried up to pack.

Clothes and shoes and games were thrown into cases, with books and damp, sandy towels. She couldn't stop Gaston tagging along, but she did not intend to be responsible for him when they arrived in England.

Ten minutes later they were all back in the lobby, dragging their cases behind them.

'Well?' demanded Candida.

Margaux flung up her fat arms in distress. 'There are no taxis. Word has got out the boat is leaving and everyone is heading for St Malo. Even my people! What can we do?' she wailed.

Louise spoke, her voice surprising for its steadiness. 'Couldn't we take the tram that runs down the middle of the road? Or the bus? We've gone to St Malo before by bus.'

Gaston, who had so far remained silent, spoke. His English was not as good as his mother's, and he had a bad accent. 'I saw a bus go. It 'as left. There is no bus again, for thirty minutes.'

His complacency infuriated Candida. It was obvious now that Margaux had known of the emergency, but had kept them here until the arrival of her beloved son.

'For God's sake, don't just stand there!' she snapped at him. 'Someone must have a car?'

Margaux's expression changed, as if she'd just thought of something. 'Wait!' She turned to rush back into the kitchen.

'Waiting is a luxury we don't have,' Candida shouted at her

228

retreating back. Then she swung on Gaston. 'How did *you* get here?'

'I came from Amiens, on my bicycle.'

Candida stared at him, recognizing with shock her own grey eyes and, even more disturbing, Henry's hands, resting on the reception desk.

'Dear God!' she muttered, turning away, confused and shaken. Margaux came rushing back. 'You are saved! The baker will take you all in his van. He will be here in two minutes.'

Candida sprang into action. 'Marina, Juliet, let's get our luggage into the road, so there'll be no more delays.' As she spoke, she dumped a bundle of French notes on to the reception desk. 'I think this will cover our hotel bill,' she said curtly.

'*Merci*,' said Margaux, knowing they'd never see each other again, and knowing she wouldn't be able to renew their new-found friendship, even if they did.

As they stood waiting by the roadside, Margaux embraced her son, pushing him towards the others, but clinging to him at the same time, as if she couldn't bear to let him go.

Watching them, Louise felt a lump in her throat, and scalding tears pricked her eyes.

'*Au revoir, maman*,' Gaston murmured, patting her shoulder, his face grave.

At that moment the little white van swung into view and stopped abruptly by the curb with a screech of brakes.

'Quickly, throw your cases in first,' Candida ordered the girls. A minute later they'd jumped into the van, sitting on their cases or on the floor, all of them covered with white flour from the dusty interior.

'Quick as you can,' Candida urged the bemused driver. 'There'll be a good tip for you if you get us there before the boat leaves.'

As the van rattled and jiggled along the tree-lined boulevards, Louise and Marina got the giggles, which soon became unstoppable, almost hysterical, because it was such a relief to be on their way. Gaston watched them with an amused expression.

Candida looked morose. She'd blamed Margaux for their predicament, and now she regretted it. It was her fault. Her sanguinity had placed them in danger, not only Marina but her niece too. Henry had told her repeatedly to return to England, and she'd called him a fusspot.

Then she looked at Gaston. It was a damned nuisance having him come with them, but at least an extra pair of strong arms wouldn't come amiss with the luggage. Though what she was going to do with him when they reached Southampton she had no idea.

Nine

'There's no answer,' Henry groaned, replacing the receiver. 'There must be *someone* at the Château Forêt?'

It was September 1st, and there'd been no word from Candida for the past two days.

'There's nothing more you can do, Henry,' Lady Anne reasoned. 'If there's no answer, then they can no longer be there.'

'God, I wish Candida wasn't so obstinate. Where the hell are they?'

'We'd have heard if anything had happened to them, my dear. Try not to worry.'

Henry's face was drawn. 'The worst part is not knowing; I feel so bloody helpless, and Liza is driving me mad because she *still* believes there won't be a war. If only she read the newspapers! Or saw one of the leaflets that have been distributed, telling us what to do in an emergency when it starts.' He sighed deeply, filled with anguish, so that his voice croaked. 'Did you read in the newspapers that seven thousand dogs and five thousand cats have been put down in London in the past week, to prevent them suffering when the bombing starts? And that thousands of children have already been evacuated to the country?'

Lady Anne looked anxiously at her son, and spoke briskly.

'Well, we don't need *both* you and Liza panicking, for goodness' sake! Amanda and Charlotte are too young to be told the full horror of what's happening, which I know only too well, seeing I've lived through both the Boer War and the Great War,' she added drily.

Henry couldn't help looking at her with admiration. She sat upright, her hands folded in her lap, looking serene, determined not to be ruffled by the likes of Hitler.

'You're right, Mother. But God knows what the future holds, and I can't help worrying about the girls.' He went and stood in the window, looking out at the two younger sisters. They were playing on the lawn, Charlotte with her new hoop, and Amanda trying to master a yo-yo. They looked as if they hadn't a care in the world, and at their age, that was rightly so.

Henry just wanted to have Louise safely back now, and until that happened he couldn't rest.

St Malo's dockside was swarming with people, frantically trying to board the already crowded *Dinard*.

'*Vite! Vite!*' yelled Nico, the baker, as he and Gaston grabbed the heavy cases. Candida, Marina and Louise stayed close behind, scared of becoming separated.

The two men pushed and shouldered their way with brutal force through the clamouring mob. The atmosphere was panicky. People with large trunks were blocking the way as they tried to get nearer the ship, and others were yelling at them to move out of the way.

'Do you think we'll ever get on board?' Louise shouted above the din. Her face was white. She had visions of being stuck here for ever.

Candida bellowed urgently to Nico, 'I have some money . . . *argent.*' He nodded in understanding. Bribery was the only way they were going to get on board.

People were shouting frantically, calling out the names of relatives and friends as they were pushed aside by new arrivals. Men lifted small children on to their shoulders to prevent them getting lost or crushed. A baby started screaming. Louise saw the panicked faces around her, and thought how ugly human beings looked when they were frightened.

Bemused fishermen with weathered faces stood and watched from a distance, their expressions implacable. Their country was under threat. But unlike all these tourists, they had no option but to stay and face the consequences.

231

At last they reached the bottom of the gangplank. Candida handed Nico a wad of French notes. He started speaking, loudly and quickly, to the ship's steward, indicating the money in his hand. It didn't do the trick.

A violent argument followed, with the steward insisting they go to the back of the queue. Nico upped the pitch of his voice. Those who were also trying to board started shouting in protest, waving their fists, trying to push Candida and the girls out of the way.

'Who the hell do you think you are?' shouted an angry English male voice. This was taken up by other English tourists, who burst into a furious chorus of 'Wait your turn!' and 'Get to the back of the queue!' Others were less polite, as French, Belgians and Americans joined in, and it began to turn into something closely resembling a lynch mob.

'Oh, my ribs . . . my ribs are being squashed . . . !' Louise wailed, frightened, as the crowds pressed closer. 'Help me . . . !'

At that moment, Nico accidentally trod heavily on Marina's foot, and she screamed, her piercing cries of agony rending the air and making the ship's steward wince.

'OK,' he muttered tersely, grabbing the money. A minute later they were hurrying up the gangplank to safety.

Eight hours later, lying on deck and wrapped in an assortment of picnic rugs, beach towels and woollen cardigans, Louise and Marina lay huddled together, trying to keep warm. Candida had managed to secure a deckchair after a confrontation with a Frenchwoman who had also tried to grab it, while Gaston roamed the ship, talking to people and smoking incessantly.

Juliet lay looking up into the thick fog that had descended over the Channel. Through the haze she could see the ship's red and black funnel, which towered mistily over them. The *Dinard* was edging slowly and cautiously forward as visibility was down to a few hundred yards, and the foghorn was booming with monotonous regularity.

Echoing horns from other ships sounded through the swirling blackness, warning of their presence, calling eerily to each other like primeval beasts in the mists of the first ages of the world.

Louise shivered and, sitting up, turned to Candida. 'How much longer until we're there?'

'I don't know.'

'We seem to be zig-zagging, instead of going straight?' Louise observed.

Gaston appeared out of the darkness, stepping over recumbent figures, his cigarette glowing in the dark.

'Why are we zig-zagging?' Candida asked him. 'Instead of going straight?'

'It's the minefields,' he said casually.

'Minefields?' Candida repeated, stunned. 'What minefields?'

'I 'ave been told the British laid minefields already, in the Channel. In case England is invaded.'

'And we're weaving our way around them?' Candida asked incredulously, the enormity of their situation taking her breath away.

'*Oui, mais certainement.*'

'Right.' She thought for a minute before saying drily, 'It wouldn't be very clever to be blown up by one our own mines, would it?'

Gaston looked at her as if she was mad.

'*Non,*' he muttered, drawing deeply on his cigarette.

It was obvious, she reflected, that this half-brother of hers had no sense of humour.

Henry led the way into the village church, followed by Lady Anne and the rest of the family.

When he was at Hartley, he always read one of the lessons, while the Granville family filled the first and second pews on the right of the aisle. Matins was a regular part of village life, and the Church of St Mary's was always packed.

Today was no exception. Anxiety was making everyone turn to God for comfort. People were grim-faced, clutching their black prayer books. Singing the hymns with robust fervour. Praying with profound hope that war could still be avoided.

Rosie, sitting beside her grandmother, while Charles stayed at home with the children, saw that some of her favourite hymns were to be sung: 'Lead us, heavenly Father, lead us' and 'Nearer, my God, to Thee'.

Liza sat admiring the flower arrangements by the steps of the chancel; the autumn colouring was so pretty, she reflected, all golden and russet, shades tinged with sadness that another summer was over.

Henry sat beside her, clenching and unclenching his jaw, as he gazed with unseeing eyes at the sixteenth-century stained-glass window. He'd hardly slept for the past two nights. If anything had happened to Louise . . . he knew he must keep a grip on himself, and watched with envy his mother's serene face. Lady Anne, though also worried, had great faith in the Lord. And she believed there was nothing to do but accept His will.

'Dearly beloved brethren . . .' began the local vicar, the Reverend William Temple. 'We are gathered . . .'

Amanda and Charlotte were bored and wondered what was for lunch. Looking around the church, they craned their necks to see where the Emery children, who they often played with, were sitting. Maybe they could invite them to tea? Nanny nudged them, frowning, indicating they should look straight ahead all the time.

'Let us say the Lord's Prayer,' intoned the vicar.

Rosie had been saying the Lord's Prayer to herself every morning for ages now. It helped get her through another day of facing the fact that she was tied to Charles for the rest of her life.

Morning service continued, the first hymn had been sung, and when it ended the Reverend William Temple emerged from the vestry and came and stood on the chancel steps. His face was pale and grave, and his hands shook as he looked at the words he'd jotted down on a piece of paper.

'A few minutes ago,' he began, 'I received the news that the Prime Minister issued a second and final ultimatum at nine o'clock this morning to the German government, giving them until eleven o'clock to answer. Having received no response, Mr Chamberlain has just announced on the wireless that Britain is now at war with Germany.'

The silence in the church emphasized the shock of the people, even though this had been expected.

Henry wasn't even surprised. The Prime Minister had issued his first ultimatum to Germany two days ago, on September 1st; the day Hitler had attacked Poland. The inevitable blow had already fallen. It had been only a matter of time before Britain entered the fray; and today was that day.

A date that would go down in history and herald a greater war than even the one he'd fought in.

Liza clasped her gloved hands in anguish; her lovely, lovely life really had fallen apart now. She'd never forgotten the last war, when she'd been a young woman of nineteen, newly married to Henry, and living in permanent fear in case he was killed. When he was invalided out of the army in 1916, because of a back injury, she'd gone down on her knees and thanked God for his return. Now, she thanked God that at least she had no sons.

Loud weeping from the pew behind made her turn to see Charlotte, who had tears streaming down her face, her small chest rising and falling with sobs. 'I d-don't want there to be a war!' she cried. 'I d-don't want my daddy to get killed.'

When they returned to Hartley after church, Parsons had taken a telephone message for Henry.

'It is news of Louise?' Henry asked, turning pale.

'No, sir. Mr Ian Cavendish called.'

'And . . . ?'

'He phoned ten minutes ago, to say the air-raid sirens had sounded in London. He said he'd telephone you later to let you know what was happening.'

Henry turned away without saying a word and shut himself in the library.

Charlotte, having been comforted by the fact that, at the age of fifty and with a bad back, her father was too old to be a soldier, now clung to Lady Anne.

'I've been working on some interesting plans, darling,' she told the little girl, 'and I need your help. Amanda, I need you too.'

Holding their hands, their grandmother led them into her sitting room.

'What is it?' they chorused, looking around the prettily cluttered room as if searching for clues.

'Soldiers get very cold when they're out in the open,' Lady Anne said, in practical tones. She went to a chest of drawers in the corner, and started taking out skeins of khaki and navy-blue wool, and several pairs of knitting needles.

'I'm going to teach you how to knit warm scarves to begin with, and then we'll knit socks and balaclava helmets . . .'

'What's a bala ... what you said?' asked Charlotte.

Their grandmother produced a knitting pattern, with pictures on the front.

Nanny, coming to fetch them to wash their hands before lunch, nodded approvingly.

'That's the ticket, M'Lady!' she said. 'Everybody must keep busy. We can't let Mr Hitler get us down.'

Liza slipped upstairs to her bedroom, and threw her hat and new mink coat on the bed. Then she sank on to the chair in front of her dressing table, and looked despairingly at her reflection in the mirror.

Now that the terrible moment she'd been dreading for months – years even – had arrived, she felt cold and sick with the horror of it all. What was going to happen? Was her beloved London being destroyed by bombs at this very moment? Would the Germans invade Britain by landing on the south coast, only seventy miles away? What would become of her and her family? Would they be made prisoners of war? Shot? Liza covered her face with her hands and sobbed with fear.

Everything was ruined and nothing was ever going to be the same again. The life she so loved had ended and she wondered how they were all going to survive the terror and hardship that lay ahead.